TEEN
AND

05/02/23

Anders,Charlie Jane

Unstoppable: Book 3: Promises stronger than darkness

PROMISES STRONGER THAN DARKNESS

PROMISES
STRONGER
THAN
DARKNESS

CHARLIE JANE ANDERS

TOR
TEEN

TOR PUBLISHING GROUP

NEW YORK

PROMISES STRONGER THAN DARKNESS

Excerpt from "One Trick Pony" by Major Powers & the Lo-Fi Symphony © 2016, used with permission

A Tor Teen Book
Published by Tom Doherty Associates / Tor Publishing Group
120 Broadway
New York, NY 10271

www.tor-forge.com

Tor® is a registered trademark of Macmillan Publishing Group, LLC.

Library of Congress Cataloging-in-Publication Data

Names: Anders, Charlie Jane, author.
Title: Promises stronger than darkness / Charlie Jane Anders.
Description: First edition. | New York : Tor Teen, 2023. | Series: Unstoppable ;
3 Identifiers: LCCN 2022056776 (print) | LCCN 2022056777 (ebook) |
ISBN 9781250317506 (hardcover) | ISBN 9781250317490 (ebook)
Subjects: CYAC: Space warfare—Fiction. | Human-alien encounters—Fiction. |
Gender identity—Fiction. | Science fiction. | LCGFT: Science fiction. | Novels.
Classification: LCC PZ7.A51876 Pr 2023 (print) |
LCC PZ7.A51876 (ebook) | DDC [Fic]—dc23
LC record available at https://lccn.loc.gov/2022056776
LC ebook record available at https://lccn.loc.gov/2022056777

Our books may be purchased in bulk for promotional, educational, or business use.
Please contact your local bookseller or the Macmillan Corporate and Premium
Sales Department at 1-800-221-7945, extension 5442, or by email at
MacmillanSpecialMarkets@macmillan.com.

First Edition: 2023

Printed in the United States of America

0 9 8 7 6 5 4 3 2 1

For Annalee, who showed me the way home

They've got a head start.
They're going to need it.
We're falling apart,
But we're making a plan.

**—Major Powers & the
Lo-Fi Symphony**

PROMISES STRONGER THAN DARKNESS

PROLOGUE

.

THE ROGUE PRINCESS

Dark times, desperate people. The stars are dying and the peacekeepers are corrupted. There are no more righteous fighters—just monsters and prey. We have no place left to run, but we all keep running anyway.

Except if you're lucky—if the Ardenii smile upon you—there's still hope. When you find yourself in a danger you can't see a way past, you may yet be saved.

Maybe the Rogue Princess will come to your rescue.

Six of the seven princesses stay within the Palace of Scented Tears, anointing themselves, drinking from the river of sweetest fears, and trying to find some answer, some clue, to help save the doomed suns. But the seventh princess travels far and obeys nobody. She saves people—she saves entire worlds—and she always tells the truth.

The Rogue Princess journeys in a starship that was made half for art, half for science, and she appears without warning. Her companions aren't fighters: they're scientists, diplomats, scholars, artists, and musicians. Survivors of the Battle of Antarràn and the Fall of Irriyaia, they search for a cure for the Bereavement, the strange sickness that menaces every last star that supports life.

And along the way, they help people in need. People like us.

Many believe the Rogue Princess is a legend, but she saved our lives. Our ship was broken, we were spewing air through a hole the size and shape of a floatbeast head, and Scanthian raiders were about to fire one last missile to finish us off. All of us chanted the Yarthin Prayer of Not Dying as we said our goodbyes and reminded ourselves that life had been sweet.

And then it appeared: the strangest vessel we had ever seen. We glimpsed a stone wall covered with graffiti, and the sweep of a Royal daggership's upper hull. The ship cradled us with its ion harness, holding our air inside so we could keep breathing, and moved between us and the bandits' ravager-class starship.

That's when I heard her voice.

"Stand down, raiders. This is Princess Elza, and my pronoun is *she*, and I will not allow you to hurt these people. Your ship has a radiation leak and you bought faulty gravitators from a scrapyard at Vandal Station, and there are a dozen other ways I could make sure you never threaten innocent lives again, without firing a single weapon. You have one chance to leave in peace."

The Scanthian raiders hesitated for just one moment. And then they were gone.

We never had a chance to thank the Rogue Princess. Or to tell her all the ways we would honor her, if we made it to a new planet to start over and rebuild our lives. She stayed long enough to make sure we were safe and repaired, and then she disappeared into the endless. We never learned why she would take the time to help us, when she has so many worlds counting on her.

But I heard a story from someone who saw her once, at the Irriyaian exile citystar. She wept into a cup of bitter snah-snah juice, and they heard her say to her friend that she would save as many people as she could, to honor the memory of the love of her life. She knew what it was to love— and to see that love stolen by fate—and she would never let that happen to other people if she could prevent it.

This is a cruel universe, and it's getting crueler. But there's one person out there who fights for all of us. When hope seems beyond all reach, pray she finds you.

1
.

ELZA

Of *course* the heist went sideways. What did anyone expect?

The *Undisputed Training Bra Disaster* had made it to the supergiant planet made of pure diamond without being detected because Elza had done her part: she'd learned all the details of the planet's defenses from the Ardenii, the ancient supercomputers that speak to her through the crown she wears: a silver filigree that casts an amber light.

Their party had managed to sneak all the way under the glittery surface without falling into any of the gravity traps or force fields, because Damini and Zaeta's soul-deep connection made them the best pilots alive.

Everything was going perfectly.

And now? Elza, Yiwei, Kez, and Wyndgonk hang inside a living net that keeps saying sarcastic things to them, like: *Oh, it's such a privilege to have these distinguished visitors caught in my fibers, I'm practically fraying with excitement. Oh wait, I'm not fraying at all, you're completely trapped. Sucks for you!*

Their captor's footsteps approach—the Great Alucian (*she/her*).

Elza can't turn her head far enough to see the Great Alucian, but the Ardenii are bombarding her with every fact there is to know about this scary lady who's one of the richest people in the entire galaxy. She's wealthy in ways that go beyond just money: rare items, secrets, influence.

"You thought you could steal from me?" The Great Alucian chuckles.

"Yes." Wyndgonk (*fire/fire*) breathes a gout of red flame. "We don't just think we *can*, we know we *should*. It's our duty to rob you. You have too much stuff for one person." Wyndgonk looks a lot like a fire-breathing beetle the size of a sofa, with a thick iridescent shell, hooked mandibles, and long segmented legs ending in tiny claws.

"We need that chalice more than you do," says Kez (*he/him*). Kez has stopped wearing his gold-threaded junior ambassador uniform. Instead, he sports a red-and-yellow-swirled shirt and crimson pants from Miscreant Station, which set off his dark brown skin and high cheekbones.

"Ahh," the Great Alucian sighs. "You came to steal the chalice that no lips have ever touched. Of course you did. It's the rarest item I own, and that is a high distinction."

Elza can't concentrate. The net whispers strange insults to her. The Ardenii fill her head with terrible information (armies of refugees fleeing their doomed stars, a small child who just watched their parents freeze to death in a blightstorm on an asteroid colony). But mostly, she's too full of grief to think about anything else. Grief siphons the life out of her, and it never seems to let up.

This heist went wrong because the person who made everything go right wasn't here to help: Tina.

"Look. Just let us borrow the chalice." Kez puts on his most reasonable negotiator voice, the one he practiced in diplomat school. "We promise we'll bring it right back, and we won't let our lips touch it, so you won't have to change the name or anything. We believe that chalice is the key to saving all of the worlds from the Bereavement."

"So you're telling me that the chalice is even more invaluable than I already thought," says the Great Alucian. "Hardly a strong argument for me to lend it out."

The Great Alucian comes around the side of the net and Elza sees her face. She's a Makvarian, a tall humanoid with shimmering purple skin and big round eyes, and she wears jewels embedded in her cheeks and jawline. According to the Ardenii, the Great Alucian rejected all of Makvaria's teachings about taking care of each other, and chose to become totally selfish.

For just a moment, the Great Alucian looks just like Elza's girlfriend Tina. A needle-thin blade goes all the way inside Elza's heart.

Elza blinks, and the Great Alucian is just another Makvarian, wearing a dark cowl and a diamond-studded black cape.

"Listen," Yiwei says. "See our friend here? She's a *princess*. She will guarantee on her royal honor that she'll bring the chalice back to you." Yiwei has let his black hair grow out into a shaggy mane around his lean baby face, but he still has the cockiness of a Royal Fleet cadet. "This doesn't have to turn ugly. Elza, tell them."

Elza snaps out of her reverie, and realizes Yiwei is talking about her. "Right," she says. "On my honor. I guarantee it."

"Or," says the Great Alucian, "I could keep the chalice here, and be the only collector in the galaxy to have an actual princess as part of my collection of rarities. Why, that sounds so much better!"

We're going to have so much time to get to know each other, whispers the net. This can't be how everything ends. The suns are dying, the galaxy is ruled by a monster, and Elza's going to be stuck in the "collection" of some rich egomaniac who would fit right in among the São Paulo elite. *Come on, get your head right,* Elza tells herself.

But the Ardenii have more facts to share: a city just died. A tree murdered all its friends.

"Take them to the immobilizing chamber," the Great Alucian says to the net. "Once they're frozen, I'll figure out where to place them inside my vault."

Wyndgonk, Kez, and Yiwei are all yelling at the Great Alucian that she's making a mistake. The net is already lifting them off the polished diamond floor, carrying them toward the immobilizing chamber. Elza knows there's got to be a way out of this, but the Ardenii are giving her nothing but unthinkable thoughts.

"Ummm," says a barely audible voice from below them. "Umm. I'm uh, I'm here to challenge you. To a game. If I win, uh, then you have to let my friends go and we borrow the chalice. If you win, we stay here. Okay? I heard that's one of your things." A small human girl with a round face and curly reddish-brown hair stands, cradling a robot monkey.

Rachael sounds so shy, so tentative, her challenge somehow feels even more brave.

"Oh, you heard correctly," the Great Alucian says. "I love a challenge, and since you are free of my net, you have the right to issue one. Very well, I accept! If you defeat me, you may take the chalice and your friends. If you lose, I keep you all, forever. What game do you choose?"

Rachael steps forward—face bright red, fists balled. "How about," she mumbles, "we play a little game of *WorstBestFriend*?"

A cycle later, Elza and her friends trudge onto the *Undisputed Training Bra Disaster,* and Rachael cradles the chalice that no lips have ever touched. It looks like . . . a big cup. Made of some tarnished alien metal, like brass or bronze. (Even the Ardenii don't know who made it, or what it's made of.)

"Thanks for saving us down there." Yiwei shoots Rachael a look that obviously puts a warm flutter inside her. Elza feels a stab of jealousy.

"Uh. Thanks." Rachael squirms and looks at the paint on the wall, the way she always does when somebody tries to tell her how heroic she is. "I guess all that time I spent in Gamertown paid off after all."

"Don't worry," Yiwei says. "Not going to try and give you a medal or anything. Dinner later?"

"Um, yeah." Rachael turns and smiles back at her boyfriend. "I just re-membered something I have to do. See you soon." She wanders away.

Elza wants to go back to her tiny quarters and stare at the floor. But Yiwei follows her down the hallway covered with murals (including a heartbreaking new one by Rachael: a flagon of snah-snah juice with com-ets and stars floating on the surface, surrounded by wildflowers like the ones Tina used to wear on her uniform sleeve).

"Can I talk to you for a moment?" Yiwei asks.

She wants to say no, but she nods. Neck spasm.

The Ardenii give Elza an update about the resettlement of all the Irri-yaian refugees: it isn't going well.

"Listen, I know you're still grieving for . . . for what happened to Tina," says Yiwei. "But what in the thousand flaming lakes was that just now? We nearly got turned into part of that egomaniac's collection, and you weren't even paying attention. We need you focused on the mission, or we're all doomed."

What happened to Tina.

Meaning the thing where Tina's mind—her whole personality—was erased, and she transformed into an arrogant jerk named Thaoh Argen-tian. Elza bottles up a scream.

"You ought to be the biggest asset to our team. The Unstoppables, or whatever we're calling ourselves this week," Yiwei is saying. "You have a direct line to the super-advanced computers that know everything there is to know. But you're not helping. I'm sorry to put pressure on you, but . . ."

Yiwei's still trying to act like Captain Othaar, his idol. Elza was right there when Othaar died from Thondra Marrant's touch, which means she can't even think of the man without feeling a wave of disgust. And the more Yiwei imitates his mentor, the more he grosses Elza out.

"I get it," Elza says. "Thank you for your concern." She really hopes the EverySpeak can translate the right amount of low-key sarcasm from Brazil-ian Portuguese to Mandarin. "I'll try to be more of a team player next time."

The Ardenii freak out inside Elza's head, because these all-knowing su-percomputers have been dying to study the chalice for hundreds of years.

And they bombard Elza with news about the chaos and disruption from the tiny black holes getting ready to gobble up every sun that supports life.

Elza's so distracted, she walks right past the hallway that leads to her quarters. She winds up in the flight lounge, which is half the gray metal control center of a Royal Fleet daggership and half an artist salon with wood-and-velvet walls and big couches.

Damini and Zaeta sit in teacup chairs in front of a bunch of holographic blobs, happily chattering to each other. Damini is a human with medium-brown skin, with wide, laughing eyes and long black hair worn up, with red kumkum between her brows. Zaeta has ninety-nine eyes in between the tiny scales on her face, and her arms end in flipper-claws.

"Did we get it?" Damini bounces up and down, and the bangles on her bony wrists chime like bells next to the red thread she always wears.

"We got it, right?" Zaeta chimes in, her top layer of eyes sparkling. "I can't wait to see it, it's the oldest artifact ever discovered—"

"—from any humanoid civilization," Damini says.

Damini and Zaeta always finish each other's sentences, ever since they became psychic best friends. It's not always obnoxious.

"We got it," Elza says. "It looks just like a regular cup. I hope we can get something useful out of it."

"I'm sure we will," Damini says. "The Ardenii helped us find it. And it's the closest thing to a clue we've found so far."

"Everyone is scared back home on Wedding Water," Zaeta says. "They can see a black hole getting ready to gobble up the sun, like a speck of death. If the ice doesn't thaw on time, a whole generation of eggs could be trapped forever."

"Speaking of which," Damini says, "we wanted to talk to you about something."

"All these side missions you've been having us do?" Zaeta says. "Like rescuing those poor Yarthins from the Scanthian pirates? It's incredibly noble—"

"—but we just don't have time," Damini says. "If we can't solve the Bereavement soon, there won't be a future for anybody."

Why is everybody getting on Elza's case today? She already has the Ardenii to remind her *every second* that the stars are dying, she doesn't need her friends piling on.

"I'm just trying to honor Tina's memory," Elza says in a quiet, toneless voice. "If Tina was here, she'd want to save as many people as possible."

They're still nattering, but Elza mumbles an apology and walks away. Being a princess is not as glamorous as she thought it would be. She chose not to stay on the *Invention of Innocence,* the deluxe starship she inherited from Princess Constellation, where she'd have been pampered by attendants and caretakers—because then she'd have had to follow orders from the Palace of Scented Tears. And that meant she didn't get to claim a fancy princess name, like Princess Nonesuch. Instead, she's here with her friends on this rickety ship, which is half Royal daggership and half artist colony, held together by daydreams and duct tape.

Elza used to think all of that luxury was wasteful, selfish. But now she sees that it's just a way to make the burden of the Ardenii more bearable. The Ardenii fill her head with random terrible things every second—like a small town in the middle of Makvaria's swampland just got destroyed by a freak storm.

Back home in São Paulo, Elza's only real friend was another travesti named Fernanda, who had creamy brown skin and short hair that she styled differently every day. Fernanda always spoke in an undertone, but she had a laugh you could hear from two streets away. The two of them were inseparable, until Fernanda stopped talking to her, and Elza had to go live at a hackerspace. What would Fernanda say if she saw Elza now: wearing a wreath of golden light on her head, but still sleeping in a run-down old shack? She'd probably think it was hilarious.

Elza almost makes it back to her quarters without getting dragged into another conversation. When she reaches her door, Rachael comes around the corner and waves at her.

"Hey," Rachael says in a voice almost too small to hear.

"Hi." Elza stiffens, ready for Rachael to tell her another way that she's ruining everything.

"I wanted to give you this." Rachael holds out something small and bright red in her left palm. "It's some kind of candy, supposed to taste kind of like cinnamon and cherries. Those people we saved from the pirates? The Yarthins? They asked me to give it to you, as a thank-you present. I didn't get a chance until now."

Elza looks at the glistening red dessert. The Ardenii fill her head with information about what a delicacy this is, and it's a hundred percent safe for human stomachs.

"Are you . . . Are you sure you don't want—"

"It's for you," Rachael says. "They wanted to thank you, and I . . . I also want to thank you. I miss her all the time, and I know we need to keep going and do what we can, and everyone is terrified. But I feel totally lost without her here. So thank you for doing good in her name. It's everything."

Elza is crying—not serious grown-up weeping, more like a little kid who fell off a bicycle. Helplessly bawling, heaving with huge tears. She takes the candy with one hand and covers her face with the other.

"Hey," Rachael whispers. "I'd really like to hug you, if that's okay."

Elza holds back for a moment, then falls into Rachael's arms, clutching the candy.

"There's enough to share," Elza says when she can talk again. "Let's eat it together."

Rachael squeezes her tighter. "Sounds good."

2
.

Elza used to waste her energy worrying about all the things she didn't know. She spent so many nights alone, dreaming up horrendous things that could be happening to the people she loved, or disasters that she wouldn't find out about until it was too late. When she found out there was a way to know everything, so she'd never have to wonder again, she knew she'd do anything to have the Ardenii in her life.

Now Elza wakes up with her head full of bad news, and goes to sleep with a weary mind. She never has to imagine the worst things that could happen, because she already knows.

And every once in a while, the Ardenii tell her a number so enormous it's impossible to comprehend, and she has no idea what it means. Except that the number keeps going up.

Everyone sits around the flight lounge, staring at the goblet they just risked everything for. The five Earthling kids, plus Zaeta, Wyndgonk, Cinnki, Kfok, Naahay, and Gahang.

"So . . . what now?" Kez holds the cup, which is still just a cup.

Elza says nothing, because she's busy losing an argument with the Ardenii inside her head.

You can't ask that of me, she pleads. In response, they send her more images of disaster: people on a thousand worlds going berserk, hurting their neighbors under blighted suns.

"Damini, what do you think?" Yiwei asks, since Damini's usually the one who solves puzzles.

"It's a total mystery, sorry." Damini shrinks deeper into her sofa cushions and glances at Zaeta, who gives her an *it's okay* smile.

When you know the answer, it becomes your responsibility. When Elza first heard that saying, she felt empowered, as if she'd been given permission to make trouble. Now those words feel like an entire planet resting on the back of her neck.

"According to our research, this cup is actually a space probe," says Kez. "A probe that was sent out a very long time ago, by people we know nothing about. And it probably saw where the Bereavement was launched from."

Long ago, a mysterious species called the Shadow Galaxy lost a war with some creeps called the Vayt. And the Shadow Galaxy took revenge by launching the Bereavement: a swarm of black holes that spread throughout the galaxy and nestled inside stars, waiting for the right moment to start gobbling them up. The Vayt tried to sabotage this weapon in the most hideous way possible, by twisting people into weird antibodies to neutralize the swarm.

These black holes have remained frozen in time inside little beach balls made of flesh, but now they're starting to wake up—and when they do, it's all over. For everyone.

"If we figure out the origin point of the Bereavement, maybe we can learn more about the people who sent it," says Cinnki (*he/him*), a foxlike Javarah who moves with a languid grace inside his silken clothes.

"So what are we waiting for?" Naahay turns her skull-face toward Elza. "You're a princess now. You just look at the cup, and the Ardenii will figure out everything."

"Thank you for telling me how to do the job that I was more qualified for than you," Elza says.

Naahay was one of the kids competing for the crown that Elza now wears, along with Wyndgonk. After everything went wrong at Irriyaia, Naahay's friend Robhhan went back home to Oonia Prime, but Naahay decided to stick around, and she's been putting a scream in Elza's throat ever since.

The Ardenii show Elza the most embarrassing thing that ever happened to Naahay: she tried to show off during a game of aahrkon when she was ten years old and toppled into a lampfish bog, in front of all her friends. Elza stifles a laugh—then she surfs a wave of guilt over invading Naahay's privacy. She can hear Fernanda in her head: *This is just like you.*

Elza realizes Yiwei has been talking to her for a minute. "Are the Ardenii telling you anything useful? Elza?"

"There's only one option left, but I hate it." Elza's skin crawls.

Please don't ask that of me.

Rachael leans close to Elza and whispers, "It's okay. This isn't on you."

Everybody looks at Elza differently—even her friends—now that she has a silver lattice woven into her scalp, casting a honeyed light onto her face. Like they want to curtsey every time she's standing next to them in the line to use the bathroom.

"But there's something you're not telling us," Yiwei says. "Isn't there?"

Elza sighs. "Yes. The Ardenii found the interface immediately, but the data is corrupted. There's an algorithm that could restore it, but I would need the full power of the Ardenii to run it. Which means . . . I would need to be inside the Palace of Scented Tears."

She can feel a shudder go through everyone in the room.

The Palace of Scented Tears is where Elza used to live when she was trying out to become a princess. It's at the center of Wentrolo, the capital city of Her Majesty's Firmament—the seat of power of Marrant, the garbage-fiend who's now in charge of everything.

"That's the most secure place in the entire galaxy. We'd have to go through two whole armies to get inside," says Kfok (*she/her*), a big slug with five eyes, two mouths, and three arms ending in stingers. "The Royal Fleet *and* the Compassion. And if we got past them . . ."

". . . we'd be facing Marrant," says Naahay. "This is not happening."

"Hush, child," whispers Gahang. "Your certainty does violence to the memory of the rain-scarred priests."

"You're the one who can't tell the difference between competence and luck," Naahay taunts Gahang.

Elza had expected Naahay to make friends with Gahang (who was part of the crew of the *Undisputed,* along with Tina and Damini). After all, they're both skeleton-people from the planet Aribentora. But Naahay and Gahang *can't stand* each other, because they each think the other is a bad Aribentor.

"There's no time for a debate," Yiwei says. "If getting inside the palace is the only way, then that's what we're going to do."

"Whatever it takes," Damini agrees.

"We can't just walk into the palace," Kez says. "Everyone who's still there is loyal to Marrant."

"We're the Galaxy's Most Wanted," Yiwei says. "Because apparently stopping a few rebels is more important than finding a way to save everyone from a frozen death."

"The queen hasn't been seen since Marrant's takeover," says Wyndgonk. "Her Radiance is either a prisoner, or . . ."

Time to drop another unpleasant truth. "The Ardenii know what's happening with the queen," Elza says, "but they will not tell me."

"We could drop into the palace from above—" says Damini.

"—using personal impellers, or hoverboots!" says Zaeta.

"We should just burn down that whole corrupt place." Kfok gestures with one barbed arm. Wyndgonk nods at her.

"We're not talking about one of the stinkpalaces of Orvan IV," Naahay says. "The Palace of Scented Tears is the most well-protected place in history and none of you has what it takes to get inside."

Everyone falls silent, just staring at the old cup and trying to think of an idea that's not instantly doomed.

"Okay, please don't hate me," Rachael says. "But there's one person who probably knows how to tap-dance inside the palace without anyone noticing."

"Don't say it," Yiwei says.

"We promised we wouldn't mention her anymore," says Kez.

Elza sighs and massages her temples. "No, Rachael's right. We need her help, and I know exactly where to find her. Thaoh Argentian has been hiding out on Vandal Station ever since she told us to go to hell."

3
.

RACHAEL

. . . 294 Earth days until all the suns go out forever

Thaoh Argentian is on a date.

Two cute young Makvarians surround her and gaze adoringly while she keeps their cups overflowing with Yuul sauce. All three of them kiss each other with their mouths full of the spicy, tart liquor, in the gloomiest corner of the sleaziest nightclub at the bottom level of Vandal Station, the Bump Dump. Thaoh has attached new gems to her strong cheekbones and jaw, bigger than the ones Tina used to wear.

Of all the things Rachael expected to find the woman who stole Tina's body doing, partying was at the very bottom of the list. Next to Rachael, Elza is as stiff as a board, and her mouth scowls under the hood that conceals the glowing circlet on her head.

". . . go dancing next," Thaoh Argentian is saying to one of the two beautiful people on her arm. "I used to love dancing, when I was young and breathless the first time around. Or perhaps we should just go back to my quarters and finish this bottle there."

The two young Makvarians giggle and twine their bodies around Thaoh's.

Elza just marches up to their corner table and sweeps the bottle of Yuul sauce onto the floor with one fluid motion. Crash, splash. She glares at Thaoh's two hookups until they disentangle themselves from Thaoh and make a retreat.

"I'll find you later! Thaoh Argentian *always* keeps her promises." Thaoh waves at her two new friends. They smile back, nervously, and then they're gone.

The nightclub is playing Javarah screech-break music, which is just as distracting as it sounds. The lyrics are all about clawing your lover's face off.

Thaoh groans at Elza and Rachael theatrically. "I *told* you. There's no way to restore your friend, and we have bigger things to worry about. I didn't ask to be brought back to life."

"But you certainly seem to be enjoying being alive again." Elza snorts.

Rachael wishes she could do something more for Elza—her heart must be breaking. Even worse than Rachael's, which is saying something.

"Yes. I am," Thaoh says, with a sudden heaviness. "I am enjoying being alive again, more than I ever expected to. I am truly sorry. If I could snap my fingers and bring Tina back, I would, but you yourself told me that even the Ardenii don't know how to do that. So all I can do is try to help fix this mess. I'm spending my time building alliances, working to undo Marrant's takeover of the Royal Fleet."

"When you're not drinking and hooking up with random people," Elza says.

Rachael feels shy, even more than usual. How weird is it, to be standing in front of her best friend but feel like she's talking to a total stranger?

"I will not apologize for blowing off steam. I came back to life in the middle of the apocalypse, and everything I spent my life trying to protect lies in ruins. If I'm going to be forced to be alive, I might as well have a little fun. I had honestly forgotten what it's like to be young—these hormones are a beast."

"Except that's my girlfriend's body you're using."

"Not anymore." Thaoh Argentian gestures for more Yuul sauce to replace the bottle that Elza smashed.

"You did not just say that," Elza says.

Rachael hates feeling so powerless. She doesn't usually wish she was the kind of person who could raise her voice and command attention—someone who could smack the table and say, "Everybody shut up," and bring an argument to an end. But now, with worlds and worlds at stake, she wouldn't mind being able to make a little noise.

"Let's stay focused on the mission." Yiwei steps forward, with his robot Xiaohou raising his little monkey face to pick up some musical cues from the screech-break. "We don't have time for personal issues."

Rachael's boyfriend keeps saying things like that lately, and it's getting all the way under her skin. Ever since Tina turned into this obnoxious woman, Yiwei has been stepping up and trying to be more of a leader, and his leadership style has a little too much "tough love" for Rachael's taste. She hasn't managed to talk to him about it, even when they've been alone together.

"Oh, great." Thaoh rolls her eyes. "Are you also here to tell me what to do with my body?"

"It's *not your body*," Elza says.

"This has been fun." Thaoh stands up and wipes spilled booze off her shirt. "But I need to get going. Listen, I have no shortage of things to feel guilty for, but living my life is not one—" Then she stops and stares at Yiwei's right sleeve.

Yiwei is no longer wearing his cadet uniform from the Royal Academy, since he dropped out ages ago. But he found a way to program the same design onto the right sleeve of the casual V-neck shirt he's wearing now: a picture of Panash Othaar, the captain of the *Indomitable*. The guy who gave his life to save Rachael and her friends.

"Panash," says Thaoh. "You know, it's weird. He was one of my closest friends, and now when I think of him, I feel sick and confused."

"That's the Marrant death-touch," Yiwei shakes his head. "Anyone he touches melts into a noxious puddle that everyone hates. Tina was right there when he touched Captain Othaar."

"The effect is worse in the long term," Elza says. "It seeps into every memory that involves the dead person in any way. Soon your whole past is soiled."

"I suppose I'm experiencing half the effect, because I have the same body but a different mind." Thaoh shakes her head.

"We need your help," Yiwei says. "We think we've found a clue that could lead us to the people who created the Bereavement—the Shadow Galaxy. But we need help to make sense of it."

"There's no point." Now Thaoh seems like a sad old warrior in the body of a teenage girl. "The stars are dying and there's no way to fix that. All we can do is try to redeem the Royal Fleet, so there's at least someone to help save whoever's left. Now if you'll excuse me? I need to finish getting properly drunk. See you again sometime."

She shoves her way past Elza and Yiwei, leaving Rachael staring at the back of her best friend's head as she walks out the lightning-bolt-shaped door.

Vandal Station packs even more sensory overload than Rascal Station, the space city that Rachael visited a billion years ago. Bustling crowds, blaring music, smells that turn her stomach—all the things that Rachael could barely deal with on her best day—fill every narrow passage between the sun towers, which rise up so tall that Rachael can't see their spires. She clenches her fists and chatters under her breath, keeps her head down.

Tunnel vision closes in on her.

Rachael should be feeling better, right? She confronted the Vayt, and purged these ancient monsters from her dreams. She regained the ability to make art, and now she can hide away and draw, when everything becomes too much. So why isn't she feeling better? If anything, it's all hitting her so much harder now—maybe because she's no longer having to hold it together in the eye of a crap-storm, or maybe because she can't talk to her best friend anymore.

Whatever the reason, anxiety chews Rachael up, and she has to force herself to move forward, through all these bodies and scents and noises. Everybody is shoving each other, and a brawl constantly seems a heartbeat away from breaking out—most of the people here fled from doomed worlds with whatever they could carry, and they're all wishing they had someone to hit.

A group of Aribentors and Yarthins block the alleyway between two sun towers as they huddle over a holographic cloud. Rachael tries to squeeze past them, and then she sees what they're looking at: Thondra Marrant, the new leader of the Royal Compassion, giving a speech in front of a roaring crowd. Rachael can't hear what Marrant is saying over the jangle of music and voices, but he's smiling, genial, looking for all the world like any other politician.

The holograph flashes a series of pictures: Rachael, Elza, Yiwei, Kez, Damini, Zaeta, and Tina.

Rachael pulls her hood farther over her face and pushes ahead.

Her friends are probably wondering where she is, especially Yiwei. People are going to freak out and maybe organize a search party. But Rachael can't bring herself to just walk away from Tina again—her mind knows this isn't Tina, but her heart doesn't—and she can't give up on the swashbuckling Captain Argentian, after all that hype.

A while later, Rachael sees a few worm-faced Undhorans, swaggering and wearing the red slash of the Compassion on their jackets—and they're holding plastiform pads with the faces of Rachael and her friends on them. *Damn. We really are the Galaxy's Most Wanted now.*

Rachael could trawl this city forever and not find Thaoh, especially if she doesn't want to be found. She tries all the sleaziest, darkest, grungiest bars and clubs, which means she sees things she can never unsee.

Just when she's about to abandon hope, she spies an old friend moving through the crowd.

Thanz Riohon wears a big cloak and a Makvarian opera mask covers his eyes, but he still moves like a Royal Fleet officer. And Rachael would know that face anywhere: full lips, square jaw, and the same fizzy purple skin as Thaoh herself. He steps through a tiny doorway that Rachael had overlooked, and she follows him inside a dark cavern where people gamble with razor-sharp corkscrews.

By the time Rachael pushes past all the Kraelyors and Ainkians tossing pieces in the air, hooting, and trying not to cut themselves, Riohon is already sitting next to Thaoh Argentian.

Rachael thinks at first this is another hot date, and the tunnel vision closes in. But then she hears what Riohon is saying.

". . . most of the daggerships and about half the shortswords are on our side. But the longswords and broadswords are more conservative, and they won't go against the Firmament, even now. When we're ready to make our move, we'll still be absurdly outnumbered, but . . . we'll have a fleet."

Thaoh starts to say something, then she spies Rachael standing over the tiny concave table in the darkest corner of the gambling den. "You again." Thaoh squints. "You're the one who doesn't talk, right? This should be interesting."

You're not worthy to wear Tina's face, Rachael almost says. But she's speechless, as advertised.

"Rachael Townsend!" Riohon leaps to his feet. "May you walk in gentle sunlight and sleep under bright stars. Of all the people to run into, I'm so happy to see you. I heard what the Royal Fleet tried to do to you and I'm sorry. This is—"

"We've met." Thaoh grimaces.

Riohon starts chattering to Thaoh about Rachael's amazing feats of heroism—as usual, this kind of talk makes Rachael want to barf. But at least the look in Thaoh's eyes changes a little, and she gestures for Rachael to pull up a fluff-chair.

"What brings you here?" Riohon asks.

Rachael half closes her eyes, and tries to pretend she's just talking to Tina and Riohon.

"You're wasting your time. Both of you," she mumbles, eyes still half-shut.

"She's blunt at least," Captain Argentian says to Riohon. "It's refreshing."

"Don't condescend to me." Rachael feels her face get hot. She grips the rim of the table with ten white knuckles. "You know I'm right. You're wasting your energy trying to fix the Royal Fleet, when *all the suns are dying*. We found a clue. There's a space probe that saw where the Bereavement was launched from—that swarm of black holes that are about to chow down on every important star."

"And . . . if we locate the origin point of the swarm, we might find some way to shut it all down. A fail-safe." Riohon purses his lips. "There are still stasis generators around all of those black holes, for now. If we could reactivate them all . . ."

"It's the slenderest of chances." Thaoh Argentian shakes her head. "I learned the hard way when I commanded the *Inquisitive*: some gambles aren't worth the risk." She gestures at all the people scraping themselves bloody trying to wager with sharp objects at all the other tables.

"I've learned to trust Rachael's instincts," Thanz Riohon says. "And even a tiny chance of stopping the Bereavement . . . we can't ignore that." He turns back to Rachael. "What's your plan?"

The trust and respect in Riohon's eyes are better than a thousand medals. "We have the space probe already. We need to sneak Elza—the Rogue Princess—into the palace so she can decrypt the information."

"Oh, is that all?" Thaoh laughs and swigs Yuul sauce. "A ninety-nine percent chance of dying, for a one percent chance of finding a clue that might not lead anywhere."

Thaoh's laughter gets inside Rachael through every pore.

There's so much more that she wants to say—needs to say—but she's done. She's used up her talking-to-jerks quota for the next week.

"What else do we have?" Riohon says. "Rachael is right: what's the point of restoring the Royal Fleet if there's no more galaxy for them to protect?"

"We could build artificial suns. We could create safe havens for refugees. We could—"

"—save a tiny fraction of all the people who will surely die." Riohon fixes her with an intense stare. "I promise, I will keep building this alliance, so our fleet is less puny when the opportunity comes. Recruitment would be easier if I could let everyone know that you're alive again."

"If everyone knew I was back, Marrant would blast this whole city to rubble just to eliminate me," Thaoh says. "I wouldn't wish to be egotistical, but I'm a bit of an obsession to him." She gestures at Rachael. "According to this one and her friends, Marrant's wife, Aym, faked her own death and hid from everyone—even me—just to escape from him."

"In any case, you can leave this with me. If Rachael and her friends need your help, then that's where you should be."

Thaoh closes her eyes and braces herself against a sudden shiver. "I'm already dead. This is a borrowed life." She pushes her chair back and stands, then opens her eyes and gives Rachael the same grin Tina used to flash when she was about to jump out of a spaceship. "Very well. Let's go break into the palace."

Rachael wants to thank Riohon for his help, but Thaoh is already halfway to the exit. She settles for giving Riohon a thank-you look.

"We'll see each other again, Rachael Townsend," Riohon says. "May the Hosts of Misadventure shield and guide you."

"Umm, yeah. Back at you." Rachael smiles and waves, and then runs to catch up with Thaoh, who's already disappearing into the crowd on the street.

4.

"Could you please explain again, with less attitude and more explaining?" Kez (*e/em*) says to Thaoh Argentian. (Kez came out as gender fluid a while back, and now eir pronouns change every once in a while. It's easy to use the right pronoun thanks to the EverySpeak, the translator that everyone carries.) "We have a stolen Compassion knifeship, thanks to Riohon and your other allies. That's bloody wonderful. So why are we going to so much trouble to disguise it as a derelict freighter?"

E gestures at the candy-apple-red ship, which looks sort of like a fighter jet except that the front is shaped like a frog's head. Cinnki, Kfok, Damini, Zaeta, and Gahang are busy covering the ship with layers of junk, including pieces of the hull from a broken-down cargo ship.

The bootleg knifeship appears especially sleek next to the *Undisputed Training Bra Disaster,* side by side in a secret hangar of Vandal Station.

"Old smuggler trick." Thaoh beams and rubs her hands together. "We change our appearance at the right moment, and we can slip inside the Glorious Nebula without anybody seeing us coming."

"That reminds me," Wyndgonk, the fire-breathing nine-eyed beetle, says. "What exactly are you calling this group of officers who want to stand against Marrant? The resistance? The holdouts? The rebels?"

"We're calling them the Royal Fleet," Thaoh says firmly. "Because that's who they are."

Wyndgonk snorts a dark flame. "The Royal Fleet is gone. You need to let go of that dream."

Yiwei steps forward and changes the subject. "So who's coming on this mission? Besides you and Elza, I mean. This ship can only carry six or seven people without maxing out life support."

Elza hears her name and wanders over. "I'd like to bring Wyndgonk, if fire is willing to come."

"Ugh." Wyndgonk turns all nine eyes upward and clicks fire mandibles together. "Sure. Going back to the palace. Sounds like a party. Why not."

"And we'll need your best pilots." Thaoh gestures at Zaeta and Damini—their faces light up at the compliment. She turns to Kez. "I heard you know your way around starship engines and esoteric physics. We could use your help too, if you're up for it."

Kez nods. "If I can help, I'm in."

That just leaves one spot on the mission.

Yiwei turns to Rachael, and she gives him an encouraging smile. But she's not ready for what comes out of his mouth: "You should take Rachael. She's good at noticing things that other people miss."

Elza nods. "I'd really like it if Rachael came with us."

Rachael is lost for words. There are literally a half dozen people in this hangar who would be a better choice. But she looks at Yiwei, and he raises one eyebrow. So she just nods and says, "Okay, sure," in a small voice.

"The artist. Seems fitting, since you're the one who talked me into being part of this disaster." Thaoh looks around at her team. "We leave at first cycle. If you have any last business in Vandal Station, now's the time. I am going to go dance and see how much Yuul sauce I can drink without passing out."

She strides away, leaving Rachael still stunned.

"So, I just have one question," Rachael says to Yiwei later, when they're wrapped around each other in their shared quarters on board the *Undisputed Training Bra Disaster*. One wall is covered with Rachael's latest sketches. "What in the actual flaming lakes? Why would you want me going on that mission instead of you? Or Gahang, who was a Royal Fleet officer?"

"This is a stealth mission, and I'm not brilliant at those," Yiwei says. "You're good at improvising when everything goes wrong, which I'm sure it will. But also? You can stay close to Thaoh and keep tabs on her, just in case. She's on her guard around me, but she underestimates you. We can use that."

"You don't trust her?" Rachael props herself up on one elbow and looks into his gorgeous brown eyes.

"You do?" He clicks his tongue. "She's definitely not what I was expecting."

"I hate being around her. She's like a walking reminder of how much we messed everything up."

Rachael feels like there's a thing she's been wanting to say to Yiwei. Her nerves have been stripped raw, a breath caught in her lungs, every time they've been together in public. And now the two of them are alone, and he smells so good, and she doesn't know when she'll see him again.

So she finds some broken words and tries to make them fit.

"I love you and I trust you, and I feel good about us," she says in a flood. "But . . . it sucks being in a relationship when we're both freaked out and depressed. That's not your fault, it's not anybody's. Things fell apart so fast, and we couldn't stop it, and the man who messed it all up got rewarded. *Again*. I just feel angry all the time, and I know you do, too."

He looks up at her, blinking. "Yeah. Yeah. I know. It's like . . ."

There's a long silence. Even Xiaohou doesn't try to fill it with tunes—the musical robot just sits on the edge of the bed looking at the two of them with his fuzzy head cocked to one side and his gumdrop eyes watchful. Like he can tell that this is supposed to be a quiet moment.

Yiwei flinches, like he touched a live circuit. Then he tries again to speak. "It's like, I look at you and I know exactly how you're feeling, because I'm feeling the same way. And I'm scared if I even talk about it, I'll realize that I'm held together by a thousand cheap patches, just as much as this ridiculous ship." He takes a slow breath, broken up by choppy heaving sounds. "Neither of us can afford to fall apart, with literally everything at stake."

"So that's why." Rachael has that joyful/miserable feeling. Like when you finally admit how terrible things are, and it's a huge relief—except that it means you have to face up to all the terribleness.

"That's why I haven't been opening up to you," she says. "It's not that I want to shut you out, it's just, I feel like you and I are carrying around big balls of poison, and if we share our poison balls, we'll just have double poison."

Yiwei startles her with the most tragic smile she's ever seen. "You know that's not how feelings work, right?"

"In theory. In theory I know how feelings work. I used to be good at feelings, even. Right now? I . . ." She chokes. Her face feels like a hot mask, laced with salt. "I don't think any of it is working. At all. I can't grieve the people we lost. I can't feel bad about the person I killed, or all the people we left to die on a doomed planet. All I can do is try not to spill poison everywhere."

Yiwei gestures with his left hand, and now Xiaohou is playing some sweet, sad erhu music with a lot of trailing high notes.

"I'm scared everybody thinks I'm a dick." He sits up and kneads his own left shoulder. "Every time I say things like 'we don't have time for personal feelings.'"

"Yeah. I don't know how to deal with it when you say stuff like that. As if we're all just supposed to shut ourselves down, like robots." She shoots a look at Xiaohou, as if to say: *No offense.*

"I don't want to be that person. I'm trying to be strong, and help everyone cope, and it's making me hate myself. I don't know how to do the thing you do, where you bring people into the group and make them want to pitch in just by being kind to them."

Rachael looks past Yiwei at a picture she painted long ago: all six of the Earthlings sitting in the bluehouse on the *Indomitable,* staring into a well of stars. "I feel like when we first met, you were an optimist."

"That was a long time ago."

"Just promise me you'll stop trying to be the tough-love guy, okay?" Rachael reaches for him, and he reaches back.

"I'll do my best." Yiwei pulls her close. "But in return, you need to let me know what's going on with you. Okay? We can share our poison when we're alone in this room. I promise you we'll each have less poison to carry afterward."

"Okay. Yeah." She cries harder, and now he's crying, too. The two of them just weep on each other's shoulders while Xiaohou serenades them. Soon she'll have to get up and put her face back in neutral, so she can follow Fake Tina around and make sure she doesn't screw all of Rachael's friends. But for now, she and her boyfriend are two crying machines.

5.

The Glorious Nebula shimmies: a big fried egg the color of peach sorbet. Rachael has seen this incredible vista twice before, when she first traveled to Wentrolo and when she was running for her life inside a makeshift artist starship, but still, seeing such a massive swirl adds a couple extra secret chambers to her heart. What kind of materials would she use to draw this thing, anyway? Pastels? Watercolors? Some kind of high-tech nano-paste with hyper-ultra colors that are more vivid than anything on Earth? Maybe Rachael will try all of those, because *she can draw again,* and it's all she wants to do.

Then Rachael sees the refugees.

They go from pinpricks to shapes in an eyeblink. There are thousands of them, all circling the outside of the Glorious Nebula, trying to find a way in. A wall of Royal Compassion ships, including a half dozen broadswords, fires an occasional warning shot at any ship that gets too close.

"I don't get it," Kez says. "The first thing we were told when we arrived here before was that refugees are welcome here. The buildings will always make more space for people to live in."

"Marrant." Wyndgonk spits dark smoke. "As soon as he finished taking power, he decided to keep out almost all migrants, except for the ones from 'civilized' worlds like Irriyaia or Makvaria."

"Revulsion! That is horrible—" Zaeta says.

"—even for Marrant," Damini chimes in.

Damini, Zaeta, and Thaoh sit up front, at the controls of this stolen Compassion knifeship (which still has no name), while Wyndgonk, Rachael, Kez, and Elza huddle in the back.

"This is shameful," Thaoh says. "But it's good for us at least. We'll just appear to be another refugee ship, until we get in the middle of a confrontation with some Royal Compassion vessels."

"And then we drop our disguise and turn into a Compassion ship in the confusion," Kez says. "Cynical, but brilliant. Brinical? Cylliant? Anyway, the timing will need to be perfect."

Rachael hates being cooped up on this tiny ship, unable to get much space from Fake Tina.

"Can I ask your advice?" Kez says to Thaoh.

Thaoh raises one eyebrow. "I thought you didn't want to talk to me."

"That was before. When we'd just lost Tina." Kez kneads the back of eir head. "I just wanted to know . . . how do you keep going? I mean, you came back from the dead, and found everything you worked for was ruined. How do you get out of bed, or whatever it is you sleep in?"

Thaoh starts to crack a joke, then thinks better of it. "I gave a lot of thought to vanishing, pretending to be some random young Makvarian. But I couldn't run away from myself, and fighting is a habit by now." She tilts her chin at Kez. "I guess you've known some loss, too."

"I had my heart broken." Kez blows into eir clasped hands. "There's a boy named Ganno the Wurthhi, who's not speaking to me anymore. But way more than that, I had my *dreams* broken. Which I think is possibly worse?"

"You were wearing a diplomatic services uniform when I first met you." Thaoh tilts her head.

"I had this notion I could become an ambassador, go back home to Earth, and welcome my people to the galactic community, but I realized I couldn't speak for the Royal Fleet or the Firmament, even before Marrant took over."

"So you need to figure out how to be a peacemaker, *without* being a mouthpiece." Thaoh lifts her gaze to the carbonfast rafters. "You've chosen a difficult path. It's always easier to break things than to repair them, and people will inevitably accuse you of compromising too much. Still, sometimes an independent voice can bring people together more easily than an emissary from one side or another ever could."

"I get that. I just . . . I wanted to go home as the representative of something grand and ancient, with pomp everywhere. Just buckets of pomp. So people would have to listen to me."

Thaoh is replying, but Rachael can't listen anymore, because something vicious is trying to claw its way out of her and her face feels hot. She suddenly has an image of popping an airlock and shoving Fake Tina out into the vacuum of space—she feels ashamed right away, because that's the last thing she'd ever do, but the rage still eats away at her.

She's a ball of poison.

Rachael finds the least noisy corner and pulls out a lightpen and pad. She sketches furiously, making dark slashes and curves, until she finds the shape she's looking for. The voices around her fade as she gets lost in her picture, and oh wow, she missed this so much. The art just flows out of her, like old times.

When it's finished, she goes and finds Elza at the very back of the stolen knifeship, staring out of a viewport at the retreating stars.

Rachael wants to say something like "I drew you something," or "This is for you," but she's still in her art daze.

Elza turns away from the starscape—maybe she was hearing more bad news from the Ardenii—and gazes at the picture, then Rachael's face. "This is . . . this is beautiful." Elza's face goes blank again, then she shakes it off. "I love this. Wish we could make it real."

Come on. Do some words.

"We could use the ship's fabricators to make it," Rachael whispers at last. "Like on the *Indomitable* when they made uniforms for us."

"So you designed this for me to wear? I didn't know you did fashion design." Elza's smile is the candy coating around a whole lot of pain.

"I haven't in ages, but I was feeling inspired. I bet this would look amazing on you. I call it a tactical ballgown." High-waisted, with a big sash tied with a bow and a low neckline covered by lace, the dress in the picture has knee-length billowing skirts and sleeves that start puffy and then taper. The whole thing looks frivolous, except Rachael shows Elza where she could attach weapons and tools to the satiny folds, and the sleeves conceal silken ropes with grappling hooks. "I just . . . hate that you're going back to the Palace of Scented Tears like this. You deserve a huge ceremony, with people throwing flowers and doing dances in your honor, instead of sneaking inside like . . . like a thief."

"A tactical ballgown. Wow. Nobody else . . . nobody's . . . You are the only one who's tried to do things for me—instead of asking me for things, or telling me to stop doing things. And I . . ." Elza is never lost for words, but now she's stammering and shivering with her face flushed.

Rachael wishes she could do way more than this for Elza—she feels like a beacon of lonesomeness, a lighthouse among jagged rocks. Rachael doesn't know what it's like to get lost in visions of distant worlds, except that she kind of does. And maybe her longing resonates on the same frequency as Elza's.

Rachael wants to find a way to say some of this—but alarms start alarming.

Zaeta says, "It's time—"

"—to make the switch," Damini says.

The stolen knifeship has worked its way into a crowd of refugees, and now a group of Royal Compassion ships are moving to intercept.

"Be careful now." Thaoh moves to the pilot station and takes the empty third seat up front. "If our timing is off by even a microcycle . . ."

"We don't need piloting advice," Damini says without looking at Fake Tina.

"No distractions, please," adds Zaeta.

Thaoh makes a chef's-kiss motion against her lips: *I'll be quiet.*

Everybody holds their breath (except for Wyndgonk) while the knifeship scoots into the middle of a tangle of ships, half Royal Compassion and half refugees. The Royal Fleet and the Compassion only just reunified, and they probably haven't had time to get everyone on the same page with codes and protocols and things—so in theory, this should work.

"Wait for it," Zaeta mutters.

"Just a little longer," Damini says.

Ships crowd around the stolen knifeship on all sides, like a space scrimmage . . . and right when Rachael is sure they're about to collide, Damini hits a button and their ship throws off its shell of garbage. Suddenly, they look exactly like the other Royal Compassion patrol ships.

Then the refugee ships retreat to a safe distance, and the Compassion ships return to their formation around the perimeter of the Glorious Nebula.

"We did it!" Damini says.

"I cannot believe this worked," says Kez.

Of course, that's when the nearest Royal Compassion ship hails them. "Attention unidentified knifeship. Please transmit your clearances and mission identifiers immediately."

"Anxiety!" Zaeta squawks.

Elza steps forward and hits the comm link, putting on a perfect imitation of a Royal officer. "New alliances and forgotten vendettas. This is the knifeship *Healing Embrace*. We are returning to Wentrolo for emergency repairs, and our identifier is, uh . . ." Elza closes her eyes, like the Ardenii are giving her the correct answer. "Our identifier is parcel.5nx.burst7. Sorry for any confusion."

Rachael can feel the tension radiate off everyone around her, like Wyndgonk is spewing noxious red smoke. Their tiny ship is surrounded and they won't last a second if this goes bad.

The Royal Compassion ship says, "Sweet reunions and easy forgiveness, *Healing Embrace*. You are approved for approach to the Glorious Nebula. Good luck with the repairs."

"Said and done," Elza says in her "officer" voice. Then she turns off the comms and gives Thaoh a look of pure fury. "So your plan to go from refugee ship to Compassion ship was a failure. I'm starting to wonder what use you are."

"I ask myself that same question all the time," Thaoh says. "But I knew if things got tricky, the Ardenii would probably bail us out. We should be fine until we reach Wentrolo, and then the hard part begins: getting you inside the palace."

"And how exactly are we supposed to get Elza inside the most secure place in the galaxy—" Damini says.

"—without anyone noticing?" Zaeta says.

"That part is simple." Thaoh only smirks a little. "We're going to turn off the sun."

6

.

The NewSun holiday was a strong candidate for the worst day of Rachael's life. This was supposed to be a chance to bask in love and friendship and the rays of a newborn star—but instead, everything went rotten, right around the time they shut down the old sun to make way for the new. She can't think of that "party" without going back into the feeling of being stuck in the tragic dark.

So Rachael hates Thaoh's plan to get Elza inside the palace.

"It's the only way," Thaoh says once again. "We sneak inside the sun station and initiate a shutdown. It'll take them a few cycles to get the sun restarted, and Elza and Wyndgonk can slip inside the palace in the confusion."

"It's a solid plan," says Kez. "Except that people are already terrified because all the other suns are getting ready to die out. This artificial sun is the only one that's still okay, for now. If we shut it down, people will panic. There could be violence, riots, stampedes."

"Yeah," Damini says. "There are lines I won't cross, and I think this is one of them."

Wyndgonk, Kez, and Zaeta all start talking at once, going back and forth.

Then Elza steps forward, with one hand raised and her crown so bright it hurts to look at. Everybody stops talking.

"There's no time for a debate, and no other plan," Elza says. "Time is running out, countless lives are at stake. One thing I've learned since I became a princess: suffering is everywhere, and we have to do whatever we can to prevent a worse hurt."

"That is the slipperiest slope," Kez says. "You start out this way, you could end up justifying almost anything."

"If Tina was here—" Damini starts.

"Tina's gone." Elza looks at Thaoh, who meets her gaze. "We're all we have. We have a responsibility to everyone who's still alive."

Elza's tone leaves no room for argument. The ship is once again silent, except for Damini's and Zaeta's muttering as they set a course for Wentrolo, the city at the heart of Her Majesty's Firmament.

Seven Firmament Security officers guard the tiny floating platform that controls Wentrolo's homemade sun: two fox-faced Javarah, two moss-covered Yarthins, one pile-of-rocks Rosaei, one fizzy purple Makvarian, and one skull-faced Aribentor. They all wear shiny armor with the Joyful Wyvern on one shoulder, and they're standing alert with cloudstrike guns in thigh holsters.

Thaoh studies their movements from above. She's sitting on an orbital funnel (a kind of round elevator platform that flies on its own) with Kez and Rachael, while Damini and Zaeta are already ferrying Elza and Wyndgonk to the palace.

"Seven of them, three of us," she says. "I've faced worse odds."

Kez and Rachael look at each other.

"Umm," Kez says. "It's only three against seven if you consider moral support really helpful."

"You . . . don't fight. Either of you." Thaoh has a way of sighing, laughing, and groaning all at once.

"I'm kind of a pacifist," Kez says. "Rachael used to do this thing where she controlled blue energy with her hands, but that's gone."

Rachael holds up her hands: *See, no blue fire.*

Sigh/laugh/groan.

"And Tina, the person whose body you're, uh, using. She was also pretty pacifist," Kez says. "She wouldn't want you to hurt anyone using her body. I know, she's gone and it's your body now. I'm just saying."

"I'll . . . keep that in mind."

Rachael lived in Wentrolo for months, but she never saw the whole thing until now: five curved shapes, like the blades of an old-fashioned ceiling fan, with agate-blue water between them.

"Can you at least make a distraction?" Thaoh folds her arms.

Kez eyes Rachael and nods. "Sure, we can be distracting."

Rachael digs inside her bag and finds a can of noxious spray paint—which was left behind by Nyitha, her old art teacher (who turned out to be Marrant's ex-wife, Aym). Rachael shakes it until she's ready to unleash stinky graffiti on any surface she aims at.

For sure, those blue-glow powers would come in handy right about now.

She could be imprisoning these guards inside energy cages, or knocking them unconscious without hurting them, if she could still move walls of energy around like she did before. Rachael was so eager to get rid of them, especially if it meant getting back her artistic skills, but maybe she was being selfish.

This is one of a dozen things she wishes she could talk to Tina about.

The orbital funnel arcs underneath the sun station platform, and then Rachael and Kez clamber up an access ramp to the main walkway encircling the station—where the seven guards are patrolling.

Rachael takes out her can of paint and then pauses, staring at the blank gray carbonfast wall in front of her.

"Are you scared?" Kez says. "Because—"

"No, no, not scared. Just trying to figure out what to paint. I want this to be something cool."

Most people would snap at her, remind her that this isn't about self-expression. But Kez just nods. "Take your time."

Rachael frowns a tad longer, then starts spraying a picture of the plushie dinosaur costume that she and Tina used to wear back on Earth, when they pranked scumbags as part of a group called the Lasagna Hats. The paint stinks worse than Rachael remembers, to the point where she has to hold her nose with one hand as she sprays. The wall starts to melt and it's so satisfying, you have no idea.

Kez is talking to someone. Rachael realizes they're surrounded by four guards in shiny Firmament Security armor, and she was so in the zone she didn't notice.

". . . purely peaceful intentions. I'm not wearing the uniform at the moment, but I'm a fully enrolled junior ambassador in the diplomatic service. If you have any disputes, I am qualified to mediate. My friend here is just going to make some artwork to beautify your space, and then we'll be on our way."

Yech, eyes watering from the (basically) tear gas spraying out of this can. The wall is going to have a permanent dinosaur-shaped hole.

". . . under arrest for violation of the . . ." says a Rosaei (person made of rocks) who towers over both of them.

"Need I remind you, free expression is guaranteed under the charter of Her Majesty's Firmament," Kez says.

Someone shouts from the other end of the walkway, but they get cut off mid-yell. Even over the hiss of the spray can, Rachael hears the unmistakable sound of a brawl in progress. Thuds and yelps, then a cloudstrike gun firing wildly.

The guards surrounding Kez and Rachael look at each other. "Go," the Rosaei says to the others. "I'll handle these two."

"We don't want to be a bother," Kez says.

Rachael puts down the can, because she's melted the wall down to some fancy high-tech guts and she's gagging a little. More punchy-kicky noises come from the other side of the circular walkway, then there's just silence.

The Rosaei tries to look over their shoulder without taking their eyes off Rachael and Kez. "I've got your friends," the guard shouts. "Surrender peacefully, and they will not be harmed."

Thaoh Argentian comes running around the corner, just as Rachael sprays some vandalism juice on the guard's armored chest. The guard recoils, and stumbles into Thaoh's right hook.

Kez steps over the prone body of the guard. "Let's do this fast, in case any of them had a chance to trigger an alarm."

"No need to worry about that," Thaoh says. "But by all means, let's hurry." She hustles inside the sun station, with Kez and Rachael on her heels.

The middle of the sun station is one big octagonal room, with a high ceiling and picture windows on all sides showing an incredible view of the whole city. Kez rushes to the center of the space, where a big holographic workstation shows the current status of the artificial sun.

"Okay, give me a beat." Kez wipes eir brow. "I want to make sure I know what I'm doing. I'm guessing it'll be easy to shut down the sun—the hard part is making sure they'll be able to start it up again without too much fuss."

Kez pokes at the interface and starts muttering "wow" to emself over and over.

If people get hurt after the unscheduled sun failure, Rachael will never be able to live with herself. She hears Kez saying *slipperiest slope* in her head, while the real Kez tries to find the most humane way to plunge everyone into night. At least unlike the actual NewSun holiday, this time all of the other lights will still be on, so nobody will really be in the dark.

Rachael turns to ask Thaoh Argentian where exactly they're supposed to draw the line.

Thaoh is gone.

When Rachael gets to the doorway, she sees Thaoh in the middle of stealing a floating barge that's parked alongside the walkway. Thaoh is almost done hot-wiring it, or whatever you do with a super-advanced flying gondola. She sees Rachael and gives a sheepish expression.

Rachael still doesn't have it in her to talk to Fake Tina. She runs back inside the sun station and tells Kez, "She's ditching us."

"Of course she is." Kez shakes eir head. "Go after her. I'll be fine."

"Are you sure?"

"Yeah. I can take the orbital funnel to the rendezvous. And we're responsible for whatever she gets up to while the sun is kaput. Go!"

Rachael hesitates—what if something happens to Kez? Except she knows that e can take care of emself. And this could be the last time she ever sees Tina's face, the moment when she gives up once and for all on getting Tina back.

"Hug?" Rachael whispers.

"Hug," Kez agrees.

Rachael throws her arms around em and whispers, "I'll see you soon."

Then she runs and jumps on board the barge right before it drifts away from the edge of the walkway.

"What the hell are you doing?" Thaoh blurts. "You do not want to come with me. This is going to be dangerous and you will not like what I'm about to do."

Rachael shrugs, like *Too bad, you're stuck with me.* She goes and sits on one of the benches along the side and starts sketching on her lightpad, as if she was in the back seat of her parents' hatchback on the way to her grandma's house.

7

.

WYNDGONK

Sing fire, sing water, sing blood. The cries of Dnynths above, the hissing of the earth below—they remind us that life is a never-ending sprint, under poison skies, with no reward except to keep running another daynight. Keep me in your flaming orison, microscopic saints of the air.

Wyndgonk prays so quietly, nobody can tell. Except that Elza smiles at fire. Because of course the Ardenii know, and they let her know, because they respect nobody's privacy. Wyndgonk turns away from Elza and prays more quietly.

From above, the Palace of Scented Tears looks like one of the cabbages that used to fall from the clouds when Wyndgonk ran fast enough, fire legs pistoning and chopping on the red clay. Fire used to think it was hilarious that the queen lived in a cabbage-shaped building.

"How much longer?" Wyndgonk asks Elza.

Elza shrugs. "Any second now. We'll need to move fast."

Wyndgonk nods, though fire shell scrunches a little with annoyance at Elza's bossiness. She might be an actual princess now, but that doesn't make her Wyndgonk's ruler. Fire can't bring fireself to bow and scrape, or to call her *Your Radiance*.

The two of them sit on board a stolen barge, hovering almost directly over the palace, ready to lower themselves onto the roof as soon as Kez and the others shut down the sun.

Wyndgonk thought fire would never return to the palace—which would have been no great loss.

The princess selection program was every bit as exhausting as fire had expected. Except for one saving grace: Elza went out of her way to find the most friendless candidates and befriend them. Every time Wyndgonk had a panic attack or got revolted by the levels of unexamined privilege inside those fairy-tale walls, fire remembered that fire was part of a team. A guild, even.

And now everyone back home is watching to see if the cloud rivers are going askew, the first sign of the sun turning into a cold ball of death. *This has to work.*

Elza always looks sad and distracted, ever since she gained a crown and lost her love. She sits motionless, staring at nothing, as the Ardenii fill her head with dreadful news. That crown is cursed, and Wyndgonk gives thanks every day that fire never had any hope of winning it.

Wyndgonk wants to say something to comfort Elza, but they come from such different cultures, and what makes Wyndgonk feel better might just upset an Earth person, even with the EverySpeak translating everything. Wyndgonk has mostly settled for being "the sarcastic friend" and making grouchy observations, instead of trying to open up about fire own hope-fears.

(Wyndgonk realized after a long time that "hope" and "fear" were two separate words in most other languages, whereas in Thythuthyan, they're the same concept. Every hope contains a fear, and the other way around.)

How would Elza react if Wyndgonk shared what was really going through fire head, instead of serving up wisecracks? All the fear and regret and dread and longing? Would Elza be annoyed, or tell Wyndgonk to shut up? Especially now that she's a *princess.*

Elza breaks the silence. "Thank you for coming with me, I know this must be really scary for you. The way they treated you in that palace before . . . it was unforgivable. You're one of the bravest people I've ever met. Are you sure you're going to be okay, though?"

Wyndgonk wants to say, *No, in fact I'm about to spew flaming chunks.* But fire just snorts. "What are they going to do, feed me more over-seasoned cake? As long as the palace itself doesn't try to kill us, it's all good."

"I think the Ardenii are keeping us a secret. For now. I hope." Elza rolls her head. "The Ardenii have been telling me about your home, Thythuthy. It sounds like an amazing place, I hope I get to visit someday. They tell me that there are three pronouns: fire, water, and blood."

"That's right. Three breeds, three jobs. My pronoun is *fire* because I was chosen as a run-farmer, running super fast to pull our food crops down from the clouds, and my fire helped to keep the Dnynths away. If my pronoun was *water,* I'd be a run-fisher. If my pronoun was *blood,* I'd be a priest or an inventor, and I wouldn't run at all."

Wyndgonk sighs: white fire. "I would have been happy to stay home and run, but the Echelon needed someone to try their claw at this 'princess' business. So they held a race and announced that the slowest person would have to come to this palace. I lost because I had a stomachache from eating too many rootberries."

"I'm glad they sent you." Elza raises the sides of her tiny humanoid mouth, which Wyndgonk has learned to recognize as a "smile."

"I'm not." Wyndgonk clicks mandibles. "But I am glad that I met you."

Elza starts to say something else, but then she stops. "It's happening. Kez just sent the signal. We're about to have an unscheduled lights-out. Let's go." She's already pulling silken cords from the sleeves of her ballgown, using them to swing down onto the palace roof.

Wyndgonk teeters on the rim of the barge, clutching a tiny cube that's supposed to provide a slow descent to the cabbage-shaped roof. Fire almost says, *Nah, I'm gonna stay up here and watch the show from a safe distance.*

Instead, fire takes a deep breath—and feels the flame inside burn a little brighter—then jumps off the barge. The roof rushes closer and all the other buildings streak past, then the impeller kicks in and Wyndgonk drifts gently down. Elza's already there, perched between two leaves of the cabbage and looking for the secret way inside the Palace of Scented Tears.

A noise deafens Wyndgonk from overhead—sounds like someone yelling, but it's the fake sun letting go of its hydrogen—and the sky darkens. Even though they were waiting for this to happen, it's still a major shock. The scream stops, but then countless other voices start crying out, all over the city.

"Come on," Elza says. "Won't take them long to get the sun up and running again. We need to get inside the queen's contemplation suite before anybody figures out we're here."

Wyndgonk's got the same lung-stomachache as when fire used to eat too many rootberries.

The palace is nothing like what Wyndgonk remembered. No crystal wings overhead, no chattering adorable cartoons, no swaying silk curtains. The walls and ceiling are colored a deep red, like the blood of humanoids, and shadows move at random, with no light source to cast them.

This place was creepy before, but now it's unbearable. Wyndgonk knows that the palace reflects the thoughts and feelings of the Ardenii, the super-genius computers that share their knowledge with the queen and with princesses like Elza. So it looks like the Ardenii are feeling pretty unhappy.

Elza adjusts the fuchsia tactical ballgown that Rachael designed for her, and the lacy front section tightens into an armored breastplate. "The queen's suite is at the top of the palace, so we should be close. The Ardenii are telling me contradictory things, like they're confused. Or they don't want to admit what's going on here. Help is on the way."

Wyndgonk doesn't know what Elza means by "help is on the way," until someone comes running around the corner on five clawed legs.

"There you are," breathes Gyrald (*they/them*), the Flavkin with the fleshy petal face and hooked claws, who was Wyndgonk's other friend in the princess program. "Thank goodness you're here. Flenby's tears, I've been so scared since you left."

Wyndgonk stares at Gyrald. "You're still here, in the palace? Even after Marrant killed everyone else?"

"Where was I going to go?" Gyrald cracks open their petals in a queasy sort of smile. "I can't go home, and the rest of this city isn't safe for me either. I never officially dropped out of the princess program, so the palace helps keep me safe and hidden from Princess Nonesuch and Marrant's people."

As soon as Gyrald mentions Marrant's people, heavy footsteps ring out. Dark shapes twitch and skitter on the cracked red wall, as if even the shadows are seeking a place to hide.

"It's not safe here," Gyrald says. "Well, it's not safe anywhere. But I think we can get to the queen's suite without getting caught, if we move now."

"We can't decipher that rusty cup here? I thought you said we needed to be inside the palace," Wyndgonk grumbles.

"I need direct access," Elza says. "Sorry."

"Oh! Congratulations, Your Radiance." Gyrald does a sort of five-legged curtsey. "Your acquaintance is a blessing."

"No time for that." Elza does the face-raising thing again, but her eyes don't change. "It's so good to see you, Gyrald."

"Same to you. I kept hoping you would come back here and chase all of the creeps away."

"I . . . I don't know how to do that." Elza hunches over, fiddling with the sleeves of her ballgown. She closes her eyes—maybe the Ardenii tell her something, or maybe it's a lot of things—and then she straightens up and strides forward. "Let's go. We don't have much time. I just hope Thaoh is ready to help with our extraction."

The three of them crawl forward, stopping every few heartbeats to hide from more footsteps. Elza tells Wyndgonk and Gyrald to climb to the top of a pointy arch in the middle of a crumbling chamber, and then to do a sudden left turn followed by a sudden right turn—the Ardenii are giving her the exact route to get to the queen's suite without being noticed.

The queen's suite is at the end of a drab reddish-gray plaster hallway, with a simple black door, the least fancy part of the palace Wyndgonk has seen. The door swings right open and they creep inside a dark chamber where something rustles and creaks. And there's a groaning sound, not too different from the racket the fake sun made when it spewed its fuel.

Elza reaches into a big pouch on the side of her tactical ballgown and pulls out the old cup that all of this trouble has been about. "Here we go. I just need a little time." She gropes in the darkness until she places the cup on a recessed shelf.

The moaning gets louder, and then it turns into a voice that wheezes, "Run. Run now. Go."

A figure with a tarnished crown over pointy ears, and a black lace dress stands at the center of a web. It looks like the silken threads the Dnynths use to ensnare Wyndgonk's people back home: a thousand strands, criss-crossing around her.

When Wyndgonk gets closer, fire sees the sticky wires aren't just interlacing around the figure—they're going inside the skin. The figure writhes and struggles against the trap.

"You must leave now," the queen says. "Please, you must go. You're in terrible danger."

8
.

Queen Amnesty greeted Wyndgonk when fire first arrived in the palace: a giddy Javarah who asked impossible questions and seemed to see through everyone's deceptions. Seeing her trapped and broken makes Wyndgonk's lung-stomachs churn worse than ever. If they can do this to the queen, what hope is there for anyone?

"Flenby's tears," Gyrald says. "How did this happen? We need to get you out of here, Your Radiance. Just hold still, just . . . we'll get you out."

"We are beyond rescue, and you can do nothing for us," the queen rasps. "You were foolish to come here."

"I'm taking you to safety," Elza says. "Let them try to stop me."

"Princess." The queen bows her head a little. "That we missed your coronation is one of a thousand regrets that tax us as much as these threads. We could have helped you choose a splendid new name. Alas, you are so new to your crown, you will be defenseless if found here."

Elza shudders. "These threads . . . the Ardenii won't explain. But Marrant and the others are trying to take your crown away from you. They want a new queen, one who will do their bidding. Right? Someone with no moral center, someone like Princess Nonesuch."

This just gets worse and worse. Wyndgonk is battling the urge to run, as if a swarm of Dnynths were on fire tail.

"Just leave." The queen coughs. "We cannot protect you. We are hiding your presence as best we can, but our control is waning." She makes a sound like a rusty hinge. "Princess Nonesuch will know your whereabouts soon."

Elza points her chin toward the rusty old cup in the alcove. "You know what I brought here. This is more important than anything else."

The queen nods. "We had believed that cup to be a myth. Technology so ancient, its secrets lay buried deep and its gaze might have beheld the very beginnings of our troubles. It is impressive that you and your friends somehow found it. You must not let it be consumed by the blight that has overtaken this palace."

"Your Radiance." Gyrald steps forward on great hooked feet. "Let me take your place inside that web. I believe I can trick those threads into attacking me instead of you, and then you can escape and keep your crown out of the grasp of these wretches."

Wyndgonk thinks, *The time to worry about the crown falling into the wrong hands was back when you were designing a system that gave one person this much power.*

The queen stares at Gyrald, astonished. "Gyrald from Flavkin. You would really offer yourself? After everyone in this palace treated you like an inferior because of the shape of your body, and because they never bothered to try to understand your culture, why would you sacrifice yourself for us?"

Wyndgonk is thinking the exact same thing.

"Well, umm . . ." Gyrald's face-petals fold inward a little. "I can't help but love this place, in spite of all the unkindness I've experienced. And if Marrant and Princess Nonesuch obtain that crown, it will be bad for all of us, everywhere. The things they could do with full access to the Ardenii . . . they could do even more harm."

"Are you kidding?" Wyndgonk steps forward. "You've spent so long in this palace, you've fallen in love with your oppressors. These people? Are not your friends."

"I don't make decisions based on what the worst people think about me," Gyrald sputters.

"Enough." Elza steps forward. "I will take Queen Amnesty's place inside this web. My crown for hers. I should be able to trick the threads into holding me instead of her, for a while at least. The rest of you take the cup back to our friends."

The queen shakes her head slowly, painfully. "None of you is taking my place here. You would not last an eyeblink against these life-siphoning strands." She turns to look at the cup. "We have unlocked the secrets of that ancient cup already, including the origin point of the Bereavement, the place from whence the swarm of tiny black holes was launched. You must journey to the Plains of the Endless and seek the wedding feast of the gods. Now go."

Elza takes the cup and tucks it back inside her gown. Then she looks back at the queen. "This isn't the way it should be. None of this is right. I know, I know: knowledge is ugly. I can't change the facts. But this is garbage, and I hate it."

"There are so many things we regret. We should have done more to stop Marrant, before it was too late. We wish you could stand by our side as part of our court, instead of skulking about the palace. But you must leave: they're coming, and we cannot conceal you."

Elza nods, and it turns into a shudder. And then the three of them are running away from the doomed figure shrouded in black lace and white threads.

They run, and the palace closes in around them. The very walls seem to encroach, the passageways getting narrower and darker. Whispers, hissing laughter, and skittering feet come from nowhere and everywhere. They pass through a gauzy curtain that smells like death, and nearly topple into a pit.

Something does not wish them to leave this place.

"There's no way back to the roof," Elza says. "We need to find another way."

"Follow me," Gyrald says. "I may be a dupe who's in love with my oppressors, but at least I've gotten to know this palace much better while you two were gone."

Gyrald leads Wyndgonk and Elza downward, into the depths of the palace. Wyndgonk's skin feels soft and clammy underneath fire shell—bad memories, plus absolute evil closing in.

They arrive at a dark, cavernous space, with hundreds of shapes fluttering on the ceiling. Wyndgonk doesn't recognize the Royal Receiving Room at first: those twitching things are what's left of the crystal wings that used to beat overhead, and the walls are coated with something that looks like rust, or mold.

"Too exposed in here," Elza says. "Gyrald, how do we get out?"

"Too late, 'Rogue Princess.'" Princess Nonesuch steps into the center of the room, flanked by five other princesses and a host of attendants. Palace guards, with the red slash of the Compassion added to their dark blue uniforms, surge forward from every direction.

They're surrounded, outgunned. Trapped.

"You may have become a princess, but you dishonor this court," Princess Nonesuch says to Elza. "You do not belong here, no more than that diadem belongs on your head. Your ascension was a mistake, a folly perpetrated by Princess Constellation. I tried to warn her."

Elza bristles and steps toward the other princesses. "I deserve this as much as any of you. I'm not doubting myself anymore."

"There are six of us, against only one of you. And we've spent years mastering our connections to the Ardenii, with the help of each other and the most experienced mentors and advisers. We can pry that crown off your head like a cheap hat."

"You are welcome to try." Elza stands tall, hands on her hips. "I haven't been hiding away in a fancy palace, I've been fighting to survive, and it's made me strong."

Princess Nonesuch laughs, her bone-covered face cracking open. "A duel, then? Or a test? We can see which of us can better stand to witness the unbearable: a test you failed once before, if memory serves."

"I'm ready this time."

These humanoids are doing their fighting stances again: feet planted, arms squared, tiny faces full of scowls.

Elza is getting drawn into a fight she can't possibly win, and her pride won't let her back down. And everyone, everywhere, is doomed if they don't complete their mission here.

Wyndgonk knows from experience that when humanoids get into their status games about which of them can hold their tiny head higher, it's almost impossible to get them to stand down. And Elza is stubborner than most.

So Wyndgonk does the only thing fire can think of—the thing fire has been longing to do since fire first arrived in this palace.

Burn the whole place down.

The jet of flame that comes out of Wyndgonk's mouth is mostly for show, and can't really be used as a weapon, most of the time. But in extreme life-or-death situations, Thythuthyans can spray a jet of flame, hot enough to melt anything short of reinforced carbonfast, for up to about twenty meters.

The bright orange flame catches on the fancy dresses of the princesses and the clean, shiny uniforms of the guards and attendants. Wyndgonk sees one guard drop their suddenly red-hot gun, and then the air is full of smoke.

"Please move." Wyndgonk doesn't try to hide the disgust and terror in fire voice. No more cute sarcasm. "I don't want to die here, and I don't want you to, either."

Elza, Wyndgonk, and Gyrald sprint toward the nearest exit under cover of the smoke. The palace probably has a hundred ways to put out a fire, so they don't have long.

They're still surrounded by a small army.

Elza sees a strange symbol on the floor and rushes to step on it. The floor opens up, and she leads Wyndgonk and Gyrald down into a dark cellar.

Elza stalks forward, fists clenched and teeth gritted, past a group of people who are having a tearful argument. One of them looks like Elza's girlfriend Tina, or maybe it's Thaoh Argentian.

"Flenby's blood, that was terrifying," Gyrald says. "What is this place?"

"It's a secret part of the palace where you can see anything that happened in the past." Elza doesn't slow down or look back. "We'll be safe down here. We just need to find another way out."

Wyndgonk slows down to watch Thaoh Argentian shouting at another Makvarian—who looks a lot like Thondra Marrant.

"Ignore them," Elza says. "They made these mistakes a long time ago, and we've got our own mistakes to make."

Gyrald and Wyndgonk both slow down, because . . . what if you could actually make sense of all this past, and figure out where things went wrong in the first place? Wyndgonk imagines being able to see the moments when fire first arrived here, all the things the other princess candidates said behind fire back.

"We need to get to the extraction point as fast as possible, and pray that Thaoh is ready for us." Elza is giving orders, just like any other princess. "Even if Princess Nonesuch and Marrant eventually get the information from that cup, we might have a head start."

"I'm not . . ." Gyrald flaps their petals. "I'm not coming with you."

"What? Why would you stay here?" Wyndgonk growls.

"I still have so much to learn here, and I'm not cut out for spying or fighting or racing against time. Especially now that I know about this basement, where I can witness the real past, I need to spend as much time as I can down here."

Elza steps forward with one foot but keeps the other foot planted, as if she's being pulled in two different directions. "But—"

"I've lasted this long because the palace keeps me hidden. As long as I'm no threat to anybody, I think I'll be fine." Gyrald's petal-face spreads open wider. "And . . . I still can't let go of the idea that I'm going to become a princess. It could happen! I keep studying and passing tests, even if the selection program is officially over."

Elza nods. "You would be a great princess." She leans forward. "Is it okay if I hug you goodbye?"

Gyrald wraps three of their five legs around Elza and leans into her chest. "I'm going to miss you. Again."

Wyndgonk balks for a moment, then squishes fire shell against both of their bodies.

Just then footsteps come from behind them, and a voice sounds out. "I'm coming for that crown," Princess Nonesuch says. "Your coronation is a mistake that I intend to correct."

Blood-faced Dnynths.

Wyndgonk and Elza start running deeper into the basement, as the princess's voice and a host of footfalls come from behind them. There's no way out. They're trapped, here in the past, with some of the worst people alive. This is not how Wyndgonk wanted to die.

9

.

RACHAEL

Of *course* Captain Argentian takes Rachael to the one place she hoped she would never see again.

The bird-shaped front of the Royal Command Post seems to glower at Rachael from the shadows, as if the feeling is mutual. This is where they tried to give Rachael a medal—and now it's become Marrant's seat of power.

Rachael does a double take. "This is why you bailed on us? You want to have some kind of reunion with Marrant?"

"Not a reunion, exactly." Thaoh shakes her head. "Millions would be alive today if I had killed that man when I had the chance, when I was alive before. I need to repair my worst mistake."

"I hate him too, but stopping the Bereavement is more important," Rachael hisses. "I thought your whole thing was that you make the tough choices. Plus Elza is counting on you to help her get out of the palace."

"Elza is a princess. She'll do just fine on her own."

"You're going to get caught," Rachael says, "and then all of my friends will get caught."

"I'm not going to get caught, unless you get in my way."

Giant banners hang from all the buildings nearby: Marrant's face, the size of a skyscraper, flashing white teeth and saying something Rachael can't hear.

Rachael wants to point out that Marrant is just a symptom of a larger problem. The Royal Fleet and the Firmament were founded by, basically, the same people who used to run the evil Seven-Pointed Empire back in the day. And even though they were trying to be kinder and better, they never really dealt with their past, or made real amends. But she's having a hard time talking to Fake Tina, and their barge is gliding toward the heart of evil.

As they get closer, the Royal Command Post starts to look different, even apart from the fact that everything is shrouded in gloom. Marrant has fenced off a huge stone-paved plaza around the building, with Firmament

Security officers checking everybody going in and out. Rocket-shaped drones circle overhead. Two large statues, at least twenty feet tall, stand at either side of the bird—except they're not statues, they're mechas, like in anime. People are walking around inside their heads.

"I do love a challenge," Thaoh says.

Banners on the front of the building proclaim: HOPE IS HERE. Floodlights at ground level cast salty triangles upward onto the sides of the building.

Their stolen barge glides through the shadows on the edge of the compound, while Thaoh studies every inch of the security. They come around to the back of the building, and Marrant is standing at a podium on a floating stage, like the one where Rachael accepted her medal. He's wearing a simple rust-colored suit, with the Compassion's slash on his chest and the Royal Fleet's winged-serpent emblem on one shoulder. Maybe a thousand people are clustered in front of the stage, in another fenced-off area, listening to Marrant speak.

Behind Marrant, a dozen Royal Compassion leaders wear crisp uniforms with medals all over their left sleeves. "It's a mockery." Thaoh's lip curls. "Where the Royal Fleet had explorers and visioners, the Royal Compassion has enforcers and vindicators. They look like a military occupation."

Just like in the hologram Rachael saw on Vandal Station, Marrant is putting on an easygoing smile, though his whole body is wound tight. His voice echoes across the slate-tiled square: "—these terrorists think that attacking our artificial sun will stop us, as if we were children afraid of the dark, but they do not know our resolve—" Every few lines, the packed audience cheers and stomps their feet.

"Our values, our very way of life, are at risk," Marrant says. "Wentrolo must be purged." He gestures, and some Royal Compassion enforcers drag a group of people, maybe twenty of them, onto the stage. "No doubt you recognize some of these people. They served in leadership roles in this city, or they were instructors at the academy, and they chose to undermine people's faith in our institutions in the midst of a crisis."

Marrant beckons. One of the people, a Zyzyian, gets dragged forward—bright pink bubbles stream out of the blowhole on top of the head.

"Instructor Caynu," Marrant purrs. "You were heard telling people that I was spending too much time consolidating my power, instead of addressing the problem of the Bereavement. That type of malicious paranoia only causes panic and disorder at a time like this."

Instructor Caynu starts to say something, but Marrant lashes out with his right hand.

Marrant is standing in front of a greasy puddle, which looks especially nasty in the low light. Everybody in the audience shudders, because they all knew and respected Caynu, and they're feeling those memories curdle. Even Rachael, who never met Caynu before, feels the surge of loathing.

Marrant is already beckoning the next prisoner forward.

"So that's the famous death touch." Thaoh's voice drips with bitterness. "He's learned to use it to discredit anyone who gets in his way. Quite an effective tool of statecraft." She scans the perimeter fence and the side of the building. "I don't suppose it would do any good for me to tell you to wait here."

Rachael feels like hiding for a month, but she shakes her head. The barge drifts downward toward a supply vehicle that's bound for the inside of the command post.

After they hop off the supply drone, Thaoh leads Rachael through a series of maintenance ducts and a laundry passage, and then they climb a narrow elevator shaft and creep through several floors of archives. "I used to sneak into this building constantly," Thaoh mutters. "I know its bones."

They're pretty close to the top of the building, where Rachael met Marrant before. Thaoh won't stop quizzing Rachael about Marrant's weaknesses: he shrugged off a pulse cannon at close range, but Yiwei made him bleed by throwing an ugly ornament at his face. And if any part of him touches you, you're finished. The whole conversation is nauseating.

It's just sinking in that Thaoh is planning on assassinating Marrant, and Rachael is along for the ride. If Rachael heard Marrant was dead, she wouldn't feel bad, but helping to murder him feels like a different thing entirely. Plus Thaoh is going to use Tina's body.

You will not like what I'm about to do.

The big chamber inside the raptor's head looks much the same as before, with the panoramic view of Wentrolo (still in the dark, for a little while longer). The opposite wall has a big display, showing the entire galaxy and highlighting the stars that are being affected by the Bereavement.

"So it's mostly affecting some main sequence stars," Thaoh murmurs. "Just the ones you'd want to live close to." She finds the control to open up the hidden chamber at one side of the room. A bed, a few chairs, some clothes. This must be Marrant's bedchamber.

"What do we do now?" Rachael asks, but Thaoh shushes her.

Footsteps are entering the big chamber with the picture window and the giant map. Marrant's voice rings out, and a few other voices answer. "Wait outside," Marrant says.

A few voices respond in unison, "With a will." Heavy steps move outside the chamber. The door whooshes shut, with Marrant's guards on the other side.

Thaoh creeps closer to the doorway, and Rachael follows. Marrant shakes his head as three attendants bustle around him in silken, cream-colored uniforms with hoods: making snah-snah juice, lighting candles, arranging everything for Marrant's comfort.

One of the attendants has her back turned to Marrant, and her hood is pulled all the way forward to cover her face. But the motion of her hands as she stirs a carafe of snah-snah juice looks super familiar. The tendons in her wrists flex, and her feet stumble a little. Rachael would know that crooked neck anywhere.

Rachael's former art teacher. Nyitha.

She's hiding in plain sight—right behind her ex-husband.

"Wait," Rachael hisses to Thaoh. "There's . . ."

But Thaoh is already springing through the doorway, ready to end Marrant once and for all.

10

.

One of the attendants cowers, while another one runs for the door to warn the guards. Thaoh throws a wooden statuette and a candle, and both attendants fall unconscious on the floor. The third attendant—Nyitha—just stiffens and lets her ladle fall back into the snah-snah container.

Marrant turns to confront his assailant. He sees Thaoh—his posture stiffens, while his eyes soften. Rachael can see the emotions at war, like some part of him still wants to reach out to his oldest friend, even now.

Then he puts on a bored expression. "Tina Mains again. I must confess I was wondering when you would turn up, since we seem overdue for yet another pointless confrontation in which you mistake naïveté for principles."

Thaoh shakes her head. "Tina isn't here. I made you a promise a long time ago, to hold you to a higher standard, and I'm going to keep it the only way I know how."

Marrant laughs so hard that milky tears come out of his eyes and he starts to shake.

Thaoh recoils. "What exactly is so funny?"

"You've tried this tactic one time too many, is all. You really thought you could confuse me by pretending to be *her,* yet again? I can't believe your Thaoh Argentian impression has actually gotten worse since the last time."

Thaoh reels, because this is the last thing she was expecting. Then she shakes it off.

"Doesn't matter if you believe it's me. I did not come here to talk."

Thaoh throws a chair at Marrant, and while he's busy ducking, she's hurling the carafe of snah-snah juice. The carafe hits him in the arm and knocks him sideways.

Marrant lashes out with one hand, but Thaoh has already leapt out of his reach.

She throws more blunt instruments at her former best friend, careful to stay far enough away to avoid his death touch. "Lucky for me this room is soundproofed."

Rachael can't help looking at Nyitha: she isn't watching the two people she loves most in the world try to kill each other, she's staring down at the ladle that fell out of the snah-snah container. Her hands shake, her whole body is rigid.

"Well, this is new after all," Marrant chuckles. "You're really trying to do me harm this time. Every other time you just taunted me and ran away."

"I told you." Thaoh sounds calm, matter-of-fact. "I made you a promise, the night before we shipped out on the *Inquisitive*. I swore I would hold you to a higher standard than anyone else. You fell so far below that standard, there's only one remedy left."

Right around the time Thaoh snaps a carbonfast chair leg in half and hurls the sharp end at Marrant's chest, he realizes she's actually trying to kill him.

"You . . . you're really her. I'd given up hope." Marrant's pale blue eyes are a map of hurt and longing. Rachael almost feels bad for him, until she remembers who this is.

This conference room is looking completely trashed; all the furniture lies in ruins and the walls have some brand-new dents and gashes in them. Thaoh is holding a chunk of conference table in each hand, long enough to bludgeon Marrant without getting too close.

"And you only came here to kill me? You don't even want to talk first?" Marrant pleads.

Thaoh doesn't answer, just swings one of her conference-table clubs at Marrant's head.

Rachael sneaks over to Nyitha. "We need to help her," she whispers.

"You've ruined everything," Nyitha whispers back.

"I'm sorry. I tried to stop her. But—"

"—but nobody ever tells Thaoh what to do. I know."

Nyitha turns and throws off her disguise, advancing on Marrant and Thaoh.

"Great hunger of sages, Thaoh. I spend days upon days waiting for the right moment to kill this fool. And you just storm in and make a mess. I thought you were supposed to be a strategist."

Marrant turns and sees his ex-wife coming up behind him. He sinks to his knees. "Aym. You're alive. You're alive, and you've been here this whole time, and you . . ." He looks from Thaoh to Nyitha and back again. "Both of you, here. We're finally together again. I never close my eyes without seeing your faces. I gave you both everything, and would have given more if I could. And now you're here, but you won't even speak to me?"

"You're not worth talking to," Nyitha says crisply. She turns to Thaoh. "I've got this. Take Rachael and get out of here."

"He's hard to kill," Thaoh protests.

"Yes. He is." Nyitha sounds like she's explaining basic facts to a third-grader. "That's why I spent so much time preparing, instead of just blundering in here and throwing furniture."

Nyitha walks toward her ex-husband, her face completely empty of emotion. He's still kneeling on the floor, looking up at her.

"You're really here," he whispers. "Please, let me tell you, explain why . . . I didn't ever want to hurt you. We could start over."

Thaoh moves forward to help Nyitha, but she casts a look that stops Thaoh in her tracks.

"Do you remember what you told me, when we were first in love?" Nyitha looks down at Marrant, her voice quiet. "You had visited a dry-root seer, and she'd told you the best future for you and me." He nods, and she continues. "It's all come to pass. We commanded a ship together. We achieved greatness, and the secrets we stole lifted you up. Only one part remains."

Nyitha leans over and kisses Marrant on the cheek.

"Wait," he gasps. "Don't. My skin—"

Rachael can't breathe. She braces herself to see Nyitha melt into nothing.

"All that's left," Nyitha says, "is the part where you and I die looking into each other's eyes."

Nyitha suddenly has a long, slender-bladed knife in her right hand, with a gorgeously carved handle made out of some kind of bone. She slides it into Marrant's chest, all the way to the hilt.

A bloodstain spreads across Marrant's shirt, turning the red slash darker and making everything shiny and sticky.

Marrant sways and then falls to the floor in a fetal position.

Nyitha stands over his body as he twitches, looking up at her with tears in his eyes.

"I thought I would feel relieved, or sad," she says. "But I just feel angry at myself for not doing this long ago." She turns to Thaoh and Rachael. "We'd best be gone."

Thaoh takes one last look at Marrant lying in a pool of his own dark purple blood, his eyes milky with tears. Then she indicates the heavy front door, with guards on the other side. "I'm assuming you had some kind of plan for getting out of here in one piece?" she says to Nyitha.

"Not an amateur. You and my former student forced me to move up my timetable." Nyitha gestures at Rachael. "And my escape plan wasn't meant for three. But we'll make do."

Nyitha pushes one spot on the wall, revealing another way out of the room, full of food-preparation supplies and attendant uniforms. She ushers Thaoh and Rachael into the dusty space—just as alarms start blaring, and guards rush in and see Marrant twitching with a knife in his chest.

11

.

Nyitha leads Rachael and Thaoh through a series of servant quarters and kitchens. Guards and attendants run past, yelling, and they have to duck under a counter, then keep moving. Nyitha opens a panel in one wall and reveals a tiny room with shelves piled high with Undhoran flap-hoppers and tubes of Cydoghian eggbursts. She pulls a carbonfast panel out of the way, revealing a disc made out of burnished metal.

Rachael is still reeling from watching Marrant bleed out, so she almost doesn't recognize the elevator platform. These things are supposed to take you up from the ground to a starship in orbit, not sit in a supply closet surrounded by walls on all sides. She gives Nyitha a WTF look, but Nyitha and Thaoh are already standing on the circle. Rachael sighs and climbs on, too.

"An orbital funnel—clever," Thaoh says. "But how do we get out of the building?"

"Watch." Nyitha pushes something on her sleeve, and the big circle turns sideways, so the three of them are standing on the wall next to the doorway of this oversized closet. Rachael expects to get the worst head rush, but instead the wall feels like a regular floor. Her center of gravity is the same as always.

The platform glides "upward" toward the opposite wall—and then they slide through a hidden opening, and they're racing over the skyline of Wentrolo, looking down at all the walkways and plazas and flying barges.

"I can't believe you're not dead," Thaoh whispers. "I saw your body. I organized your funeral."

Nyitha sighs. "Thanks for doing that, I heard it was nice. Anyway, you were also supposed to be dead."

"I actually was! I wasn't just pretending, like some sort of munthit."

"It was the only way to keep that man away from me."

Rachael has spent enough time with Nyitha to know that something is very wrong—apart from the fact that she just stabbed her ex-husband and got reunited with the girl she was in love with back in school (who looks exactly the same as she did back then).

"Wait," Rachael says. "How are you okay? You touched Marrant's skin. I saw. You kissed him on the cheek."

"Yes. That was my entire plan. I knew there was no other way to get close enough to stick the knife in."

"So . . . you figured out a way to protect yourself from the death touch?" Rachael says.

Nyitha shakes her head. "No. I did not."

"But . . . but you *touched him,* and you didn't melt into a puddle."

"Yet. I didn't melt into a puddle yet." She swallows something heavy. "I found a way to slow down the process a little, by drinking a highly unpleasant draught of Undhoran nightweed juice."

Thaoh stares at her oldest friend. "How long? How long do you have?"

"Not sure. But I definitely won't live to see tomorrow's artificial sunrise. That was smart, by the way, creating an unscheduled lights-out."

Grief is a pulled muscle somewhere deep inside Rachael—it spasms and flares every time she moves.

A voice deep inside Rachael says, *Any art you can make in the face of sorrow is good art.* Rachael never even knew how much sorrow Nyitha was nursing until it was too late—but Nyitha still risked everything to help Rachael, and took her to the ends of the universe. Literally.

"I can't," Rachael says. "I can't believe you touched him on purpose. I can't let you go. I only just learned who you really are. Please tell me there's a way to fix this."

That last part, Rachael says to Thaoh as well as to Nyitha.

"There is," Thaoh says briskly. "We're going to get you into stasis," she tells Nyitha. "A bubble of timelessness, keep you frozen until we figure out a permanent solution. We'll find a way to save you, and then—"

Nyitha shakes her head. "You of all people should know that it's a mistake to try and cheat death."

Thaoh starts to argue, or maybe explain that she never asked to be brought back, but Nyitha waves one gnarled purple hand.

"I met her, you know: the girl whose body you're occupying," Nyitha says. "She was a sweet kid, clever and cheerful—even though I could tell she was wearing your legend like a cloak of broken glass. I really thought Tina was going to do better than you and I ever could've. It's funny, I keep finding new ways to be disappointed."

"Why didn't you tell me you were still alive? Before, I mean." Thaoh brushes her face, even though Rachael didn't see any crystalline tears. "Why fake your death? You and I could have taken Marrant down together. None of this would have needed to happen."

"You had already chosen Marrant over me once," Nyitha says sadly. "And he worked so hard to isolate me, taking away my support system. Especially you. He tried to make me hate anyone who could take even a sliver of my love, after what I had tried to build with you. When I learned years later that he had turned his skin into an instrument of ruin, it only made sense." She makes a face like she's swallowing something bitter that hurts her throat. "I was scared to face him again. I was sure he would destroy me—or worse, win me back to his side."

Now there are definitely tears on Thaoh's face, glimmering between the jewels on her light purple skin. She heaves and shudders, and Rachael has to fight the impulse to reach out to comfort her, because this isn't Tina. It's a stranger.

The orbital funnel arrives at the rooftop of an apartment building, and Thaoh seems to snap back into being Captain Argentian. "Time we got ourselves in order. I'm declaring Situation Green Sprint: we're surrounded in hostile territory, with an injured member of our party. We have to get to safety, and we have to get you into stasis." She looks around. "Unfortunately, we've missed our rendezvous."

"Whose fault is that?" Rachael mutters. "You left our friends high and dry so you could go on your own side mission."

She hopes Kez, Elza, and the others already left without them, because it's just hitting Rachael how selfish Thaoh was: assassinating Marrant is probably the best way to turn the entire Royal Compassion into a mob. This city is about to become inescapable.

"Using an orbital funnel was clever, bought us some time," Thaoh says to Nyitha. "They're impossible to track, even in the most heavily surveilled city in the universe. But we can't stay here—we need a new extraction plan."

Nyitha nods and removes a section of the fancy decorative molding around the rooftop, revealing a sleek baby-blue ship. It's about the same size as the Mazda Miata that Rachael's ex-boyfriend Sven's dad got on his forty-fifth birthday, and looks about as roomy. "I didn't think I would have to bring anyone else with me when I ran."

"Why did you even need a getaway ship if you were going to let him touch you?" Rachael's heart is shattering.

Nyitha purses her lips. "I just wanted to get far away from anyone who might remember me fondly."

Oh, right. Because when Nyitha *does* melt into a toxic sludge, anyone who's within a million miles of her will hate her. Including Rachael.

Rachael's been lucky—if you can call it that—with Marrant's death touch up to now. She was hit with the effects when Marrant touched Vaap and Iyiiguol, two random crewmembers from the *Indomitable*. But she had barely known those two, and it was easy to avoid thinking about them. Every other time Marrant touched someone Rachael knew, she was far enough away to be spared.

If Rachael can't remember Nyitha the way she was, can't mourn for her, it'll be a whole extra death. Nyitha deserves to have someone know how wonderful she was.

Thaoh must be thinking the same thing, because she seems to snap into a decision. "Take the escape ship. Go. Far away from us and from everybody else. Rachael and I will find another way out of here."

Nyitha shakes her head. "I can't do that."

"You don't deserve—"

"I'd rather you be alive to hate me than die thinking well of me. If I can get you two to safety, that's all that matters." Nyitha pushes a button on her sleeve and the roof of the ship slides back, like a convertible. "Let's go."

Thaoh is about to argue some more, but the sunless sky grows even darker.

A swarm of knifeships and barges and daggerships, too many to count, is descending toward them on all sides.

"No time to argue," Nyitha says.

Thaoh and Rachael jump into the ship, and Nyitha clambers painfully into the pilot seat. They do a swan dive off the roof of this building so fast, Rachael's guts lurch. She can't help thinking that Damini will be sad she missed this.

12

.

When Rachael first came to Wentrolo, everything looked pristine: gleaming towers that changed their shapes while you slept, gorgeous walkways, gardens everywhere. Then Nyitha showed Rachael the underside of the city, full of greasy pipes and ducts and layers of old crud. Nobody knows this lower half of Wentrolo better than Nyitha, who hid from the world down here.

From inside this tiny ship, all Rachael can see is dark shapes gliding past, but her stomach and inner ear feel the turbulence as the ship darts in and out of different hiding places. Nyitha is crisscrossing the underside of the city, spinning around, racing through narrow spaces. Every time Rachael thinks they've gotten away clean, another cherry-red knifeship appears, shooting showstopper missiles at them.

Rachael is squished between Thaoh and Nyitha, who are arguing over her head. In the canned air, she can smell sweat and Thaoh's surprisingly sweet breath. Most of all, the air is thick with the noxious sickly odor of Nyitha's body starting to lose solidity—the same stench that always came off Marrant's skin.

"Leave us behind," Thaoh says. "We've passed a dozen perfectly good hiding places. Rachael and I will be fine. If we can't save your life, then you need to be far away."

"Stop," Nyitha says. "Just . . . just stop."

"I can't. I never even had a chance to love you."

"You had a chance. You threw it away."

"And now I'm going to hate you, and I just can't."

Their tiny ship scoots into another hiding place, behind a big black light bulb that hums.

Nyitha turns her gaze to Rachael. "What did you mean before, about a side mission? Yes, I heard you. I spent enough time with you to know that everything important, you say under your breath."

Rachael squirms—two giant purple women are staring at her and it's a lot. She finally mumbles, "We didn't come here to kill Marrant. I hate him too, but killing him won't solve anything as long as the stars are still dying." She explains about the cup, and how it could have a clue to find the people who launched the star-killing swarm, the Bereavement.

"I wanted to restore the Royal Fleet," Thaoh protests. "We can't help anyone, we can't save anything, as long as the Royal Fleet remains compromised. Maybe now that Marrant is dead, we can—"

Nyitha twists both hands, knuckles popping out, and the ship goes from zero to lose-your-lunch in a split second. They're racing across the blurry underside of the city, and Nyitha's jaw is clenched. Rachael has never seen her this angry.

"You wanted to kill that bastard too." Thaoh sounds exactly like Tina.

"I didn't endanger anyone else to do it. I didn't betray my friends. I don't know if we actually succeeded in killing him, or if his people got him into surgery in time. And Rachael's right: solving the Bereavement is far more urgent," Nyitha spit-snarls. "You haven't changed at all. You already died for the Royal Fleet, and now you're back to do it again."

Nyitha's face sags on one side, just a little. The toxic skin-melting odor is getting stronger.

"Those showstopper missiles stop time in a small area," Thaoh says. "If we could catch one using our ion harness, we could use it to freeze you until we can find a way to save you."

"This ship doesn't have an ion harness." Nyitha makes another wild turn, her whole face screwed up with fury. "I'm already dead. Worry about the people you just double-crossed."

"I took a calculated risk."

"You did what you always do."

It's all too much: the missiles flying past their tiny ship, the rusted crags of the under-city rushing toward them, the two women sparring on either side of her. Rachael hunches over and draws nothing in particular, an abstract design, on a tiny plastiform pad in her lap.

The shouting has stopped, even if the shooting is still going on.

Rachael looks up.

"It's okay," Nyitha says. "The old ladies aren't going to fight anymore. That is not how I want us to spend our last moments together. The two of you have touched my life in so many ways." She glances at the pad in Rachael's lap. "I see you regained your ability to draw."

Rachael nods. "Elza helped me, after she became a princess. But it only worked because of all the help you had already given me. You basically saved my life."

"I didn't do much." But Nyitha beams. "Listen, I'm going to get you both to safety. And then you have to make all this worthwhile. Find out about the Bereavement. Save the stars. Promise me."

Rachael can't talk. She just nods, she hopes that's promise enough.

"As for you," Nyitha says to Thaoh. "I have a dying wish. We don't really do dying wishes on Makvaria, that's more of an Oonian thing. So just take this as a piece of advice: give that body back. Let Tina have her life again, give her a chance to screw up and make a future and do all the things we already did."

"I can't," Thaoh says. "There's no way. Even the young princess couldn't think of a way."

"There is a way. They used a mindstone, right? Gotta be a mindstone. All you do is go to the acid swamps of Wamgha, find the mind-threaders, give them something they've never seen before. They'll sort you out."

Thaoh leans her head back, as if she's got a nosebleed. Then she nods.

"I'll do it on one condition. If you won't let me get you into stasis, then you have to get away from me, as far as you can, after we get to safety. Otherwise, I won't care about any promises I made to you."

"I'll do my best. I don't know how long I have left." Nyitha coughs and her face gets a little less solid.

Their tiny ship has reached the lower rim of the city. Thaoh and Nyitha both scan the tactical display, which still shows too many ships in every direction.

"There's one break in their formation." Thaoh points at the display. "We'll run for it when that ship passes. Listen . . . I know you think I rejected your love, or I chose Marrant over you, but that's only true if you think that romance is more valid than friendship. I never stopped wanting to be your friend, and I'm sorry. I'm sorry I made you feel like you mattered to me less than Marrant."

Hearing Tina's voice say that friendship is just as important as romance stirs something inside Rachael: a hunger, a sadness, a hope.

"Wow." Nyitha wipes tears from her eyes. (At least, Rachael hopes they're tears and not liquefying flesh.) "Never thought I'd hear Thaoh Argentian apologize. Almost makes it worth dying twice."

"Great hunger of sages, I'm saying I love you, okay? And maybe it's enough if we know we loved each other, even if this is the end for both of us."

"Maybe." Nyitha doesn't say she loves Thaoh back, but she squeezes Thaoh's hand. "Just keep your promise, okay? And I'll try to keep mine."

Nyitha can't get out of the driver's seat of the Mazda Miata by herself. Thaoh has to climb out and run around so she can give Nyitha a shoulder to lean on, and then Nyitha nearly spills over onto this tiny robot watch station at the fringe of the nebula.

"Easy," Thaoh says. "I've got you."

"Guess I got you as far as—" Nyitha hacks a wet, sickly cough. "—as far as I could. Up to you now . . . Way should be pretty clear from here."

Rachael gets out of the ship, too. "I just wanted to say thank you. For everything."

We all lose pieces of ourselves.

Thaoh is already restarting the Mazda's engines. "We need to go. Now."

Rachael's face burns. "Just let me . . . just let me say goodbye. Nyitha changed my life. I need to tell her." Loss feels slippery inside her, it rises up and then slides through her grasp.

"I already know." Nyitha puts on a mockery of a smile. "Please just go. I need you both to remember me fondly, so Thaoh won't renege on our deal."

Rachael can't weep, but she also can't move.

Sometimes they're gone forever.

The few feet around the front of the ship and into the passenger seat are the hardest steps she's ever taken. She climbs in and a protective bubble forms over her head.

Nyitha goes from a person to a speck in a blink of an eye as the tiny ship lifts away from her—almost as if she was melting right before Rachael's eyes.

Then they're racing past the edge of the Glorious Nebula, letting the towers of Wentrolo resolve into a single point of light.

"Tears of my ancestors, we can't go to spaceweave yet." Thaoh's eyes scrunch and her forearms are taut inside the holographic jelly interface. "Come on, come on, give me spaceweave, you piece-of-junk ship."

Rachael's chest has an unbearable weight inside and her brain is caught in a loop, replaying her last sight of Nyitha. Coming up with all the words she wishes she'd gotten to say to her teacher.

"How will," Rachael stammers. "How will we know if we made it? If we got far enough away from her before the full effect hits?"

Thaoh's face turns grim. "If we still love her tomorrow, we made it. No other way to tell."

13

.

ELZA

The Ardenii break Elza's concentration with a piece of news like an electric shock: *Somebody just stabbed Marrant.* Which is excellent—except that the entire city is hunting for the perpetrators, and escape just became twice as impossible.

Elza tells Wyndgonk and Gyrald what happened.

"Flenby's tears, I hope he's dead," Gyrald mutters.

"He's in surgery," Elza says. "They're trying to save his life right now."

"Wait," Wyndgonk sputters, with gray smoke. "Who stabbed Marrant?"

Elza focuses her mind. "Even the Ardenii don't know yet."

The three of them are still making their way through the basement of memories, which literally goes on forever—it's not a real place, so it can be as big as it needs to be. Elza walks past long-dead queens and privy councilors chattering about old controversies, like the Irriyaian-Oonian War, and the petition of the Kraelyors for full membership in the Firmament.

Elza should have been prepared for this noise in her head: the Ardenii are so much louder here in the palace, where every wall sings with their presence. She has to fight to stay present, to keep from losing herself. She can't even make out one thing, it's like ten pieces of music playing at the same time.

Princess Nonesuch has had years to get used to this racket, and she's right behind them. "You can't escape, fledgling princess," she taunts. "You are only venturing deeper into the bowels of the palace."

Elza feels brittle inside. What if they're cornered, because she can't concentrate enough to make the palace work for her—because she's not a real princess? What if Wyndgonk and Gyrald are about to die because Elza isn't worthy?

Then she shakes it off. Elza deserves to be here, she earned her title, she's done doubting herself. The queen herself just greeted Elza as a princess.

So she tries to clear her head and focus on moving forward, and she calls out to the Ardenii. *Please help me get out of here. I deserve your help as much as Princess Nonesuch does.* If they respond, it's lost in the flood of cosmic gossip.

"All exits are closed to you," Princess Nonesuch says.

"Is she right?" Wyndgonk's voice actually trembles. "Are we just getting more trapped?"

"Not if I can find what I'm looking for," Elza says.

This basement has gotten darker gradually, and now Elza strains to see her own hand. Feral shadows play around her, and long-dead people whisper. Princess Nonesuch is closing in on her.

Elza should just hide. She should find the dimmest corner of this memory hole and try to conceal Wyndgonk, Gyrald, and herself there. She pictures the three of them cowering inside a burrow made of forgotten transgressions, jumping at every noise, never knowing when it might be safe to emerge.

No more hiding, Elza tells herself firmly. She pushes ahead, through ever-darkening layers of the past.

Then she finds what she's looking for: herself.

A younger Elza is standing with hands on her hips, saying to someone, "You think it's so great that I'm paranoid?"

This other Elza looks so fearless—so clueless—Elza can't help staring. She whispers in her other self's ear: "Keep talking. I know how you like to talk."

Elza hustles Wyndgonk and Gyrald forward, with her own voice ringing behind her. Pure defiance, beautiful snark.

Princess Nonesuch won't be fooled for long, but that might be enough for Elza to make a way out. She concentrates: space means almost nothing here, but she must be underneath the Wishing Maze by now. She finds a scrap of paper in her pocket and a lightpen. She writes: "I wish I could walk free of this place."

"So you've decided to stand and face me," Princess Nonesuch says to the holographic Elza. "What do you hope to gain?"

"You keep asking me questions with no good answers," Past Elza says back.

Elza takes her scrap of paper, with her wish on it, and holds it up, as if trying to get it into the heart of the Wishing Maze.

The next thing she knows, a slice of light appears: a doorway ajar.

The three of them duck through the doorway while Princess Nonesuch spars with the decoy Elza. They stumble out into Peacebringer Square, near the entrance to the maze. Firmament Security officers in shiny armor swarm onto all of the walkways and search everyone getting on and off barges.

Elza pulls Gyrald and Wyndgonk behind a barge that just landed, and they creep toward the nearest walkway, staying low to the ground.

The further Elza gets from the palace, the more the roar of the Ardenii fades back to a hum. She doesn't know how to feel—she feels small and lonesome, and her brain no longer reaches all the way to the distant star nurseries at the edge of everything, but at least she can think now. It's like a caffeine buzz just wore off.

At least the stolen knifeship is at the rendezvous: a courtyard, crammed with rusted metal sculptures, in the smokiest part of the Stroke. Kez pokes eir head out of the hatch: "There you are. We were starting to get worried."

Wyndgonk rushes on board the ship, but Gyrald hangs back.

"You're still staying?" Elza says. "After everything that just happened?"

"I can't do much good out there," Gyrald says. "But if I can get back inside the palace, I might make a real difference."

"Just promise you'll be careful." Elza takes one last look at her friend. "I don't know how your species says goodbye—we didn't get the chance last time."

Gyrald's petals spread wider: a smile. "Is it okay to touch you?"

Elza says yes, and Gyrald's front legs reach out and touch Elza's forearms with their hooked toes. "I'll be thinking of you, Rogue Princess."

"I'll be thinking of you, too," Elza says.

"Then we won't really be apart at all. Be careful yourself."

And then Gyrald is disappearing into the crowds of the Stroke, and Elza climbs on board the tiny stolen ship, eager to tell Rachael everything that just happened.

There's no Rachael. Or Thaoh. Just Kez, Damini, and Zaeta.

"I don't think Rachael is coming," Kez says. "Thaoh went off on her own side mission, and Rachael went with her."

Elza feels a million years old. "I think I can guess what that side mission was."

The Ardenii won't let up, it's like a never-ending head rush. Elza keeps learning more about the people who were injured in the chaos all over town since the sun went out. And the desperate attempt to save Marrant's life.

Most of all, the Ardenii are yelling about the trap tightening around Elza and her friends.

"According to the Ardenii, Rachael and Thaoh were seen escaping from the Royal Command Post, along with another person," Elza tells her friends. "We don't know what happened after that."

"I should've stopped Rachael from going with Thaoh," Kez says.

"We never should have trusted that wet-mouth in the first place," Wyndgonk says.

"If anybody can get Rachael out of the mess Thaoh created, it's Thaoh," Damini says.

"We'll just have to hope she's safe," Zaeta adds. "But how do we make it out of here without Thaoh's help?"

Everyone stares at Elza. She raises one hand, like *Let me think*. She reaches for her connection to the Ardenii. They tell her someone just discovered a flower the size of a planet, delicate petals soaking in the rays of a white giant star.

That gives her an idea. "The sun is about to turn back on, right? When that happens, there'll be a solar flare—everything will be out of operation, except for a ship like ours."

"It'll only last a handful of seconds, though," Kez says.

"Split-second timing—" Damini says.

"—is our specialty," Zaeta says. They both have identical grins.

"Okay. Get ready." Elza closes her eyes and tries to tune out all of the million other things that are happening, so she can focus on the sun platform, where engineers are struggling to restart a giant fusion reactor.

The engineers reach for the power-up switch, up there in space—and Elza almost says *Now*—but then they stop for one more round of tests.

Wait . . . wait . . . the engineers start the power-up sequence.

"NOW!" Elza shouts.

The tiny knifeship leaps like a grasshopper, soaring up from the ground—just as the sky fills with blazing light, and all of the buildings and barges and Joiners go dark all around them.

Wentrolo shrinks from a place to a set of shapes, and then it's just a twisty bowl-shape, silhouetted against the sherbet of the Glorious Nebula. The nameless ship overheats its engines, burning hard to break away from Her Majesty's Firmament.

Elza's stomach is turning upside down, but next to her Wyndgonk growls, "Can't this thing go any faster?"

"We're going—"

"—as fast as we can—"

"—and then some."

The pressure starts to crush Elza's chest and face. She can't breathe.

What's the point of having all of the knowledge in the galaxy and thoughts that reach to the edges of everything when you're still a frail human being with spindly bones and blood vessels and a tiny squishy brain?

They're approaching the edge of the Glorious Nebula, which is surrounded by even more Royal Compassion ships. They're covering the entire surface, in a tight grid.

"Nobody is getting through that," Kez says. "We're going to, what? Run a space blockade?"

Elza's head still throbs from the acceleration with no gravitators. She closes her eyes and asks the Ardenii, *Any bright ideas?*

The Ardenii have nothing.

"We're on our own," Elza says.

"I've got an unforgivably horrendous idea," Damini says. Those words coming out of her mouth are never a good thing.

"Oh no," Zaeta says. "No, no, no. We're not doing that."

"You trust me, right? Of course you do! And I've done the math—well, I've done half the math. The point is, thanks to Fake Tina, we have a bit of a situation on our hands, and we need to work the angles, and the angles are very acute right about now. We really have no choice but to exercise a bit of creative thinking, and . . ."

Kez breaks into Damini's chatter. "What exactly are you planning?"

Damini gestures at the tactical display, where one especially ginormous broadsword ship is dead ahead, nestling up against the edge of the nebula. "See that big ship?"

Kez nods. "Hard to miss."

"We're going to ram it." Damini laughs in harmony with the screaming of the engines.

The broadsword is called the HMSS *Unforgettable*: a frog the size of a city, with six curled "legs" and a cute sloping belly. Elza would want to drink in this gorgeous sight, if they weren't about to crash into it at top speed.

"You see, a ship this size is bound to get struck by random objects all the time, like asteroids, ice chunks, or space detritus—it's basically a giant fly-catcher," Damini says cheerfully. "You need a lot of countermeasures to neutralize these impacts by absorbing most of their momentum and then sending them on their way so they don't hang about causing problems."

"And an object coming out of the nebula won't look like much of anything at first," Kez says. "That's quite good, even by your standards."

Damini blushes—but next to her Zaeta snorts. "We'll see how clever you think this is soon."

Elza wasn't sure if Zaeta and Damini were capable of having disagreements until now. Even the Ardenii don't know much about the vunci bond that the two of them entered into.

"Get ready to cut the engines as soon as we come out of the nebula," Damini says.

"If we crash and I have to come back as an antimatter wraith, I am going to be very upset!" Zaeta shouts.

"I wouldn't let you reincarnate as anything that wasn't beautiful," Damini says. "Hold tight, everyone. This could get—"

The tiny ship bursts out of the edge of the nebula, with the slick hull of the *Unforgettable* dead ahead.

The engines cut out. Elza's stomach and throat change places.

Their momentum keeps the stars blurring into blue-tinged spaghetti. They roar toward a cluster of sharp spikes coming off the *Unforgettable*'s undercarriage.

Kez is yelling, "I take it back, I take it back, this is not good!"

"Too late, you already gave me validation!" Damini laughs.

"We're about to hit," Zaeta shouts.

The spears and knife-points sticking out of the broadsword are close enough to see every tiny crag and serration. Elza tries to think of some last message to give the Ardenii, in case anyone ever cares to know what she thought of her short tenure as a princess.

The knives are about to stab at them . . . and then they just coast to a stop.

"See?" Damini says. "See?"

The *Unforgettable* has snagged their little ship and is gently pushing it away.

"It's working," Kez says. "They think we're just a random piece of junk now that all our systems are powered down."

"This ship *is* a random piece of junk," Wyndgonk says.

The *Unforgettable* gives them one last push, and they start drifting away, out into the endless blackness of space.

"Best get comfy," Damini says.

"We'll keep drifting until we're out of range," Zaeta adds.

"Anybody know any good card games?" Kez says.

Wyndgonk belches smoke. "I liked it better when we were about to crash and explode."

Elza hasn't had time to think for ages now, and it feels like a debt piled up to the ceiling. Too many terrible thoughts she hasn't been letting in, too much ugliness that she hasn't had time to process—and that's without the Ardenii sensing her mind is ready to receive an extra-large dose of bad news from a thousand worlds.

Plus they tell Elza another number with too many decimal places to count, and as usual, they won't explain.

Elza wishes Rachael was here, so they could talk about how badly Thaoh Argentian screwed them both. Wherever Rachael is, Elza hopes she's okay and not dealing with too much of Captain Amazing's bullshit.

14

.

RACHAEL

The Mazda Miata jerks up and down like a lowrider as it tries to descend through the atmosphere over the famous acid swamp of Wamgha. "The swamp gas separates out in the air," Thaoh explains in a chatty tone. "Makes things a bit turbulent. I've seen worse."

Rachael is too nauseous to talk back.

At least she still has all her happy memories of Nyitha. There was one moment, when she and Thaoh were racing away from the Glorious Nebula, when Rachael felt herself being swept away by dark, bleak feelings—and she was sure the death touch was kicking in. Then she realized: she was just pissed at Nyitha for dying for no good reason, and at Thaoh for making everything worse.

Now they're here, at the place where Nyitha said they could bring Tina back. While they were flying here, Thaoh kept saying things like, *Trust Nyitha to know about all the strangest miracles. She always had a knack for poking around in places where nobody else would bother to look.*

Now Thaoh is grimacing and reciting Makvarian poetry to herself as she fights the turbulence—like she's trying to hold on to being Thaoh Argentian for as long as she can.

The ship comes down on a rocky ledge over a swamp the color of fancy dijon mustard, which smells worse than Nyitha's spray paint. The sky is Barbie pink, with ropey gray clouds.

Thaoh climbs out of the ship, then winces. "Raised glasses and last dances," she says under her breath.

"This is a noble thing you're doing," Rachael says.

Thaoh cocks her head. "I've broken my word too many times already. I owe it to the dead to honor my vow this time."

A round, lumpy creature with thick, muddy gray skin glides across the surface of the swamp. "We don't get many visitors here. I'm Marshwell, and I don't use a pronoun. Are you looking for the mind-threaders?"

"That's right." Thaoh explains the situation, then reaches into a storage space in the back of the Mazda Miata. "My friend said I had to bring you something you'd never seen before. This is a light fixture from the best nightclub on Vandal Station." She pulls out a bent piece of metal that looks sort of like brass, with a light emitter on one end and THE BUMP DUMP written on the side.

They talk for a while, and Thaoh's gift seems to be accepted. At last, Marshwell says, "Well then, we better get started."

Thaoh talks the whole time, even as she lies down on a table and the mind-threaders apply an anesthetic cocktail to her forehead to put her to sleep. "You'll find all the navigational information on my Quant," she tells Rachael. "That ship's engines are going to need major repairs, and I'd advise you to head for Miscreant Station."

"We'll figure it out," Rachael says. "Thank you."

Thaoh keeps trying to make sure Rachael has everything she needs, until her voice peters out into a mumble and at last she goes still.

"Now we can begin." Marshwell gestures to the other mind-threaders and they gather around Thaoh's head. Rachael stands at the edge of the operating room, which has walls made of chalky stone and a furrowed roof, and watches as the mind-threaders slide translucent slime-needles inside Thaoh's skull.

The mind-threaders work in silence for a long time, occasionally reshaping themselves to have more pointy edges or lumpy curves.

Then Marshwell stops moving, seeming to get taller and thinner. "Oh. Oh dear."

"This is a problem," says another mind-threader.

Rachael almost asks what's wrong, but she doesn't want to distract them.

"The strata are too deep," says Marshwell. "The other mind is buried."

"We've gone too far now," says a third mind-threader. "If we stop, the patient will die."

"If we continue," Marshwell says, "the patient may also die. But yes. We have no choice. Let's just hope this 'Tina' is as strong-minded as Thaoh claimed."

The mind-threaders keep working, faster and faster, thick gray skin turning more and more angular and jagged.

Please, Rachael begs silently. *Please save her. Please, Tina. I need you.*

Thaoh—Tina—is twitching and jerking her hands, and she breathes harder and faster, as if she's fighting for her life.

15

.

The *Undisputed Training Bra Disaster* is waiting at the rendezvous point, thank goodness: in the middle of an old decommissioned minefield from the long-ago Pulsar War. The thousands of mines won't explode anymore—Elza hopes—but they generate a magnetic field that'll hide a ship just fine.

"Thank god at least one thing is going right today," Kez breathes. "I can't wait to be back in a cozy chair with a nice cup of hot snah-snah juice."

The *Undisputed Training Bra Disaster* is already opening up the back of its art-shed side, to allow this tiny, nameless ship to dock.

"Don't celebrate too soon," Wyndgonk says. "We didn't make a clean escape after all."

There's a Royal Compassion ship on their tail, burning at top speed to catch up.

"They followed us from the Glorious Nebula," Kez says. "They must have stayed just outside the range of our sensors, trying to see where we were going."

"And we led them right to our friends," Damini groans.

"They're called the *Unconquerable*," says Zaeta. "They're a dagger-class ship, and they want us to surrender."

"Not happening," Elza says.

"Can we lead them away from the others?" Kez asks.

"And then what?" Wyndgonk says. "We can't outrun them."

Zaeta and Damini are already plotting a course around the minefield, hoping to lead the *Unconquerable* away from the *U.T.B.D.*

"One thing at a time," Damini says.

"Yes," Elza says. "Let's protect the rest of our crew."

Sometimes Elza wishes she could just make foolish decisions—without immediately knowing all the reasons why they're foolish. Like right now, the Ardenii are letting her know that the *Unconquerable* has them trapped, and the Royal Compassion ship has already figured out that they were rendezvousing with another ship here.

Sure enough, the *Unconquerable* doesn't bother chasing their knifeship—instead, it keeps heading for the deactivated minefield, searching for the *Undisputed Training Bra Disaster*.

Damini curses. "Why won't they take our delicious bait?"

"This bait is so fresh and tempting! I'm insulted!" Zaeta says.

"Maybe we just need to put more sauce on it." Damini offers a fist, and Zaeta bumps it with a flipper.

The tiny nameless ship takes a hard right turn and swerves into the ancient minefield, bobbing and weaving around jagged shapes that look like old gnarled tree roots. One of them comes close enough to see a layer of frozen grease still clinging to it.

"Careful!" Wyndgonk shouts. "These mines won't blow up anymore, but they can still wreck us if we crash into them."

Damini and Zaeta are too busy joking about bait, and making the ship buck like a young stallion.

Now the *Unconquerable* is following them, closing the distance way too quickly. A beam of hot red fire scorches across the hull of the tiny knifeship: a warning shot from the *Unconquerable*'s pulse cannons.

"They've got us trapped," Wyndgonk says. "Why am I the one who has to keep pointing out bad news?"

"I think we made a mistake," Zaeta says in a tiny voice.

"We didn't make any mistake!" Damini protests.

"This is a mistake. They're no longer even trying to take us alive." The whole left side of Zaeta's face is freaking out, like it physically hurts her to argue with Damini.

"Listen to me," Damini says. "We've got this. You and me. There's nothing the two of us can't—"

Everything goes sideways. Elza is thrown out of her seat along with Kez and Wyndgonk, and she loses all her breath as she slams into the opposite wall. Her whole body spasms with pain and she can't replace the breath she lost, and the ship is spinning out of control. A cacophony rings in Elza's ears—alarms and screaming engines.

Elza doesn't need the Ardenii to tell her that they just took a direct hit. They tell her anyway.

"Can't stabilize our attitude control," Damini grunts.

"Concentrate on keeping our engines from blowing up," Zaeta retorts.

The *Unconquerable* is swinging around to finish them off.

And then the *Unconquerable* isn't there anymore. At first, Elza isn't sure what's happened—did the whole ship just vanish into a hole in space or something?—then the Ardenii show her a cloud of gas and debris. Two dwarf-star ballistic missiles came out of nowhere and blew the *Unconquerable* to pieces.

The *Undisputed Training Bra Disaster* sails toward them, in between two clusters of mines. A brand-new missile tube still glows faintly on the right side, right on the line between "art shed" and "daggership."

Yiwei's voice pops up on their comms. "Are you all okay? That was a close one."

Nobody answers. Elza stares at the pale light of the new weapon system that wasn't there the last time she looked.

As soon as the knifeship docks, Yiwei stumbles on board, face flushed. "Rachael! Rachael, are you—"

Then he stops and looks around, with his mouth open.

"She's not here," Elza says. "She's with Thaoh."

Yiwei keeps looking, as if this could be a prank, and maybe Rachael is hiding under one of the seats. "She's . . . What the hell happened?"

Everyone fills Yiwei in on all the disasters, and the life slowly drains out of him.

"I . . . asked her to keep an eye on Thaoh." Yiwei slumps against the wall of the knifeship, mashing his face against his fists. "I didn't even think about what might happen."

"You did that because you know Rachael can look after herself," Elza says. "Wherever she is, you can bet she's holding Thaoh accountable."

"And speaking of accountability," Kez says, "what the hell just happened? When did we start blasting weapons and blowing people up?"

Yiwei straightens up. "You were all about to get slaughtered, and I saved your lives. You're welcome." (Actually, the Ardenii tell Elza, what he's saying in Chinese is closer to "Don't be so polite," or "Don't bother to thank me.")

"Nobody is thanking you," Kez says.

"*I'm* thanking you," Damini says.

"You saved all our lives," Zaeta adds.

"How many people did we just kill?" Kez asks Elza, the bringer of horrible facts.

"Thirty-seven," Elza says. "Almost all of them were in the Royal Fleet until a couple months ago."

"We killed thirty-seven people," Kez says to Yiwei. "Where did those weapons even come from?"

"You left us behind at Vandal Station, and we had time to make some upgrades," Yiwei says. "Someone was selling missile launchers and pulse cannons, and we were able to come to an arrangement." He curses under his breath. "Rachael's gone, we're barely holding on, and you're mad at me for rescuing you from certain death?"

They all stream out of the totaled knifeship, into the *Undisputed Training Bra Disaster*'s wood-paneled cargo hangar.

Elza's eye lands on one of Rachael's brand-new murals on the far wall: a big basket-shaped object against the backdrop of a shimmering hole in space. Her breath catches and she feels utterly lost, like every direction is the same.

Kez is still arguing with Yiwei. "So this is who we are now. We just kill anyone who gets in our way."

"We kill anyone who's trying to kill us," Yiwei says, as they all stream onto the flight lounge.

"That's a lot of people, though," Cinnki says from the comms station. "Pretty much everyone is trying to kill us." His ears curl all the way back on his head.

Yiwei doesn't say anything—he just stares at a lightpen and pad that Rachael left on a chair, as if she was coming right back.

"Yiwei's correct," Gahang says from the pilot station. "When you're under assault by superior forces, you don't always have the luxury of qualms."

"You make it sound so easy. Where's your righteous doubt now?" Naahay snipes, because she never misses a chance to fight with her fellow Aribentor.

Elza feels weary, deep inside her soul, and she's only half listening to this argument because the Ardenii have decided to tell her everything they know about the thirty-seven people who just died. One of them was a Yarthin named Iangual (*she/her*) who was known for her prize gardens.

"We've definitely killed some Compassion soldiers before, when we had no choice," Damini says.

"Yeah, but that was the Compassion," Kez says. "Those people knew what they were signing up for. And we talked about never doing that again."

"*You* talked about it," Yiwei says. "I went to the academy and studied combat tactics."

"If this is the way it's going to be," Kez says, "then I need to leave this ship. The next time we stop at Vandal Station or Miscreant Station, or on an inhabited planet, I'm out. I don't care if the fate of all the worlds is blah blah blah. I already helped plunge a whole city into darkness, and I'm not interested in turning into my father."

"I'm out, too," Cinnki says. Yiwei stares at the lead singer of his band.

Another member of the *Unconquerable* crew was an Undhoran named Caycaycaycay (*he/him*) who was passing information to Riohon's rebel fleet and planning to defect soon. Elza silently pleads with the Ardenii to stop—she doesn't want to think of these enemies as people.

"You're being childish, both of you," Damini says. "We can't afford—"

"They have a point," Zaeta says. "I don't know if I can be part of this either."

Damini and Zaeta stare at each other.

Elza finally pushes all of the life stories of the newly dead out of her mind, and stands up. Everybody stops talking and looks at her.

"We can keep having this discussion on the move," Elza says. "We've got a long voyage ahead of us. We need to get to the Plains of the Endless, which is halfway across the galaxy. We probably have a head start. Let's not waste it."

Nobody speaks or moves for a long time. Then Damini and Zaeta nod at each other, and they take over the pilot station from Gahang and Kfok. The ship moves away from the old minefield, on course for the other side of an endless void.

As soon as the ship is under way, everybody starts yelling at each other again. Elza sighs. This is going to be a long trip.

16
.

YATTO THE MONNTHA

. . . 270 Earth days until all the suns go out forever

Yatto the Monntha came back to life slowly. They still tried to make things better for the people around them, but for a long time they were acting in a daze, as if they had gone into a facing-day dream and never quite woken up. Their hands and their feet moved on their own, without much direction from their brain.

For the past thirty metacycles, Yatto's whole world has been one small compartment on the Irriyaian exile citystar: a snake-shaped space made of tarnished carbonfast, full of recirculated air and uneven gravity. This is the new home of the Monntha nation, and Yatto has been hiding at the tail of the snake, where they've been doing their best to help two Monntha families to get food and medicine from what passes for the government here. It's only mostly futile.

Yatto used to believe that they had the power to help masses of people. Twice, in fact: the first time, Yatto started acting in patriotic light-dramas, or what the Earthling kids called "action movies," believing that they were lifting up the whole Monntha nation and making all of Irriyaia proud. Later, Yatto joined the crew of the HMSS *Indomitable* and hoped in the heights of their spirit that they would be saving worlds and lifting people up.

Now, Yatto is helping twenty people, and it feels like a lot. Every one of those twenty people has medical conditions and acute trauma and a need to find the people they've lost, and Yatto tries to stay on top of every one of their situations. Yatto themself was exposed to hard vacuum for ten or twelve microcycles after being sucked into space, so their skin is still brittle, their eyesight is slowly recovering, and their joints hurt when they move. The burns on Yatto's face kept them from being recognized as a "movie star," and since then Yatto has worked hard to disguise themself, changing their name to Nathy the Monntha.

Their main friend here is Karthel the Monntha, a smooth-headed child who hasn't even chosen a pronoun yet. Karthel is a practical joker who makes up random songs and dance routines—who acts as if this is some kind of deep-space vacation. Yatto is never sure if Karthel is making the best of things, or is just too young to grasp the direness of the situation.

Yatto tries to stay busy, because when they stop moving, they get trapped in a memory: standing on a high platform, shouting at their people, trying to use their fame to stop a tragedy, only to fail. They didn't witness the death of their homeworld, Irriyaia, because they'd already been pulled into space and taken aboard an escape craft, but they've watched the recording a thousand times. *My fault.*

The Compassion used Yatto's performances to light a fire of hatred in the Irriyaian people—a fire that ended up consuming everyone. Yatto never found a way to speak louder than that false image of themself.

Now Yatto is repairing one of the gravitators in their tiny compartment, so everyone can sleep without being awoken by a low-gravity pocket. Karthel watches over Yatto's shoulder, curious, and occasionally helps when a delicate adjustment is too difficult for Yatto's still-clumsy fingers. *If I never hear the name Yatto the Monntha again, I will die happy.*

As soon as that thought passes through Yatto's head, a voice says, "Yatto the Monntha. I've found you! God, I've found you. Miraculous reunions and faint hopes. It's me. Look up. Please look up! I need to look you in the eyes."

Yatto doesn't look up.

So Thanz Riohon, Yatto's crewmate from the *Indomitable,* squats down until they're face-to-face. Riohon looks the same, as if the world hadn't ended: his square-jawed purple face remains eager, his deep blue eyes widen as if to take in some fresh wonder instead of beholding nothing but ruin.

"Why is this person calling you Yatto?" Karthel whispers. "That's not your name."

"It's a mistake," Yatto whispers back. "He'll be leaving soon."

"I've been searching for you everywhere," Riohon says. "I couldn't give up hope. Listen, we have a chance. Thaoh Argentian is back, really back. We have a plan to save the Royal Fleet, so it can once again become a force for good and help everyone who huddles afraid in the dark. We can't do it without you. Will you join us?"

Yatto gets up and walks away without looking back at Riohon.

Yatto doesn't get far, because there isn't far to go: the Monntha unit is sealed off from the other nations' tiny habitats, and Yatto doesn't want to risk going through the checkpoint. No hiding places—at least, none that aren't already occupied by people with their own reasons to hide from what's left of the world.

So Riohon finds them a short time later, staring out a viewport at the outside of the citystar, curving away from them. Gleaming in the light of a pair of stars that everybody calls the Rain's Eyes.

Riohon stands there whispering in Yatto's ear as both of them stare out the same viewport. "We need your help," he says. "Time is running out. We have a fleet—mostly smaller ships, but the crews are good people. We can fight smart. When people see us standing up to Marrant and the Royal Compassion, they will flock to join us."

He talks and talks.

Yatto closes their damaged eyes and says just two words in response. "Another war."

"Not another war," Riohon says. "The same war. It never ended. I want the same thing as you: to help all of these refugees and everyone else who's going to be displaced soon. We can't do any of that until we get rid of Marrant."

There's a long silence, except it's not silent at all: there are the cries of the injured, the prayers of the heartbroken, and the creaking of the deck-plates. Yatto just wants this conversation to be over.

A voice comes from behind them. "I can't believe it. A Royalist here, in our last refuge. Haven't you done enough damage already?"

Yatto doesn't need to turn around. They already recognize the voice of Ganno the Wurthhi, Kez's one-time lover.

"I'm not staying long," Riohon says. "But you should know that we are not your enemy. I'm so terribly sorry about what happened to your world."

"What *happened*?" Ganno chokes on bile. "It didn't just *happen*. Take some responsibility." Then Ganno realizes who's standing next to Riohon. "Oh god, it's you. Yatto the Monntha. You have more to answer for than anybody."

Ganno and Riohon argue back and forth while Yatto stares out at the stars. They feel broken inside—and not a clean break. A shattering, a splintering, too many stray pieces to reassemble.

Everything Ganno says is true: Yatto has much to answer for, and no answers to give.

"I've known Yatto the Monntha for half my adult life," Riohon is saying. "They aren't who you think. I've seen them risk everything for others, so many times, and they want nothing more than to make up for—"

"Stop saying what I want." Yatto's deep voice warbles, as if it's vibrating through all the shards. "You don't know what I want."

"I'm here to remind you of who you are," Riohon says.

"You can't escape from the harm you've done," Ganno says.

Yatto finally turns to face the two of them. And behind them, the crowd of a dozen or so other Irriyaians, mostly Monnthas, who've slowly gathered. Everyone is about to know who Yatto really is.

"What exactly is it you want me to do?" Yatto asks Riohon.

"Come with me. We need experienced starship personnel, and you can inspire a lot of people to join us. You're still a beloved figure."

Yatto turns to Ganno. "What do you think? Should I go with him?"

Ganno scowls. "Why should I care what you do?"

"You cared enough to follow this man into the Monntha section. You care enough to stand here shouting at me. So tell me: Do you think I can still make a difference?"

Riohon bristles. "It doesn't matter what this hothead thinks."

"It does to me," Yatto says. "In Irriyaian culture, the image you put out into the world matters. It's the center of prenthro, and it's how we decide who controls the land and all the resources. If my fellow Irriyaians don't believe in me, then I can't believe in myself. So I'm not the one you have to convince, Ganno the Wurthhi is."

"Wait," says Ganno. "That's not what . . ."

"If you can make Ganno the Wurthhi believe that I still have the power to do good—that you can do good with my help—then I will go with you," Yatto says, hoping more than anything that Riohon fails to convince Ganno.

Ganno almost starts yelling again, but then Yatto's words sink in. "Okay," he says. "I'm listening. Tell me why Yatto the Monntha should join with you to help resurrect the rotting corpse of the Royal Fleet. I promise you I will be difficult to convince."

Riohon looks around at the growing crowd of curious Irriyaian refugees and sighs. Then he puts on a big smile. "I'll be delighted. The Royal Fleet by itself is nothing. It's a rotting corpse, as you say. What matters is us, all of us, working together, under whatever banner makes sense."

Ganno yawns theatrically and a couple of the Irriyaian spectators hiss.

Riohon's smile dims a little, but then he straightens up and tries again. He's starting to realize that Ganno was telling the truth about being difficult to convince.

17
.

TINA

. . . 260 Earth days until all the suns go out forever

Oh god, my head hurts so much, and everything smells like battery acid, and I have a weird feeling that I forgot something really important, but I can't remember what. I used to have this feeling sometimes, back on Earth, when I woke from an extra-deep sleep. I would lie on my lumpy futon and recite Dua Lipa lyrics in my head until the world became world-shaped again.

I can't see or hear anything, I'm in some kind of hazy smogscape. Four out of five senses conked out—except for the sharp tang of acid in my nostrils.

So I try the Dua Lipa thing, just reciting the lyrics to "IDGAF" to my-self, trying to remember how they go. It's been so long since I even listened to Dua Lipa—how long? I don't know. Weirdly I also don't know what day (metacycle?) it is.

I get to the chorus about how you can say you're sorry, and a voice be-hind me says, "Excuse me, do you mind?"

It's my voice, except that it's not.

I turn around (even though I don't seem to have arms or legs exactly) and come face-to-face with the person I would have given almost anything to meet.

"Do you mind?" she says again. "We only have a short time to talk, and I don't want to waste it listening to you reciting poetry."

Captain Argentian smiles at me, but sadly—like she planned a whole elaborate birthday party for a kid who then announced they just wanted to go to Chuck E. Cheese.

I start to explain that I wasn't reciting poetry exactly—but then I catch the part about us only having a short time together. "How . . . how are you and I in the same place? Am I dead? Are you dead? Are we both dead?"

"I've been dead for a very long time. You know that." Captain Argentian moves closer and reaches out an insubstantial hand. I take it with both of mine. "You're alive, and you're about to be rid of me forever. I need to say a great many things to you, and it starts with: I am sorry."

"You're sorry? Why are you sorry? You . . . I'm the one who totally failed to . . ." I choke on acid fumes, or feelings, or both.

"I'm sorry for so many things. I'm sorry that anybody ever told you that you were born to be me, instead of being born to be yourself. I'm sorry I left behind such a heinous mess for you to deal with."

I didn't even know how much I needed to hear her say those words to me. My chest is caught in a vise and my eyes—do I have eyes?—are misty.

I say, "It's okay. You don't have to—"

"I do. I do have to." She takes a deep breath. I can see through her face. "I'm sorry for the things I've done since I came back to life, the uses I put your body to. I hurt your friends. I was selfish. I didn't realize how intoxicating it would feel to be young again. I'm sorry that I tried to use your body to commit murder."

"You . . ." All of a sudden I feel light-headed and sick. A tiny speck of light, so bright it's almost black, appears at the center of my vision. "You did what?" I pull my ghostly hands away from hers.

"I was selfish," she says again. "I'm sorry. We tried to kill Marrant. Maybe we even succeeded, though I wouldn't bet on it."

"You said you hurt my friends. What did you do?"

"It doesn't matter." She shakes her head. "You'll learn the whole story soon. Here's what's important: you have to do better than I did. Better than my whole generation did. We had good intentions, but we kept trying to keep a broken machine working. You need to build something new."

"You aren't supposed to be selfish. That's the whole point of you. You're supposed to be self-sacrificing and noble and, and . . . you're supposed to be better." My not-a-body is shaking.

Thaoh Argentian sighs. "It's easy to convince yourself that you're hurting people for the 'greater good'—and that can mean anything you want it to mean."

"You . . . you enjoyed being in my body." I feel heartbroken, like something precious has been taken away from me, and I can never get it back.

"Of course I did. What was I supposed to do? You're the one who gave me your body to do with as I saw fit."

If we weren't both ghosts—if I could hurt her right now—I don't know what I'd do.

"Listen," she says. "We don't have much time left, and I'm about to die a second time. They're in the process of evicting me from your brain once and for all."

I was just wishing I could yeet Captain Argentian into a black hole. But now it's hitting me: I only have one chance to talk to her, and there's so much to say.

"I'm not ready to come back," I find myself saying. "I already blew it, right? I don't know what I'm doing, and everything is a mess, and I can't take this burden back on my shoulders."

Thaoh shakes her head. "I know how you feel. It never gets any easier."

Acid smell is getting all in my eyes and my sinuses. Waves of anxiety rock my chest.

"I'm scared I'll have no choice but to fight," I say, "and I don't want to kill anyone. That's your job."

Thaoh nods. "They told me you were a pacifist. Listen . . . when I was your age or a little older, I felt the same way. I didn't want to do violence anymore."

"So you're saying I'm going to grow out of it." I want to scream bloody murder at her again. Then I see the look on her face.

"No, I really hope you don't. Killing is the clumsiest, cruelest solution to any problem." The watchful look in her eyes reminds me of my mom. "I'm trying to tell you, there's another way. From what I heard, you have all my old skills, including muscle memory. But you don't even know what skills you have until you try. Correct?"

"Yeah," I say.

She looks like me, but somehow more glamorous. It's in the way she holds herself, but maybe she's also putting some product in her hair? She has this magnetism that I only wish I could lay claim to.

"When I was young, I studied a Ghulg fighting style called nahrax. It's designed to incapacitate an opponent without causing serious injury or death. I should warn you that those skills were rusty when I died, so they'll be rusty for you, too."

I take that in. I can't help remembering when Lyzix trained me, back on the *Indomitable,* and it was all about being ready to kill when necessary. All this time, I had another way to fight, but nobody told me.

"So how do I practice this, uh, nahrax?"

"Start by getting into the inward rush stance, and it should flow from there." Thaoh demonstrates what the inward rush stance looks like: left leg raised, with the thigh at a forty-five-degree angle to the ground, right arm pointing straight up. Makes sense, considering how much the Ghulg love to harmonize with their tusks.

She takes me through it a few more times, until I'm sure I can get into it on my own. I'm going to have to spend a few hours a day practicing this until it's sharp again.

"I wasn't scared to die the first time, but this time I'm rickety with fear." Thaoh lowers her head and purses her lips. "I guess I forgot how wonderful it is to be alive. Promise me you'll enjoy it. Even if all the worlds are ending, even if everything seems hopeless, promise me you'll find reasons to celebrate. Don't try to put your emotions on lockdown."

I don't know what to say.

"I'm scared to be alive again. I don't think I can do this."

"It's your life. Just please listen to someone else who got a second chance at life: don't let any of it go to waste. You might find it's sweeter the second time around."

Thaoh is turning see-thru, like a faded decal on a car window.

"I'll try," I say. "I'll do my best, okay? Listen, I don't know if I forgive you or not, but I hope you find peace after this, and . . . thank you for bringing me back. Thank you for giving up your life for me."

She opens her mouth to say something, but I can't hear whatever it is. She's more ghost than person, and I can barely make out her face now.

Right around the time that Thaoh Argentian fades to nothing, this entire weirdscape starts to melt away too. I feel like I'm falling asleep, but then I realize it's the opposite: I'm waking up.

"I'm not ready." I don't even get the words out before it's over.

I open my eyes and see Rachael looking down at me. She's smiling, but nervously. Like she's scared this won't work, and she'll be smiling at Captain Argentian and it'll be weird.

"It's me." My voice sounds froggy. "Good to see you with my own eyes."

Everything hurts and I can't sit up or even raise my head to see my surroundings. The ceiling overhead looks like the underside of a boat, curving downward, with a big opening in the middle that shows a pink sky full of lint-colored clouds. That battery-acid smell is a lot stronger now, like we're near a big old acid bath.

Oh, I know what planet we're on: Wamgha, home of the famous acid swamp. Great place to dispose of a few thousand bodies, if you're a galaxy-spanning serial killer.

I try to move again and let out an involuntary gasp. My whole body feels messed up.

"Take it easy," Rachael says. "You just got brain surgery from some giant bags of slime, and they said you'll be knocked sideways for a while."

"You did it. I can't even. You did it, you brought me back." I've never been so glad to see anyone, ever.

"I had some help from Captain Argentian, once she got her head out of her ass." She bites her lip, like she doesn't know how to say something. "How much do you remember about the past few months?"

"Um . . . nothing?"

"A lot has happened. A *lot*. I don't even know where to start."

She goes silent, but my brain is noisy enough on its own. The last thing I remember . . . the Compassion tried to stop the Bereavement and it backfired? Irriyaia's sun ate itself? Oh god. Yatto. Just the stuff that I personally witnessed was bad enough, I can't imagine what's worse.

I still can't move without pain shooting through me, and my brain is made of wet sand. Then I suddenly realize: it's just me and Rachael here.

"Uh, so where's Elza? And the others?"

"We, uh, got separated. I don't know where they are."

I can tell from Rachael's face that she's trying to hold back a flood of bad news. But I'm suddenly way too tired to take in anything.

I close my eyes and grit my teeth. "Tell me later, I guess."

"Okay. But I want to show you something."

Rachael fishes in a bag and pulls out something. A lightpad. She holds it up to me, and I can't even believe what I'm seeing.

It's a sketch of the acid swamps of Wamgha: I can see the froth on the surface and the streaks of toxic gas wafting through the air, and those spiky "trees" (they're actually a blend of silicone and fungus) sticking out here and there. The sky is full of gray clouds and puffworms. It's a picture of one of the most revolting places in the universe.

And yet, it's so beautiful, I cry like I just invented crying.

"You . . . you drew this. You made this art. You did it, you got your gift back."

Rachael nods. "Elza helped me."

My heart feels supermassive, incandescent. "And you've been practicing. Look at these lines. This is next-level. Look at the shading here. I can actually see this puffworm moving, like you captured the way they zigzag through the sky. This is the coolest thing I've ever seen in my entire life."

"I had a lot of time to kill while you've been recovering."

"This is what we're fighting for." Oh god, I'm bawling again. I've only been alive for like five minutes and I've already cried more than my first time around.

"We're fighting for my sketches?"

"Shut up! We're fighting for beauty, okay?" I sniffle. "We're fighting for beauty and friends to share it with. That thing that turns all the garbage that we have to live through into pictures and stories. I'm not saying it right. But you know what I mean."

Rachael's mouth quirks upward, her cheeks redden. The coruscating swamp light puts pastel colors on her skin. The two of us being together again feels like a clutch of miracles. "I'm afraid if I hug you, your head is going to break like an egg," Rachael says. "But can I . . . can I rest my head on your shoulder or something, with extreme gentleness?"

I nod, crying all over again.

Rachael climbs next to me on this table/platform thing, and lays her head on my shoulder. "I've missed you so much," she whispers. "I haven't even known what to do with myself."

We stay like that for a long time, at peace, with her face against my chest. I can feel her breathing, and feel her hair nestling my neck and upper arm. If I had to come back to life from an endless nothing void, I'm glad my best friend was the first person I saw with my new/old eyes.

18

.

I'm sitting on a big grungy rock, surrounded by bubbling acid, with Rachael on one side of me and Marshwell, one of the mind-threaders, on the other. Like pretty much everyone on Wamgha, Marshwell has a skin like an elephant's hide, wrapped around a soupy slime interior, and keeps changing shape, from pointy star to spiral swirl. The three of us watch the suns change places in the sky—there's no sign of the Bereavement taking hold yet, but it's just a matter of time.

"If it's really true," Marshwell says. "If you really can help rekindle the suns, then we would have brought you back from the depths of the mind-swamp for free."

I squirm. Time was, I would have given anything to have people put all their faith in me.

"Who told you that I could help rekindle the suns?" I ask, staring out at the faint glimmer on the soupy horizon.

"The other you," Marshwell says. "Thaoh Argentian."

Marshwell doesn't exactly have a pronoun. In the Wamgha'a language, you either refer to somebody by name, or you list all of their titles and achievements and food preferences, which takes a while. And if you leave out anything, you're in big trouble. Safer just to use someone's name every time you mention them.

"I need to go check on my other patients." Marshwell turns bowl-shaped, which is how the Wamgha'a say "BRB," and then wanders off.

Rachael and I sit together for a while on this chalky rock. She's sketching, I'm brooding. I know she'll wait as long as it takes for me to say what's on my mind, because that's what I've always done for her.

The sky isn't a cute pink, it's a cough-syrup pink. Makes me nauseous, or maybe it's the brain surgery.

"I can't make sense of any of it," I say at last. "Too many feelings at once. I can't settle on one of them. I'm here and you're with me, and I want to Snoopy-dance forever. But I'm so scared for Elza and the others. Like even if they escaped after Thaoh threw them under the bus, they're heading into the lair of the creatures that even the Vayt were terrified of. Plus every time I look at the sky, I remember how we already failed." I gesture at the doomed suns.

Rachael nods and carries on sketching.

"But then I think about Thaoh, in my body, doing things that I could never live with myself . . ." A chill settles onto my skin. "It's like I cheated on Elza, and then hung her out to dry. Elza tried to warn me, back when she first found out about the mindstone. I just feel . . ."

I can't find the words, or gather the breath to say them. Head spinning a little.

At last I say, ". . . dirty." Saying it out loud makes the feeling worse. "Like I can never get clean again."

Rachael puts down her plastiform sketchpad. "When Thaoh was doing those things, we kept saying over and over, *That's not Tina.* Those three words became like a chorus. Because it's true." She fidgets with her pen. "The way I think about it is, Thaoh did all kinds of things before you were born, and you're not responsible for any of them. So this is just more of that."

"Except this time, it was my body. And she hurt the people I love."

"Yeah. I can't imagine. I'm just saying, you didn't do any of those things. You could have had a brain worm, or been hypnotized by a mind-control ray, and your actions wouldn't be your fault. But this wasn't even you. The way I see it is, you made a major sacrifice to save all of us when the *Unity at All Costs* was blowing up, and you paid a price. We all owe you. Also, I need to know if brain worms are a real thing."

I try to remember. "Uh, sort of? There are mind parasites on Kthorok VII, but they just make you worship the singing volcano fish, and it only lasts a short time before you drop dead."

"That's lovely." Rachael shudders.

My skin crawls every time I imagine Thaoh making out with a stranger in front of Elza. "I can already tell that I'm going to have some really gross nightmares."

I have to close my eyes and bite my tongue. A wave of ick washes over me.

"I know." Rachael's voice sounds like it comes from a long way off. "And I'll be there every single time when you wake up, to remind you that you're you. And that you have people who care about you."

I open my eyes and look at Rachael and the sketchpad in her hand, lit up by the sunlight reflecting on the acid swamp.

Warmth rises up and drives out the ick.

"Gratitude," I say. "That's the one feeling I can latch onto. I'm grateful to be here with you. I love you, Rachael Townsend. I don't think I've ever said that out loud before."

She blinks and says it back: "I love you too. Can we hold hands?"

"We sure can."

We clasp hands and look at the horizon. Bask in the light of these suns while they're still here.

I'm still new, still unstuck from myself. Her palm against mine feels like an anchor to the past.

"Nyitha and Thaoh lost out on so much time together because they put romance ahead of friendship. I never want anyone or anything to come between you and me."

"Same." I turn and gaze into Rachael's green eyes. Her face is a little flushed, maybe just from breathing acid fumes all the time, and her reddish-brown hair frizzles in the wind. I'm knocked sideways once again by the miracle that is the two of us being here together, so far from home.

Rachael starts to say something else, but my head spins and my mouth tastes like liverwurst. She catches me right before I keel over into the nearest pool of acid.

Marshwell sees me wobbling and dashes over. "You should not rush your recovery. Your neural pathways are still resetting themselves, and your species has brains that are inconveniently far away from your other organs. Do not exert yourself too much for a while."

"I will try to keep my brain in neutral." I can just glimpse the thick soup sloshing inside this shape-changing crusty shell. It catches the light and makes pretty ripples and streaks of red and blue.

"Let's get you back to bed," Rachael says. I nod, feebly.

A few days later, I still can't process all the bad news. Random bits of information pop into my head when I'm thinking about nothing in particular, like: *Nyitha is dead.* Or: *Thaoh hung Elza out to dry.* I can't even consider the possibility that anything could have happened to Elza—I have to believe we'll see each other again, or I'll just crawl into a hole forever.

I'm giving first aid to the ship, which Rachael calls the Mazda Miata. The impellers took a couple hits when Rachael and Thaoh were escaping, and the best I can do is patch them with the high-tech equivalent of duct tape.

Rachael sits next to me, doodling and talking about nothing in particular. "I hope our friends are being careful, but I know they're not. We kept having the same conversation. Someone would say that something was too big a risk. And then Yiwei or Elza would say that no risk is too great, because everything is on the line." She shudders. "I hate it. This shouldn't just be on us. We shouldn't have to carry it all by ourselves."

Ack. I can totally picture Elza trying to be pragmatic and do what's necessary, especially after the way the palace schooled her to look directly at suffering without losing her cool.

All I can think of to say is, "Can't exactly second-guess the choices you all made while I wasn't myself. I'm sure everyone did their best." I poke at the engines.

"Do you think it's weird that I haven't drawn people since I got my art back?" Rachael changes the topic again, like she's surfing anxiety. "All I draw is things, and places. Sometimes I worry that I'm still partway blocked."

"Nah." I jam the fuel intake into place and barely avoid blowing myself to pieces. "You're just trying new stuff. You've been through a lot, and you're working through it, right? Maybe you just need to explore your own feelings without trying to capture anyone else's for a while."

"I wish I could talk to Nyitha. It still hasn't sunk in that she's gone, 'cause I'm a slow cooker. I'll probably feel wrecked in a while. At least I get to mourn for her, because we got far enough away in time."

"I'm really sorry about Nyitha," I say to Rachael. "She was a really generous person, in spite of what a raw deal she got."

"I'm going to try and honor her." Rachael holds up her sketchpad, which shows a tattered banner floating across the entrance to the Stroke on Wentrolo, saying ARE YOU SURE YOU DON'T ALREADY KNOW?

I slot the last component into place. "I think we're good to go. We can take off in a little while, and we should be able to make it to Miscreant Station for proper repairs. And then we go looking for our friends."

Our last few hours on Wamgha go really quickly. I haven't even gotten to see much of the place—the acid swamp is just one region, there's also a forest of giant teeth and a permanent bomb cyclone that writes epic romance novels.

We load our junk into the Mazda Miata, and say goodbye to Marshwell and the rest of the Wamgha'a, and I realize Rachael is looking at me funny.

I stop singing. "What?"

"You . . . were singing. You were singing that Olivia Rodrigo song that I tried—in vain—to get you to do at the Mitchells' backyard karaoke party."

Oh. Yeah, I was. Wasn't I?

"When I got to talk to Thaoh for a minute, she made me promise that I would enjoy being alive again," I say. "And I guess, the cough-syrup sky and golden acid swamp look nice, and you and I are together again, and we're going to find my girlfriend. So I guess I'm in a not-terrible mood."

Then I sit in the pilot seat, and shiver. I don't want to put my hands back into the grape jelly interface, I don't want to go back out there and have people shooting at me and putting things on me again. I can't make my arms reach forward.

"I don't know if I can do this," I say in a weak voice. Hard to believe I was singing a moment ago. "First I tried to be Captain Argentian, and then I tried to be me. And both times, I failed."

Rachael doesn't answer, like she's processing. Then she says, "The only thing we have to hold on to is that we believe in each other. That's how I know our friends are still alive. And it's how I know you're going to figure this out."

I stick my hands into the high-tech pudding. The machine wakes up in response to my touch, and I activate the launch sequence, as if I've done it a hundred times before. A moment later, we're arcing upward, into the air and past the sky, as the ground becomes a mosaic. And then we're in space again, rushing to the stars.

"Let's just hope those repairs can hold up until we get to Miscreant Station," I say. "Otherwise this could be a really short trip."

19

■

Our engines are melting—we're basically flying with fondue under our hood. The stench is way too similar to the sulfur from that acid swamp, and my fingers are getting singed inside the holographic jelly. I don't dare let go of the controls, or we'll get blown to pieces. We've already come too far to get back to Wamgha.

"I swear I did my best with those repairs," I say between curses. "We're definitely not going to make it to Miscreant Station, and I'm not sure we're going to make it anywhere."

I scan the tactical readout for anyplace we could reach before the ship goes boom. Dust cloud, asteroid party, another dust cloud, a whole lot of empty nothing, and . . . a solar system with one inhabited planet. A planet we've visited before, in fact.

"Okay," I say. "We have one shot. If our duct tape holds, we might barely get to Second Yoth."

"Second Yoth . . ." Rachael frowns. "Isn't that . . . the home of the Grattna?"

"Yup."

The Grattna have three of almost everything: three limbs, three wings, three eyes. Their culture is based on there always being three options, or three sides to any conflict. Marrant took a bunch of them prisoner and used them for his horrible experiments, but we rescued them—well, most of them—and helped them steal Marrant's advanced ship, so they could copy it and be able to protect themselves next time.

"Hopefully they'll be happy to see us," Rachael says.

"If they don't look at us and get reminded of the worst thing that ever happened to them." I sigh. "They'll probably have some third choice of how they could react, but I can't think of it right now."

I set a course for Second Yoth and try to handle the controls gently even though they feel like a hot stove. The smell gets more acrid, and the engines make a horrible grinding noise. *Come on,* I plead silently. *Just be a starship for a little longer. You can do this. That's a good Mazda Miata.*

We don't exactly crash outside Kufn, the main city on Second Yoth. We sort of half land, half face-plant, with noxious smoke spewing from the Mazda Miata's engine compartment.

We're in a stand of trees that look like toothpicks with doilies on top, and I look around for some kind of Grattna welcoming party. They have a whole ritual for welcoming strangers, with three types of greetings. But I don't see anyone at all.

Then I realize we're surrounded by Grattna holding guns that look like modified superstream cannons in two of their three limbs.

"We don't welcome or tolerate outsiders," a voice says. "You can't stay here—so either leave or die."

On our way down, I was concentrating on keeping the Miata from blowing up, but I noticed a shipyard in orbit, building supersized warships exactly like the one we liberated from Marrant. Half a dozen of those warships already patrol the space around Second Yoth, and I barely snuck past them, especially with the Mazda Miata's engines belching radiation all over the place.

"Um," I say. "We're friends. Remember us? We helped you."

They just point their weapons at us with more emphasis.

"The Royal Fleet chose to join with the Compassion—so we can't trust any of you, and we don't want to get involved in any more of your struggles," says the leader.

"Let's just slow down. My name is Tina and my pronoun is *she*. This is Rachael, her pronouns are also *she/her*. Who are you?"

"I'm Eldnat, my pronoun is *he*. You can't stay, and I don't want to hurt you, so please just leave."

I try to explain that our ship is damaged and we can't go anywhere without fixing it, and it's partly thanks to us that they have all those fancy new ships in orbit.

Eldnat is bigger than the other Grattna I've seen, with three deep-set eyes that seem made for scowling and a wide, toothy mouth. All three wings flex as if they're about to reach out and slap my face, and muscles strain inside a set of overalls made of thick, dark green fabric.

"You aren't welcome or necessary here." Eldnat seems to choose his words with care, to make sure I can understand.

"We just need to stay long enough to repair our ship—"

At last, Eldnat seems to lose his cool, and I understand less and less of what he's saying. "You are not _____ with _____ and we do not _____."

"Please! We just need a few parts to fix our engines!"

More Grattna show up to rubberneck—literally, their necks are kind of rubbery. I feel like an asshole standing here haranguing these people who've already been through a lot, but I don't know what else to do.

"Your sun—the Yothstar?—is about to go dark," I say, "just like all the other suns that support inhabited planets. We're working on a solution, and we just need to get back to our friends."

"We _____ and we are working on building an artificial sun," Eldnat says. "We will _____ ourselves _____."

We're surrounded by a crowd of Grattna, arguing amongst themselves and yelling at us. At last, I see one Grattna that we've met before.

"You're back," says Halred (*she/her*). Her three eyes are wider than usual, with blue-and-yellow-swirled irises. "We figured you were dead or imprisoned. You can't stay here, but you can't leave either." She pauses, deciding. "We'll help you to repair your ship, and then you can be on your way."

"Thank you thank you thank you." I bounce with relief, not to mention I need to pee because I've been stuck for ages on that tiny starship with no toilet.

They don't exactly have day and night on Second Yoth—instead, they have ziyy, zyaa, and sayyn, which are times where the wind blows in a particular direction or the light turns paler or redder. It only gets dark occasionally, so everyone just naps all the time. Rachael and I try to get on the Grattna sleep schedule, but it leaves me cranky and disoriented because I'm not a napper.

Every time I sleep, I have nightmares where I make out with a stranger in front of Elza. I try to stop myself, I can't stop myself, I want to say *I did not agree to this,* but my mouth is busy kissing. I wake in a sweat-puddle, wrestling with my fancy sleeping bag.

True to her word, Rachael is next to me, and she sits with me, saying: "It wasn't you. It wasn't you."

A couple of ziyys later, Rachael and I are sitting at a hexagonal table

outdoors, with Halred, Eldnat, and a couple other Grattna. The ship repairs are taking a little longer than we'd hoped, because the Miata needs a
bunch of parts that have to be scrounged or custom-made. The Grattna are
being pretty nice to us, but they're also really clear that as soon as our ship
is fixed, we'd better get gone and stay gone.

The longer we talk to the Grattna, the harder it gets to communicate,
because we've run out of simple topics. I've never tried to have a real conversation with them—before, we just talked about escaping or fighting, basic
survival stuff. When we start talking about politics or friendship or religion or some other big things, the EverySpeak conks out, and half the stuff
they say turns into gibberish.

I sit and stare at the confusing food on my twist-shaped plate. (The
Grattna don't have "raw" or "cooked"—instead, they have three different
states for food to be in.) I'm wondering whether we'll even be in time to
help Elza and the others.

Halred shows up every now and then to make sure Rachael and I stay
out of trouble, and each time, I try to have a conversation with her.

"We could help each other," I say to Halred. "I don't want this to be just
a one-way thing."

Halred says something that makes no sense. Is my EverySpeak broken?

"Listen," I say. "You believe there are three sides to every conflict, right?
But now the Royal Fleet and the Compassion have merged into one side, so
you need a third side. The Royal Compassion keeps coming after me and my
friends, and you could be our allies. As equals this time. You have all those
amazing ships, plus you think about everything differently than we do."

Halred crosses two limbs with the third. "You don't understand how
things work. It's—" And then the EverySpeak craps out again.

I get a charley horse in my neck and a tightness in my chest when I
imagine leaving here without having accomplished anything.

"We don't just want your help standing up to the Royal Compassion,"
I say. "We need to build a new alliance. Something better than the Firmament and the Royal Fleet ever were—an alliance that gives you a real
say. Please."

Everything Halred says in response turns into noise. The harder we try
to communicate, the less we understand.

I find my way through the three-way streets to the hexagonal aerie
where they're letting Rachael and me crash. Rachael sits in the corner,
sketching, while I collapse onto a pile of cushions.

I wake up thrashing, marathon-breathing. Rachael is already sitting next to me, saying, "Hey."

"Ugh." I shiver and wipe away sweat.

"Another nightmare about her?"

I start to say yeah, but then I remember. "Actually, no. This time, I was me, and I was at that platform at Antarràn, and the Grattna were inside these cages, begging for my help. And I just turned and walked away from them." I make a noise deep in my throat. "At least this is a shitty thing that I did, instead of something Thaoh did in my body. That's something, right?"

"Yeah." Rachael stares out the window, at the doily trees and the three-faced spires. "And maybe this is a wrong that you have a chance to try and make right."

Rachael and I sit at the top of one of the tallest structures in Kufn, built into the side of a massive tree. The view is incredible—the whole city stretches out in three segments, surrounded by doily trees, basking in the mid-zyaa sun.

"How soon can we get out of here?" Rachael asks as I stare out at the skyline.

"Soon, I hope. Halred says we should have a new spaceweave core in a while. I just hope I find a way to start a real alliance with them first."

"No offense, but it seems like you're not getting anywhere." Rachael purses her lips and gazes at her sketches of Kufn and the forest. "Maybe you can't solve hundreds of years of misunderstandings overnight—sorry, I mean overzyaa."

I sit with that.

It's not just that the Royal Fleet never had a place for the Grattna or the Kraelyors or anyone else who doesn't look like us. It's also that Captain Argentian and people like her got used to zooming around in big starships, viewing planets like this one from a distance and maybe dropping down for a quick visit.

And the EverySpeak is part of the problem too, because we think we can understand everybody, and we really, really can't. From talking to Elza, I know there are so many words in Portuguese that the EverySpeak can't handle—so how the hell can I hope to understand people from an even more different culture?

"No more looking down at people from orbit," I say out loud. "No more pretending that everybody can speak English, even if that makes things easier in the short term. I know what I have to do."

I pull myself upright, nearly bonking my head against the low ceiling, and trudge down the ramp before I can lose my nerve.

Behind me, Rachael asks, "Wait, what? What are you going to do?"

"You'll see," I say over my shoulder.

I wander the outskirts of Kufn until I run into Halred, who gives me a weary look because she's sick of my garbled lectures.

I walk up to her and do the scariest thing I've done in a long time: I turn the EverySpeak off.

I point to myself. "Tina." I point to her: "Halred." Then I point at the nearest doily tree, and hope she gets it.

Halred looks at me like I've grown an extra head, then she sighs and tells me the word for the doily tree in Grattna: *nmatk*.

I try to say it: "Martuk."

Halred sighs louder and says it again: "Nmatk."

I try again, and again. Takes us forever, but eventually I can pronounce a single word in her language.

One word down, ten thousand to go. I've got no place else to be, and I'm not going to quit until I can speak at least a little bit of street Grattna. Because if I can understand how they talk, I'll be closer to understanding how they think.

And then maybe we can actually be friends.

20

.

. . . 238 Earth days until all the suns go out forever

The farther Elza travels from the Glorious Nebula and the central worlds, the weaker her connection to the Ardenii becomes. Now they can only talk to her if she's close enough to one of the main "civilized" planets, or a Royal Compassion ship that can boost their signal.

Elza thought she'd feel relieved . . . but she misses them. Like an empty socket from a missing tooth, which you can't resist probing with your tongue. The Ardenii feel like part of her now, like her mind includes all this extra space, and when they're gone she feels . . . emptier. She even misses the massive numbers they kept sending her with no explanation.

Still, even when she's cut off, the Ardenii find ways to dish some dirt, whether she wants it or not.

She'll be walking around the *Undisputed Training Bra Disaster,* and she'll run into Gahang, the skull-faced young Aribentor who served on board the *Undisputed* with Tina, Zaeta, and Damini. And way-too-personal details about Gahang will pop into Elza's brain: like, he was involved with a radical religious sect that tried to sabotage a government building on Aribentora. After Gahang was arrested, his family made a deal for him to enlist in the Royal Fleet, instead of doing hard labor in the mountains.

It's creepy to know the most intimate secrets about someone you only just met. What would Fernanda say if she was here? Probably the same stuff she said when their friendship ended.

There's only one way the Ardenii can still be telling her things, so far from their home: The Ardenii must have crammed anything that might be useful to Elza into her crown, the last time she was within range. And the crown on its own seems to have enough awareness of Elza's situation to know what information to give her. Not just about Gahang, but also about ships whose course might intersect the *Undisputed Training Bra Disaster*'s—once or twice, they've flown within scanning range of another ship, and Elza has suddenly known the name of the captain, and the exact cargo the ship is carrying.

It's hard enough being cooped up on this tiny ship for weeks. Knowing everybody's business is making it a hundred times worse—Elza can't get through a conversation with somebody without a knowledge bomb going off in her head.

Elza has been hiding in her tiny quarters as much as possible, looking at the deep pink folds of her tactical ballgown and wishing she could talk to Rachael. Elza knows all the things she wishes she could say to Rachael, but even her crown can't tell her how Rachael would reply.

Or Tina. Except . . . Tina is probably gone forever. Elza is trying to get used to the idea.

While Thaoh Argentian was hanging around, Elza could convince herself there was still hope—like maybe they would stumble on a way to bring Tina back. But Thaoh is on the run, with the whole Royal Compassion on her tail.

As for Rachael? She wasn't captured, the last time Elza got an update, and the Ardenii believed she was probably still alive. Elza wants to reassure Yiwei and the others, but she doesn't know what to believe.

Elza walks into the one big space on the ship, the flight lounge: half decadent artist salon, half sterile Royal Fleet operations center. Zaeta and Damini are back at the ship's controls, after letting Gahang and Cinnki take a turn for a while, and they're having one of their moods.

"Stop fighting me," Damini grumbles to Zaeta.

"Why don't *you* stop fighting *me*?" Zaeta snarls.

Every time they swerve, the ship's hull creaks louder, like it's about to break.

"It's clearly this way," Damini says.

"That's not clear to me," Zaeta retorts.

"Can we just wreck this ship and get it over with?" Wyndgonk snorts. "Maybe the self-destruct from the *Undisputed* still works."

Elza suddenly knows that suffocating in space is Wyndgonk's deepest phobia.

Ugh, stop it, Elza thinks. *I don't need to know everybody's secrets.* The crown doesn't respond. She imagines Fernanda clicking her tongue: *This is what you always wanted.*

"So," Cinnki says. "We're here. We're at the place the cup told us to go. And there's nothing but a few solar systems and a big ugly asteroid field."

Cinnki once stole a priceless moon-ruby from the slash-temple on Javarr, and he thinks nobody knows it was him. He hid the moon-ruby somewhere, and it's never been found.

"That's a whole lot of asteroids," agrees Kfok—who became an artist after she was dishonorably expelled from the defense force back on Kraelyo Homeglobe for deserting her post, the crown says.

"There better be something more than just rocks," Kez (he/him) says. "Thirty-seven people died so we could get here." He and Yiwei still aren't looking at each other.

"Maybe you just didn't understand what the queen was telling you," Naahay says to Elza.

Gahang rolls his giant exposed eyeballs at Naahay, like *Ugh, not again*. The two Aribentors only loathe each other more deeply, after this long voyage.

Naahay is exactly who Elza thinks she is according to the crown. When Naahay was in formation school on Aribentora, she failed an important test but her fancy parents pulled strings so she could retake it. She's failed upward, over and over.

Yiwei speaks up at last. "Look. This place has probably been untouched for hundreds of thousands of years. The people who sent the Bereavement to kill all the stars—the Shadow Galaxy, or whatever they're called—they could have left a whole city behind, and it might've crumbled to dust by now."

The crown can't tell Elza any secrets about Yiwei, Damini, or Kez, because the Ardenii have no presence on Earth.

Elza walks over to the pilot station where Zaeta and Damini are still squabbling over which way to steer the ship. "—so impatient," Zaeta says. "Sometimes you need—"

"Don't lecture me," Damini hisses.

They both realize Elza is standing over them, and fall silent.

"So there's nothing unusual out there?" Elza says. "No weird radiation, no particles, no big neon sign?"

"Nothing but rocks," Damini says.

"And a few high-magnitude stars," says Zaeta.

"Aff," Elza says. Then something occurs to her. "Are all of the habitable stars being affected by the Bereavement? Same as everywhere else?"

"Umm . . . yes," Damini says. "Except. Oh, wait."

"Mystification!" Zaeta says. "There's one star that shows no sign of a tiny black hole. It's right there, at the edge of this asteroid field."

"Clever," says Damini, smiling again. "The one star that's not being affected by the Bereavement—"

"—is probably where the Bereavement originally came from," Zaeta says.

The two of them are already steering the *Undisputed Training Bra Disaster* toward that one untainted sun. Cinnki rushes over to the glowing flower bed next to the pilot station and starts scanning.

"Looks like a whole lot of rocky planets without much of anything," Cinnki says.

"Wait a minute." Yiwei jumps to his feet and crosses the room until he's looking over Cinnki's shoulder. "This one planet has five moons, and check the closest one. There's something there."

Cinnki squints, and his ears twist a little. "There's a power source."

"The Shadow Galaxy?" Yiwei says.

"It's probably not the Sparklefriends of Mirth," says Wyndgonk.

Kfok makes a surprised noise from the ottoman in the far corner. "Look at this," she says. "I don't think that asteroid field is really an asteroid field. I think it's . . . debris."

"Debris?" Yiwei rushes over and looks at the 3-D display next to Kfok. "Yeah. Those are starship chunks, from thousands of ships. I've never seen anything like it. You'd mistake them for rocks, unless you know what you're looking for. They must have had some kind of next-level stealth technology that our scans mostly bounce off of."

Gahang clicks his tongue against his exposed teeth. "It's a starship graveyard. Probably all that's left . . ."

". . . after the final battle between the Shadow Galaxy and the Vayt," Yiwei says. "We definitely came to the right place."

21

.

The *Undisputed Training Bra Disaster* gets caught in gravity twists as it approaches Larstko IVb, the moon with the mysterious power source. The ship's eggshell hull screeches in protest.

"Watch out for that magnetic flux," Damini says.

"*You* watch out," Zaeta snaps back.

Kez watches the two pilots, like he's wondering if he should try to make peace. He meets eyes with Elza—she shakes her head.

This moon has lower gravity than Earth, but it's still a bad choice for the first place to try and land the *Undisputed Training Bra Disaster*. The magnetic field acts weird—like, the poles move around—and it spews electromagnetic waves. The ship lurches, worse than the boat Elza's parents took her on, near Praia Grande, when she was six years old. She thought she'd never stop throwing up.

At the other end of the flight lounge, Yiwei and Gahang sit together, making plans. "This moon is where the Shadow Galaxy made their last stand, after they lost the battle against the Vayt that left all that debris," Gahang says in a sober baritone. "They retreated to their stronghold, where they launched their ultimate weapon."

"So we have to be prepared for anything," Yiwei says.

Gahang's bony head bobs up and down. "There could be traps, deadly security measures, any number of things."

"We'll need to follow Situation Blue Crawl protocols." Yiwei slips into Royal Fleet jargon almost by instinct, and Gahang follows suit.

"We don't have the equipment to perform a thorough RealTac scan," Gahang says.

Why didn't Elza notice sooner? Gahang is becoming a mentor, or maybe a big brother, to Yiwei lately. Maybe Yiwei is trying to salvage the version of himself he was finding in the Royal Fleet, and it doesn't hurt that Gahang is an Aribentor, like Captain Othaar. Or maybe Yiwei's just trying to

distract himself from worrying that Rachael didn't survive Captain Argentian's side mission.

Either way, ever since Yiwei blew up that Royal Compassion ship, he's
been spending more and more time with Gahang.

"Everybody hold tight," Damini says from the pilot station.

"We're entering what passes for an atmosphere," Zaeta adds.

The *Undisputed Training Bra Disaster* thrashes like a person fighting a
bad dream, and Elza barely stays in her chair. Kfok flies across the room
and lands on the empty sofa with a muffled thump. Damini and Zaeta
chatter back and forth over the screaming of the engines and the croaking
of the hull.

Up close, the surface looks rocky, barren. No sign of any stronghold or
fortress.

"Let's not land just yet," Yiwei says to Gahang. "We can fly over the
surface and keep an eye out for any remains." Gahang nods in agreement.

"I love your confidence that we'll be able to land at all," Damini cracks.

"We *will* be able to land—if we're careful, for once." Zaeta gives Damini
thirty-three eyes' worth of side-eye.

Yiwei and Gahang whisper back and forth, staring at the ship's instruments, while Naahay gives Gahang the evil eye. Damini and Zaeta squab-
ble nonstop.

Elza hides at the far side of the ship, in the crewmaster's office from the
Undisputed, which somehow got saved when most of the useful stuff was
wrecked. She sits on a big velveteen cushion from the *Training Bra Disaster*
and tries to reach out to the Ardenii with her mind. Nothing. Instead, she
falls into obsessing about Rachael and Thaoh. What are the chances that
Elza will ever know what happened to them? And how do you mourn for
people if you don't know whether they're dead—and if so, whether their
deaths were worthwhile?

Some gear inside her shaves its teeth when she tries to hope.

Elza goes to the cubby where she's been sleeping and hunts inside a tiny
wicker box until she finds a lump of fuchsia satin: her tactical ballgown. She
looks at its rippling folds, thinking, *This is ridiculous*—and then she pulls it on
over her practical black explorer pants. The moment those folds and billows
settle around her waist and hips, she feels better, as if Rachael is still with her.

Someone approaches as Elza is smoothing the dress into place.

"Oh, good," Wyndgonk says. "You've put your armor back on. We found something."

Elza follows Wyndgonk back to the flight lounge. Yiwei, Gahang, and Cinnki are staring at a holographic bubble that shows the rocky surface below. Yiwei points at a big hill, or mound of dirt. "This is way too symmetrical and even. And it's hollow on the inside."

"So there was a building," Cinnki says. "And it got buried."

"We can use the ion harness to remove the dirt," Gahang says.

Soon, all the dust is whisked away, revealing a building that's about the size of the Palace of Scented Tears, and the shape of a xequerê back home: wide round base, with a big-mouthed spout coming off the top.

"It probably looked pretty," Kfok says.

"Let's try and land nearby," Yiwei says. Before Zaeta and Damini start arguing again, he adds: "I'm sure you can do it, and we can take our time."

Elza finds a seat just before the *Undisputed Training Bra Disaster* starts twisting onto one side and then the other. The ship drops several meters, and Elza's knuckles stand out—then they level out and glide to a stop on a flat piece of ground facing the structure.

"See?" Yiwei says. "That was an excellent landing."

As soon as Yiwei thinks nobody is looking, though, he shrinks into himself, face downcast and fingers tangled in his hairline.

Elza wants to say something to him, like, *I'm worried about Rachael too.* But she doesn't have the words, and there's no time—the hatch is opening and they're about to go explore yet another ancient monument to evil.

If only Tina was here. Damn, if only Tina was *anywhere.*

Tina made a promise to Elza, that she would stay by her side, as her consort. She only lasted a few minutes before she broke her word.

"I should go out there first," Gahang says. "I'm the most experienced, and the most expendable."

"Excuse me, we're all pretty experienced," Damini says.

"This isn't our first weird monster world," Zaeta chimes in.

"Nobody's expendable. We should go in a group and watch each other's backs," Kez says.

"I definitely think we should let Gahang go first," Naahay taunts.

Elza stands up, looking at each of them in turn. "We go together, whoever wants to come. That's how we've gotten this far."

Everybody looks at each other, then nods and starts packing up their gear.

The air outside the ship crackles with something like static electricity, and the wind gnashes its teeth. But Elza can breathe, and she doesn't keel over.

"Doesn't look that impressive." Kfok squints at the big xequerê. "For the home of the people who condemned every sun to death."

They walk around the outside twice without finding a way in.

"Well, this was fun," Cinnki says.

"I think this bit of wall looks different." Damini reaches out and feels around until her fingertips land on something, and then she pushes. Part of the wall pushes inward, revealing a doorway large enough for everyone to fit through.

"Well done, Damini," Yiwei says. She blushes.

"Everybody be careful. Literally all we know about these people is that they created the biggest weapon of mass destruction in history," Gahang says. "We have to be ready for any—"

Gahang stops talking, and stares.

The inside of the structure is painted with bright reds, blues, and purples that look fresh. Signs everywhere say things like NEVER LET US PART and LET'S FALL IN LOVE. As soon as Yiwei steps inside, colorful lights whirl around and beams of light play around the bright high-ceilinged space, painting rainbows everywhere. Glittery confetti swirls in the dusty air.

LOVE RULES ALL, a message pops up.

"Are we sure we came to the right place?" Kfok says. "This does not look like the armory of the people who killed all the stars."

Elza can't help bristling. "This is where the data from the chalice led us to."

"Is this like the Compassion?" Zaeta asks. "Where their name is the opposite of what they really stand for?"

"I don't think so." Kez's nose wrinkles. "I think this is for real. Look at all this poetry." He gestures at one wall full of flowery words. "And this love questionnaire. These people, whoever they were, had a culture that was obsessed with romance. A bit like the courtly love tradition on Earth: knights and maidens, sonnets and bonnets. When in real life? Love is a bloody nightmare."

Of course. Kez is still hurting over Ganno the Wurthhi, his sort-of boyfriend who kicked him to the curb. Elza tries to give Kez a sympathetic look—she herself is living proof that love comes and goes like a daydream.

When Yiwei steps further into the space, silken threads gather around him, and now he's wearing a bright red robe with semi-detached puffy sleeves and a hood that covers the back half of his head. He recoils, like he's just been attacked, then looks down, realizes what's happened, and shakes his head.

"Definitely not what I was expecting," Yiwei says.

"No fancy clothes for me," Elza says loudly. "I already got enough make-overs at the Palace of Scented Tears."

"It's . . . a wedding venue?" Damini says. "We toured several of these, when my uncle Srini was remarrying."

"I was going to say it reminds me of a bonding shrine," Kfok says.

"Or a love/hate crucible," Cinnki says.

"It's definitely something," Zaeta says.

At the other end of the space is a large doorway, made of some dark metal, scored with lines of corrosion.

"Any ideas how to get that door open?" Yiwei asks Damini.

Damini hurries forward, then stops and looks at Zaeta. "Want to help me figure this out?"

Zaeta's uppermost eyes widen, then she says, "Sure. Let's do this."

Something hits Elza—like a burst of lightning. She sways until Wynd-gonk catches her in fire front legs.

The Ardenii haven't reached her in so long, she can't understand for a moment. Then it falls into place, and fear blossoms inside her.

"What is it?" Yiwei asks.

"The Royal Compassion. They know about this place, and they sent their fastest ships. Four of them. They'll be here in . . ." Elza squints. Total head rush. "They'll be here in four cycles. A few hours."

All of the spinning lights and candy-colored messages suddenly feel even creepier.

Gahang shakes his skeleton-head. "We'd best move quickly. Whatever's in this building, we need to find it before they do."

22

.

Damini and Zaeta search all around the tarnished doorway yet again, but there's no sign of an entry mechanism. "And I don't see any instructions, or clues," Damini says.

"Me neither," Zaeta says.

Gahang is staring at his Quant. "Whatever's behind that door, it's protected by reinforced walls that a missile strike would just bounce off."

"Like a bunker?" Kez scratches his head. "So these people were all about romance until they went to war with the Vayt and they turned part of their love shrine into a fortress."

"So maybe the way to open the door is to show that we believe in love, in spite of all the ugliness and hurt," Cinnki says.

Everybody looks at each other.

Elza could swear the temperature in this wedding chapel (or whatever it is) just dropped a few degrees.

"Okay, sure," Yiwei says. "Let's give it a try. We're running out of time."

He trudges back to the ship and returns holding a guitar and an instrument called an ayyxa, which is mostly used in Javarah screech-break. "'My Heart in Your Hands,' in G-flat. Got it?"

Cinnki and Kfok, the other two current members of Yiwei's band Not on My Trash Pile, make scoffing noises and reach for their instruments. Xiaohou perches on Yiwei's shoulder with all four metal paws, and produces a syncopated, slow beat that has a little bit of trap and a little bit of Blot music. Kfok plays a haunting melody on a vokvog, an instrument that's a little like a flute, except she sucks in air through five flared tubes instead of blowing out. Yiwei joins in on his homemade guitar, strumming out some chords that sound a little bit like Elza's favorite São Yantó ballad.

Then Cinnki strums the ayyxa and sings in Javarah, except that Elza can understand the lyrics, of course. The chorus isn't actually "My heart in your hands" at all, because Javarah don't associate that organ with love or emotion—instead it's just, "Take off your fur! Take off your fur! Give me your fur, I'll give you my fur! We'll be furless together! I trust you with my skin, I trust you not to hurt me the wrong way. I dream about you whenever I'm able to dream."

Cinnki puts so much vulnerability and longing and tenderness into every line, Elza wants to weep in front of everybody. She also wants to take all of their instruments and smash them into scraps of wood and metal. Even Xiaohou—she wants to take the little robot monkey and break him into tiny pieces.

Elza followed this song's advice, she took off every layer of protection around her skin, around her whole sense of self. And it near destroyed her.

The song is still going, and nothing is happening with that ugly door. Cinnki puts everything he has into that last chorus, begging his lover to go furless with him, please, just lose your fur, it'll be okay.

"Well," Cinnki says when the song ends. "That didn't work."

"And the Royal Compassion will be here soon," Gahang says.

"Screw this," Kez says. "The people who murdered every sun don't get to hear our sappy declarations of love. I tried sharing my heart, and I got crushed. I'm over it."

There's a tiny click from the giant tarnished door, almost too faint to hear.

"Something just happened," Damini says.

"Keep going," Zaeta says.

"No more candy-mouth lies," Elza says. "I gave someone everything I could, and she's gone, and I'm more alone than if I'd never let anybody in."

The door clicks a bit louder.

Elza steps back, because she doesn't have it in her to say anything more. Something has cracked inside her, leaving jagged edges and brittle folds.

Everybody stands there and stares at each other. Except for Gahang, who's scanning on his Quant for the Royal Compassion ships.

"Okay, fine." Yiwei steps forward. "You know what? I didn't think I could ever love anyone the way I love Rachael. I didn't even know what love really meant. And she's gone, because we trusted the wrong person, and I see her smile when I close my eyes, and it's all ruined, and I wish I could just sleep for a month—but I can't, because I'd dream about her, and that would be worse. I've been trying to stay positive because so many people are going to suffer and die if we don't fix this mess, and we can't afford to fall apart now, but love is a joke."

"Hey," Elza says.

"I know, I know, I went from not sharing to oversharing. But I—"

"That's not what I was going to say." Elza moves closer to him. "First, do you want a hug? And second, you did it." She gestures at the door, which swung wide open while he was saying the part about wishing he could sleep for a month.

"Oh. Okay. Let's go." Yiwei puts his serious face back on, like nothing just happened—except that Elza can still see the pain in his eyes.

The other side of the door looks completely different: gray walls, long-dead tactical displays, and a structure at the center of the room that looks like a big ceremonial fountain gone dead: a flat octagonal bowl atop a flared base. This must be the weapons control station.

"And here it is," Kez says. "The moment where love and sweetness turn into war and hatred. The first story ever told, and probably the last. They held on to their romantic notions as long as it suited them, and then they reached for weapons."

Kez's face is wan, like he's remembering why he ran away from home. Elza tries to send him a comforting look.

"I found something." Zaeta pokes at a kind of interface, in a stone alcove on the far corner of this cavernous gourd-shaped space.

"Yeah, you did," Damini says. "Great work."

Zaeta rolls her topmost row of eyes at this transparent attempt to butter her up.

A creature made of knives appears at the center of the room, next to the dry fountain. Like a hologram, or a swarm of little robots holding a single shape. The creature has a long, sloping body that starts with a slender neck and widens into a round belly, with four spindly legs ending in claws, and a spiked tail. And big wings, like a bat.

"It's . . . a dragon," Yiwei says.

"We traveled everywhere, and we finally found a dragon," Kez says.

"This could be what inspired all the legends of the Joyful Wyvern," Cinnki says.

Elza strides over there and notices something that looks familiar, like she's seen it before—but she hasn't, the Ardenii have, and they left that piece of information nestled in her crown in case it came in handy while she was out of range. A tiny waterwheel catches a thin spray of blue-gray liquid from a spout in the slate wall. Elza nudges the wheel, and some water dribbles onto the floor.

The dragon made of tiny blades comes alive.

"Ah. Visitors, after so much time," the knife-dragon says. "And I see why. The weapon has been deployed, the fail-safe has been triggered. Sundeath will soon be irrevocable, and you have come to learn why. My name is Laynbone. My body is long since ashes, but should you require a pronoun for me, you may use *she/her.* I was a leader of the Fatharn people."

"Just tell us how to stop it," Yiwei says.

"We're sick of ancient mass murderers trying to tell us sob stories," Cinnki adds.

Laynbone seems not to hear either of them. "We were the greatest civilization this galaxy will ever see, and all of our traditions revolved around love and discovery."

"Shut up and tell us how to turn off your doomsday weapon," Kfok says.

"Wherever we traveled, we made alliances," Laynbone says. "And when we found a civilization as exalted as our own, we always proposed a marriage: our two peoples would combine, blending our DNA and creating hybrid offspring. We did this with six species, and grew stronger and richer each time. Until we became enamored of a seventh species: the Vayt."

"Wait a minute," Elza says. "The Vayt said you attacked them."

For the first time, Laynbone seems to pay attention. "We did not attack them. We loved them—and they loved us. We held the most beautiful wedding any two peoples ever had, with a whole season of dancing and feasting. You stand inside the building wherein our union was consecrated. We were as happy as any living things can be, for a time."

"So this, all of this, was because of a messy divorce," Damini says.

"That's just really disappointing," Zaeta says.

"Alas, the Vayt realized that we planned to carry on as we always had: making alliances, finding new civilizations to join with in sacred matrimony," Laynbone says. "They grew wrathful, for they had believed they would be the last, that they completed us forever. We'd never concealed the truth, and we tried to explain so many times."

"So you went your separate ways and lived your lives in peace, like mature, reasonable people?" Kez says.

"We fought a war," Laynbone says. "No ordinary war, either: a war of total annihilation. The Vayt ravaged us across a thousand thousand stars, breaking worlds like eggs, and they would not rest until we were no more.

At last, we came back here—the place where our love had begun—to die. Our hearts were so broken, we could see no future for anyone, and so we took our ultimate revenge, launching a weapon that none could detect or counteract until too late. A weapon that can only be stopped—"

"Yes?" Yiwei says.

"How do we stop it?" Naahay demands.

"—by restoring the flower of our love." Laynbone sheds a single pearlescent tear from above her left eye, and then vanishes.

"'The flower of our love,'" Cinnki says. "That's the worst song title I've ever heard."

"That doesn't even mean anything," Kez says.

Damini clicks her tongue. "So these people, the Fatharn, believed in biodiversity and introducing new genes to themselves—"

"—and the Vayt responded to their ultimate weapon by trying to make every creature in the galaxy the same shape," Zaeta says.

"Almost as if the Vayt were still trying to punish these dragon people, even though they were long gone," Yiwei says.

Elza plays with the waterwheel, trying to get Laynbone back. Everybody searches this high-vaulted space, which is full of little cubbies and hidden alcoves, for any more clues to what Laynbone meant by "flower of our love."

"Check this out." Kfok gestures at some carvings on top of the dry fountain at the center of the room. There's a little hollowed-out space, like a light bulb socket.

"Sure looks like something goes in there," Yiwei says. "Hard to say what. But look at these raised sections, they're like an interface. Maybe if you had the right key, you'd access the controls that make all of the tiny motes in the Bereavement stop murdering stars and shut down for good."

"But what goes in there?" Damini squints. "It could—"

"—be anything," Zaeta says.

Elza turns away from the ornately carved socket, because she has just noticed someone sneaking out on six legs while everyone else is distracted.

23
.

Wyndgonk hears Elza following, and turns to face her. Fire head is wreathed in what look like storm clouds. She's seen fire scared and upset, but this—whatever this is—is new.

She approaches slowly. "What's wrong?" she asks. "Whatever it is, you can talk to me, if you want. You've been there for me so many times."

Wyndgonk's eyes are smoke-veiled. Fire mouth glows red. "Why are we still friends?"

Elza steps closer, near enough that Wyndgonk's breath could scald her. "What kind of a question is that?"

The smoke clears. Wyndgonk looks up at her, with all nine eyes undone by some unspoken misery.

"I just need to know. Why do you keep me around? Is it just because I make you laugh? Why did you ask me to go to the palace with you?"

How do you answer a question like that? Until recently, Elza would have said she was somebody who didn't really have friends, especially after Fernanda—and now she has a bunch. She has no idea what makes someone a real friend, except that it feels right. "I . . . I like you. I trust you. I enjoy your company, you make me happy."

"It just . . . made sense for us to be friends, back at the palace, because we were the ones nobody else would talk to. You, me, and Gyrald. I thought the three of us would go on being losers together—and then you *won*." Wyndgonk sighs: gray wisps. "And you have the crown and your whole family, and now you're about to ask me for something bigger than anyone ever has."

The thin atmosphere gets thinner. "What am I going to ask you for?"

"It's not fair," Wyndgonk says. "We shouldn't have to give everything to save everyone."

Part of Elza, some old defense mechanism, is boiling up. She's already let go of so much, and people keep testing her, and she's so tired.

But she sees her friend in pain, even if she doesn't understand why, and so she leans forward, almost touching fire face.

"I asked you to come to the palace because I knew I could count on you," she says. "But more than that, I was scared, and I wanted to be close to the people who make me feel like I can go on, including you. I knew going back to the palace would be more dangerous for you, because of how you look, but I couldn't face it without you."

Wyndgonk raises fire head, front legs crossed. The look in fire eyes calls out to all the crumbling sharp edges inside her. "If I never made a wise-crack again, would you still want to be my friend?"

Elza nods. "Your wisecracks aren't that funny, to be honest."

Wyndgonk clicks fire mouth. "I need to know that you're not going to sacrifice my people for the sake of the greater good."

"I won't. I swear it, on my crown. Now can you please explain?"

"I'll show you."

Fire marches back inside the inner chamber, and walks up to the alcove. Wyndgonk's long insectoid leg goes into the alcove, and the carvings vibrate, like they're starting to come to life. Then nothing.

"What . . . just happened?" Cinnki says.

"I recognized that Laynbone creature, and these carvings look familiar too," Wyndgonk says wearily. "We have legends, on Thythuthy. These creatures, the Fatharn, must have visited a long time ago."

"When you stuck your leg in, something happened," Yiwei says.

"But not enough," Wyndgonk says. "I know what's supposed to fit in there. But you'll never convince my people to give it up."

"Give what up?" Elza says in a gentle voice. "Please tell us."

"The hearthlight," Wyndgonk says. "It's our genetic material and our most important stories, all in one place, and we guard it with our bodies and souls. We're not even supposed to talk to outsiders about it."

"Your people will die too," Damini says. "If the Bereavement isn't stopped. You'd be saving yourselves as well as us."

"We'd be paying the entire price. And if anything happened to the hearthlight, it'd still be the end of us." Wyndgonk closes fire eyes and shivers so hard, fire shell trembles. "There would be no more children, no more next generation, no more anything."

"You were right before," Elza says. "This isn't fair. But we won't let that happen. I already swore."

Wyndgonk shrinks inside fire shell a little. A hoarse, gravelly sound comes from deep inside. Elza traps her tongue between two teeth and tries not to rush her friend.

Then fire emerges and looks up. "Let's go then. At least Thythuthy isn't far from here, so we don't have to spend another thirty metacycles trapped on a tiny ship together."

Fire turns and walks away without another word. Kez shoots Elza a helpless, guilty look, and she sighs.

"Let's see if we can seal up this chamber on our way out," Gahang says. "Maybe the Royal Compassion won't find their way in."

"Just to be clear," Elza says to Gahang and Yiwei. "The only way we get this 'hearthlight' is if Wyndgonk's people agree to give it to us."

"Agreed," Yiwei says. "Though if Wyndgonk's attitude is anything to go by . . ."

". . . we're going to have a tough negotiation ahead." Kez's eyes light up for the first time in a while. "At last, a chance to use all that diplomatic training!"

24
.

Four Compassion ships appear in orbit while the *Undisputed Training Bra Disaster* is still straining to rise out of Larstko IVb's atmosphere.

The ship rattles like an old barn as its engines fight the jet streams and eddies of the upper atmosphere. Kez huddles in the corner, with his mouth in an empty xargar-shell bag.

"Stop fighting me," Damini says to Zaeta.

"*You* stop fighting me," Zaeta hisses.

"Listen, I know this is scary and the ship isn't in good enough shape for flying through this magnetic flux," Yiwei says. "And they'll shoot us down as soon as we reach open space . . ."

Damini grunts. "Not—"

"—helping," says Zaeta.

". . . but you're the best pilots I've ever met. Just, please, work together. I don't know how this vunci bond between you is supposed to work, but it must hurt to be fighting when you're linked together all the time," Yiwei says. "I know you care about each other."

"It's just, Damini said she wanted to share everything with me," Zaeta says.

"I did," Damini protests. "I do."

"But she spent years being impulsive and taking chances and doing whatever she felt like in the moment! And she just expects me to go along with whatever she decides! I don't get any say."

"I thought you liked that about me." Damini looks crestfallen. "I thought we had that in common."

"I do, I think it's great that you're so fearless. I just want to be part of making the decision."

"Uh, I hate to interrupt," Cinnki says. "But we've got missiles."

"The Royal Compassion didn't wait until we got out of the atmosphere after all," Gahang says.

Above them, the blue-gray sky is full of bright red spots, right where it bleeds into starry blackness.

"That's a lot of missiles!" Damini says.

"I'd say that's too many missiles," Zaeta says.

"What do we do?" Damini says. "We could try to sneak past them."

"We need to drop down," Zaeta says. "Let the—"

"—magnetic storm—"

"—take care of some of them." Zaeta cackles. "Exactly. Everybody hold on to something!"

The *Undisputed Training Bra Disaster* drops like a rock, and Elza's stomach rises up. She spots the xargar-shell bag that Kez was holding over his mouth earlier, and checks that it's empty before putting it over her own face.

Just when Elza's nausea peaks, the ship tumbles head-over-stern, going upside down and right side up again.

"Aaaaa," Kfok cries. "Little warning next time."

"I'm trying to keep these engines from melting," Kez says from the back of the ship, "but this is definitely not helping."

"We lost about half the missiles," Gahang says. "Good work."

"Still looking for a way out," Yiwei says. "They've got us boxed in."

"We've received a message," Cinnki says. "Someone wants to talk."

Everybody looks at Yiwei. He shrugs. "Sure. Why not?"

A second later, a hologram appears at the other end of the flight lounge from Damini and Zaeta's pilot station. A familiar porcelain-doll face under a shock of blue-black hair glares, with eyes like hot coals. And a tiny scar on one cheek.

Marrant.

"Where is she?" Marrant says. *"Where is my wife?"*

"Where is who?" Gahang says.

"Stop feigning ignorance! I know you have Aym. She tried to kill me— she even succeeded, for a short time. And somehow she withstood my touch. I know this ridiculous ship belongs to her. Deliver her now, and she will be the only one who dies slowly."

Yiwei looks at Elza. She makes a "chef's kiss" sign: *Don't tell him anything.*

"Nyitha doesn't want to talk to you," Yiwei says. "And we're all very busy over here."

Marrant's mocking smile is long gone, and so are all his attempts to charm people into seeing his point of view. All that remains is fury.

Elza did not think it was possible for Marrant to get any more terrifying.

"You are all traitors," Marrant spits. "You had a chance—you could have done the right thing and joined me—but you're too selfish and weak-minded. You all deserve a worse death than the one I'm about to give you."

Elza feels weak, drained, her arms and legs won't work. She can't face this man again.

Then she straightens up. *You're a princess, and that man is trash.*

She rises and walks over to where Yiwei and Gahang are facing the hologram. She nearly falls—twice—because the ship is bucking like a wild horse.

"You need us alive," Elza tells Marrant. "You only found this place because of us, and now you need to know what we've discovered here. We have information you need."

Marrant stares at her, then barks out a laugh. "Anything you figured out, I can learn on my own. And I refuse to let traitors draw breath. Goodbye, 'Your Radiance.'"

Marrant's hologram evaporates.

"I think we made him mad," Damini says.

"There are way more dreamkiller missiles and dwarf-star ballistics and pulse cannon bursts coming our way," Zaeta says.

"At this rate, he's going to risk hitting his own people," Gahang says.

"He's . . . making mistakes," Yiwei says. "Marrant is ruthless, but he's not reckless. Not like this."

"I guess almost dying has pushed him over the edge," Cinnki says.

"Psychoanalyze our mortal enemy later!" Wyndgonk shouts. "Right now, we need to avoid choking to death on our own flash-frozen guts."

Elza closes her eyes and reaches out with her mind. *I know you're here,* she thinks to the Ardenii. *Each of those four ships has a piece of you. I know most of you is far away, and I still haven't had half the training I need. But I could really use some help.*

No response, for an agonizing age. Then Elza gets a flash, like a mental image.

One of the four ships up there in orbit is the *Inarguable,* and one of the people who built it was a Yarthin named Tyanoul (*he/him*), who was suffering a crisis of faith. Tyanoul spotted a tiny rust patch inside one of the ship's deck plates, where nobody else would ever see it, and decided to leave it in place as a religious offering—because Yarthins worship rust. That spot of rust is still there, and it's been slowly growing ever since.

Elza staggers to the front of the crew lounge, her head still throbbing.

"That ship." She points at the *Inarguable*. "If we hit it in this exact spot with our ion harness, it'll suffer a tiny hull rupture, and get knocked off course."

"It'll drift too close to the other ships," Gahang says.

"That's the opening we needed," Yiwei says. "Thank you thank you thank you."

Damini and Zaeta pull the *Undisputed Training Bra Disaster* into a steep climb, heading straight for the *Inarguable*. "This better work," Damini says.

"Or we'll be getting up close and personal with that ship," Zaeta says.

The walls and floor judder so hard, the whole ship seems like it's about to fly to pieces, and Elza can feel a massive weight bearing down, even with the gravitators.

"Hold on," Yiwei says. "Just a bit closer."

Missiles streak past, like a hailstorm. One of them comes close enough for Elza to see the air sizzle as it slices through.

"Almost," Yiwei says.

A beam of pure energy slashes through the ceiling, right next to where Elza's standing.

Kfok rushes to patch the hole, and Elza looks around wildly. They took a direct hit, and nobody got—

Oh. Gahang's dead body lies on the floor, almost close enough for his charred hand to touch Elza's ankle.

"Mourn later."

Yiwei sounds as though those two words cost him dear. One layer beneath his hard mask is purest agony—he won't look at Gahang's corpse.

The *Inarguable* is close enough for Elza to read the writing on its hull, and to see that a jagged red slash has been added to the Royal Fleet crest—so now it looks like the Joyful Wyvern is wielding red lightning.

"Now!" Yiwei shouts.

Cinnki fires the ion harness, and hits the exact spot that Elza picked out. Nothing happens.

The *Inarguable* looms, a wall of guns and missile launchers.

Then the *Inarguable* lurches as the rusty deck plate gives way. The ship spins out of control, on a collision course with its neighbor, a former Compassion barbship.

"Let's get—"

"—out of here!"

Damini and Zaeta crank the *Undisputed Training Bra Disaster*'s impellers up to top speed, and they race away from the tiny moon.

"We did it!" Cinnki says. And then he looks down at Gahang. "The cost was too high. But at least the rest of us are alive, and we have a chance to save so many other lives, thanks to Gahang's sacrifice."

Yiwei crouches down next to the body of his friend. "We'll need to figure out a way to do a proper memorial . . ."

"Oh no, oh no," Damini says.

"We didn't exactly get away," Zaeta says.

Marrant's new ship, the *Vision of Peace,* is racing toward them, weapons hot.

"We just need to get far enough away from the atmosphere to make it to spaceweave, and then we're free," Cinnki says.

A missile explodes, so close the entire ship quakes.

"We've got more hull breaches!" Kfok twitches her stinger-arms. "We can't spaceweave unless they're patched."

"I'm on it." Cinnki is putting on an atmosphere suit already. "Just hold it steady."

"We'll do our best," Damini and Zaeta say.

"Be careful out there," Yiwei says. "We'd hate to lose our lead singer."

"I'm just warming up." Cinnki climbs through a force-shielded hatch.

Then the clunk of his boots on the outer hull echoes through the ship.

"Last chance," Marrant says over the comms. "Give me Aym, and I will consider the rest of you enemy combatants rather than treasonous criminals. One way or the other, you die today."

Yiwei looks around for Cinnki, who usually handles comms—but Cinnki's footsteps are still thundering overhead. So Yiwei reaches over and silences Marrant's transmission himself.

"Our luck finally ran out," says Kfok. "We're going to die this time." Her stinger-arms twitch and her slug body vibrates with anxiety.

"We're certainly doomed, yes." Naahay sounds bored.

Elza can feel the fear in the stale air, thick and clammy. Elza's been scared, too many times, but she's never marinated in so many people's terror before.

The Ardenii are gone again. Everything's quiet, except for the straining of the hull, Cinnki's footsteps overhead, and Damini and Zaeta wrestling with the controls.

"Just a little further," Yiwei says.

Another ear-crashing noise. The walls rock and every loose object flies across the room. Elza thinks it's another near miss, or an actual hit, then she realizes: they just broke out of the atmosphere.

Space has too many stars—and then Elza realizes all those extra points of light are missiles and pulse cannon beams heading their way.

Another explosion goes off, close enough that the walls tremble like shutters in a windstorm.

"This isn't how it ends," a tiny voice says. "It can't be."

Elza doesn't know who just spoke, and she probably never will. But she tries to take those words into herself, make them true.

"Cinnki," Yiwei says. "You better come back inside."

There's no answer.

"Cinnki?" Yiwei pleads. "Please acknowledge. Cinnki!"

Elza can't remember the last time she heard Cinnki's boots on the hull.

"We can't wait any longer," Damini says.

"We need to spaceweave now," Zaeta says.

Yiwei's whole face is screwed tight. "Do it," he says.

Space and time fold, in that sensation that Elza will never get used to, and she gets a buttery-sweet taste in her mouth. Marrant's ships, and the moon, are far away.

"We made it," Kfok says. "I can't believe we survived that."

"Not all of us did." Yiwei looks down at Gahang's charred corpse. And at the hatch, where Cinnki climbed out and never came back.

25

.

TINA

. . . 232 Earth days until all the suns go out forever

Turns out learning an alien language from scratch is really hard. Like, really *really* hard.

I took two years of high school French, and I still barely know how to say "I like cheese." And French is spoken by human beings, who have mouths and brains and bodies just like mine, more or less. Trying to get even the basics of Grattna, a language that you speak with three tongues—they're not exactly tongues, it's a whole thing—is way different.

Took me a whole day to learn how to say the most basic phrase in Grattna, which is "Food, drink, and hyith." ("Hyith" is a third thing, which is neither food nor drink.) Every time I want to give up, I imagine Thaoh strutting around in my body, treating my friends like dirt—and I resolve to be different.

I've gotten hold of a basic reader that the Grattna give to their children. *See Spot Run,* sort of. Except it's not a book, it's a translucent yellow figure-eight that's full of liquid and if you shake it right, bubbles come out with words and pictures inside.

"Here's what I've figured out so far," I tell Rachael. "They don't have verbs. Because, y'know, the whole idea of verbs is that we have a subject and an object. Which is two things."

"Sure," Rachael says. "Except that English can have more than one subject or object, and verbs can be indirect, right?"

"They sure can." I suck my tongue into the roof of my mouth. "Most of the worst things that ever happened to me, happened indirectly."

I still can't close my eyes, even to blink, without seeing Thaoh use my lips to kiss a stranger while Elza watches. Or imagining Elza trapped and dying because Thaoh abandoned her for a private revenge mission. Feels like I swallowed a two-pound bag of ice cubes.

"I've definitely heard the Grattna say things like, 'You can't stay here,'" Rachael says.

"Yeah. I think they figured out how to say things in their language that make sense to us, but it doesn't come naturally." I shake my figure-eight until it spits up words. "Grattna grammar is all open-ended—you list a few nouns at the start of the sentence, and then at the end of the sentence you mention some stuff that happened, or could happen."

Rachael frowns. "So if you wanted to say that someone murdered your brother and married your sister, you would just list the three people, and then later you mention that someone was murdered and someone else was married?"

"Yeah. But instead of saying 'murdered,' you'd use a word that means both 'died' and 'killed.' Because nobody gets to be the subject and act on everybody else."

"That's . . . pretty confusing."

"Yeah. I think the middle of the sentence is where you explain the re-lationships between all the different words. It's a part of speech we don't have in human languages, and nothing makes sense without it."

Rachael has been trying to copy a piece of Grattna artwork: a jumble of colors and shapes that maybe looks different if you view it with three eyes instead of two. She puts her sketchpad down and gives me her most earnest look.

"I think it's really great that you're trying to understand the Grattna better," she says.

"But—?"

"But they're repairing the Mazda Miata, and they say it'll be ready to leave in a zyii or two. And when that happens, we're going to have to leave and find our friends. So I don't know if it's that realistic for you to become fluent in a radically different language by then."

I sit down next to her, heavily. "I have to try. You know? I have to make this count for something. There has to be some reason I came back, some-thing that I can do because I'm me. And I need to think about something besides . . ." I gesture, as if all the ways Thaoh misused my body are dust specks floating around my head.

"I'm just saying, I hope you don't get too crushed if it doesn't work out."

I stare out at the colors playing across the nearby fen as the light re-fracts. Every rainbow I've seen here doesn't have any red or violet, because of the weird sun—which was weird even before the Bereavement.

I'll never know how many people Thaoh kissed when she was in my body, or how many people she hurt. It was my choice to become her, but I still feel like something was stolen from me, something I'm going to be missing forever.

"Maybe I can try something else," I say. "I mean, I think I understand the basics of their grammar. What if I could reprogram the EverySpeak? So I can at least get closer to saying stuff that actually makes sense to them? And I can understand what they're actually saying, instead of just the cliff notes?"

"Can you do that?"

I laugh. "I have no freaking clue. Never tried before. But it's worth a try."

I pull my jacket inside out so I can get at the EverySpeak, which is woven into the actual sleeve. This is going to be interesting.

"I've been thinking about what you said before," Rachael says while I poke at the jacket's circuitry. "You said that you tried being Captain Argentian, and then you tried being you, and both times you failed. But . . . I don't think you actually tried being you."

"I did, though. I tried being me the whole time when I was in the academy, and on the *Undisputed*. And I got nowhere."

"Nah. I think you were trying to be Not Captain Argentian. And now that I've spent an unhealthy amount of time with her, I know for sure that there's a lot of her in you. Not just because of genes or whatever, but also just . . . temperament. Before you even knew you were a clone, you were trying to stand up to bullies and prank jackasses. So you don't have to reject everything about her, any more than you needed to try and copy her. Just find your own way."

I nod, warm glow rising in my chest. "That actually helps a lot. Thank you."

This EverySpeak circuitry is, not surprisingly, pretty tamper-resistant. Gonna need some tools.

I look at my hands, and try to make myself believe that they're mine. "She asked for my forgiveness. Thaoh did. When we were together, inside my head. I told her that I didn't know if I forgave her or not. Now I wish I had just said no: I don't forgive you."

Saying something this selfish and mean gives me an instant guilt-crash. But also relief—because that feeling has been killing me, and now it's finally out in the universe.

Rachael doesn't say anything, just nods and offers me her hand. I take it, and we watch the fen sparkle with half rainbows.

I can't stop thinking about when hundreds of the Grattna were in cages, begging us to release them—including Halred—and I just walked away. I can see their eyes wide with fear, the light fuzz on their heads and necks quivering. I can still smell the stink from all those bodies crammed into a box.

But now I'm wondering, what were they actually saying to me? All I know is what the EverySpeak translated their words as.

The Grattna don't have a way to say, "Please help us." The closest thing to "help" in their language is a word that means something like "to shorten the distance between X and Y." But you can't shorten the distance between X and Y without increasing the distance with Z. Complicated relationships.

The EverySpeak is pretty hard to reprogram, and I might've voided the warranty. But I finally get access to a kind of language matrix, where it sets the rules for each language. This matrix tries to read your mind and figure out what you're actually trying to say—but no two brains are the same, and no two languages work the same way.

Anyway, the matrix for Grattna-ese is trying really hard to make me comfortable speaking such a different language—like, the priority is making sure I don't have to think too hard. I make a bunch of tweaks, using everything I've learned about their actual grammar.

But mostly, I change the priority: away from "make Tina not have to do any work" and toward "let Tina speak clearly and understand better."

Worst case? I stop being able to speak any language, maybe even including English. (Seriously, I could try to say something to Rachael in English, and the EverySpeak would turn it into Pnoft-wobble.) Risk I gotta take.

Once I'm pretty sure it's fixed—or at least broken better—I go and find Halred.

All three of her eyes narrow when I show up, like: *You again*.

"Your ship still isn't ready to leave," she says, except now the EverySpeak turns this into something like, "Ship you us someone else [visitation-possession] repair prepare launch." Like, the ship that brought Rachael and me here, which used to belong to someone else, is in the Grattna's keeping for now, and it can't fly away yet.

"That's not what I wanted to talk to you about," I say. Except it comes out a lot more complicated, because my sentence acknowledges there are two other things I could be doing, instead of talking to her. "I wanted to apologize, for when you were in a cage and I just left you. That was awful, and there's no excuse."

Every sentence I'm saying packs in a ton of extra information, like when I talk about the cage, I start out by mentioning the Compassion and the Royal Fleet, and I clarify my relationship with both of them in the middle. All of this hurts my brain.

But it's worth every bit of brain freeze to see Halred's eyes widen, and her mouth hang open with astonishment.

She says something back that I don't understand at first. I have to sit and untangle it. It's like, Halred was scared of the Compassion in that moment, but also scared of me, because I was acting like another cruel humanoid. She understood why I walked away, but still hated me for it, and she knows that humanoids will always put other humanoids first. But we did fight together in the end. There's a lot more—she packs a lot about the distance between me and the Compassion, versus the distance between me and her.

Takes me way too long to figure out a way to say that I want us to be real allies now.

Halred crosses her wings, which is the Grattna equivalent of shaking her head, and says something that I eventually understand as basically "Too little, too late."

26

.

I keep trying with Halred and Eldnat, and a few of the others. Everybody is weirded out when I open my mouth, maybe because I'm making sense in a way that people like me usually don't. Eldnat does an actual spit-take. I get the impression that usually people from the Royal Fleet show up and just blurt out demands, in a way that barely makes sense.

Even with my tweaked EverySpeak, I still can't say what I really want to: We need to work together as equals this time. I stumble and struggle, and no matter what, I can tell it's coming out wrong.

The second time I try to talk to Eldnat, he's cooking some swamp grubs (I guess) on an electrified sheet of metal. He wears a big smock that I guess is a Grattna apron, except it doesn't say anything about kissing the chef. I trot out all the phrases I've been practicing, and he just crosses his wings over and over.

At last he says, "You will never be _____ with my people."

No matter what I do with my EverySpeak, I can't make sense of the missing word. It's just a collection of tongue-clicks and low grunts.

Rachael is still studying Grattna artwork when I go find her again. "Hey," she says without looking away from the glittering mosaic in the middle of an arch over her head. "I heard the Mazda Miata will be ready to leave soon."

"Yeah." I sit down on the crumbly clay ground next to her. "I keep getting nowhere."

"It's good that you're trying. But you were never going to be able to undo centuries of paternalistic garbage in a few weeks, even if you spoke better Grattna. You know that, right?"

"Yeah." I sigh and stare up at the mosaic—it twinkles like a Christmas tree in the weird sunlight.

I just wish I could understand that word that Eldnat said. The thing that we will never be with his people.

Then I realize why this Grattna artwork looks odd. "Remember in eighth grade, when you taught me about perspective?" I say. "How things get smaller as they get further away? This artwork doesn't do that, exactly."

Rachael nods. "The Grattna have three eyes, so their depth perception is different, I guess. I don't entirely understand it."

I coax the EverySpeak to produce a list of recent vocabulary, and there's that word Eldnat used. I slow it way down and it sounds like two other words stuck together: that word for when you get closer to A but further away from B, plus a word that means "rooted in the ground." Like one of those weird doily trees.

"What if that word means that you are always the same distance from someone else, no matter who else is in the mix?" I say. "And Eldnat was saying that we'll always get closer and further away, as time goes by? Because we'll forget about them as soon as we don't need them anymore?"

"Yeah, maybe," Rachael says.

"I think I know what I need to do."

The Grattna have finished repairing the Mazda Miata, and the engine is running like a dream. The hull gleams so bright, you would never know how many hits this thing took. Rachael and I didn't want to give this ship a proper name, because why get attached to a ship we're just taking for a joyride that'll lead to it being thoroughly trashed? But this ship carried me back to life—I'm tempted to start calling it the *Unlikely Resurrection*.

I want to thank the Grattna for fixing the ship, but I'm pretty sure they don't say "thank you" any more than they say "please." I say the most Grattna thing I can, which is more like, "I'm staying the same distance from you, even if someone else pulls me away."

Eldnat, Halred, and the others just cross their wings behind their backs.

I wait around a bit longer, hoping they'll say something else. But they just stand there, wings crossed, waiting for Rachael and me to leave.

"Well, this sucks," I say as I climb into the pilot seat next to Rachael. "I really hoped to leave here with some new allies."

"You did your best." Rachael shrugs. "Building a relationship takes a long time. Maybe the seeds we just planted will sprout into something beautiful eventually. I'm just glad I got to learn more about Grattna culture. I kind of love it here. And I got to glimpse a whole other way of thinking about art that breaks up the whole division between looker and lookee, or whatever."

"Yeah." I start the launch sequence.

"So do you have any ideas about how we're going to find our friends? They could be anywhere by now."

"I have exactly one idea, which is that we let the Ardenii know that we're trying to find Elza, and they can reach her wherever she is. As long as she made it out of there in one piece."

I'm done with all the launch calculations and the engines are powering up.

"Hang on." I jump out of the pilot seat and run back to the handful of Grattna waiting for us to leave. "I just wanted to say, if you are ever in trouble or under attack, like if the Royal Compassion ever shows up here, you can call for us and we'll come as soon as we can," I say to Halred. "Here's a secure transmitter."

I hold out one of the two safebeam nodes that I found in Thaoh's pockets.

Halred takes the node and crosses her wings again. "I hope the godparents keep you in their sight."

"Same to you."

Then I run back and jump into the cockpit right before it seals up and the ship lifts off.

"What was that about?" Rachael asks.

"Just had to try one more time." I shrug while also wrestling with the controls. This atmosphere is a nightmare to climb out of. "You never know, maybe we can stay in touch. Maybe I'll even find a way to say 'I like cheese' in Grattna."

We only get a little ways out into space before we pick up something. Not a signal, exactly? More like a fuzztone in the fabric of space—like when a car drives past playing loud music with the bass turned way up and the windows down, and all you can hear from the outside is this BARRRP BARRRP BARRRP sound.

"So it's a trap, right?" Rachael says. "We've walked into so many traps lately. It's kind of our thing. Like, there was a net that seemed hell-bent on damaging our self-esteem."

"I . . . maybe?" The fuzztone feels random, but also personal. "My gut is telling me this might be what we were hoping for: a message from the Ardenii. Something nobody else would notice."

"Okay." Rachael rolls her neck and watches Second Yoth shrink into a pinprick. "If it's another trap, you owe me a snah-snah juice."

"Deal."

I set a course for the space-bass, and hope against hope that I'm not being led astray by my longing to see Elza and the rest of our friends again.

27
.

ELZA

. . . 217 Earth days until all the suns go out forever

Somehow the funeral went wrong.

The white silk was supposed to meet a tiny candle and evaporate into a dazzling mist, which would settle on everybody's skin so they could carry a reminder of Cinnki and Gahang with them. That's how they'd done it on board the *Indomitable* whenever someone had died in battle.

They tried to make the funeral silk using the ship's fabricators, but the recipe must have been off. Instead of evaporating, it came apart, filling the air with nasty white fluff that stuck to everything. Even a while later, scraps of lint still cling to everyone's clothing. A burnt-polymer smell hangs around, turning Elza's stomach.

As soon as the funeral ended, Yiwei rushed back to his new makeshift tactical station in a gray carbonfast nook underneath the flight lounge. He's been there ever since, watching for danger with one hand on the weapons-firing controls. If anybody comes near, he grunts about threat awareness until they go away.

Meanwhile, Zaeta and Damini needed a break from piloting—but the only other people who knew how to fly the *Undisputed Training Bra Disaster* together were Gahang and Cinnki.

"We can't be here all the time," Zaeta said from her customary seat on the right side of the flight lounge.

"My butt hurts from this chair," Damini chimed in. "And sleep is non-negotiable."

In the end, Elza and Kfok offered to try their luck at the pilot station.

Kfok hunches forward in a teacup chair, frowning with one mouth. She mutters under her breath: "Keep it steady, hold it steady."

"It's okay," Elza says. "I've watched Damini and Zaeta enough times, and I think we can handle this between us. Plus we're light-years away from anything, and nobody knows we're—"

An alarm that Elza has never heard before starts screeching.

"There's a ship," Yiwei yells from below their feet. "Unidentified. It's headed straight for us, on an intercept course. Probably just a few crew-members, judging from the size."

"Can we talk to them?" Elza asks.

"We can't open a channel without letting the Royal Compassion know exactly where we are," Yiwei says. "I've already armed our missiles. If they keep coming . . ."

"Don't shoot," Kez (she/her) protests. "They could be friendly. They could be anybody!"

"They could be a flying bomb," counters Naahay. "Can we be smart for once?"

"By the time they're close enough to scan properly," Yiwei says, "it'll be too late. After what happened to Gahang and Cinnki, I'm not taking any—"

"I get it," Kez says. "I'm twanged out and exhausted too. But—"

"I'm just trying to keep us safe," Yiwei says.

"So we're actually going to kill anybody who gets in our way?" Kez says.

"Of course not." Yiwei's voice strains. "But we only just barely survived a coordinated attack—"

"How did these people find us?" Kfok demands.

Everybody is yelling, and Yiwei has his hand on the trigger for the ship's new missile launcher. Elza feels trapped, with her hands stuck in the pilot-ing goop, and the Ardenii are still giving her nothing.

"We haven't survived by being paranoid," Kez says.

"Some of us didn't survive," Yiwei says.

Elza straightens up as much as she can at this pilot station, and calls out, "We are not shooting anybody. Else. Not unless we're sure they're a threat." The flight lounge goes quiet, which Elza chooses to see as a good sign. "Yiwei, you said it's a tiny ship. Could they even have enough room for weapons?"

Long pause. "Maybe. Hard to tell."

An alert sound comes from the velvet-covered alcove to Elza's right, where Cinnki used to monitor comms. Kez rushes over and looks. "There's a kind of hum. Or a rumble? A humble? Coming from that ship. To anyone watching, it would seem like random interference. But I think it's a . . . greeting."

"Very well," Yiwei grumbles, but Elza can hear him pulling his hand out of the weapon-control jelly. "Let's hope you're right, and we're not about to get blown to pieces."

28

.

By the time the ship drifts inside the *Undisputed Training Bra Disaster*, Yiwei has scanned it properly. And sure enough, there are no weapons, just a single row of seats and an engine core. The ship itself could easily be a bomb—even if the people flying it don't want it to be. But everyone agrees to let the sky-blue cruiser on board anyway.

Zaeta and Damini take back the pilot station so Elza can rush down to watch the tiny ship glide inside the art studio/hangar, next to the knife-ship. The front opens upward, revealing two people in the front seat: Rachael. And Thaoh Argentian.

Elza reels. Something hard and shapeless is lodged in her chest.

She wants to wrap her arms around Rachael—but also, to hurl Thaoh back out into space.

Thaoh gets out of the ship first, running and shouting Elza's name.

Elza watches her approach with a head full of noise, almost as if the Ardenii were somehow back in touch. She tries to keep her face impassive, disdainful—*don't give that bagaçeira anything*—but she's just so tired. She's still spitting out funeral lint and it's been one battle after another, and she can't do another terrible conversation right now.

She braces herself for Thaoh to say something cocky.

Instead, Thaoh bursts into tears, wheezing and shaking. "We made it," she says. "I never thought I'd see—"

Elza does the only thing she can think of: she ignores Thaoh and walks toward Rachael.

Rachael's climbing out of the ship and massaging her numb legs. She makes a face, like *Oh, oh no,* and looks at Thaoh.

Thaoh has just dropped to her knees next to Elza.

"It's me, I'm back," she says in Tina's voice. "I'm so sorry. I would have given anything. I'm sorry I left you. I'm sorry for all of it. It makes me sick just thinking about how she hurt you. I can never make up for it, but I'm going to try forever."

Rachael whispers, "It's really her. We fixed Tina."

Tina's eyes are wide, pleading, overflowing with tears, looking up at Elza. Her lip trembles.

Elza feels blood flowing back into all the parts of her she's been letting go numb. She can't speak, can't move, she's tripping over herself like a drunk person.

She looks down and sees her girlfriend—she doesn't even look like Thaoh, she doesn't have that angry swagger.

Elza would know Tina anywhere.

At last Elza chokes out, "I thought you were lost forever."

"I would only be lost if I didn't have you to come back to."

She tries to help Tina to her feet, but Elza's still unsteady, and the two of them land in a heap on the scuffed stone floor, embracing and talking a stream of nonsense to each other.

But when Elza leans in to kiss Tina, a thought flashes through her mind: *How many other people did that mouth kiss?* No way she'll ever know, which makes it worse. She pushes it aside, but it keeps coming back.

Kez rushes into the hangar, yelling and laughing with tears in her eyes. "You're back, you're both back. Tina, is it really you? Please tell me it's you."

"It's me." Tina gets to her feet at last and helps Elza up.

"Oh, thank goodness." Kez shakes her head. "I didn't hate Fake Tina, but she was . . . a lot. She was vastly more horny and violent than I was expecting."

"So I heard." Tina rolls her eyes. "Wait . . . Fake Tina?"

"We started calling her that," Rachael says. "Though not to her face."

"That's the most beautiful thing anybody's ever said to me," Tina whispers. "I'm going to start crying again."

Elza still can't make sense of her feelings—one second she thinks *My girlfriend's back,* the next she feels a chill pass over her.

Yiwei rushes into the cargo hangar and sees Rachael and Tina. He smiles, and then the smile curdles.

Elza was so knocked sideways by seeing Tina again, she forgot about the missile they almost launched.

"We made it," Rachael says.

"You made it," he says. "I was so sure . . ." He closes his eyes and shakes his head, still not touching Rachael. "I'm sorry. I'm so sorry."

"Why are you sorry?" Rachael whispers.

"I know what you're sorry for." Tina charges toward Yiwei. "Yeah, I saw it. The brand-new weaponry you were targeting us with. How close did you come to blowing us out of space?"

"A little too close for my comfort," Kez says.

Rachael stumbles back, like someone just shoved her. All of the color drains from her face. "Why didn't you say something?" she asks Tina.

"Didn't want to worry you." Tina shrugs. "By the time I saw the guns, it was already too late to do anything."

Elza moves toward Rachael. "It's okay," she says quietly. "You're safe. We figured it out in time." Rachael just stares.

"I never would have forgiven myself," Yiwei says. "I understand if you hate me. But the entire Royal Compassion has been hunting us. Your alter ego tried to take out Marrant—"

Tina bristles. "She's not my alter ego!"

"—and she blew it," Yiwei spits. "She only made Marrant more dangerous. He came after us, and we were helpless. He threw everything at us and we couldn't do *anything*." Yiwei is shaking. "We didn't all make it out alive. We lost Cinnki and Gahang."

"Marrant survived." Tina's face goes from flushed to drained of blood in an eyeblink. "Of course he did."

Rachael looks at the oversized dandruff clinging to everyone's clothes. "Oh wow, you literally just held a funeral." Something burns the back of her throat. She still hasn't done a proper memorial for Nyitha, and now she has more people to grieve for. Death won't let up.

Tina stalks over to the locker at the side of the hangar and starts pulling out pieces of an atmosphere suit. "I'm going out there and yanking that weapon system off our ship."

"Don't," Yiwei says. "You'll cause critical hull damage. We'll all die instantly."

"It's true," Kez says. "I hate the weapons too. But we can't remove them ourselves. We'd have to go back to Vandal Station."

"God damnit." Tina throws the gear back in the locker and slams the door. She slumps over, head resting against the locker door. "This is not how I thought we did things. This is not supposed to be a warship."

"Maybe we should talk about this after we've all had a rest," Elza says. Everybody ignores her.

"I never signed on to your pacifism pledge," Yiwei says. "You were gone—we thought you were gone forever! And we had to do whatever it took to survive."

Rachael isn't standing next to Elza anymore. She looks around—did Rachael duck out of the room while nobody was paying attention?

Then she looks down on the floor. Rachael has rolled into a tiny ball at her feet.

Elza crouches down. "Are you okay?"

Rachael shakes her head. "I need to be alone. I can't do this."

"I know a secret place," Elza says. "Nobody will bother you."

Rachael nods, getting back to her feet. She follows Elza out of the cargo hangar, toward the tiny crewmaster office that Elza discovered. On her way out, Elza turns and looks back and sees Tina staring at her with a hunger in her eyes that Elza doesn't know if she can feed.

A while later, Tina and Elza lie next to each other, fully clothed, inside Elza's sleeping cubby. There's barely enough room for two people.

Tina's breath feels so good on Elza's neck, and Elza wants to relearn her whole body, reclaim the whole of her, however long it takes.

Except that Elza remembers Thaoh sneering, *Not anymore*. And then Elza's skin feels hypersensitive, like the slightest touch would prickle.

Tina reaches out to Elza. "Can I touch you?" Her voice barely carries.

Elza wants to say yes, she's supposed to say yes. She freezes. "I don't know."

"It's weird, huh," Tina says. It's not quite a question. "Having me back, I mean. After everything Thaoh did."

Elza nods. She wants to say it's okay, but she can't speak.

Part of her still feels like she's talking to a stranger.

"I get it," Tina says. "You can't feel any weirder about this than I do."

"I know you're not her," Elza says. "It's okay."

But inside her head she hears, on repeat: *I might as well have a little fun. These hormones are a beast.*

Tina sits up. "Part of me thought I could come back and we could just pick up where we left off, but . . . I feel toxic. I'm still having nightmares. I didn't even think about how weird this would be for you. I basically cheated on you, even if I wasn't me."

Elza feels strangely relieved, hearing Tina say what they're both thinking. But also worse, like now it's out in the open and they have to deal with it.

"We can help each other, right?" Elza says. "I think talking will help."

"Yeah." Tina is opening the little door to the cubby, getting ready to climb out. "But maybe we should give each other a little space, too. Just until it stops being weird."

Part of Elza wants to say, *Come back, I need you to hold me*. But she's mostly grateful that Tina is moving away—because she was getting squicked and she didn't know how to handle it. She's terrified that she'll never again want Tina to touch her.

"I kept you waiting a long time," Tina says. "So I can wait as long as you need, even if it's years."

Tina closes the cubby behind her, and Elza is alone.

29

.

RACHAEL

Rachael knows Yiwei must be freaking out, because trying to kill your girlfriend is right at the top of the list of all-time worst relationship fails. She should go talk to him, let him explain, but she desperately needs alone time.

"I've never let myself feel guilty for self-care before," Rachael says firmly, "and I'm not about to start now." Except . . . it's hard to know that Yiwei is suffering, and not do anything to help.

Trust Elza to know the one spot on the ship where nobody will disturb Rachael. This tiny crewmaster office from the *Undisputed* was halfway blocked by a wood-paneled wall of the *Training Bra Disaster,* and you have to turn sideways just to get to the hidden door. There's just enough room for a teacup chair and workstation, where Rachael spreads out her art supplies.

She tries to draw the Grattna city, Kufn, from memory: all the triangular buildings glistening in the sunslight, with perches on top for the Grattna to fly onto. A stand of doily trees growing in the distance. The light of the mid-sayyn sun hitting just right. It comes out pretty good.

Something inside Rachel doesn't trust what she can't draw. So it's maybe bad that she's only drawing landscapes and objects for now. Is she done with people? But everybody out there is falling apart, and so much is at stake.

She sits in there long enough to make three fairly decent sketches.

Now she's ready to talk to exactly one person. She figures out how to use the ship's system to send a private message to Elza, and a couple minutes later there's a knock on the office door.

Rachael lets Elza have the one chair, and she sits on the floor. "Some homecoming," she says.

Elza laugh-groans. "This has been the worst day. But I'm glad you're back. I didn't have anyone to talk to, except for Wyndgonk. And fire is dealing with a lot right now."

Rachael almost says, *We're all dealing with a lot.* Instead, she just nods and massages her drawing hand.

Neither of them talks for a while, but it's a comfortable silence, not a staticky one. Like they know each other enough that they don't need to make noise.

"When did we become the helpers?" Elza says. "I'm supposed to be the malcriada hacker, and you're the art hermit. When did we become the people that everybody leans on?"

"Probably when you got yourself a hat that literally says 'I know everything.'" Rachael gestures at Elza's faintly luminous crown. "And I guess I'm just a good listener? I like listening, when people aren't screaming."

"I hated wearing a uniform on the *Indomitable,*" Elza says. "But I get why we wore them. It meant that we were all there for each other."

"Groupthink sucks, though," Rachael says. "If everybody just went along with the group, you might have launched that missile, and me and Tina would be dead." She shivers. "I still haven't talked to Yiwei. I need some hot snah-snah juice and I'm afraid to leave this room to get some."

"I will fetch you snah-snah juice. There's a little bit left, I think." Elza stands up, then pauses. "I do think we could use something to remind us to listen more. Everybody is hunting us, and all we have is each other."

Rachael nods. "We're the Galaxy's Most Wanted." Then something strikes her. "We could make patches."

She starts sketching a design, with GALAXY'S MOST WANTED written across the top, and she gets so engrossed that she barely notices when Elza comes back with the last of the snah-snah juice.

Yiwei is waiting in their shared quarters when Rachael finally looks for him. He hangs his head and says "I'm sorry" over and over, spiraling.

She wants to let him off the hook, but she doesn't know how, or if she can. The "ball of poison" feeling is back, stronger than ever.

"I know I said I wouldn't ever give up," he says in Rachael's ear. He almost sounds drunk. "But . . . I gave up. On ever seeing you again. I can't even process that you're back. And I almost blew you out of space. I'm so sorry."

It's kind of like how Elza understands that Tina's not responsible for the things Thaoh did, but she still can't look at Tina without seeing Thaoh.

The best way that Rachael can make sense of it is that when you take extreme measures, they tend to get out of hand. Both Thaoh and these new missile launchers were supposed to make everyone safer. But.

"I'm not mad at you," Rachael says. "But you are scaring me. When was the last time you slept?"

"We've been living from crisis to crisis." Yiwei sits askew on the edge of the bed. "I've been watching the tactical scans all the time."

Everything in this tiny room looks the same as before. Earth-style mattress, a few of Rachael's pictures pinned to the wall, a set of cubbies for their clothes and supplies . . . it's like she never left. Except something looks off, and Rachael can't figure out what.

Then she realizes what's missing. "Uh . . . where's Xiaohou?"

"Oh." Yiwei looks around blearily. "I think I stashed him somewhere. There hasn't been any time for music since . . . since we lost Cinnki."

Rachael sits down on the bed next to Yiwei. "I was so scared I wouldn't be able to mourn for Nyitha, because Marrant touched her. But she found a way to slow down the process, and we got far enough away from her before the effect hit. But now, I'm still not really grieving her, because there's been too much to think about. And that's not healthy. We have to grieve, and it takes time and energy."

"I don't want Cinnki and Gahang's deaths to be in vain. Or Captain Othaar's. Or Nyitha's." Yiwei sits down next to Rachael, fidgeting two-handed. "I want their deaths to mean something—which means we have to win."

"Yeah." Rachael looks at the side of his head. His taut jaw works clenched teeth. "But we can't give up what we are. I love this ship because it's so impractical. It's like a foolish wish, flung out into the cosmos. It's such a mess, it forces us to be creative and weird instead of just powering our way through every situation."

"That's not enough for me anymore," Yiwei says. "I would trade this flying collage for a proper daggership like the *Indomitable* in a heartbeat. If we had better countermeasures and a stronger hull, I wouldn't be so twitchy." He looks at his Quant. "I'd better get back to the tactical station."

"Get some sleep," Rachael says in a don't-argue tone. "You know who eats tactical scans for breakfast? Tina. I'll get her to take a shift on there."

Yiwei starts to argue—then he nods, and takes off his shoes. "I gave up on seeing you again."

"I love you. Get some rest."

Yiwei mumbles something and rolls over on his side in a fetal position. Rachael pulls the space blanket over him and then goes to find Tina.

"It's true, I eat tactical scans for breakfast," Tina says, with a theatrical sigh. "But you know what else I eat for breakfast? Breakfast."

Tina's eyes flick in the direction of Elza's cubby, like she's battling the urge to try and talk to her girlfriend again. She's been doing extra nahrax practices to distract herself. It hasn't helped.

"Give Elza time," Rachael says. "On top of all the stuff Fake Tina did, Elza also had to go back to the palace for the first time since her coronation, and she was sneaking inside instead of getting the welcome she deserved. And I see how much that crown is stealing her peace of mind."

Rachael should have realized sooner—every time she says *Fake Tina*, the real Tina gets a happy flush, and the red stones on her cheeks get a little redder.

"I should have been there for Elza." Tina stares at her shoes. "I made her a promise, and I immediately flaked."

"You tried to keep everyone safe, the only way you could," Rachael says. "The same way Yiwei did when he tried to shoot down our little ship."

Tina snerks. "Well played. Ten out of ten. Okay, I'm going to celebrate not being blown to pieces by sitting at the tactical station. Like old times. Just please bring me a snack. Also, I have no idea where the tactical station is."

"Me neither. Yiwei's finally sleeping." Rachael sees Wyndgonk at the other end of the hallway, on fire way to the crew lounge. "Wyndgonk! Do you know where the tactical station is?"

Wyndgonk rubs fire front legs together, which means *Yes*. "It's where the games used to be. I miss the games."

Everyone checks Tina out, when they think she's not looking—like they're still seeing the afterimage of Thaoh.

Rachael walks Tina down to the space under the flight lounge where the games used to be.

They pass by Kfok, staring at a piece of artwork that Rachael hasn't seen before: one of the portraits Cinnki made of his friends who died too soon. It's made out of a special moss that will slowly change, so the picture will grow old even though the real person won't get to. "I wish I knew how to make this kind of art, so I could make a portrait like this of Cinnki," she says.

"I hope you figure it out," Rachael says. "I'll help, if you can find any instructions."

Kfok nods. "I just hope the time comes when we can be artists again."

Oof. That hits Rachael right in the feels.

Damini and Zaeta are up front in the flight lounge, poking at the controls. Neither of them looks up when Rachael and Tina come in, and they're not being their usual chatterbox selves.

"Mind the—" Damini says.

"I see it," Zaeta says.

"What about—"

"It's handled."

"What's up with them?" Tina whispers to Rachael.

"They've been having some trouble," Rachael says. "This bond between them, the vunci, it doesn't work so great if you can't agree on everything."

Tina stares at the two of them, narrowing her eyes. Then she walks down the ramp to the lower level. "Starting to look forward to spending some alone time at the tactical station. I bet it'll be relaxing, like needlepoint. Although I've never actually tried needlepoint, so I have no idea?"

She scoots into the little teacup chair and gets her hands into the holographic sludge. Rachael goes to find her a snack.

30

.

ELZA

. . . 217 Earth days until all the suns go out forever

Elza knows the *Undisputed Training Bra Disaster* is almost at Wyndgonk's home planet, Thythuthy, without anybody saying anything—because the Ardenii come rushing back into her head.

One moment she's sitting in the corner of the flight lounge, trying to look dignified and princess-like while sitting on a beanbag. The next, her mind is in a thousand places at once—witnessing a rare merger between two white dwarfs, watching a comet shatter, seeing the Yarthins declare war on their neighbors. Once again, there's an unthinkably giant number—and once again, it's gone up. Whatever this means, Elza somehow *knows* that it's bad news.

She felt so empty without the Ardenii, she forgot how easy it was to drown in their minds.

Somewhere in all that noise is one actual piece of information: the Royal Compassion hasn't figured out about the hearthlight, and they haven't sent their own mission to Thythuthy, though they still have plenty of ships out looking for the *Undisputed Training Bra Disaster*.

Elza looks up and sees someone standing over her—for a moment, she can't see past the comet fragments—and realizes it's Tina. She hasn't really talked to Tina since they agreed to give each other space, so she tries to be present. "Olá."

"Hey." Tina fidgets. "Sorry for . . . I mean, I'm sorry to bother you. But we can't find Wyndgonk. We're almost at fire home planet, and we thought fire ought to know."

"Oh, fire is too cool to hang out with the rest of us," Naahay grunts from nearby. "I'm sure fire is off brooding somewhere."

Elza ignores Naahay as usual. "I'll help you look for fire." She pulls herself up from the beanbag with as much grace as she can manage.

They walk around the ship twice, in silence, without any sign of Wyndgonk. A couple of the hallways lead nowhere, and when the ship is traveling at full speed, the only way from the front to the back is by going through Kez's bedroom.

The Ardenii have a new simulation of how badly the galaxy will be destabilized by turning so many suns into black holes, all at once—Elza feels all the gravitational eddies in her inner ear.

"I swear I'll be ready to talk soon," Elza says to Tina. "I am really trying."

Tina nods. "Take all the time you need."

Wyndgonk is crouching under the ramp made of tree bark that leads to a gray carbonfast storage space.

Fire breath casts an orange glow on the rough underside of the ramp. "I was hoping you would find me."

"Really?" Tina says.

"No. Of course not. Would I be hiding down here if I wanted to be found?" Wyndgonk scoffs. "Did they take away your ability to detect sarcasm when they rid you of that annoying other persona?"

"We just wanted to tell you that we're almost at Thythuthy," Elza says.

"I know. That's why I'm hiding."

"You told me that I was going to ask too much of you." Elza makes a heroic effort to push the Ardenii to the back of her mind. "Are you . . . scared to go home?"

"I failed to accomplish any of the things I was supposed to do at the palace." Wyndgonk grinds fire mandibles. "And now I'm coming back with a group of aliens who want my mother to hand over the most important object in our culture? Ugh. Pass."

"I already swore that we'd protect the hearthlight," Elza says, then the thing Wyndgonk just said hits home. "Did you say your mother?"

"The Ardenii didn't tell you?"

She probes with her mind, and, *oh*—the Ardenii are reminding her that they did tell her Wyndgonk's mother is the keeper of the hearthlight. It's just that they also were telling her at the same time about three planets that were exploding for different reasons.

"If your mother is the keeper of the hearthlight," Elza says slowly, "then I really do need to ask for your help. You can talk to her."

Wyndgonk doesn't answer. The flame glows a little brighter.

"I'm sure your people will be proud of you, if they're not total assholes," Tina says.

"That body part isn't considered a negative thing in my culture," Wyndgonk says. "If anything, it's a nice thing to call someone."

"Well then, I'm sure everyone will think you're an asshole. Possibly the biggest asshole in their entire history."

"Stop trying to win me over with compliments. It doesn't matter: my mother is not going to give us the hearthlight."

"Your mother will have to understand," Tina says. "Everyone's lives are at stake, including—"

"See? You're going to show up and start lecturing. I should come along just to laugh at your feeble attempts at diplomacy."

"Actually," says a voice at the top of the ramp, "the feeble attempts will be one hundred percent mine." Kez has put on a golden mesh jacket that sort of resembles her old junior ambassador uniform, and she's wearing a twitchy smile.

A raucous noise rings out in the flight lounge, like a sick floatbeast that's about to fall out of the sky. Nobody can identify the source of the screeching, until Tina searches the clothes she was wearing when she arrived with Rachael. In the pocket of Thaoh Argentian's jacket, there's a tiny device that looks sort of like a Quant.

Elza's never seen one of these things before, but the Ardenii recognize a safebeam node, which allows you to communicate for a short time without anyone else listening or knowing where you are.

"I forgot I had this," Tina says. "They're super rare, but Thaoh had two of them. I gave the other one to the Grattna. Maybe that's who's calling now."

She pushes something. Riohon appears in an egg-shaped holographic blob.

"There you are," Riohon says. "I was starting to think something went wrong with the palace mission after you failed to check in. But I have news. We've won over a dozen more daggerships to our side. I hope you're not angry, but I have been telling people privately that you're with us, and it's working."

"I'm sorry—" Tina tries to say.

"So many people want the chance to fight alongside you. Your name still carries a lot of weight."

"Uh, I'm not—" Tina sputters.

"And that's not all," Riohon says. "You'll never guess who I tracked down."

Riohon shoves someone else forward, into the glowing egg.

Yatto the Monntha.

Kez falls out of her chair. Damini stares with tears in her eyes. Tina is speechless.

Elza's heart rises up and flutters like a dragonfly's wings. Even the Ardenii did not know that Yatto had survived. A snatch of a joyful song from childhood, that she can't even name, plays inside her.

"You're alive," Rachael says. "Yatto, you're alive, how are you alive? We thought—"

"I also thought so," Yatto says. "I have felt myself to be half-dead. But the fight isn't over and I can't give up."

"And with you on our side," Riohon says to Tina, "we will—"

"It is good to meet you, Captain Argentian," says Yatto the Monntha. "I have heard tales of your exploits for as long as I can recall. Whatever meager assistance I can provide is yours."

Tina finally gets a word in edgewise. "Um, about that. I hate to break it to you, but . . ."

Riohon stares, and his face falls.

There's no sound but the faint pinging as the last remaining seconds of secure transmission count down.

"It's also good to see you, Tina," Yatto says. "I believed you were gone forever."

"Uh, back atcha," Tina says. "Listen, we're heading to Thythuthy, because we think they have an artifact that can help us stop the Bereavement."

"We can rendezvous with you afterward," Yatto says. "Send coordinates. I only hope—"

Right before the egg turns white and then disappears, someone else comes into view: Ganno the Wurthhi, Kez's ex. Kez stares with her mouth open, long after the image has faded completely from view.

31

.

WYNDGONK

. . . 216 Earth days until all the suns go out forever

The last thing Wyndgonk's mother said when fire left home was, "Don't come back without a crown." Wyndgonk eyes the glowing threads around Elza's hair and thinks, *Close enough. I brought a crown home, even if I'm not the one wearing it.*

But Innávan probably won't see it that way.

Wyndgonk would way rather have to distract some Compassion guards again, or get chased around another exploding starship, than go home a failure. Tina keeps saying, "You're so lucky, you get to see your family again."

Elza sits next to Wyndgonk, in the same stolen knifeship they used to sneak into the Glorious Nebula. Kez putters with the ship's engines, while Naahay and Tina are in the two pilot seats. Elza is still keeping her distance from Tina, and the longing feels as thick and noxious as the cloud layer they're about to descend through. Soon they'll catch their first sight of the City of Braids.

Kez asks Wyndgonk endless questions, as if she could learn to understand Wyndgonk's whole culture in a single ride.

"I spent so much time training to make peace, and then my chance was ripped away from me. I could never make Ganno understand why it was so important to me," Kez says. "Plus there's so much riding on this meeting. I just want to make a good first impression."

"You're a few hundred years too late." Wyndgonk chortles. "Countless other humanoids have already left an impression here."

"This time, we're bringing an actual princess," Naahay sneers from the pilot seat. "We're probably the most important people to visit this backwater planet in generations."

"The most important thing," Wyndgonk says, "is when you're talking to someone important, you have to list everything you *don't* know, before you say what you do know. That can take a long time, but it's impolite to skip it."

"I understand," Kez says. "So please tell me about the people we're going to meet with. Is there some kind of ruling council or something?"

Wyndgonk sighs. "No. We just need to talk to my mother. Fire is the one who's in charge of the hearthlight."

"That's convenient," Naahay says. "Family connections are always useful."

Kez stretches the sides of her mouth upward. "At the very least, we've got a leg up."

"Keep your legs down at all times," Wyndgonk says.

"It's a figure of speech."

Tina tries to make eye contact with Elza, but she's staring into space and swaying a little—because she's reconnected to the Ardenii, and her brain is drowning in nonsense.

Wyndgonk would rather have a million tons of rock piled on fire head than that crown.

"My mother has three emotional states: disappointed, angry, and angrily disappointed," Wyndgonk says.

Kez wails. "Sounds all too familiar. Just lovely."

Their knifeship descends into the cloud layer, and then they're surrounded by poisonous gray vapor and the lethal claws and teeth of the Dnynths. Wyndgonk cringes, even inside this metal cocoon.

The last scraps of Wyndgonk's chrysalis had barely fallen off when Innávan taught fire to make a carve-snare for the first time. The shape looked deceptively simple: a kind of scythe made of sharp fibers, on a long rope that turns into a rigid pole when you run fast enough. But weaving together the seed-husks and Dnynth-hairs into a form that was supple enough but could hold its shape was nearly impossible, and Wyndgonk's first five efforts were broken. And meanwhile that business of running fast enough to make the carve-snare pull down the vegetation growing in the clouds? It was a sport and a game, but also a matter of timing. Wyndgonk was constantly out of breath, claws scrabbling against the loose, rocky soil, falling head over tail. Sucking in breaths of noxious air, because of *course* this was a high-toxicity day. People barely bothered to hide their laughter.

Everything changed one day, when Innávan heard Wyndgonk whispering numbers in between scant breaths as fire ran with the carve-snare in one claw.

"What was that you were doing?" Innávan asked when Wyndgonk finally came to rest, with dirt smudged along one side of the supposedly aerodynamic running clothes.

"What was I doing?" Wyndgonk couldn't help venting a sad wisp of white smoke. "I was trying, Mother, the way I always do. I can't run the right way and my carve-snare is still too loose, and I'm sorry I can't be perfect."

"No, no." Innávan brushed all of that aside with one claw, mandibles looking impassive. "Everything you just said is true, but that's not what I meant. What were those numbers? I heard you muttering."

"Oh." Wyndgonk stiffened, sure this was about to turn into mockery. "I realized that everything about run-farming is math. Physics, really. It's all about velocity and angle of motion and air resistance and cloud patterns. If I could do all the math in my head, I could make it work."

Wyndgonk braced fireself for Innávan to say that run-farming is all about skill and instinct, and you shouldn't get too much in your head. Instead, fire just turned and walked away.

The next day, Innávan brought a stranger, with an especially pearlescent shell and expressive antennae, to visit. "This is Ernati. Blood is a math tutor. From now on, you're going to spend half your days at school, half your days training, and half studying with Ernati."

That was three halves to every day, and Wyndgonk started to protest. But Innávan was already walking away.

The City of Braids looks even more beautiful than Wyndgonk remembered: strands of living rock twined together in complicated patterns, with tens of thousands of people living inside each strand. From above, the pale light from both suns plays on the interwoven threads, picking up seams of metal and precious stones. As they get closer to the ground, Wyndgonk sees the central basin, the wildschool and tameschool, the game library, and all the other places where fire spent fire childhood.

I hate to admit I missed this place. Part of me wishes I'd never left, but another part wishes I'd stayed away forever.

Right when the knifeship reaches the wide ridge-sided basin in front of Wyndgonk's parents' strand of housing, Elza stirs from her trance. She looks around, disoriented, and makes eye contact with Tina. Then she turns to Wyndgonk.

"I'm sorry you're having to go home under these circumstances," Elza says. "You've been there for me, and it's time for me to return the favor. Maybe it'll help that I'm a princess, and I can give my word to help as much as I can. That means something, right?"

Wyndgonk doesn't know what to say: Elza's presence will just remind everyone that Wyndgonk fell short.

As soon as they all step out of the knifeship, everybody runs outside to look at the returning prodigy and the visiting aliens. Including a princess! Watha and Manto are there, looking for all the stars like nothing has changed, and Wyndgonk feels fireself get younger, looser, just looking at them.

The grouchy, sarcastic persona that Wyndgonk created for dealing with all these humanoids is flaking, ready to slough off like another chrysalis. It's an itchy, prickly feeling.

Mostly? Wyndgonk is conscious of anxiety, stress, all of these quintuplets of eyes staring. When your whole culture is based on handling lethal situations with cleverness and coordination, people who screw up are not treated well.

"Well." Naahay grimaces. "This isn't quite as squalid as I'd envisioned."

"Please be quiet," Kez says. "You're going to make my job so much harder."

Naahay just rolls her exposed eyes.

Innávan comes running out of the braid where Wyndgonk grew up, white smoke pouring out of both sides of fire mouth. "You're home. Oh! You're home. Our baby is home!"

Wyndgonk nearly falls over. "You're . . . I'm . . . You're happy to see me?"

Innávan wraps all of fire legs around Wyndgonk. "We've been so scared. I would have given anything for you to return home safe. That's all that matters, it's all that ever mattered."

Now Wyndgonk is gushing white smoke too. "I'm sorry. I tried to represent our people."

"You did. Look at the friends you've made." Innávan crosses her mandibles at Elza, Tina, Naahay, and Kez. "Wyndgonk was always different. When fire wasn't stealing sweetfish from the market, fire was doing mathplay and sciencedance at a higher level than any adult. Nobody was surprised when fire got the highest marks on our mathematical aptitude tests and got sent to the princess program."

"Hold on." Elza stares at Wyndgonk. "You told me that you got sent to the palace because you lost a race due to a stomachache."

Wyndgonk snorts. "I guess that crown doesn't tell you everything." Fire turns back to Innávan. "So you're not upset that I failed?"

"Oh, sweetie." Innávan's voice has never sounded so tender. "So much has changed since we sent you away. Everything is going dark, and the people with whom we sent you to gain influence have shown their true natures. I'm sorry we sent you alone into a monstrous situation. You did what I needed most, which was to make it home alive."

Wyndgonk is totally losing fire composure in front of Elza and the others. This noxious air smells sweeter than any perfumed chamber in that palace, and everyone Wyndgonk grew up with is watching and rejoicing. To come home, to be *welcomed* home, is more joy than Wyndgonk can handle. Fire rolls over on fire back, legs in the air, and doesn't even mind how ridiculous this must look to the humanoids.

I couldn't allow myself to miss this place the way my heart wanted to. I feel like I could run faster than anyone, if my legs ever return to the ground.

Fire gets back upright, and then turns to Innávan. "Well, in that case . . . my friends have something to tell you." Wyndgonk gestures.

Kez steps forward, fiddling with her two tiny forelimbs. "Umm. Here's what we don't know. We don't know if we can stop all the stars from going out. Including yours. We don't know for sure that the Royal Compassion hasn't figured out we're here. And if they did, we don't know how soon they'll arrive. We don't know if our ship will fall apart at any given moment. We don't fully understand what will happen if we succeed in our mission. Here's what we do know: we found an ancient facility that seems to control the Bereavement—the thing that's killing the stars—and it appears that we need to borrow your hearthlight to access it."

Oh. The humanoid actually did pretty good.

"I don't understand." Innávan turns and looks at Wyndgonk. "Why would you all need the hearthlight, specifically?"

"I was there when we visited that facility, and we couldn't get the interface to work," Wyndgonk says. "There was an empty space, and it responded to my DNA. It was exactly the right size and shape for the hearthlight. And it appeared the Fatharn, the people who created the Bereavement, had visited our world a long time ago. They looked exactly like those old pictures in the *Howlstory*."

Innávan crosses her antennae and mandibles in a frown. "Why would these 'Fatharn' visit our world, among so many others? I'm not going to be happy until I know the answer."

32

.

RACHAEL

Yiwei pulls up every kind of tactical scan, until he's covered an entire wall with threat warnings. "We have to be ready in case they show up." He holds his body taut, like a catapult waiting to fire. "We can't have a repeat of last time."

"What happened to Cinnki and Gahang wasn't your fault," Damini protests.

"Let's blame Marrant for his own actions," Zaeta adds.

Yiwei dropped out of the academy and swore that he was better off without the Royal Fleet—but now he's acting more uptight than any actual Fleet officer Rachael ever met.

"The Thythuthyans have their own defenses, but they're stretched thin trying to protect a dozen worlds. If the enemy does show up, it'll be Situation Yellow Fall. Our job will be to slow down the enemy long enough for the landfall expedition to finish their mission, while safeguarding their extraction."

"Some things you can't prepare for." Kfok is crawling along the ceiling trying to patch up any cracks, since her slug bottom sticks to any surface.

"We need to do what we can." Yiwei doesn't look away from the wall of danger. "There has to be some way to use that cloud cover as camouflage for a sneak attack. Trouble is, it's too low. We'd have to be so deep inside the atmosphere, we'd probably get torn to pieces. Maybe if we bounce radiation off it, we can create a glare on their scans."

Nobody says anything in response.

Finally, Damini speaks up. "I think we should agree that if Marrant shows up again, we're not fighting him on our own."

"We could improvise some sort of minefield in orbit," Yiwei says.

Rachael doesn't know how to talk to Yiwei when he's like this, especially in front of everyone else. His neck and shoulders are tight, like he's trying to shoulder a burden that's rolling away from him.

"We can't put mines in orbit around Thythuthy—" Damini says.

"—without getting the Thythuthyans' permission first," Zaeta says.

"Right, right." Yiwei kneads his forehead. "We're running out of time. We won't even know they're coming until they're almost here. We can't let them catch us unprepared. Again."

Rachael gets close enough to Yiwei to whisper, "Hey, can I talk to you? Alone?"

Yiwei clicks his teeth. "Now's not a good . . ." Then he catches himself. "Sure. Let's talk."

Yiwei's DIY guitar and other music stuff are piled up in the corner of the quarters he's been sharing with Rachael—he hasn't touched any of it in ages, as far as Rachael can tell. She still hasn't found where he put Xiaohou.

Rachael sits on the bed. He sits too, but he doesn't exactly come to rest.

"Listen, I've already seen this movie once, with Tina. I hated it the first time, and the reboot is even worse."

"Just say what you mean."

"I mean that you're pushing yourself too hard. You're trying to take on everything yourself, and be a superhero, instead of just doing your best and letting everyone else help you. You're obsessed with living up to the legacy of a dead captain."

Yiwei goes from sitting bolt upright to slouching over, his head on his chest.

"I'm not trying to be a superhero. I'm not."

"We talked about this before. I know you're trying to be the person Captain Othaar wanted you to be, but—"

"It's not about that. It hasn't been for a while. I'm just . . ."

He's trembling a little, and his feet turn against each other.

"You're just what?"

"Trying. Not to fall. Apart." She can barely hear his voice through his arms. "You weren't here. Gahang, Cinnki, and me, we were a good team. Gahang was helping me to feel more confident about all this, like I had found another mentor. Cinnki kept supporting me but also challenging me. And then . . ."

"And then they both died. Damini was right, though. That wasn't your fault."

Rachael can feel his grief, like a second skin between them.

"I never said it was. I couldn't do anything, none of us could. Marrant threw everything at us, he was relentless, and we couldn't even catch our breath. We only escaped because of luck, plus some fancy flying from the miracle twins."

How did Rachael not realize before? Yiwei is deep in the grip of PTSD. Not as if she doesn't know what that's like.

"I'm sorry I wasn't there," she says.

"You were busy bringing Tina back to us. You couldn't have done anything here."

"I could have given you someone to talk to." She chooses her next words with care. "I was really traumatized after the mausoleum, and not just because I lost my art. You helped me to deal with it, once I let you in. I'm still messed up, but as long as I remember that I'm not okay, I can be sort of okay. And I know I can lean on you, and Tina, and everyone else."

"Yeah. Except . . . I'm just sick of feeling helpless, you know?"

"I am familiar, yeah."

He's finally straightened up enough for her to see the haunted look on his face.

"Hey," Rachael says. "I could really use some touch, if you're up for it."

"Yeah."

He turns toward her and lets her into his embrace. She can feel his heart beating way too fast, and the nervous flutter of his breathing.

"We're not going to get through this by being tough," Rachael says in a low voice. "When you're outmatched as bad as we are, toughness isn't much. We just have to be sneaky and slippery and like an annoying bug that they can't swat."

"That makes a lot of sense." Yiwei lets go of her and climbs off the bed with a slight stumble. "And that gives me an idea of how we can survive if Marrant does show up here."

Yiwei steps back into the flight lounge, and everyone holds their breath.

"Damini was right," he says. "If the enemy does show up again, our best option is to hide. And be there to pick up our friends when they need a ride."

Damini and Zaeta both sigh with relief, in unison.

Yiwei points to something. "See that orbital structure? That's got to be the atmosphere scrubber that Yatto said they helped install here, when they were on the *Inviolable*. It's made of the same stuff as we are, and it's got a similar radiation signature."

"And we can hide next to it, and nobody will notice us." Kfok whistles with her left mouth. "Not bad."

"Seems fitting, to use the only good thing the Royal Fleet ever did here to keep us safe from the Royal Compassion," Yiwei says.

"Nice and easy," Damini says.

"We'll find a cozy spot," Zaeta says.

The *Undisputed Training Bra Disaster* glides toward the Royal Fleet's rectangular orbital platform, which is the size of a grain of rice one second and a skyscraper the next.

"I'm glad we worked this out," Kfok says. "I don't like it when the humanoids fight."

Yiwei nods. "Yeah. I just want to keep everyone safe. At least this way, if the Royal Compassion shows up, we'll be—"

The ship's engines go dead. Rachael is so used to hearing that constant drone, the silence feels incredibly creeptastic.

No sound but the creaking of the distressed hull and the floorboards under their feet.

"What happened?" Kfok's neck stretches out, so her head is sticking up like a periscope. "We had some kind of power failure?"

"Not a power failure." Yiwei is staring at his Quant. "Something took out our engines, without breaking a sweat."

Rachael's skin feels clammy, she's short of breath. "Marrant?"

"No." Yiwei's face is a mask of terror in the pale light of his Quant. "Someone worse."

33

.

TINA

I feel like I realized something important, after I came back to life—and now it's slipping away. I need to find a way to hold on to it with both hands.

When I was alive the first time, I was so focused on surviving the next battle, solving the next problem. I never had time to pay attention to the bystanders and victims, all the people who had just been swept up in a war they didn't ask for. I fought to save them, but I didn't really see them.

So right now, we're on Thythuthy, and Kez is trying to convince Wyndgonk's people to lend us their most prized possession. The hearthlight is a repository of their culture as well as all their genes, and I hate that we're even asking for it. Of course, their sun is just as doomed as everyone else's, but they're still taking an incredible risk. Even with Wyndgonk's mother being the keeper of the hearthlight, it's a tough sell.

"You should give us what we want, because it's in everyone's best interest," Naahay says. Everybody looks daggers at her until she quiets down.

"Maybe the princess stays with us," says Wyndgonk's mother, Innávan. "As a guarantee."

"She's not a hostage, she's my friend," Wyndgonk says.

Elza is still in a trance, like she's been ever since we got to this planet. I'm supposed to be her consort, the person she talks to when the crown gets too heavy.

I'll give her space for as long as she needs, but I'm scared we're running out of time before the next tragedy. And I don't even feel like I'm really all the way back to life if I can't see the recognition in her eyes. I can't help being thirsty—like every time I try to give her a supportive, I'm-here-for-you look, I feel it turn into a please-see-me look instead. Ugh.

She just stares past me. I'm going to just drop dead of longing.

Please don't let me be half a ghost in your eyes. I can't handle any of this without you.

I try to keep busy, inventorying everything in my satchel, until I find a cloudstrike gun that must have belonged to Thaoh, like a final taunt from Fake Tina. I open up the back panel and remove all the links from the cloud chamber to the rest of the weapon—guns are like miniature starships, they're just batteries that shoot energy into the world—and now, at least, this gun will never hurt anyone again.

Kez is talking to the Thythuthyans about making some kind of deal, or treaty. "We need to make sure you get what you want, too. We need this to be an equal exchange."

"Yeah. When this is over, we gotta build a new alliance, which doesn't put humanoids on top." I tell them about my conversations with the Grattna—though I leave out the part where the Grattna told me where to shove my ideas. "And if you need a hostage, I volunteer. I'll stay here until my friends save the day."

Elza comes out of her reverie and turns to me with a whole world of hurt in her eyes. "You're going to offer yourself up without even talking to me first? You're doing it *again*."

"No! I just . . ." A dizzy spell catches me off guard, like my actual head is spinning. I can't bear the look in her eyes. "I know I'm just reminding you of her, and . . ."

"If I could just trust that you'd be there for me." She turns away from me again so I just see the crown with its hooks going into the spaces between her braids, and the back of her neck slightly hunched over.

I can't think what to say to reassure her, in front of Wyndgonk's mother and everybody else. Frozen half-solid. The words won't come.

"Well, I'm certainly not staying here any longer than strictly necessary." Naahay's skull-face fixes into a grimace.

"Nobody is going to be a hostage, Mother." Wyndgonk steps forward and gets in Innávan's face. "We are not using people as bargaining chips." Black smoke comes out of fire mouth. "That's what the Royal Compassion does, and we need to be better."

Innávan crosses her antennae. "We just need some assurance—"

"You have all the assurance you need. You sent me to that palace because you believed I could handle myself, right?" Wyndgonk shifts into an unmistakable power stance, putting all fire weight on fire front legs. "This isn't about whether you trust *them*, it's about whether you trust *me*."

Innávan starts to argue, then shows Wyndgonk a tiny blue flame instead. "Very well. You may take the hearthlight, since the circumstances are so dire. A word of warning: I will not be able to deactivate the security measures around it. I can give you the cipher key, but you will need to do a large number of complex calculations in a short time."

"Not a problem," Elza says. "This crown isn't just for decoration. The Ardenii can help me crack any code instantly." She's still turned away from me, her voice still trembles.

"Indeed." Innávan bows fire head. "I will show you to the chamber where the hearthlight is kept. Good luck."

Even with most of my attention focused on Elza, I keep one eye on Naahay. She's glancing around, like she's checking all the angles. Something about this bratty Aribentor is making the hairs on the back of my neck stand up.

Innávan leads us through a tangle of stone braids under a nasty gray sky. Every now and then, I glimpse these flying predators, the Dnynths, soaring overhead, looking to feast on an unsuspecting person.

Elza told me before that Wyndgonk's people depend on the Dnynths to plant their crops in the clouds, but the Dnynths are still an apex predator—so Thythuthyan culture is all about having balance, so they can harvest enough to eat without getting eaten.

We reach one of the biggest rock-braids. "It's in here." Innávan holds out a strip of plastiform in one claw. "And this is the encryption key, to help you solve all the equations and remove it safely."

Elza takes the slip from fire. "Thank you. I'm glad to be making a difference using pure math, for a change."

"I'll return to my duties, but please come say goodbye before you leave," Innávan says.

I fall behind the rest of the group, with Naahay by my side. "I saw you holding a gun earlier," Naahay whispers. "I heard you don't even like guns for some reason. You should give it to me, just in case there's trouble. They gave us weapons training at the palace."

Naahay's bony plates pull sideways, forming a weirdly eager expression. I almost explain that I sabotaged the gun.

But something makes me pause. Why does she want a gun so badly? Most of the answers I can think of are really bad.

"If we get attacked again, or if Wyndgonk's people change their mind, we'll need someone who's ready to defend us," Naahay adds.

That does it. I hand her Thaoh Argentian's fancy paperweight. "Here you go. Just don't go shooting any of the locals."

She hefts the gun in one hand. "I'll stay out here, on guard. You won't regret this."

"I'm sure I won't."

I rush ahead to catch up with Kez, Elza, and Wyndgonk. They're already walking through a passage between two strands of stone. Inside is a big high-ceilinged round chamber, with a platform at its center.

On the platform sits a figure eight the size of two baseballs, made out of dense strands that look like crystal, or spun glass, with spiky strands twirling off at right angles. The hearthlight.

As we get closer, kite-shaped transparent creatures flit around the edges of the room, hissing. At the thin end of the kite, their mouths open to bare razor-sharp spectral teeth and spiny tongues, and they brandish seven pairs of legs that end in suction cups surrounded by sharp claws. Holograms, I guess.

"They're Dnynths." Wyndgonk's carapace trembles. "I wasn't expecting this. They've created copies of the most vicious predators in the world to guard the hearthlight. This is giving me terrible memories of wildschool." Fire turns to Elza. "We'll get eaten alive if our math is wrong."

"Our math won't be wrong." Elza is still smiling. "Just leave this to me."

She reaches out, and a holographic cloud appears. She starts poking at symbols, faster and faster, like a piano player performing a fiendishly complicated piece at double speed. Her crown glows brighter and brighter, like the Ardenii are having fun.

"There," she murmurs. "This won't take long."

As she solves the math problems, the ghostly Dnynths seem to shrink further away.

Elza's crown blazes with a white light, until it's too bright to look at. So instead, I stare at her face, with the glow playing over her cheekbones and the tiny dimple in her chin, her eyes suddenly as deep as the middle of the ocean. She's talking to herself—or the Ardenii—too quietly to hear. I can't see a smile on her face without smiling myself.

Then . . . the light of her crown goes out.

Elza stops in the middle of solving three different math problems at once.

"It's her," Elza says. "I can hear her in my head, taunting me. She's here to take my crown away."

"Who?" Kez says. "Who's here?"

I've already guessed. My stomach is full of tiny crawling things.

"The new queen," Elza says. "They finally put Princess Nonesuch in charge, and she just cut off my connection to the Ardenii."

34

.

ELZA

You thought you could come into our house and take what you wanted. You never belonged with us, Rogue Princess. You embarrass the whole Firmament by wearing that unearned crown.

Elza can't respond to Queen Nonesuch, because her crown can't send a response—any more than it can do anything else. No matter. Everything Elza wants to say to the new queen, she's already said, back in the palace. *I deserve this as much as any of you. I'm not doubting myself anymore.*

All around Elza, the Dnynths take on more substance and move closer, snapping their jaws and lashing out with the sucker-claws that ring their triangular bodies. Spiked tails whip around.

In front of Elza is a wall of math. These problems seemed so easy a moment ago.

We pledged we would correct the error of your coronation.

"We're trapped!" Kez yells. "There's no way out."

The Dnynths are closing in—Elza can feel their breath against her neck. She and her friends are surrounded.

The only way out is to finish solving these ridiculous math problems, which use a whole system of notation that Elza isn't used to. She can't even figure out how to pick up where she left off, before the crown went offline.

We are on our way to strip you of your title. Prepare to beg for your life.

"I can't do it," Elza says out loud. "I'm . . . I can't, not without the Ardenii helping me."

"Then we're all dead," Wyndgonk says.

Someone is standing between Elza and the haze of math problems.

Tina looks down at Elza, with the rippling light from the holo-Dnynths playing across the jewels on her face.

Her eyes dilate, driving out the blue. Fixed on Elza, without a flicker of doubt.

"Ignore the queen. Ignore the Dnynths," Tina says. "You did just fine before you had the Ardenii." Tina's voice has the same soothing tone that

Elza uses when she's trying to help someone else crack a problem. "This is just math. There's no bullies, no monsters—just numbers. You got here because you solved problems that nobody else could, remember?"

Your time is over. We have put your ship out of operation. Nobody can help you, Rogue Princess.

"You are Elza Monteiro, and I will always believe in you, even if I doubt everything else," Tina says.

Tina's face is full of love and trust—she looks just like when she was encouraging Elza to wear this crown, on a doomed starship.

Thaoh Argentian doesn't seem to matter so much anymore. Neither does the queen.

"I missed you so much," Elza says. "Please don't ever leave me again like that." Her heart bangs a broken rhythm and all of her senses are elevated. She can smell Wyndgonk's rising flame and hear Kez scrambling to get out of the way of the Dnynths.

"I won't," Tina says. "I promise. I'm here, it's me. I love you."

The queen is still ranting, but Elza shuts her out.

Elza takes a deep breath and looks at the math in front of her. "I'll finish this. Can you buy me some time?"

"Sure." Tina grabs a piece of broken vine and swings it like a whip, distracting the transparent Dnynths. She dances around, keeping just out of their reach.

"I'll help with the math," Wyndgonk says.

"Me too," Kez says.

Elza nods, too busy reconstructing where she left off to speak. She points to one of the problems she was in the middle of, and Kez and Wyndgonk start on it, while she tackles the others. If she doesn't think about the monsters all around her, this is actually fun.

"Eeep!" Tina yelps.

Elza pauses, almost loses her place.

But Tina's voice comes again. "Don't worry. Keep going."

There are so many variables to hold in Elza's head, and the queen is still trying to throw her off—but she closes off one problem. And another. And another. The math is so clear in her mind, she holds on to it and ignores everything else.

"Got it," Elza says.

"Me too," Wyndgonk says.

"Yep," Kez says.

The Dnynths vanish. Tina crouches, clutching at a tiny scrape on her knee. This cavernous space is suddenly much too quiet.

The queen's voice is gone, too.

Wyndgonk steps forward nervously and takes the crystalline double-twist in one claw. "We did it. Let's just hope we can bring this thing back intact."

"We will treat it like the most precious thing in the world, since it's actually the most precious thing in your world," Kez says.

The exit is visible once again, and Elza makes a beeline for it. "We need to get going. Right before we were cut off completely, the queen told me that she put the *Undisputed Training Bra Disaster* out of operation."

"At least we still have the knifeship." Wyndgonk hisses in fire throat.

Elza and the others rush through the passage toward the outside. There's nobody around.

"Where in the flaming lakes is Naahay?" Kez says.

"Who cares?" Wyndgonk says. "We can get some peace for once. Let's move."

Tina sidles up to Elza and whispers, "I have a plan. But you're going to hate it."

The sky turns overhead, even though it's the middle of the day, and the clouds pulse with slashes of lightning. "It's the weather-stabilizing satellite." Wyndgonk makes a disgusted face with fire mandibles. "The one the Royal Fleet installed for us. The Ardenii are making it go haywire."

Elza shakes her head. "The Ardenii have a code: they won't cause direct harm to anyone. This is just to throw us off our game. And when the new queen gets here, she can kill us herself."

"We won't be here by the time she arrives," Tina says. "Listen. I'm still your consort until you tell me otherwise. And part of my job is to help you stay safe, although I know you can take care of yourself. Do you still trust me?"

Elza makes a face. "You just said I won't like your plan."

"I think it's our only shot. Can you shut down your crown completely, so the queen can't use it to track us?"

Elza nods. "But I still don't—"

"It's going to be okay," Tina says. "I promise. Can I touch your hand?"

"Um, sure."

Elza squints, wrinkling her nose, and deactivates the last of her crown's functions. The silence grows even more absolute. She and Tina rush hand in hand back to where they left the knifeship, with Kez and Wyndgonk behind them.

"Listen, Rachael said something to me after I came back to life," Tina says. "She said I never really tried being me, after I decided I didn't want to be Captain Argentian. So this is me trying to be me. Playing to my strengths."

Wyndgonk puffs dark smoke. "As long as we're all risking a gruesome death for the sake of your personal growth."

Elza starts to say something—

—but there's a gun pointed at her head.

Naahay steps out from behind one of the braids of rock and wraps her free arm around Elza's neck, while holding her at gunpoint.

"I swore an oath to serve the queen," Naahay spits. "So did both of you." She looks at Wyndgonk and Elza. "I'm taking this traitor to Her Radiance, and then perhaps certain injustices will be rectified. I can at last resume my princess training."

Naahay drags Elza toward their knifeship parked next to the big stone braid where Wyndgonk's mother lives.

Wyndgonk rolls fire head. "We don't have time for this. The Bereavement is—"

Naahay scoffs. "If anybody is going to solve the Bereavement, do you think it's going to be your charming little crew? Or Her Radiance, who has access to all the information in the galaxy? I will make sure to share with her everything we have learned, and I'm sure she'll put the knowledge to good use. Which reminds me: hand over that hearthlight."

Elza squirms. "Don't give her anything."

Naahay tightens her finger grip on the trigger. "I could shoot her, and they'd probably still be able to salvage the crown from what's left of her head. Do not try me."

Wyndgonk goes stiff, shrinking inside fire shell. Tina gives fire a tiny nod.

Fire belches some dark smoke and hands the hearthlight over.

Naahay holds the precious crystal in her left hand, but keeps the gun barrel pressed against Elza's temple.

"You helped me get this crown," Elza says. "I thought you were on our side."

"I've been patient." Naahay drags Elza into the knifeship, then shoves her into the rear compartment. "I knew eventually a chance would arrive to get back into the princess selection program." Naahay seals the door, trapping Elza.

She activates the ship's comms. "This is Naahay Ontahra, formerly a candidate in the princess selection program. I have captured the Rogue Princess, and I'm bringing her to you. I'll turn on a beacon so you can home in."

Naahay leans over and sparks a beacon like the one that used to be embedded in Tina's chest: a glowing ball of stars.

35

.

TINA

Finally. Took you long enough.

As soon as Naahay turns the communicator off, I step forward. "Okay, fun time is over. You're not going anywhere."

"I have no desire to shoot you." Naahay levels the gun at me. "I've never killed, and I would detest having your death on my conscience. But if you step any closer, you're absolutely dead."

Elza is watching all of this with her eyes wide. I look past Naahay at her.

"I already died for Elza once. And it's time I took this 'consort' thing seriously. I mean, it's not healthy to define yourself by your relationship, right?" I advance on Naahay. "But I made a commitment, and you know what? I see it as a badge of honor. I'm proud to be the consort to the Rogue Princess."

I lunge forward and Naahay squeezes the trigger.

Nothing happens, of course.

My momentum carries me forward and I tag Naahay right at the base of her exposed jawbone. She topples over, unconscious, still clutching the useless gun.

I step over Naahay's body and open the compartment to let Elza out. "I did say you weren't going to like it."

"So that was your plan?" Elza stares at me. "You figured out that Naahay was going to betray us?"

"I knew that after spending five minutes with her. She's not exactly subtle. So yeah. I gave her a deactivated gun. And when I saw that she'd snuck away instead of standing guard like she promised, I figured she was making her move at last." I fiddle with the knifeship's controls, step off, and hand the hearthlight back to Wyndgonk. "Now we just launch this ship into space with that jerk on board, and that beacon going. Hopefully this buys us a little time."

"The queen won't easily be fooled." Wyndgonk takes the hearthlight back. "She knows everything it's possible to know."

Elza shakes her head. "Marrant outwitted the previous queen, who was much more experienced. It might work."

I step back on board the knifeship long enough to pull some components out of its comms, but I'm careful to leave Naahay's beacon transmitting. As soon as Elza and I are out of the knifeship, I slam the hatch shut behind us. The ship rises up into the air on a path toward low orbit.

"Did you mean what you said?" Elza asks me. "About being my consort?"

"Nah." I grin. "I was massively understating because I didn't want to get sappy in front of that creep. Being your consort is one of the main things that shapes my life, along with being Rachael's best friend. All I want is to help lift you up so everyone else can see how bright you shine."

Elza's perfect face becomes a prism. Tears streak down her face and her lip trembles. "Don't scare me like that again."

"Yes. I'm sorry. I know I need to earn your trust back, and this was a lousy way to do it. I'm going to spend the rest of my life, however long that is, giving you reasons to rely on me again." Now I'm splash-eyed, too.

I feel weak inside—but also, like I just got my heart back.

"Good." Elza leans forward and presses her lips against mine. Warm glow spreads all the way through me and I get tingles on the palms of my hands and the soles of my feet.

I pull away from her. The sky darkens some more and the thunder rings out. "I ought to know by now that who I belong to is at least as important as who I want to be."

"We're only as good as the people in our life." Kez nods.

"Enough processing," Wyndgonk says. "We need to find a way out of here before my mother realizes we're doing a truly terrible job of safeguarding my people's most vital treasure."

The sky is getting blotchy and purple. Even though I know intellectually the Ardenii won't hurt anyone, I'm getting a fear-pocket in my gut. A couple of low-flying ships pass overhead, buffeted by the winds—or maybe the Ardenii are screwing with their guidance systems a little.

"So how do we get off-world?" I ask.

"I have an idea," Wyndgonk says. "But it won't be very comfortable for your humanoid bodies."

A short time later, we're riding on, basically, a grain elevator. "Ugh, I'm getting muscle spasms under my shell," says Wyndgonk as we huddle in between big bales of something that looks like barley. "The perfect ending to a visit home."

Wyndgonk seems to be in a worse mood than usual. Probably something about going home, and dealing with fire mother, not to mention suddenly being responsible for the whole future of fire planet.

I don't know what to say to Wyndgonk, but Elza leans forward and looks into fire watermelon-seed eyes. "Hey," she says. "I'm sorry that you had to come home and take something away from your people, instead of bringing them something. But I promise, we will make sure Thythuthy gets rewarded."

"It's not just that," Wyndgonk says. "It's Naahay. I spent so much time putting up with her attitude, because she was part of our crew. She constantly found ways to make me feel worthless. And I guess I figured that was the price I had to pay to be one of you."

Ouch. I feel like a bowling ball is lodged in my gut. Elza and Kez both have identical stricken expressions.

"We should never have let her stick around," Elza says. "We didn't want to kick her out, because we were trying to be welcoming to everyone."

"But by welcoming her, we were allowing you to feel unwelcome," Kez says to Wyndgonk. "That's not okay. We ignored a dozen warning signs about Naahay because she came through for us a couple of times. I kept waiting and hoping for her to be better somehow. But I should have known—I knew people exactly like her at Eton."

"Thank you." Wyndgonk trains all of fire eyes on me. "And then Naahay tried to steal the hearthlight. And for a moment, I was certain that you were all going to let her. Deep down, I wasn't that surprised."

Oof. That bowling ball of shame just went from a duckpin to a tenpin.

"I had to make her think she'd won. We needed a decoy." The bristles of alien barley stalks dig into my back.

"I know you like your schemes," Wyndgonk says to me. "But leave my people's future out of them. We promised to keep it safe at all costs. We need to act as if that promise means something."

I nod. "I get that. But—"

Elza catches my eye and shakes her head. I stop trying to argue.

"If a situation like that happens again," Elza says, "we will give our lives to protect the hearthlight. This is more important than any of us."

Wyndgonk snorts and nearly roasts some dried vegetables. "Let's just try and get away from the evil queen before we make any more vows."

Fire is giving me nine eyes' worth of stink-eye. But Elza fixes me with a tender look, like she finally believes I'm back.

The *Undisputed Training Bra Disaster* is starting to fall out of orbit, sinking lower as it swings around the horizon. My mood still lifts, seeing my home.

We manage to swing our borrowed grain elevator alongside, as if we're just making an extra delivery—but we can't get the hatch open. Our air is starting to run out, and we don't have any way to let our friends know we're back.

Someone waves to us from the top of the ship. Kfok, wearing an atmosphere suit fitted to her non-humanoid body, is climbing around trying to repair the power junctions. We all wave back.

The hatch opens and we stagger inside the ship.

"Thank goodness you made it back," Yiwei gasps. "There's a new queen, and she's—"

"We know," Wyndgonk says. "Because things could always get worse."

"I think I can guess how she put the ship out of operation," Elza says. "The Ardenii aren't gods, not really. They just know how to find every little broken thing in the world, like when I knew about that rust patch on that one ship."

Kez clicks her tongue. "I bet anything it's those 'gently used' impellers we installed at Vandal Station." She turns to Yiwei. "Give me a hand fixing them?"

"Always." Yiwei follows Kez back into the engine area.

Elza and I make a beeline for the flight lounge, where Damini and Zaeta are sitting around, waiting for the engines to come back on. Rachael is perched on a big mushroom-shaped beanbag. She notices Elza and me holding hands, and smiles.

"As soon as we get the power back on—" Zaeta says.

"—we'll need to be ready to go." Damini nods. "I'm already plotting a course."

"Indignation!" Zaeta's top layer of eyes looks up at the ceiling. "That's the worst course we could take."

"No, listen," Damini sputters. "I worked it all out. We use the gravity well—"

"You're doing it again!" Zaeta squawks.

Elza is poking at the dull gold circlet on her head, with her eyes closed. Trying to get it working again. I want to tell her that it'll be okay and her mind will touch that hugeness again, but I'm trying not to make promises that I don't know I can keep.

36

.

ELZA

The first time she met Fernanda, Elza was still living with her parents in Alto de Pinheiros, and she'd snuck out to go to a party with a group of other travestis, everyone dancing to Brazilian Funk and drinking bottles of Skol. Fernanda was quiet, but she had a fire in her eyes that made Elza want to keep looking. Elza and Fernanda ended up out on the balcony, looking out at the lights of São Paulo, and they talked about the dreams and fears that were at war in both their lives.

Elza's future was all laid out: go to college, study computer science, become a coder, get rich, live in a one-bedroom apartment in Vila Madalena upstairs from an art gallery that she never visited. Fernanda wanted to be a poet, or maybe a journalist, and tell the stories of all the people she knew whose stories never got to be told. She kept a tiny notebook with her, even at this party, with a little golf pencil tucked inside.

At this point, Elza was still a few months away from getting caught by her parents and losing her whole comfortable existence. But talking to Fernanda, watching all the people dancing on the other side of the glass balcony door, two things were clear to her: she couldn't bear to live as anything less than her full self, no matter what it cost her. But also, she wanted to be more like Fernanda and give voice to the voiceless.

It's easy, Fernanda told her. *You just have to care more about being heard than being loved.*

Now Elza nestles against Tina on the sofa at the back of the flight lounge as everybody holds their breath waiting for the engines to come back on. Elza missed the weight of Tina's body against hers, the gentle cradling of one strong arm. Elza has the worst brain fog of her life, like she feels as if someone carved out half her brain, and she's having a hard time finding words. One moment she'd been fully connected to the Ardenii, the next she was totally cut off, and her mind can't adjust.

"The queen's taking the bait, at least." Wyndgonk points. The knifeship with Naahay on board was just seized by an ion harness.

At first Elza can't see where the harness is coming from, and then it comes around the side of the planet, and she gasps out loud.

The entire Palace of Scented Tears is here, floating in space: two clasped hands, reaching to pull Naahay inside. Elza did not know the palace itself could become a starship, but she shouldn't be surprised.

"I guess the queen doesn't like to leave the comforts of home behind," Kfok says.

The knifeship is approaching the palace. Soon the queen will know Elza's not on board, if she hasn't figured it out already.

There's a low hum, which turns into a drone: the engines are back on.

"Hold tight," Zaeta says.

"We're going to take our leave from Her Radiance," Damini says.

The *Undisputed Training Bra Disaster* has sunk into low orbit, almost at the upper edge of Thythuthy's poisoned atmosphere. Elza sees the Dnynths playing in the clouds, tiny diamond-shaped creatures surfing and swimming—they look cute from up here. The clouds turn into a blur as the ship speeds up its orbit, trying to build up enough speed to break for open space.

"False princess," a voice rings out. "Twice rejected, twice disgraced. You really believe you can hide from us?"

Elza turns to see a hologram of Queen Nonesuch, glaring at her. Tina reaches out and waves one hand in front of the queen's face—no reaction.

"She must have found a way to broadcast to every holographic projector nearby." Kfok scowls with both mouths.

Yiwei returns from the engine room, and immediately runs down to his new tactical station.

"We see everything, and your fear offends our sight," the queen says. And sure enough, her eyes seem to look right at Elza, seeing her squirm.

"She's trying to freak you out," Rachael says.

"She's succeeding," Elza whispers.

"Stop running and face us," the queen hisses. "You have no dignity, no honor. You are nothing. We would be rid of you."

Elza feels transfixed by the queen's regard. She can't look away from the cruel gloating face—until something is in the way.

Tina has put herself between Elza and the hologram.

"Hey. Hey. Stop looking at that dusty fool. Look at me instead," Tina says. "Elza, she's doing this because she can't stand that we're outsmarting her. Again."

The queen's pale flickering face glares. "No matter where you go, you can never escape from us."

"I'm so sick of her," Damini says.

"I did not vote for this queen," Zaeta says.

"We're not going to make it," Yiwei says from the tactical station. "The palace is moving into position to intercept us when we break orbit."

"By now you must realize your position is impossible," the queen says, as if she just heard Yiwei.

The queen serves up taunts, while Yiwei tries to help Damini and Zaeta bolt from this trap. Elza still can't think clearly—her mind is still buffering, ever since it got cut off. Or maybe it's just all the stress and anxiety, finally piling up.

Tina and Rachael are sitting on either side of Elza, with Tina perching on the sofa's arm to make room.

"She's never going to give up, even if we escape now." Elza can't help quivering like a wet cat. "She hates me because of what I represent, and she won't stop until she destroys me."

"Her loss if she can't see how wonderful you are," Rachael says. "It's messed up that someone who has so much knowledge can be so ignorant."

"Yeah," Tina says. "You told me that they taught you to recognize patterns when you were at the palace, but they also taught you to look for the places where the patterns fall apart. Even with all that training, it's easier to believe that all the dots join up perfectly."

"I never expected much from any of those people," Wyndgonk snorts. "And they've never disappointed me."

The ship is climbing up out of low orbit, and now Elza can see the palace waiting, its fingertips extended as if in welcome.

"We will uncrown and unmake you," the queen says.

"Two minicycles to intercept," Yiwei says. "She's got us where she wants us."

"Be really nice if there was a plan," Kfok says.

Everyone is looking at Elza.

"The queen wouldn't be trying to psych you out if she really thought she had you cornered," Tina says.

"It's true," Rachael says.

Work the problem, Elza tells herself, as if she was giving someone else coding advice. *Start anywhere and work your way into the center.*

She closes her eyes and listens to herself think.

"Okay." Elza leans forward on the sofa. "The queen can't risk damaging our ship, because she wants my crown. It's almost impossible to make another one, and the only way to get it in one piece is if she captures me alive. She probably knows we've got the hearthlight, too."

"So she can't use weapons against us," Yiwei says. "I like that."

"We just need to stay far enough away to avoid getting grabbed," Kfok says.

Zaeta nods from the pilot station. "Then we know—"

"—what we need to do," Damini says.

"Are you sure about this?" Wyndgonk is hunched over, with fire pearlescent shell catching the reflected light from fire homeworld. "We're going to gamble that the usurper queen won't just destroy us, and the hearthlight, rather than let us out of her grasp?"

"I'm sure," Elza says. "I wouldn't risk your hearthlight. The queen knows she'll have other chances to capture me."

"Your coronation was never ratified," the queen is saying. "We do not recognize you."

"We're about to fly close enough to the palace to wash the windows," Damini says.

"But not close enough to snag us," Zaeta adds.

The planet's surface falls away as the ship breaks orbit, and the palace looms larger and larger in the viewport. Elza digs her fingernails into her own palm. *Please let me be right.* She can see the aquiline walls of the palace, dotted with ornate crystalline shapes.

The palace has a pulse cannon aimed directly at them.

"We give you one final chance to surrender," the queen snarls.

"Her poker face needs some work," Tina says.

Everyone holds their breath—no sound but the engines working overtime—and then the *Undisputed Training Bra Disaster* pulls away from the Palace of Scented Tears and makes for open space. Space and time fold and a sweet taste fills Elza's mouth as they race away from Thythuthy.

37

.

TINA

. . . 213 Earth days until all the suns go out forever

Everybody is repairing the ship, de-stressing, and trying not to obsess about the fact that both Marrant and Queen Nonesuch are hunting them. "We really are the Galaxy's Most Wanted," Damini says.

"That reminds me! I have something for all of us," Rachael says.

The next time I turn around, Rachael has printed some new badges for us all to stick on our shoulders, where the Royal Fleet insignia would be if we were still wearing uniforms. At the center is an angry seven-legged kite covered with feathery scales—a Dnynth—baring sharp teeth, sticking out its spiked tongue, and raising one sucker-claw. Around the top, it says, GALAXY'S MOST WANTED, and around the bottom, it says, CAN'T CATCH US.

I love it so much.

As soon as everyone has these patches on their clothes, we're all moving with a spring in our step. We're smiling a little more—at least, I think that's what Kfok is doing—and joking back and forth.

Even Elza, who always complained about the Royal Fleet uniforms, is wearing one on her jacket. Except I notice on second look that hers looks a bit different: at the bottom, instead of the thing about not catching us, it says, THE ROGUE PRINCESS.

I run into Elza folding her tactical ballgown and laying it on a shelf. "Hey," I say. "How are you holding up?"

She shrugs. "I'm okay. It's time I stopped letting people like that get to me."

"The thing where your crown stopped working, just when you were relying on it . . . that's got to be scary. I'm just saying, I'm here if you want to talk about it."

Elza starts to say something, but Yiwei's voice comes over the shipwide comms. "Hey, everybody. We need to plan our next move. Meeting on the flight lounge?"

Elza finishes putting the dress away, and I follow her back up to the front of the ship.

Soon we're all sitting in a big circle on couches, teacup chairs, and space beanbags: Wyndgonk, Kfok, Elza, Rachael, Yiwei, Damini, Zaeta, Kez, and me.

"Here's the situation," Yiwei says. "We have the hearthlight, and we believe that if we insert it into the empty space at the heart of that wedding chapel, we can shut the Bereavement down. For good."

"And then we need to bring it right back to my people," Wyndgonk says.

"Yes. We gave our word. The trouble is, Marrant's forces are occupying the ancient temple, and by now they've had time to bring in a whole fleet to protect it. They're going to be expecting us, and the queen also knows we're heading there."

"We can't let Marrant have the hearthlight," Elza says.

"Right," Yiwei says. "So we're just one ship against a whole fleet. *And* we're half shed. We need a lot more muscle, which is why we're going to go rendezvous with Riohon's rebel fleet and enlist their aid."

The way Yiwei took charge of this meeting was already fraying my nerves, and now he's telling us what our next move is going to be. I feel my neck and jaw turn into one big vise. I haven't exactly forgotten how Yiwei nearly took a shot at Rachael and me.

"So wait," I say. "You've already decided we're going to team up with Riohon and his crew? Without even discussing it with the rest of us?"

"I don't see any other option," Yiwei says. "We're not even outnumbered. 'Outnumbered' is when it's five against one, or ten against one."

"Riohon is going to be fighting to restore the honor of the Royal Fleet," I say. "It'll be just like when you all trusted Thaoh, and she decided taking down Marrant was more important than sticking to the plan." I don't mention that I'm still having the occasional Thaoh nightmare. "If we join up with Riohon, we're committing to having a big battle. There has to be some way to just sneak into the wedding chapel without throwing down."

"Marrant will protect that ancient temple with everything he has," Yiwei says. "We can't count on his security being incompetent."

"Why is this even a debate?" Damini bounces with impatience. "Riohon is our friend, and we can't do this alone."

Am I remembering the look on Riohon's face when he realized I wasn't Thaoh? Maybe, a little.

"It's a debate because we've trusted these people before," Kez says, "and it hasn't turned out great."

"We've done okay so far with sneaking around and escaping from the tiger's mouth," Yiwei says. (Actually, my souped-up EverySpeak lets me know this is a Chinese expression for slipping out of the jaws of death: hǔkǒu tuōxiǎn.) "But this time, it's definitely coming down to a fight. By now, Marrant has had time to move some broadswords into orbit around Larstko IV. He'll have the whole moon covered."

Elza turns to me. "If we don't team up with Riohon, we'll need other allies."

"My people can help," Kfok says. "If we get to be part of what comes after. We don't have a million battle-slicers, but we have a few."

"The Thythuthyans will do whatever we can to protect the hearthlight," says Wyndgonk. "But we don't have any ships that can stand against the Royal Compassion. The Grattna are the ones who managed to copy Marrant's flagship."

"The Grattna already turned us down, right?" Yiwei looks at me.

I only choke on my failure a little. "Yeah. But there's always another way. I thought we were all equals here, but now you're making decisions for the whole group."

I look around the circle, desperate to see anyone agreeing with me. Even Rachael is giving me a helpless look, like she agrees with her boyfriend. And then my face lands on Elza, and my heart crashes.

"Let's not waste any more time debating this." Elza looks at me wearily. "We need Riohon's help if we're going up against Marrant. Even if we don't agree about everything, we can use his ships for now and figure out later what comes afterward."

My jaw drops. Elza's said a million cynical things in front of me, but she's never been about expediency or making whatever compromises it takes to win.

"Then it's settled," Yiwei says. "Unless we need to vote or something."

"No need," Kez says. "If the rest of you are okay with this, then . . . so am I. There's too much at stake. Time is running out. Survival first, justice later. I hope."

"Fine," I say. I'm aware I sound like a sore loser. "I just hope we can be smart and avoid a bloodbath. There has to be a way to neutralize Marrant's advantage."

"I'm counting on you to help find one," Yiwei says. "For now, let's get in touch with Riohon and hope these safenode beacons are as secure as everyone says."

Everybody gets up and starts bustling and making plans. I'm left sitting alone in my armchair, feeling the bottomless pit of garbage emotions yawning open. I keep replaying how I snapped at Yiwei, but also how he tried to boss us around. And the way that Elza suddenly became Expediency Girl, which is so not like her.

But also . . . I can't stop seeing a big, ugly battle, almost as if it's already happened and I'm reliving it. Ships cracking in half like twigs. Bodies screaming on fire until the vacuum of space puts them out. Good people and bad people, dying just the same. There has to be some way to avoid all this death, but I don't know how.

38

.

RACHAEL

A hundred starships huddle in orbit around a supergiant star, which dazzles Rachael's eyes even with the filters on the viewport. The Bereavement left this star alone because it's too big and too hot for anyone to live near. And all that radiation makes it the perfect place to hide a honking big fleet.

Rachael sketches furiously, trying to capture the way the blazing light plays over the curved surfaces on top of the daggerships and swordships. She really could use some pastel crayons for all of these blues and pinks and yellows, and oh god, the oranges. She could spend a week sketching this view, but she only has a couple of cycles left before the *Undisputed Training Bra Disaster* arrives at the rendezvous.

Yiwei is looking over Rachael's shoulder. "That's . . . gorgeous. I think this is my favorite picture you've ever done."

Rachael scoots closer to her boyfriend. "It's funny. I know these are powerful warships packed with weapons of mass destruction, but from here . . . they're just shapes and colors. I could be drawing a bunch of balloons, or a flower bed."

"It's only when you get up close that you see the truth about something sometimes." Yiwei makes a noise in his throat.

He's wrestling with anxiety or insecurity, and Rachael doesn't know how to help him. She can't forget when he was freaking out and talking about putting mines in orbit around Thythuthy.

"Every one of those ships has forty or fifty crewmembers. Maybe a couple hundred on board some of the bigger ships." Yiwei shakes his head. "There's close to ten thousand people total. And a lot of them will be dead soon, even if we wind up triumphant. Not even mentioning all of the billions of people who'll be dead if we fail."

Rachael stops drawing and looks up at him. "You feel like you pushed everyone into a big battle."

"Yeah."

"And now you're second-guessing yourself, even though you were acting so sure in that meeting."

"Yeah."

She offers her hand, and he takes it, and then his other hand is on her shoulder. This moment is perfect: the view, the picture she's almost finished drawing, the gentle pressure of his palm. She can't bear to think of it ending, of there never being any more moments like this.

"Remember when you told me that your life can be a work of art?" she asks.

"Yeah. That was actually—"

"I know, I know. That's actually what your ex-girlfriend said. I don't care. I like it and I'm taking it. The thing about works of art is, sometimes the flaws are what make them really beautiful. The screw-ups, the bad parts, the parts that just make you upset or sick."

Yiwei is tossing Rachael a whole bouquet of looks: shmoopy and tender, but also kind of sad and . . . hopeful?

"I don't want to be perfect. I meant it when I told you that I really don't want to be a superhero, or to be just like Captain Othaar," Yiwei says. "I just feel everybody's fear, all around me, and I'm scared, too. And the way I cope is trying to figure out how we can survive, and how I can keep everyone from losing hope. And sometimes . . . that leads to guns."

Oh. That actually makes a whole lot of sense. So it's not just PTSD, it's also . . . empathy.

"Yeah," she says, choosing her words carefully. "I think you have this need to hold everyone together and be there for people, and sometimes to everyone else it can read as swagger. Because you come on kind of strong, and you spent so much time trying to be like Captain Othaar."

He nods heavily. "Yeah. That makes . . . that makes sense. Ugh. What do I do?"

Rachael sits with this for long enough for those distant ships to get noticeably bigger. Yiwei knows her well enough that he doesn't rush her.

At last, Rachael says, "I think I know who we should talk to. Come on."

Tina sits in the nook underneath the flight lounge, staring at the tactical display that Yiwei set up. At first, Rachael thinks Tina is scanning for threats in the neighborhood, but then she realizes: Tina is studying the ships they're going to meet up with.

"Yeah, I'm being kinda paranoid." Tina wrinkles her nose. "The same radiation that hides those ships from the bad guys makes it hard for us to tell exactly who we're going to rub elbows with. I just don't want any surprises."

"That's smart," Yiwei says.

Tina only rolls her eyes a little. "Thanks."

"Do you have a sec?" Rachael says. "We wanted to ask you something."

"Sure." Tina pulls her hands out of the holographic goo and swivels her teacup chair to face Rachael and Yiwei.

Somebody has decorated the walls around the tactical station with stuffed animals from Miscreant Station—the one closest to Rachael looks kind of like an otter with five tails and weird bony antlers. These plushies all chatter and bob their heads in time with the vibrations from the ship's engines.

Yiwei stumbles over words at first, then says, "I guess we need to talk." Rachael gives a thumbs-up.

Tina nods. "Yeah, okay."

"I'm not trying to be in charge. I'm not. I guess I shouldn't have assumed we were all going to be okay with joining up with Riohon's fleet."

"You're definitely acting like you want to be in charge lately," Tina says. "I know that you all went through a lot while I was, uh, out of commission. But sometimes you get seriously bossy, which just pushes my buttons."

"It was easier when Gahang and Cinnki were still here." Yiwei plays the back of his own neck like a guitar fret. "Sometimes I think Rachael and I together would make one good captain. She's really good at listening and bringing people together and seeing the big picture. And I'm pretty good at standing up and talking loud."

Rachael snorts. "I love you, but I wouldn't want to combine into one person. You would so not want to hear what I'm thinking half the time."

"But that's a great idea though." Tina perks up so much, all the stuffed animals react. "You can be captain together!"

"Wait, what?" Rachael almost falls off her beanbag.

"Seriously," Tina says. "You're totally right. You two should be co-captains. Why not?"

"You mean captain and alternate captain, right? Like Othaar and Lyzix, back on the *Indomitable*," Rachael says.

"Nah," Tina says. "I mean that you're both captain. You make decisions together."

"Like on *Legends of Tomorrow!*" Rachael claps her hands. Seeing Yiwei's blank look, she shakes her head. "It's a great show. If we ever make it back to Earth, we're one hundred percent watching all of it. We'll skip the first season though."

"You really think that would work?" Yiwei says to Tina. "Would you take orders from the two of us, in a crisis when there's no time for debate?"

"It would be my honor," Tina says. "Though I think we should ask everyone else before we make it official."

The rebel fleet is close enough to make out the individual ships now. They're all former Royal Fleet dagger- and shortsword-class vessels— but they no longer fly the Royal crest with the Joyful Wyvern, and they no longer have HMSS in their names. Instead, they have a new crest with a spiked glove and the words ROYAL FLEET IN EXILE. And under that: WE'RE TAKING IT BACK.

Rachael admires their optimism.

"They still look like toys," Tina says.

"The closer we get to these ships, the more my crown responds," Elza says. "Because all of those ships contain a tiny fragment of the Ardenii, and they're still trying to connect with me. The queen is still blocking me for now."

"You helped me get my art back, so I'll do whatever I can to help you reconnect with the Ardenii," Rachael says.

"Thanks," Elza says. "At least it's given me time to think on my own, and I've been able to study the crown a little more. It has so much storage, it's like a whole RAID array sitting on my head."

The three of them are sitting in a tiny crawlspace at the top of the *Undisputed Training Bra Disaster.* This is pretty much the same spot where the bluehouse was on board the *Indomitable,* except instead of a garden full of alien vegetation and shrooms, there are just bare wooden boards and a few piles of art supplies from Nyitha's artist collective.

Every now and then, Rachael spots something laying around the art-salon side of the ship, like a pile of tagging supplies, and she remembers that this was half Nyitha's ship. And she remembers how Nyitha was willing to be hated as long as Rachael survived. Rachael can't imagine ever making that kind of sacrifice, any more than she can imagine faking her own death for years.

"I have something to say and I don't know how to say it." Rachael catches her breath and waits for the flush to leave her cheeks. "Both of you are powerful in ways that have nothing to do with fighting Marrant or that usurper queen. Tina, you play epic pranks! And you tie yourself in knots trying to understand people that no other humanoid ever tried to understand. And Elza, you're a ridiculously patient teacher and helper, and you always want to figure out how things really work. I just . . ."

Rachael gathers her thoughts and her breath and sways a little. Telling people how she feels about them always takes a lot out of her.

Tina and Elza are smiling next to her. The rebel fleet is close enough now to see all the dents and scratches.

"I just hope that neither of you ever feels like you're not powerful just because your power doesn't help stop the bad guys in one particular situation," Rachael says. "Promise me, both of you, that you'll remember you're excellent. Not everything has to be a weapon or whatever."

"Yes, Captain." Tina squeezes Rachael's hand.

"With a will, Captain," Elza says.

Oh yeah. So they didn't end up doing a big meeting to decide whether to select Yiwei and Rachael as co-captains. Instead, they just went and asked Damini, Zaeta, Kez, Wyndgonk, and Kfok one or two at a time, and everyone was like *Sure, that's cool.* Or even, *About damn time.*

"Like, the Grattna might not come to our aid," Rachael says to Tina. "But that doesn't mean your work was a waste of time. Maybe it was the beginning of something."

"That reminds me," Elza says. "I found something buried in the memory of my crown. I think I know how you can convince the Grattna to be our allies."

Tina perks up a little. "How?"

"A few hundred years ago, the Grattna tried making more alliances with other worlds, and they came up with two kinds of allies: wing-friends and limb-friends. The third choice was just not to be allies at all. Anyway, a wing-friend is just working with you long enough to solve a problem, or to defeat some shared enemy."

"And that would be us." Tina's face brightens. "If I can get the Grattna to come help us, we might actually have a chance."

"And you could feel like you're contributing," Rachael says.

"Yeah. That too." Tina shakes her head and lets out a big breath through her nose, like a horse. "Come on. I think I can use that device Thaoh left behind to send a secure message to the Grattna, before we rendezvous with the fleet."

Tina and Elza hurry out of there, leaving Rachael staring at the fleet massing for battle.

39

.

TINA

I'm trying not to sound too needy as I talk to Halred via safebeam—which will only be secure for a minute, adding to the pressure. I've made more modifications to my EverySpeak, so it's a rat's nest of extra junctions and protocols. (I showed Elza how I reprogrammed it and she basically told me to leave the hacking to her from now on, but she also helped me make it a little less clunky.)

"We already told you that we will never be _____ with you," Halred says wearily. (Like, the distance between us is less than our distance from the Compassion, but still not short enough.)

"I understand. But listen, I believe this can be the start of a real alliance."

(Actually, I say something like "We don't have a friendship right now, but we aren't enemies either, so we have a chance to become better friends." Except that I also mention a couple other ways that things could go.)

Elza gives me a wan smile. I notice she's staying out of view of the Grattna, in case they wouldn't be happy to see that we have a princess in our midst. Makes me mad, but I also get it.

Kez chimes in, "We just visited the Thythuthyans and they trusted us with their most precious object. We have become closer to them, and we would like to be closer to you, too."

Damn. Kez is really good at this. Not surprising, but still. Damn.

"We can't be limb-friends yet. I know. We can only be wing-friends," I say. "You don't have to say yes or no right now. I'm sending the coordinates for where we're going to be." I send the coordinates for the wedding chapel.

"You understand about wing-friends and limb-friends." Halred narrows all of her eyes and crosses her wings in front. "We will not say yes or no now, but we will decide soon."

The connection ends.

"Don't get your hopes up too much." Kez is smiling and shaking her head at the same time. "The Grattna are dealing with historical injustice and recent trauma, which is a really bad combination. You don't overcome that in a few days."

"I know. I just really wanted . . ." I suck my lips inside out. "It sucks, you know? To put everything on the line and still get nowhere."

"Believe me. I know that feeling by heart."

Elza still perches on the big armchair at the side of the room, where the Grattna couldn't see her. I never want her to feel like she needs to hide. More than that, I wish I could find a way to help her get her crown back online. She insists it's a simple permissions issue, and she just needs to spoof something.

My eye lands on the viewport: so many starships, hiding next to a megasun. I feel a chill go through me and it hits me: *What the hell am I doing?* I get dizzy, thinking about heading into battle. A whole lot of us won't be alive soon, and we're just sailing forward as if that's normal and makes total sense, and I know there has to be some other way.

I spent all this time saying that I wasn't going to fight anymore.

What am I doing?

"So you say that violence should be a last resort. But the thing of it is, you tend to run out of other resorts really quickly," I whisper to Yiwei as we walk toward the shed door at the back of the *Undisputed Training Bra Disaster,* on our way into the cargo hangar of the *Unbroken,* Riohon's ship. "Especially when everybody else is already shooting. If we can't agree on the lines we won't cross, then maybe there's no 'us.'"

Yiwei tenses up because he's sick of this conversation. But he just says, "If it was just our survival at stake, I could agree with you. But we have to win, whatever it takes."

Part of me is scared that Yiwei is right. I mean, if my mom and everyone else back home dies, will it really be much consolation that I stayed true to my values?

"I just . . ." My tongue suddenly feels way too big. "I just feel like there's always another way, if you just have enough imagination to see it."

"Like I said, I'm counting on you to be there to help me see that other way." Yiwei offers me his hand and I clasp it. "Please believe me when I say that I don't want any more blood on my hands. I keep having nightmares about the ship I blew up, the *Unconquerable.*"

"I'm sorry. I've been there." I let go of Yiwei's hand. "If it does come to a fight, I'm going to be on defense, not offense."

"I figured as much."

I feel just a little of the tension drain from my neck.

We're all heading over there together: Yiwei and me up front, then Wyndgonk, Zaeta, Kez, and Damini. Elza, Kfok, and Rachael bring up the rear.

The door opens—the same metal sliding door that used to lead to a dirty corner of the Stroke, back in Wentrolo—and we're in a cargo hangar exactly like the one of the *Indomitable*.

Riohon steps up and gives us a proper salute with two fingers and a thumb held to his chest. "Shared ideals, with nobody left behind. Welcome to the *Unbroken*. It's so good to see you all."

Yiwei and I both salute back. Yiwei says, "Happy reunions and short absences," and I chime in. Everyone else behind us does the salute and the blessing, with different levels of enthusiasm.

And then Yatto the Monntha steps forward and stands next to Riohon. Yatto looks older, or maybe just worse for wear. "One last time," Yatto says. "I've missed all of you, but more than that, I've missed our fellowship. We've all lost so much, and this is our chance to make all of that loss mean something."

As beat-up as Yatto looks, they seem . . . calm. Like they've worked through some stuff.

"I still can't believe you're alive," Elza whispers.

"I cannot believe it either," Yatto says. "At least every time I almost die, I feel as though I gain more perspective."

"This is Thanz Riohon," Damini is saying to Zaeta. "He's the reason I know how to do that thing with the impellers."

"Riohon! So good to meet you," Zaeta bubbles. "I have so many questions. I wrote them all down!" Zaeta brandishes a lightpad with a list scrawled on it.

"Now that we're together again—" says Damini.

"—we're going to totally crush this," says Zaeta.

"There is one person who has helped me to find my center after all the destruction we endured," Yatto is saying to Elza, Kez, and me. They gesture, and another familiar person steps forward: Ganno the Wurthhi.

Next to me, I can feel Kez tense up.

"Ganno and I have formed a connection that goes beyond anything that either of us ever expected," says Yatto.

"Ohh." Kez's eyes widen, and she takes a deep breath. "*Ohhhhh*. The two of you are—"

"No, no," Ganno says. "Not like that! Just a deep spiritual connection. Kez, it is good to see you again, I am so relieved that you're okay, if anything had happened to you I would have—"

Kez takes a step back and her body language stiffens. "It's good to see you. I . . ." She trails off. "I should go check the engines."

Ganno starts to say something else, but Kez is already walking away.

Yatto shakes their head: *Let her go*. Ganno looks at the floor.

40

.

WYNDGONK

Everybody is talking over each other and jostling to get a peek at the holographic image at the center of the control deck on the *Unbroken*: captains and alternate captains, with their sleeves crammed with medals and honors.

The control deck is about the size of the flight lounge on the *Undisputed Training Bra Disaster,* but half the space is taken up by a big table with the holographic scan of the Larstko system over it. There's room for seven or eight chairs, but those have been removed to make way for the big crowd.

They also removed the transparent wall between the control deck and Forward Ops, where the pilots sit, and that's where Wyndgonk and Kfok are sitting, along with Elza.

Wyndgonk cradles the hearthlight in fire front pincers, wondering if fire will be remembered as the fool who handed over the future of fire people and caused their extinction.

"The objective is simple," Riohon says. "We get past Marrant's blockade and insert the hearthlight into the interface long enough to shut down the Bereavement. And then we get out."

"High stakes," Yiwei says.

"Couldn't we simply tell Marrant that we have the hearthlight?" asks a Zyzyian in a Royal Fleet uniform, spitting red bubbles. "He might let us use it to stop the Bereavement. It's in his interest to save all the stars, as much as ours."

"No." Yatto's voice drops to its lowest register. "We cannot risk allowing Marrant to have control over the Bereavement. We still do not know what that interface will allow someone to do. And we must ensure that the hearthlight is returned safely to the Thythuthyans."

That's the first time in this whole meeting anyone's mentioned Wyndgonk's people.

Wyndgonk is getting the too-many-rootberries heartburn again. Fire can't help imagining Innávan and everyone else on Thythuthy, waiting for the hearthlight to come back, and slowly realizing that it's over. No more next generation, and nothing to teach them even if they could be born.

"We can't afford a full-on assault," Yiwei says. "If we—"

"Perhaps there is a way to turn the enemy's overwhelming numbers to our advantage," says a Rosaei in a captain's uniform.

"We could try to separate their smaller ships from the heavy carriers," says an Aribentor whose uniform is full of honors. Nobody has bothered to tell Wyndgonk their names or pronouns, if any.

Why are they still wearing these uniforms, when the Royal Fleet is gone? Especially with the new queen, who doesn't deserve any loyalty?

"Perhaps a variation on the Xixthip maneuver," says another officer.

Yiwei pipes up again. "I was thinking maybe we could . . ." Nobody pays any attention to him. Wyndgonk understands humanoid body language enough to know that Yiwei is stewing. Fire knows exactly how he feels.

"Clearly our main advantage is that Marrant needs to avoid destroying the hearthlight." The Zyzyian's bubbles are very dark purple now. "If he does not know which ship it's on, he won't risk damaging any of our ships until he gets it."

Wyndgonk looks over at Kfok, who is scowling with one mouth and grimacing with the other.

"If I puffed really hard," Wyndgonk whispers, "I could light some of their uniforms on fire."

"It would be an improvement," Kfok says with her left mouth while making a fart noise with her right.

"I'm sorry," Elza says. "This is what I was afraid of."

"Why aren't you in the meeting?" Kfok says. "You're a princess. They'll listen to you."

"The first thing they'll do is ask me what the Ardenii are saying." Elza reaches up and touches her inert crown. "And once I tell them the truth, they'll dismiss me the same as Yiwei."

All of the officers including Riohon are pointing at the tactical scan and talking back and forth. Yiwei is hopping up and down trying to get their attention.

"I should just go," Wyndgonk says. "I should just take that cruiser and go back home with the hearthlight, and tell my mother it didn't work out."

"You probably should," Elza agrees. "But I really hope you don't. I'd miss you, for one thing, and I still think we can win."

"When did you become such an optimist?" Kfok cackles with one mouth and snorts with the other.

"Probably rubbed off on me from my annoying girlfriend." Elza smiles at Tina.

Yiwei tries again. "What if we—" Everybody just talks over him.

Wyndgonk hands the hearthlight to Elza. "Hold this for me." She nods.

Fire rises up and lets out a jet of flame that reaches almost to the control deck, singeing the air—it feels immensely gratifying. "Hey. HEY."

Everyone inside the control deck turns and looks, with identical stunned expressions on their faces.

"I wanted to see the people to whom I am entrusting the most precious item in my entire culture, and I am not impressed," Wyndgonk says. "My crew and I put ourselves on the line to find this temple and learn its secrets. We are not here to help you—you are here to help us. Our co-captains are Yiwei and Rachael, and you need to shut up and listen to them now."

"Okay." Riohon makes a slapping noise with his tiny humanoid mouth. "You're right. Yiwei and Rachael, you've both come so far since the *Indomitable*. What should we do?"

"You weren't there. You didn't see what Marrant was like." Yiwei's voice is guttural, and he spews fear chemicals. "The last time we faced him, we thought we knew what to expect, but we were wrong. He's changed since he almost died, like he doesn't care how many of his own people he kills. So whatever plan we come up with, we can't count on Marrant responding strategically."

Everyone goes silent. Now the fear chemicals are wafting off all of the humanoids, in one big mist that fills the room.

"So . . . what do you suggest?" The Zyzyian's blowhole spits out several black spheres.

"I'm not sure. The obvious thing would be to create a distraction, and draw off most of his forces so we can sneak inside. But we can't count on Marrant taking the bait. And he's got three ships for every one of ours." Yiwei turns to Rachael. "What do you think?"

"If we're lucky," Rachael says, "Marrant doesn't know how many ships we have. He might think there's only a handful."

Tina gestures at something on the tactical cloud. "So this weird blob here, it's a spaceship graveyard?"

"Yeah," Yiwei says. "It's the remains of all the ships that fought in the final battle between the Vayt and the Fatharn. At first, it just looks like an asteroid field. Those ships had some kind of stealth technology that makes it hard to see the wreckage."

"So if we got him to chase us in there, he might not be prepared for the number of ships waiting for him," Rachael says. "We could keep his whole fleet busy playing hide-and-seek."

Riohon scratches his head. "Might work. Marrant knows that some ships have deserted his ranks, but we've been careful to keep the existence of our whole rebel fleet a secret."

"The hard part is getting a whole fleet inside the debris field without getting spotted," Yiwei says.

Kfok stands up and waves a stinger-arm. "Some of us Kraelyors have had to learn how to steer clear of, uh, Royal Fleet patrols, because we used to get harassed and accused of smuggling. Anyway, we perfected certain tricks. When we're trying to stay off the radar, we hide inside a comet's tail. Sometimes we steal a whole comet and steer it where we need it to go."

"Comet theft!" Damini does a happy dance.

"I've always wanted to steal a comet," Zaeta says.

Now everybody in that meeting is buzzing about the plan that Yiwei, Rachael, and Kfok came up with, and pretending it was their idea.

Elza leans close to Wyndgonk. "Remember when you asked me before why we're still friends, now that we're not in the princess selection program anymore?" Fire nods, and she goes on. "I think I know the answer now. You don't stay friends with someone because it 'makes sense' to join forces—you stay friends because you make each other better."

"Yeah." Wyndgonk crosses fire mandibles in a show of affection. "Everybody lets you down, but that's not the whole story. Some people still find a way to make friendship worthwhile. I guess we'll see how good our new friends are, soon enough."

"We certainly will." Elza laughs. "I envy you sometimes. If I had a literal furnace inside me, I'd blowtorch everything, all the time."

"You wouldn't," Wyndgonk says. "You'd get tired, and you wouldn't want to face the consequences. Trust me."

41
.

RACHAEL

. . . 183 Earth days until all the suns go out forever

In third grade, this redhead named Peggy used to throw snowballs with rocks in them at Rachael's head, and luckily she was a terrible thrower. Whenever she got caught, she'd wail *I didn't knowwwww* as if gravel had somehow just snuck inside her pristine snowpack.

Funny the things that come back to you at the weirdest times.

Rachael stands in Forward Ops on the *Unbroken,* with Riohon, Damini, and Zaeta, watching three other ships getting into position to use their ion harnesses to snag a comet called Fej. Depending on whether Rachael looks at the viewport or the holographic scan, Comet Fej looks like a craggy mountaintop coated with snow, or just a big chunk of ice twinkling in the distant sunlight. A long, glittering tail streaks behind.

She has a pad and lightpen in her lap, and she starts sketching the comet in motion, plus the tiny ships flitting around like moths.

Fej spins obnoxiously, and the ships have to bob and weave to stay in position.

"This is going to take a while." Riohon turns to Damini and Zaeta. "So maybe I can help you two with your piloting problems."

The two girls give each other slow sidewise looks. Then they both start talking.

"Damini keeps making rash decisions on her own," Zaeta says.

"Zaeta doesn't trust me even though I would never hurt her," Damini says at the same time.

"Okay." Riohon raises his hand, like *Let me say something.* They quiet down. "So . . . I think a lot of your problem is to do with piloting, specifically. You have to make a thousand decisions in an eyeblink when you're at the controls of a starship, with everyone's lives in the balance. Even if the two of you are mentally and emotionally linked—especially then—you can't possibly agree on all the judgment calls."

On the viewport, Rachael watches one of the other ships toss an ion harness. It bounces off, sending Comet Fej spinning the wrong way.

"So you're saying that piloting a starship is bad for our friendship." Damini looks crestfallen.

"But we love piloting together," Zaeta says. "It's our favorite thing! Confusion."

"And you're both really good at it," Rachael says.

Now the comet is spinning so wildly, another one of the ships frantically scoots out of the way.

"There are obvious advantages to having two pilots who are perfectly in sync," Yatto says. "But not if it comes at a cost to your friendship, or your peace of mind."

"Exactly," Riohon says. "Sometimes I set a course and I get stuck on it, even when everyone is warning me it leads to destruction. Like when I was determined to work with Captain Argentian to save the Royal Fleet instead of focusing on the real problem. I'm saying, the connection between you two isn't just a means to an end, it's something precious that hardly anybody else will ever get to experience. You need to protect it."

"So, what—"

"—do we do?"

Riohon purses his lips. "You said you've tried consulting each other more, but in a crisis, there's no time. I think one of you needs to take the lead at any given moment."

"Sort of like how Yiwei and Rachael are co-captains?" Damini adds.

"Sort of, yeah," Riohon says. "Except maybe you two should take turns being pilot and co-pilot. Neither of you should be in charge more often, or it'll just cause resentment."

"Taking turns calling the shots," Zaeta says. "I like it."

"Me too," Damini says. "Thank you."

Riohon laughs. "It's partly self-interest. We need you two at your best if we're going to make it through this mess." He leans forward and starts the *Unbroken* drifting closer to Comet Fej. "Want to help me snag it?"

Damini and Zaeta clap in unison. "Yes! Yes, please!"

The whole front section of the *Unbroken* is full of people bustling around, making sure the comet heist goes smoothly and nobody else notices Fej changing course with a whole lot of ships hiding in its tail.

Kfok hangs on the back wall of the control deck with her slug-bottom, giving advice to the crewmembers who are wrangling the ion harness. "Not too much torque. You need to graze it gently." The ship's captain, a Yarthin named Bingoul (she/her) whose actual face-moss is going gray, nods and tells her crew to listen to Kfok.

"Hey, you." Kfok sees Rachael walking past with Yatto, and waves. "This is kind of fun. I miss making art, though. That's what we came out here to do, right?"

A guilty longing floods Rachael's brain. She holds up the picture she drew of Comet Fej, and Kfok smiles with both mouths.

"Good likeness. You really captured this comet's obnoxious streak. Little jerk keeps slipping out of our grasp."

Rachael smiles back. "You'll get it."

Then she and Yatto wander down the ramp toward the crew lounge. Everything looks exactly like the *Indomitable,* their old ship, and Rachael almost expects to run into Crewmaster Bul or even Captain Othaar in the hallway.

"I heard they have floatbeast liver in the crew lounge," Yatto says.

"A little taste of home," Rachael says—and then she remembers. Yatto's planet, Irriyaia, is gone. "Oh, oh, I'm sorry. I didn't mean to remind you . . . I never even got a chance to tell you how sorry I was about all of it." Now she's just babbling.

What do you say to someone whose whole world died?

"You risked everything to prevent it," Yatto says as they set off down the hallway. "That means more than a thousand sympathetic words after the fact."

The crew lounge is identical to the room where Damini dared everybody to eat an eggburst that kept getting bigger and smaller. There are three tables, one bigger than the other two, with a bunch of chairs, and cupboards full of all kinds of alien food. Rachael and Yatto have the place to themselves, and Yatto finds some salty-sweet blaycakes for Rachael.

"Wyndgonk said that you and Yiwei are sharing leadership together," Yatto says in between crunchy bites of the floatbeast liver, which looks like green-tinted glass.

"Yeah." Rachael munches her blaycake, which is crumbly on the outside, soft on the inside. "I don't really know how it's going to work. You know how I am."

"I know that you possess many of the important qualities of a successful captain," Yatto says. "You're good at bringing people together, and you are not afraid to tell people when they are doing wrong."

"Yeah, but . . . what if I need to be alone, just when everybody needs me to do captain stuff?"

"Captain Othaar needed alone time sometimes, like when he was doing poetic meditation. But it's true that in a crisis, you may not be able to abandon your duties." Yatto chomps on an emerald shard. "Back on Irriyaia, Mantho the Null was famous for staying silent, and when she did speak, she did not raise her voice—but everyone stopped to listen."

"Mantho the Null . . . she was your spiritual leader?"

"The founder of Irriyaian society. We strayed from her teachings and lost everything." Yatto sighs, suddenly weary—then their eyes focus again, and they smile at Rachael. "Mantho the Null taught that you can be alone even when you're surrounded by people, if you can create a private space within your mind and retreat into it. Rachael, I've seen you sit and make art while everyone else speaks."

"Yeah." Rachael looks at the picture she drew of Comet Fej, leading a few starships on a merry chase. "Maybe there is a way I can be present but also have space."

"If any of us are alive in a while," Yatto says, "we'll all need to find ways to reconnect with ourselves."

As they walk back toward Forward Ops, Rachael finds herself telling Yatto about Yiwei adding weapons to their ship and nearly shooting at her. "It still freaks me out, when I obsess too much about it, but I also understand? Like, Tina and Yiwei keep arguing about violence, and I love both of them, and they're both right, in different ways. It hurts my brain."

Yatto stops walking on the ramp, and Rachael thinks they're about to say something wise and gentle.

Instead, they say, "I can't help thinking that if we'd killed Marrant instead of capturing him, after Antarràn, my world might still be alive."

"Maybe," Rachael says. A chill runs over her, as her mind touches a place she's been trying to avoid. "I killed the leader of the Compassion, Kankakn, when she ended your world. I still see it sometimes, when I'm half-awake. I tore her apart."

"It's difficult to grieve when a friend dies," Yatto says. "But it's even harder to grieve for an enemy you killed. We don't even like to think of it as grief, because that implies you wish they hadn't died. Still, if you must take a life, then it's best to make space to hold a funeral, even if it's only in your own imagination."

"We could be having a lot of daydream funerals soon, depending how things go," Rachael says.

Somebody is in the bluehouse, the little garden space that sits over the ship's control deck. Yatto tenses, like this could be an intruder, then they put their fingers to their lips in a "chef's kiss" sign, and lead Rachael up the ramp in silence.

Kez (he/him) and Ganno the Wurthhi are sitting up there with cups of snah-snah juice, watching Comet Fej get bigger as the Unbroken approaches. You can see all the furrows and crags in the comet's surface now.

"Oh. Are we interrupting?" Yatto asks.

"Nah," Kez says. "We were just sitting here. It's not every day you get to watch someone lasso a comet."

"That's cool," Rachael says. She scoots next to Kez, and Yatto sits down next to Ganno.

One of the other ships has finally gotten an ion harness wrapped around the peak of the comet's mountaintop. The comet sprinkles loose ice shavings into space, where the ion harness digs in—it looks like a hailstorm at night.

"We can do so many incredible things," Ganno says in a soft voice. "It only fuels my rage that we let my world die."

Rachael nods.

"There are no words," Kez says.

Ganno looks at Kez and Yatto on either side of him, and shakes his head under his clasped hands. "I'll keep blaming the two of you until I learn to stop blaming myself."

"I get that," Kez says. "I blame myself plenty. We all made mistakes. But . . . after the childhood I had, I don't handle it well when people put their anger at other people onto me."

"That makes sense." Ganno rubs the spikes on the back of his bald head. "I wish I could be more like you, and stay kind when everyone else is screaming."

"That does not come naturally, trust me," Kez says. "That's part of why I wanted to do the diplomatic training. My first instinct is always to snap back."

"I don't know when I'll be able to let you in," Ganno says. "Maybe never."

"I'll try to be there for you however I can," Kez says. "If you ever need a friend."

A second ship has gotten an ion harness on Comet Fej. More space glitter.

"I really thought I was going to be part of making Irriyaia a better place," Ganno says.

Yatto speaks for the first time in ages. "Ganno, do you remember what you said to me before? When I said that I would only join Riohon's fleet if you convinced me to?"

"No. I don't remember. Did I say something smart?"

Yatto's striped face looks weary but amused, tinted blue by the grow lights. "You told me that nothing is settled as long as we're alive. That our legacy is a fluid thing that always changes. That the proper use for the past is to spur us to do good things in the future."

"I did say those things, didn't I?" Ganno shakes his head ruefully.

"You should definitely take your own advice," Kez says.

The four of them sit and watch as Comet Fej slowly, agonizingly, changes course, spraying ice in all directions as it veers.

42
.

We're riding inside a comet.

It doesn't feel real at all. Rachael is lying in bed with Yiwei back on board the *Undisputed Training Bra Disaster,* and she can hardly tell the ship is gliding alongside a bunch of others, inside a tail of pure ice. The entire rebel fleet has gotten lashed together, in a complicated structure that Rachael doesn't pretend to understand, so they can ride the comet all the way to the debris field. The trip will take a long time, because comets don't actually travel at the speed of light. Who knew?

Every now and then, Rachael sits up and looks out the tiny viewport in her bedroom, and sees countless flecks of ice and snow swirling around outside. And then she lies back down and snuggles up to Yiwei's comforting warmth. She could fall into his eyes forever.

Her arm starts to cramp, so she sits up and digs through a pile of junk at the foot of the bed until she finds a lumpy metal object, covered with fake fur. She digs out Xiaohou, the musical robot that Yiwei brought with him from Earth.

She holds Xiaohou up, watching his legs and tail unfurl as he comes back to life. "You should keep him with you. For luck. And in case you need a heroic soundtrack."

Yiwei shakes his head. "I can't afford to be distracted."

Rachael looks at the wee monkey face: round curious eyes, upturned nose, pointy metal teeth, surrounded by fuzz. Xiaohou looks up at her and burbles, like *Hiiiiii.* "Can I keep him for now?" she asks. "If we get separated for some reason, I want something to remind me of you."

Yiwei shrugs. "Sure."

She tucks the robot into her satchel from the *Indomitable.* She and Yiwei sit on the edge of the bed. She wants to say something about the fact that they're both having daymares about the people they've killed, or that she's starting to feel anxious about the "co-captains" thing.

Before Rachael can say any of that, Yiwei speaks first. "I wish there was time for one last tender conversation, but there's something I need to know. When Nyitha almost ended Marrant, you said she had a way to slow down his death touch."

Rachael shudders all over. "She still died. We barely got away from her in time. Her plan failed. It was no great thing."

"Do you remember how she did it?" Yiwei asks. "I'm sorry, but this could be important. If Marrant manages to lay hands on one of us, that person might have an opening to take him out. He's only vulnerable at close range."

Rachael stares at Yiwei. The intensity in his soft brown eyes looks totally different to her than a moment ago. "Tina wasn't entirely wrong. You're getting seriously hardcore, and I'm starting to worry you'll do anything to win."

"That's not—" Yiwei flinches. "I wouldn't sacrifice anyone to Marrant's touch on purpose. You know that. But he's already taken so many people from us, and I know he'll do it again. At least this way, something good could come out of it."

Rachael turns herself into a tiny ball of arms and legs. "Ugh. I don't even remem . . . Okay, she said that she drank some Undhoran nightweed juice. I think they have plenty of nightweed in the bluehouse on the *Unbroken*."

"And then everyone could be protected."

"It's not protection!" Rachael feels her face burn. "It only prolongs the inevitable. It's even more cruel than the instantaneous version."

"One week from now, I would like to be the most emo person," Yiwei says. "I want to just . . . lie around feeling my feelings. Write some slow songs. But right now, I need to think of anything we can do to improve our terrible odds, so there's even a chance we'll still be alive then."

"Okay." Rachael raises herself off the bed and finds her shoes. "Let's go find some nightweed so we can force-feed the disgusting juice to everybody. This is totally how I wanted to spend our last hours together before we go dancing around the razor tongue of death with the Hosts of Misadventure."

She low-key complains the whole way as they walk through the empty corridors of the *Undisputed Training Bra Disaster* and cross over to the *Unbroken* to search the ship's bluehouse for bitter herbs.

43

.

ELZA

. . . 180 Earth days until all the suns go out forever

They've been at it forever, and nothing works.

Wyndgonk stares at Elza's crown, until her neck is stiff from leaning forward. "The crown looks fine. You're close enough to all these ships, you should be getting as much rancid garbage from the Ardenii as you can handle." Fire reaches out one slender claw and pokes, right where the crown connects to Elza's skull.

"I know. Maybe there's nothing we can do." Elza can't see the bottom of this murky sadness.

"That's certainly what the usurper queen wants you to believe," Wyndgonk says.

She and Wyndgonk are sitting on the big sofa in the flight lounge of the *Undisputed Training Bra Disaster*. The room feels way too empty without Damini and Zaeta piloting, Kfok crawling on the ceiling, and everyone else bustling around. The ship is lashed to the *Unbroken*, being swept along by a comet's wake, so there's no need for anyone in here.

Elza used to say that becoming part of something bigger than yourself means that you need to be smaller. Now she sees the truth: she's only as big as what she can touch.

"We're dancing around the real question," Wyndgonk says. "And you know I don't dance."

"Is dancing just not a thing in your culture?" Elza asks.

"Nope, all of my people dance except for me." Wyndgonk puffs smoke. "The real question is, do the Ardenii want to cut you off? Or is that just what the queen wants?"

Elza has to stop and think about this. She tried her best to turn the Ardenii to her side when she was trapped at the palace, and they helped a little. They definitely tried to keep her safe, right up until when she was cut off. "I don't know if the Ardenii 'want' anything," Elza says. "They're so old, they've seen so much, all of our battles are tiny to them."

"But are they loyal to the queen?" Wyndgonk crosses the tiny pincers in fire mouth. "Or do they just want to share their information with someone, and she's the only one who can receive it?"

"Um, both? And neither."

Elza bites her lip. Trying to comprehend minds as big, as bizarre, as the Ardenii always felt like a good way to give yourself a headache. But because she's Elza, she's kept trying to understand anyway.

She remembers that scary number they kept telling her—the one that kept going up. Now at last, she realizes what it was.

"When the crown was working, the Ardenii used to tell me a big number every once in a while," Elza tells Wyndgonk. "I never understood what it was, but now I think it was the amount of death in the entire galaxy."

Wyndgonk squints all nine eyes. "The . . . amount of death. Like, how many people are dying?"

"Not just people," Elza says. "Plants, animals, microscopic creatures, even sentient clouds of gas. I think the Ardenii are obsessed with death, because they can't die themselves. They have some way of measuring how much death is happening every second, and they've been doing it for a very long time. They don't have any way to measure suffering, so death is the best they can do."

"I can't decide if that's kind or cruel," Wyndgonk says. "Or what the purpose of it is. On Thythuthy, one of my people dies every second, even when we're not in a crisis."

"Yeah. That's the thing. The Ardenii know that death needs to happen, for life to continue. But if they believe in anything, they seem to believe that there shouldn't be more death than necessary." Elza sighs. "Before the crown went dead, the Ardenii told me the death rate was higher than it had ever been. I barely had time to think about it, until now. I think it made them sad."

"That makes me think they don't want you to be cut off," Wyndgonk says. "As far as I can tell, your crown is working perfectly, and I don't think the queen has the power to force the Ardenii to disown you."

That word "disown" hurts someplace deep inside Elza. For a second, she sees her parents throwing a gym bag at her through the front door of their house. And Fernanda screaming at her, on a sweltering hot day. Maybe part of Elza believes she deserved to lose touch with the Ardenii.

She forces herself to think about what Wyndgonk just said. "If the crown is working and the queen can't force the Ardenii to cut me off, then what's going on?"

"That only leaves one part of the system: your brain," Wyndgonk says. "Maybe the queen got your crown to give your brain a jolt, so you disconnected to protect yourself. Or she just convinced you that you'd been cut off. And you believed it."

"She literally got in my head." Elza whistles. "So how do I fix it?"

"My guess? Sleep. If you can dream long enough, your brain will reset. You could also try meditation, maybe using poetry the way the Aribentors do. Whatever you can do to make your brain go quiet for a while."

"Oh sure, I'll just have a nice relaxing time when we're about to fly into a death trap." Elza laughs. She used to feel self-conscious about her laugh, but now she's just glad to have the occasion.

"You'll figure something out," Wyndgonk says.

When Elza and Wyndgonk walk out into the hallway, Rachael and Yiwei are holding out a big tankard full of some thick green soup, with yellow foam on top. Tina, Damini, and Zaeta are gazing at little cups of the stuff, with identical doubtful expressions.

"Come on, drink up." Yiwei holds out cups to Elza and Wyndgonk.

"The stomachache goes away eventually," Rachael promises. "I think."

Tina drinks some, and gags. "It's worse than I expected. So bitter, so slimy. With notes of cigarette ash and old socks."

"Come on," Yiwei urges. "Gānbēi! Drink up!"

"Uh. What is it?" Elza asks.

"It's the stuff Nyitha drank that gave her a little protection from Marrant," Rachael says. "She was able to survive for a day or so after he touched her. I know it's ghoulish."

"It's horrible," Damini says. "Why would we plan for Marrant to touch us?"

"We have to be prepared for the worst," Yiwei says.

"Revulsion!" Zaeta sputters. "Do we even know if this is the right dosage?"

"Nope," Yiwei says. "We're doing our best to prepare for the worst."

Everybody finally drinks some, just to get Yiwei off their backs.

Elza and Tina managed to get a slightly bigger room for the two of them. Instead of bed-webbing, there's a tiny cot, and they sit on the edge, side by side.

Just like Rachael warned, Elza has an epic stomachache now.

"So Wyndgonk thinks you need to turn off your brain and relax to get the crown working again?" Tina says. "Is there anything I can do to help?"

Elza starts undoing the snaps on her jacket. "Yes. Yes, there is."

Soon Tina is breathing on Elza's neck, and her strong callused hands are touching Elza's leg and shoulder, and who knew that someone touching your shoulder could feel so good? Shoulders are an underrated body part.

"Please don't leave me again," Elza says between gasps.

"I won't," Tina says. "I'll never leave you again. I swear. I'm your consort as long as you'll have me."

Then their mouths are too busy to talk, and their bodies are moving together, and Elza can feel Tina's arms and legs all around her, enveloping her with warmth and life.

Elza falls asleep with her body stuck to Tina's with sweat. The two of them breathe together.

The Ardenii jolt Elza awake.

A planet was just destroyed, a newborn child on Undhorah IX started speaking all the adults' worst secrets, a Zyzyian scientist just invented a dreadful new weapon, someone wrote a beautiful song, death is on the rise everywhere.

And there's one more thing.

Elza nudges Tina, who grumbles in her sleep. "Marrant knows we're coming. He's ready for us."

"Well, that's not good." Wyndgonk shivers, opening and closing fire shell. "We need to rethink this whole plan."

"I don't think we can." Yiwei glances at Rachael.

"Yeah. It's too late," Rachael says.

"Marrant's smart," Damini says. "It makes sense he'd see an attack coming."

"That doesn't mean he knows what our plan is," Zaeta says.

"And even if he knows the plan, he still can't track us in that debris field." Tina tries to put some positivity into her voice, but she's slouching and rubbing her chin. "We'll have an even playing field."

The whole crew of the *Undisputed Training Bra Disaster* is sitting around the crew lounge, looking bleary-eyed because they all got woken up with bad news. The comet has almost arrived at the ancient battlefield where everybody is going to hide.

"What exactly did the Ardenii tell you?" Rachael asks Elza.

"Just that Marrant has been preparing, and he knows there's a fleet coming to attack him. If we were hoping to catch him by surprise, we won't."

"We need to tell Riohon and Yatto," Damini says.

"Already doing it," says Kfok from the comms station. "But they're not going to be able to do much either."

"We have to stick to the plan," Rachael says. "It's our best shot."

"Sure," Wyndgonk says. "But we need to hide the hearthlight better. Marrant knows this is our ship, and it's too vulnerable. Riohon and his friends want to take the hearthlight on their flagship, the *Unbroken*. But that ship basically has a big hologram on the side saying 'Attack This Ship First.'"

"You definitely should not let Riohon and his friends have the hearthlight," Tina says. "They think of it as a strategic asset, not a sacred responsibility."

"So we should put it on a ship that Marrant won't notice," Kez says. "One that's easy to defend."

Elza's already closing her eyes and getting help from the Ardenii—thank the orixás she has them back, she missed this feeling. "Hmm. There's a tiny daggership called the *Unpredictable*. Barely larger than a knifeship. It's new, so no radiation leaks that make it easy to notice." She looks at Tina—she doesn't understand for a beat, then she gets it and nods.

"Yeah. We'll go with you on that ship," Tina says. "You need someone to watch your back over there. And where Elza goes, I go."

"You're going to bail on us?" Rachael pouts.

"We'll still be in the neighborhood," Tina promises. "We'll be tossing paper airplanes back and forth the whole time."

"I just don't like this," Damini says. "We do better when we're together."

"I'm sorry," Elza says. "I owe this to Wyndgonk, and fire people."

She looks at Rachael, Yiwei, Kez, Damini, and the others. She could be seeing them for the very last time, and something inside her insists on grieving in advance. *Be grateful instead,* she tells herself. *You had a second chance to be a decent friend, and just look at the people who chose to let you into their lives. Feel lucky, not miserable.* But the sadness rolls over her anyway.

Throw together any random group of people and they'll call themselves "family," until they face a real test. Family is the people you can't walk away from.

"Fake Tina said one good thing: friendship can be just as important as romance," Rachael says to Elza and Tina, red-faced, lip-biting. "The love I have for you two is epic and cheesy and embarassing, and my heart will be straight-up destroyed if you don't come back safe."

Elza reaches out both hands for Rachael to clasp. "I wouldn't even know who I am without you." Then she looks up at Damini, Kez, Yiwei, Zaeta, and Kfok. "Everyone here. Loving all of you only strengthens my love for each of you."

Tina looks at the GALAXY'S MOST WANTED patch on her sleeve. "I can't believe I got to have you all in my life. Fake Tina was right. I want to write terrible poetry about everyone in this room."

"I'm going to be so mad if this is the last time we're all together," Damini says.

"This is how we defy the razor tongue of death, by cherishing each other," Kez says.

Now everybody is huddling together and saying their goodbyes and trading blessings, like they're still in the Royal Fleet. Someone finds a bottle of Yuul sauce and they spike some snah-snah juice with it, and there are toasts and songs.

Elza still can't help pre-grieving. She begs the Ardenii, or the Hosts of Misadventure or whoever, to keep her family safe somehow. The Ardenii show her Marrant's fleet, massing for battle.

44
.

TINA

The *Unpredictable* is even dinkier than I expected. There's just the control deck and Forward Ops, with an engine compartment directly below, and then a small lounge and crew quarters. The maximum crew for a ship this size is about twenty people, but they only have nine, so they gratefully put me to work on tactical as soon as I show up. The captain walks onto the control deck . . . and it's Yatto the Monntha.

"There was nobody else to lead this ship," Yatto says. "And I didn't want to be one of twenty people standing around Forward Ops on the *Unbroken*, getting in each other's way."

I jump out of my teacup chair and salute with two fingers and my thumb, against my collarbone. "Righteous causes and no compromises. Welcome aboard, Acting Captain."

"Lasting friendships and short-lived hostilities." Yatto waves off the formality. "I would rather hug than salute, if that's all right with you."

"It's more than all right." The two of us hug, and then Yatto is hugging Elza, too. They reach out to Wyndgonk, but fire isn't really up for trying to squish fire body against a humanoid's.

Then I'm back at my tactical station, staring into a cloud of potential doom—just like old times.

All of the ships in the fleet stream out of the comet's tail into the ancient battlefield, taking advantage of a solar flare that'll make it hard to see what's going on. The *Undisputed Training Bra Disaster* is hanging back, since it's the most breakable and distinctive of all the ships.

The debris field is easy to mistake for an asteroid belt: just a collection of pointy shapes swirling around. But as we get closer, I can make out sheared pieces of metal with scorch marks from weapons I can't even imagine. My scans bounce off the scrap, and I can't make out the ships that have gone inside ahead of us.

Goose bumps run over my arms and shoulders. I can't help thinking this old war zone is full of ghosts, who are probably pissed off after chilling here for so long. I only hope they leave us alone.

"Let's be careful," Yatto says. "We don't want to collide with any of that debris. We don't know what it's made of."

One piece of good news: Marrant's entire fleet is holding a defensive formation around Larstko IVb, the moon with the wedding chapel on it. It looks like Marrant is still expecting us to attack head-on, instead of sneaking into this junkyard.

"Once we're in place," Yatto says, "our friends lure Marrant's fleet inside and keep them busy, while this ship makes a run for that temple where we can insert the hearthlight."

"Humanoids," Wyndgonk clacks mandibles. "You love your traps and strategies. It's apex-predator thinking."

"As long as it works," Elza says. "We had a really good plan at the palace, too, until Captain Argentian decided to pursue her own agenda."

I only get a little tiny guilt-bloom. It's fine.

"So far so good," I say. "No sign they've spotted us. We're not being scanned."

As we approach the edge of the debris field, my scans lose their cookies. It's just a lot of noise, countless pieces of trash that give me nothing. I can't see the ships that went in ahead of us, and I can barely make out a path forward.

"It's like taking a stroll in a knifestorm," says Junior Explorer Ethka, the Makvarian at the pilot station.

Almost all of our ships are already safely inside the asteroid field, with no Royal Compassion drama yet.

When we put our heads (or other brain-having body parts) together and believe in ourselves, we can accomplish anything. This might just turn out okay after all. The knot of anxiety that's been tightening inside me for ages starts to loosen.

Until I do one of my super-extra-paranoid scans and . . . oh no.

This is not good.

"Bloody hell!" I jerk away from my tactical station as if it stung me. "We need to warn the others. Yatto, you need to break comms silence, use the emergency beacon. All those ships, they need to get out of that asteroid field before—"

Too late. I can see the ships in front of us getting hit all at once.

Yatto shouts about evasive action.

Ethka wrestles with the navigation controls.

I'm frantically trying to use the ship's ion harness to move some of this wreckage into a makeshift barricade to protect our hull. But there's too many of them, and it's too late.

We're not going to be able to outrun this. Our ambush got ambushed, after all.

I should've known never to underestimate Marrant.

45
.

RACHAEL

The *Undisputed Training Bra Disaster* pulls up the rear of a gleaming swarm of daggerships, knifeships, and swordships. All the ships ahead of them are slipping out of the tail of the comet as it continues on its way, and sneaking inside the ancient starship junkyard.

"Steady," Yiwei says in the least steady voice ever. "Keep it steady."

Zaeta and Damini are having fun zipping around these jagged pieces of dead ships. For now, Zaeta is the boss, which means she starts the sentences and Damini finishes them.

Zaeta laughs. "We should turn this into a game! It would—"

"—be a huge hit in Gamertown." Damini laughs, too.

One level down, Kez (*she/her*) is keeping the ship's cobbled-together engines going somehow, while Ganno watches in silence. All of the pacifists (except for Tina) ended up on the *Undisputed Training Bra Disaster*, the least-fightiest ship in this fleet of misfit toys.

Rachael giggles at the phrase "fleet of misfit toys." She almost wants to turn that into a comic. Maybe it'll be the first comic she draws, post-Vayt. *Please let there be time for goofing off when this is all over, please let us all still be here.*

One moment, Rachael is watching half her friends work, and trying not to worry about Tina and Elza, as the debris closes in around them.

Then, everything goes to hell.

"Incursion!" Zaeta yelps.

"Oh no, oh no," Damini says.

Rachael is about to ask what's going on, but then she doesn't need to. The holographic RealTac display is full of them, thousands and thousands.

Immobilizer claws.

The *Indomitable* nearly got hit with them, the first time they faced Marrant. These metal claws, each around the size of a Boston terrier, float around looking for ships to latch on to. If they clamp on your hull, they're nearly impossible to remove. And then they shut everything down: weapons, engines, life support, the whole deal.

Marrant packed this spaceship graveyard with immobilizers.

The ship directly ahead of the *Undisputed Training Bra Disaster* goes dead in space. Just . . . lights out. And as soon as the immobilizer clamps on, it starts sending a signal to Marrant's people, like a big flashing "kick me" sign.

Another ship goes dead. And another.

All the other ships swerve and twirl, trying to stay out of reach of the claws, but Rachael sees them go dead, one by one.

Damini is hyperventilating. "What do we, what do we—"

"We fly." Zaeta grits her needle teeth. "We keep going, as long as we can."

"We can't let any of those claws touch our hull," Yiwei says. "We'd be a sitting target, like all of these other ships."

"That weapon system you attached to the side of the ship," Kfok says. "Give me firing controls. I have better peripheral vision than the rest of you."

Yiwei pokes at a holographic control fluff. "Done."

"Please tell me we're not going to try and shoot down the immobilizer claws," Kez says. "Even by our standards, that's a dreadful plan. They're so tiny you can't even target them until they're almost within clamping range."

"You're just jealous of my superior number of eyes," Kfok snarks.

"We'll have another line of defense." Yiwei is already putting on an atmosphere suit. "I can use an ion harness to keep them from touching our hull."

"If you're going out there—" Zaeta's top layers of eyes frown.

"—we won't be able to maneuver," Damini says.

"Just hold us steady. We should shut down most of our systems anyway, to make a less obvious target." Yiwei makes for the hatch.

Rachael is already there, wearing her own atmosphere suit.

"No way I'm missing out on all the fun." Rachael hopes her voice doesn't betray how scared she is.

Yiwei is about to tell her to stay in the ship—she knows that twitch in his left eye by now—then his face lights up. "It wouldn't be fun if you weren't there."

Ganno the Wurthhi, Kez's ex-boyfriend, has a third suit on. "I'm coming, too."

Rachael has spacewalked a few times. (And she's almost lost count of how many times she's been on board a ship that got blown up.) But she's forgotten how disorienting it is to step out of a ship and emerge into zero gravity, with no up and no down. Her boots clamp onto the patchwork hull of the *Undisputed Training Bra Disaster*, but her inner ear is telling her everything is turvy-topsy.

"We need to space ourselves out along the hull, so we can cover as much territory as possible," Yiwei says. Ganno walks toward the rear of the ship.

She steps over a section of the outside wall of Nyitha's artist salon, painted with some graffiti about not exporting exploitation.

"Here they come." Yiwei's voice comes through a speaker in Rachael's suit.

She can't see anything. Just blackness, with dark shapes swimming in the distance—these must be the long-dead starships.

Ganno the Wurthhi lashes out with his ion harness, and snags an object somewhere overhead. He looks for all the world like a fisherman, trying to reel in a super-vigorous trout. His arms jerk to one side and the other.

Rachael is so busy watching Ganno wrestle with his catch, she doesn't see another claw until it's right on top of her. She doesn't think—she just reaches up and fires her ion harness, and then she's lassoed an immobilizer claw. Thrashing around, snapping its jaws. Her arms are getting pulled out of their sockets.

"I got one! I think. What do I do now?"

"I could—ugh—also use some pointers," Ganno grunts.

"They trained us for this at the academy. Just pull it as close as you can, and then find a little pin right at the hinge of the clamp. And yank it out, without letting go of the claw."

"Oh, sure. No problem at all. Just . . . grab a bitey squirmy little alligator clamp and yank out a tiny rod, why would that be a problem?"

Rachael is most definitely talking to herself—she wishes she could shut down her suit-to-suit so the others didn't have to hear. She tries to drag her captive claw down, but the closer it gets to the ship's hull, the more excited it gets. The claw is squirming and flopping around, and then it wriggles out of her harness altogether.

She watches, frozen, as the metal jaws dive toward the hull of the ship. *Damn it damnit.*

Then she breaks out of her daze, and flings her ion harness just in time to grab the claw when it's just a few inches from the hull. "No, you don't." She seizes it in her hands and yanks the pin out of its side. The claw goes dead.

The hull quakes under Rachael's feet, and she feels it in her neck. The ship's one and only cannon is firing at more claws that are further away. THOOM THOOM THOOM. There's no sound, but it's still the loudest thing ever.

Then everything goes still. The ship's hull isn't vibrating under Rachael's feet anymore, and the lights have all gone quiet.

Rachael is sure one of the claws must have found its target, but then she hears Yiwei sigh with relief.

"We shut everything down," Yiwei says. "Hopefully the claws will think they got us already."

Rachael scans all around her. No more claws anywhere nearby.

"I think we made it," Ganno says. "But let's keep looking just in case."

A while later, Rachael makes her way back to the flight lounge, where Damini and Zaeta are just crouching side by side in the darkness. At least the air and gravity are still working, for now.

"Irony," Zaeta says. "We got rid of the claws—"

"—but we're still stuck with no light anyway," Damini says.

"We're the only ones who managed to go un-clawed," Kfok sighs. "We were lucky that we were bringing up the rear. Every other ship in our rebel fleet got hit immediately."

"Including the *Unpredictable*?" Rachael asks.

"Yeah. Sorry. They're a sitting target, same as the rest of these ships," Kfok says.

Tina. Elza. Hang in there. We'll find a way to help you.

"Uh-oh," Kfok says. "You'd better see this." She has a Quant in one of her stinger-arms, and she's looking at a scan of the debris field nearby.

"What's going on?" Rachael asks.

"It's Marrant's fleet."

Rachael feels sick to her stomach, looking at Kfok's Quant.

It's still hard to see what's going on, thanks to all that magic wreckage, but this is easy enough to make out. Marrant's ships are approaching in a tight formation, like they've just been waiting for their trap to spring.

One of Marrant's ships approaches the *Unbroken,* Riohon's flagship, and docks with it. And then another Royal Compassion ship swoops in on a helpless rebel ship, locking on.

"What are they doing?" Ganno sounds like he's choking.

"Remember how Marrant doesn't know which ship the hearthlight is on?" Kfok says. "His people are going to search every ship. They have enough ships to do this pretty fast."

"And once they're sure a ship doesn't have the hearthlight on board . . ." Yiwei says.

". . . they're going to destroy it." Rachael's stomach clenches with anxiety.

"They can afford to take their time, since nobody can put up a fight," Kfok says. "But this will be over soon either way."

Tina, Elza, Yatto, and Wyndgonk are trapped on a dead ship, about to be under siege. And there's nothing Rachael can do to help them.

Rachael is about to take off her atmosphere suit, but Yiwei contacts her on a private suit-to-suit channel. "Rachael, I have a plan, but I need to run it past you."

"Okay."

"Marrant's people will think our ship is immobilized, just like all the others. So they're going to send a ship for us. And when they do, we can surprise them."

Vertigo nearly knocks Rachael off her feet. "You mean . . . we can attack them."

"They won't be expecting anything. We can shoot them down."

"How . . . how many people . . ." Rachael tries to phrase this question in a different way than *How many people are we going to kill?* "Can we try to disable their ship without killing the whole crew?"

He hangs his head inside his helmet. "We can try, but . . . probably not. We'll have to act fast, and we can't afford to let them return fire. If we can take one of their ships, we can strike back. Maybe help our friends. You're co-captain, so . . . what do you think?"

Somehow an immobilizer managed to clamp itself onto Rachael's body. She can't feel her hands and feet, she can't move, she can't catch a breath. Her head is full of noise, and her vision is swimming.

But she thinks of her friends on the *Unpredictable,* helpless, under siege.

She nods, slowly. "Sounds good. I'm in."

46

.

TINA

I hear Elza yell my name, but I can't get to her. I grope around, but I can't find a handhold.

I think I'm floating close to the ceiling, which is way high up, but my inner ear is as flummoxed as the rest of me. I don't know my way around this ship, even if I could see.

"Sit tight!" I shout. "I'm coming to you."

I don't hear Yatto's voice. I hope they just got knocked unconscious.

I ransack all the knowledge in my head, which mostly came from Captain Argentian, until I come up with something. This type of small daggership has handholds in the ceiling, almost like monkey bars, for if the floor becomes, basically, lava. I manage to push off something and float in the direction that I think is "up." My hand brushes against something, and then I'm holding on to a rung. I manage to find another one with my other hand, so I can swing myself across the control deck.

There ought to be an emergency compartment somewhere . . . got it.

I find a couple of pairs of magnetic boots, an atmosphere suit . . . and a fancy flashlight.

Takes me a moment in the dark while holding on to a ladder, but eventually I put on one pair of the boots, and turn on the light. I catch a glimpse of bodies drifting around me: Elza, Wyndgonk, Ethka, Yatto. I reach down to activate the magnetic clamps on my boots . . .

. . . and that's when something goes THWACK against the wall nearby.

We've been boarded, I think with my heart racing.

Then I realize what made that sound.

"That was debris—maybe old, maybe new," I say as I get my boots working.

I land semi-gracefully on my feet, and then clunk-stomp, clunk-stomp over to Elza, handing her the boots.

"Shouldn't you save these for Yatto?" She looks at the boots I've just placed in her hands.

"Yatto's out cold," I say. "And I need to do a lot of things in a hurry, without leaving your side. Wyndgonk, please hold on tight to the hearth-light. Do not let go, no matter what."

"Sure," Wyndgonk sighs. "I was already doing that anyway. I don't suppose they make boots that would fit my legs?"

"I'll try and find some," I say.

Elza drifts down to her feet next to me. The beam from my flashlight plays over her face, but also her crown is still sputtering with faint golden light. Her lower lip trembles.

All I want to do is hold her and tell her it's going to be okay. No time.

"We still have one advantage: Marrant will have to search every ship, and he might not get to us right away." I hold out my free hand to Elza and she takes it. "Come on."

"Where are we going?"

"I need to go outside the ship and cut off the parts of the hull that have claws on them, so we can get our power back on." Another slab of debris crashes into us like a freight train.

"But if you're out there and the ship gets hit with more junk—" Elza protests.

"I know. No choice. We have to hurry."

That's when it hits me. Kind of like a gross smell, except it's inside my brain.

I suddenly hate Thanz Riohon. Like, a lot. A heartbeat ago, I was hoping that he could figure out a way to get the *Unbroken* clear of the immobilizers and take on Marrant, and now . . . all I can think is that Riohon is a rotten sewage monster.

Riohon must not have drunk the nightweed juice, the way the rest of us did.

Next to me, Elza loses a breath. "Riohon."

"Marrant is on board the *Unbroken*—searching for the hearthlight, in person. We don't have much time. Come on."

I try my best not to think about Riohon anymore, because I have a lot to do.

And I can't afford to be knocked off my game by thinking about how much I loathe him now.

A few other crewmembers have gotten magnetic boots on, and Elza and I pass them in the single hallway. "Check on Yatto," I say, "the acting captain. Last I saw, they seemed unconscious. The pilot, too. I'm going out-side to try and free us from the claws." I can't see well enough with this flashlight to tell if these people are more seasoned than me, but it doesn't matter. They wish me luck and move on.

The boots slow me down, and so does groping my way forward in mostly-darkness. We have no idea what could be floating around here, and I don't want to find out when something whacks me upside the head.

We get to the hatch and I start putting on the atmosphere suit. Feels like a million years since I did this, but it's still second nature.

"I'm going out there with you," Elza says. "Not leaving each other's side, remember?"

I want to argue, because she'd be (a little) safer inside. But I really need her close to me, on what I can already tell is the worst day of my life.

"Let's do it." I find a second atmosphere suit and hand it to her.

The hatch is stuck. I don't want to force it too hard, or it'll never close again.

"Here." Elza reaches into a compartment on the wall. "This ship was refitted at Scoundrel Station, and they always include a secondary release valve."

The hatch swings open, but there's no energy barrier trapping the air inside the ship. We just have to hustle through as quickly as possible and then seal it behind us.

"Thank the Ardenii for me."

Elza shakes her head. "The Ardenii are currently overwhelming me with details about all the people who just died on the *Unbroken*. They need to make themselves useful occasionally."

While we crawl across the hull, I try to distract Elza from the danger and the information overload by chattering about what we're going to do when this is all over. "I really want to visit Makvaria, but only if you come with me. Before, I couldn't face meeting Thaoh's family and all the people who knew her, but maybe I can, now that she chose to turn back into me. But also? I want to go back to Earth, with you on my arm. I want to show you off to everybody."

A piece of wreckage rockets toward us, sharp edges spinning like a throwing star. I manage to snag it with the ion harness on my suit and send it flying into a nearby rock.

I can't see any of the other ships in our fleet now. No idea how long we have before a boarding party shows up.

There are two immobilizers clamped onto our hull, and they're dug in pretty deep. These things are impossible to unclamp, so I don't bother trying. I just start slicing into the hull around the first one, which is right near the bluehouse, with the torch attached to my suit.

"And you know what? I bet Yiwei's new band can play a gig on Earth, once they find a singer to replace Cinnki—that would be the greatest concert in history."

"I don't want to hear about what we're going to do if we survive this," Elza says in a voice I have to strain to hear. "It hurts too much to dream up happy endings, especially while my head is full of the people who won't get to live their lives at all."

"Okay. Tell me about them," I say. "If it'll help. Tell me about the people who just died."

Damn, this hull is tough to cut through. It's almost like they designed it to be resistant to attack. It's taking me forever to get this one section.

"On the *Unbroken*, there was Crewmaster Haargon, she was an Aribentor. She wrote poetry that made people doubt their own skin and the air that they breathed, so she was basically considered a saint on Aribentora. She gave it up to come and fight for us, and they threw her out into space without a suit."

I finally manage to remove the section of hull with the first claw on it, leaving a gaping hole in the side of the ship. No way for the ship's systems to seal the hole until we get power back on, so I have to do a quick-and-dirty repair myself. This is taking too long.

Second claw is all the way on the other side of the ship, and the whole walk across, Elza is telling me little details about people in our fleet that the Royal Compassion just murdered. I start tuning her out—guilt bloom—because I need to focus on the people who are still alive.

Something is coming our way. Could be just another piece of wreckage, but nope.

It's a ship, with Royal Compassion markings, weaving between asteroids and chunks of scrap. I can't tell how soon it'll be here.

"Flaming lakes." The torch is jamming up, and there's still half a deck plate to remove.

"Here, let me help." Elza takes the torch and gets it lit again.

Then the two of us are working frantically. I'm cutting the deck as fast as I can, and Elza is pulling at the deck plate with all of her strength.

The ship is already way bigger than the last time I looked. It'll be here soon, we're a sitting duck.

"Almost got it." Elza braces with one leg and pulls with both hands, and I slice away. The hot flare dazzles my eyes and my hand is getting a cramp. There's still one strut made of dense carbonfast, holding the section of hull in place.

I give up on trying to leave a hole that'll be easy to repair later, and just hack away at the last strut, watching the metal bubble and melt slowly.

That Royal Compassion ship is close enough to see the glow of its engines, like a pair of candles against the night.

The deck plate gives way in Elza's hands and she tosses the second claw off into space.

There's no time to walk all the way around, back to the hatch we came out. I lower myself through the new hole we've made, and feel my boots snap onto the floor. I hold my hands up, and lift Elza down.

We're inside one of the crew quarters, with someone's personal junk floating all around us. I lead Elza out into the corridor and seal the door to the quarters behind us, praying the seal on the door is strong enough to keep the rest of the ship from losing all of its remaining air. Then the two of us are stomping toward the engine compartment. My own breath is deafening inside my helmet.

Before we even make it to the engine section, there's a reassuring whoosh: the life support coming online. And I get a funny sensation in my inner ear as the gravity comes back. I take off my helmet and deactivate the magnetic boots, and Elza does the same.

"That's a good sign," I say. "The systems are restarting automatically, or someone in Engineering is turning things back on."

"So can we make a run for it before that ship gets here?"

I shake my head. "Engines will take longer. So will main power." I gesture around us: the lights are still off, except for a few emergency lights at floor level. "And no tactical scans. Can the Ardenii tell you how soon that ship will be here?"

Elza closes her eyes. "They're in touch with the computers on all the Royal Compassion ships around here, but there's a lot of interference and signal delay, and too many factors to account for. We might have a minicycle, if we're lucky."

Five minutes.

"Situation Yellow Crawl." Yatto's voice comes over my shoulder comms.

"Repeat, Situation Yellow Crawl. Prepare to be boarded. All personnel, secure stations." At least Yatto's okay. For now.

Now that my boots aren't having to clamp onto the floor each time, I can run back toward the control deck. I hear Elza right behind me, her breath coming staccato in the near-darkness.

I turn my head and shoot her a reassuring look. "We'll find a way to—"

Everything goes red. My ears are full of noise.

The next thing I know, I'm on the floor, with Elza next to me. My ears are ringing.

More debris just hit us. More dead ships in our fleet.

I try to get to my feet but I'm still winded. My leg throbs with pain.

"Can you move?" Elza says.

I nod. The pain is fading, thank goodness. I take a breath, then another.

"We need to keep going." I only wheeze a little as I climb to my feet, then help Elza up.

Elza starts to follow me, then stops. She recoils as if someone just slapped her.

"Too late," she chokes out. "We're being boarded. We need to find Wyndgonk and the hearthlight, and get to safety."

A loud clang reverberates, followed by a hiss. Someone just opened the main hatch in our cargo hangar. Footsteps ring out, followed by a way-too-familiar oily voice. "Your ship is dead, and so are you. Let's not make this more time-consuming than it needs to be."

Marrant. He's here.

And we're trapped inside a tiny ship with him.

47

.

RACHAEL

How long have they been sitting there, feeling the air get colder and crappier?

They're on "minimal life support," which means they won't actually choke or freeze to death, but they might get pretty close. Yiwei has taken back firing controls on the big cannon, and Kez is waiting with one hand on the switch that will restore main power. Nobody can relax, because when whatever is going to happen finally happens, they'll have to move quickly.

Rachael wonders if she should have said no to Yiwei's plan, but she can't think of anything else they could have done. Maybe Tina or Elza would have had some other idea, but they're not here. Rachael keeps coming back to: *This isn't a battle, it's a massacre. We have to be willing to fight bloody.* The more she thinks about it, the more she's sure they're doing the right thing.

But maybe that just means that she's decided to be okay with taking the easy way.

"I have a practical question," Kfok whispers. "No power means no tactical scans. How will we even know when a Royal Compassion ship shows up to board us?"

"We'll know when they start trying to get inside our ship." Yiwei makes that sound like a totally reasonable thing. "That's why the hull sensors are still active, just on low power. With our power off, they'll have to cut their way inside. We'll have to move fast."

A loud thud echoes through the hallway outside the flight lounge. Rachael is sure this is the Royal Compassion coming to board them, but then she realizes: this is just debris from another rebel ship that got blown up.

Rachael can't think about Riohon without feeling a wave of hatred, and the worst part is that she isn't sure when this started. As far as her brain is concerned, she's always loathed Riohon, from the first time they met. She's pretty sure this means Riohon just died, but she can't make herself feel bad about it.

"So we're really going to shoot them down," Kez says in a whisper. "The Royal Compassion ship, I mean. We're going to blow them up."

"I meant it when I told Tina violence was a last resort, but here we are," Yiwei says.

Rachael is about to chime in and say that she agreed to this decision, as co-captain. But Yiwei shushes everyone.

There are some noises on the ceiling. Not the thunk thunk thunk of debris impacts, but more like a low clanging. Someone is climbing around on their hull.

The hull sensor shows three people, and they're bringing cutting tools.

Yiwei hits a switch, and all their power comes back on. The light is overwhelming after so long in the dark, and the whoosh of air sounds way too loud. Yiwei is already aiming the ship's one and only cannon at the Royal Compassion ship parked a short distance away: a spikeship called the *Friendly Advice*.

"Now who's a sitting target?" Yiwei fires a long burst, slashing through the *Friendly Advice*'s control deck, engine compartment, weapons, and cargo hangar in one long, jagged cut. At this range, the ship's countermeasures are useless, and nobody even has a chance to react to the supposedly dead *Undisputed Training Bra Disaster* coming back to life.

The three people on the ship's hull were close enough to the cannon to catch some radiation when it suddenly fired, but two of them are still running around. Rachael can hear their footsteps and see them on the hull sensors, like ants whose nest got disturbed.

"We need to shake them off," Yiwei says.

Damini and Zaeta give each other a look. "You mean kill them," they say in unison.

"They're wearing atmosphere suits," Yiwei says. "They have a chance. They'll kill us if they get any opportunity."

Tiny shapes float up through the zigzag cut in the hull of the *Friendly Advice*: dead bodies.

We could be having a lot of daydream funerals.

Damini is still hesitating. "I . . ."

"Yiwei's right," Zaeta says. "And these people would wipe out my whole world if they had the chance."

Damini has tears in her eyes, looking at Zaeta. "It's your call."

The two people on the hull have found another spot and they're moving their cutting tool into position.

"This ship is barely holding together as it is," Kfok says. "And I enjoy having air."

Zaeta is already firing up the ship's engines, putting the *Undisputed Training Bra Disaster* into a parabolic spin. Damini follows her lead.

The two surviving Royal Compassion attackers are trying to hold on. Their boots stay clamped to the hull while the rest of their bodies whip back and forth.

Damini and Zaeta twist the ship back in the opposite direction, and the two bodies are flung off into space, clutching at nothing. Yiwei is already shutting everything down again, so more claws don't come for them.

"So we took out one of their ships. Now what?" Damini is still shuddering.

"Are we just going to collect trophies?" Kfok adds.

"I don't know." Yiwei folds his arms. "There has to be a way we could use their ship to help our friends. Like if we could capture it."

"We disabled their everything," Kez says. "That ship will never go anywhere again. But . . . wait a moment. I have an idea."

Everyone stares at Kez. She starts to talk again, then just flutters her hands.

"Okay," Kez says at last. "If I share my idea, then I'll be complicit in the deaths we just inflicted. But . . . I suppose I'm already complicit, because I helped. And life is messy. So . . . there has to be some reason the immobilizer claws don't attack the Royal Compassion ships."

"We know the claws aren't networked," Yiwei says. "They all move on their own."

"Right," Kez says. "But what if the Royal Compassion ships have a beacon, or a transponder, on board, and this tells the claws to leave them alone?"

Yiwei gasps, actually gasps. "A device that identifies them as a friendly ship."

"Right. If we can find it, maybe we can clone it. Use it to give protection to any other ships that haven't already gotten destroyed. Of course, I have no idea what it'll look like, or whether we left it intact just now."

"But it's worth looking for." Yiwei is already putting on an atmosphere suit. "Who's with me?"

Kez reaches for another suit. "Since this was my idea, I'd better go along. I have some notion what to look for, at least."

"I'll keep you company," says Ganno the Wurthhi. "You shouldn't have to face this alone."

Kez stares at Ganno, like: *Make up your mind. Do you like me or not?*

"I'll come too," Rachael says. "The more eyes, the better."

"Great," Yiwei says. "Let's go."

Outside the ship, Rachael tries not to look at the scorch mark—where their cannon fired and burned one of the members of their boarding party to death in the process.

This spacewalk is just as barfy as the last one. Yiwei activates the impeller on his suit, and he's flying "up" in a big arc, heading toward the *Friendly Advice*. Kez and Ganno follow suit.

Rachael is convinced that she's going to steer wrong and end up flying a hundred miles in the wrong direction. Already Kez and Ganno are shrinking away, and she can barely see them.

Her suit pops up with a holographic message: "Follow same trajectory as other suits?" Rachael isn't even sure how to respond, so she just says, "Umm, yes please," out loud. And then she's soaring through the void, arms and legs touching nothing at all.

The next half hour or so of Rachael's life is a big blur, even while she's living through it. Some of the dead bodies in the *Friendly Advice* did not get sucked out through the hole Yiwei made, and they're still bobbing around. They're icy, wraithlike, pale in the light of her suit's glorified flashlight—trapped in the moment when they realized they were the prey instead of the hunters. There's a Makvarian who looks a lot like that trash fire Riohon, and a couple of Irriyaians who appear to be Monnthas, going by the color of the stripes.

It's even harder to grieve for an enemy you killed.

"I'm sorry you have to see this," Yiwei says over suit-to-suit to Rachael. "I'm . . . I'm not handling it well either. It's one thing to shoot at people from a distance, but . . ."

"We did the only thing we could," Rachael says. "We ought to be able to face the consequences."

She tries to pay attention to the walls and the control stations. All of the holographic displays are dead, so everything looks the same to her.

"We're looking for something that was added recently," says Kez. "They would have had to program all of the transponders to have the same codes, or the same frequencies, and install them at the same time."

Ganno is combing the engine compartment, while Rachael, Kez, and Yiwei search the control deck and Forward Ops. The captain of the ship is still strapped into his chair—a Ghulg, with yellow-red hair and unusually large tusks—and he looks like he just got the worst news of his entire life.

"I think I found it." Yiwei points at a pale green object in the middle of the tactical station, right where Tina used to sit on the *Indomitable*. Sort of egg-shaped, with spiral lines swirling along its sides and a pulsing red light on the bottom. "Seems like it has its own power source."

Kez takes the tiny egg from Yiwei and examines it. "The frequencies probably change pretty often. But we should be able to copy it, with a little work."

"Thank you. Truly, thank you. I know you don't like what we did here, but you may have just helped to save a lot of lives," Yiwei says. "Come on, we'd better go. We don't want to be here when Marrant's thugs show up to investigate."

Kez is already rushing down to get Ganno. Yiwei releases his boots from the floor and floats up to the hole they came in through. Rachael tries not to take one last gander at the frozen corpses with the identical "oh shit" expressions, but of course she gets a good eyeful anyway. Oh god, she's going to barf inside her helmet. She gags, eyes and mouth closed tight, hyperventilating through her nose.

Then she follows Yiwei back out into space.

48

.

TINA

My tactical brain goes into overdrive, the ghost of Thaoh Argentian doing the math. Marrant's ship is parked a ways off, which makes sense.
You don't want to put your best ship at risk, if the ship you're boarding
explodes or something. He most likely arrived by funnel, bringing half a
dozen mercy-killers with him, but they're liable to be his elite squad. His
main objective will be the hearthlight, but if he finds out about Elza and
me, we might become secondary objectives.

Close quarters. No place to run, but lots of places to hide.

I show Elza a cocky grin. "Marrant's trying to scare us. That's good
news. It means he doesn't think he has the advantage."

"Or he's a sadist who enjoys making people squirm."

"Or that. Come on. We need to find Wyndgonk and Yatto. Also, I'd like
to make a pit stop at the armory. Marrant's not the only one who can set
traps."

Rachael kept trying to tell me that there was a lot of Thaoh Argentian in
me, and not just because we're genetically the same. Like, I needed to stop
defining myself as not-her, because that wasn't working for me. So okay.
I put on the swagger and pretend I'm not peeing-myself scared, and creep
down the hallway.

I put my helmet back on, because I need the enhanced vision in this
darkness, even with my Makvarian eyes. Elza does the same.

As scary as Marrant's voice was, the quiet is worse—this ship should
be humming and burbling, with the engines and a dozen other systems
grinding along. I can hear my own breathing, as if I were still in space.

We only get a little ways down the hallway before a scream shatters the
silence, high-pitched and twisted with fear. And then the scream dies out,
as suddenly as it started.

"This is tiresome," Marrant says. "You weak fools are making this more
painful than it needs to be."

We're almost at the armory. I don't like messing with weapons, but we can use them to confuse and disorient, without killing anyone.

A large person in red-slashed black armor steps around the corner: a Scanthian, bristles standing out sharp inside their helmet. They see us and aim a fireburst gun.

Elza and I lock eyes, and then we're both running toward the Scanthian. I manage to get into my inward-rush stance without slowing my run, and Elza also stiffens her arms into knife shapes.

A roar of hot gas. The air goes furnace-hot all at once as the Scanthian fires their gun.

I duck just in time, and Elza just swerves past the fireball as if it was a minor obstacle. I love her so much right now: the determination in her eyes, the half smile on her lips as she dances around the naked flame.

I already know at a glance all the weak points on this mercy-killer's armor (*thanks, brain!*) and I come up swinging at them, using all the nahrax moves I've been practicing. Left leg, right leg, access port on left side of torso. The Scanthian does a drunken shimmy and lurches forward—right into Elza's fist, which strikes their vulnerable neck.

We step over the Scanthian's body, barely pausing to yank the power core out of their gun. Could come in handy.

Three more mercy-killers come from behind us, yelling and shooting balls of flame. Everything goes hot and loud and we're both running for our lives.

A short time later, Elza and I are crouching inside a locker in one of the crew quarters, as the mercy-killers stomp around the hallway outside. Everything sounds way too loud, including my own heartbeat.

We might only be a dozen yards away from Yatto and Wyndgonk, if they're still alive. We can't cross that distance.

Every time one of us starts to make a move to get out of this locker, more footsteps and voices go past. The two of us took down one mercy-killer, but we can't fight three or four of them in an enclosed space. At least our suits are masking our body heat and other vital signs.

Another agonized scream. Another abrupt end.

Marrant's voice rings out. "Stop making me work so hard. I know that your fleet must have the missing piece that will allow me to control the

Bereavement. Why else would you send all these ships to try to retake that shrine to doomed romance? Give me what I need. This can all be over."

I try to tune out Marrant's garbage. Except . . . something in what he just said bugs me.

Control.

He doesn't want to shut down the Bereavement—he wants to master it. Use it as a weapon, against anyone who gets in his way. He could choose which suns live, and which die.

Even in the darkness of this locker, I can see the reaction on Elza's face. She caught it too.

This nightmare just got nightier and more marey.

"Your pride will cause so much needless suffering," Marrant says. "You can't stand knowing that I will be the one to save us all. You'd rather see everybody die than let me be the hero for once."

We can't cower here any longer. Elza and I nod at each other and then I push the locker door open. I drop onto the floor as softly as I can in my heavy suit, and help Elza down.

Okay, *think.* Marrant doesn't know what the hearthlight looks like. He just knows there's something missing, and he might have guessed it's organic. We could trick him.

"Give me the missing piece and I might spare your home sun," Marrant snarls.

Now we're back in a dark corridor. The lights at our feet are flickering. Noises echo all around us.

Basically, full-on horror movie.

At least we're not going down into the dark basement—we're going into the cramped, spooky attic instead. Way better.

Our oversized shadows twitch on the ceiling in the weak beams from the floor lights. Everything is too quiet and echoey. I feel the cold seeping in through my suit. Every thud and creak is a team of mercy-killers coming to end Elza and me.

Just as I think that, two mercy-killers in atmosphere suits come charging around the corner. Elza and I barely duck inside an empty computer-control room in time to watch them stomp past the doorway, brandishing their fireburst weapons.

There's someone in this room with us. A Makvarian, wearing a scowl.

Takes me a minute to recognize Junior Explorer Ethka (*she/her*), part of the crew in Forward Ops, with a burn covering her whole torso. She lies on top of a rack of equipment, where they threw her body after they killed her.

I never got to know her, and now I never will.

The ramp to the bluehouse is right next to the entrance to the control deck, same as it was on the *Indomitable*. I almost try to peek inside the control deck, but that's where Marrant's voice is coming from. Dude should start his own podcast, or a Twitch stream. Then he can listen to the sound of his own voice for as long as he wants.

At the top of the ramp, I start frantically rummaging through all the vegetation and fungi growing up here. The bluehouse isn't even blue for once, because the grow lights are off.

"What are we looking for?" Elza whispers.

"I don't know. Something we can convince Marrant is the hearthlight. We just need something the right size and shape. Marrant was never interested in learning more about cultures like Wyndgonk's, so he won't have a clue what to look for."

Maybe it's good news that we haven't seen Yatto or Wyndgonk. Maybe they found a way to get the hearthlight off the ship, and we can buy them some time.

Someone is coming up the ramp. Heavy tread.

Elza shows me a few random roots and growths that are kind of the right size and shape. Too big, too obviously a Ruglian squash, too crumbly . . . I point to a dirt-encrusted lump of fungus that even I can't identify. "That one," I whisper.

An Irriyaian, a bit taller than Yatto, comes up the ramp, weapon raised. I'm already flinging clods of muddy soil onto the faceplate of their suit. The Irriyaian staggers forward, right into the power core we took from the other mercy-killer's gun, which explodes in a tiny burst of sparks and smoke.

The two of us sprint down the ramp, and then down the corridor away from the control deck. We hear footsteps behind us, and one fireball erupts over our heads.

"Don't shoot," Marrant barks. "I think they have what we're looking for."

Nowhere left to run.

I can feel the ship's systems finally powering up around us. The floor vibrates a little harder as the engines restart, and holographic screens flicker into life. The lights overhead are coming back on. Too late.

We reach the cargo hangar at the bottom of the ship.

"Maybe we could launch an orbital funnel," Elza says.

"If we can figure out a safe destination," I say. "Those things don't even work without an endpoint. If any of the ships in our fleet is still in one piece—"

Elza's not next to me anymore.

The Irriyaian we knocked down is holding her by the throat.

Marrant enters, smiling with his mouth and glaring with his eyes. My stomach curdles and my skin goes icy cold. I thought I was ready to face him again.

He sees me, and the rage in his eyes burns hotter. "You," he says. "*Again.*" He towered over me the last time we met, but now we're the same height.

He probably thinks I'm still Thaoh. Maybe I can use this, pretend to be her one last time? Or is it better if he knows I'm me again? I can't decide.

Might as well tell the truth. "I'm not her. I'm—"

"I. Don't. Care." Marrant's voice is suddenly so loud and fierce, the whole cargo hangar rings. "Makes no matter which one you are. You're dead either way. Where is my wife?"

"Your *ex*-wife didn't make it," Elza says, choking a little. "She died."

Marrant screws his eyes almost shut. A sound between huffing and gagging comes out of his mouth and he balls his fists. "She's really gone. All this time, we could have been . . ."

Then he shakes his head, focuses. "No matter. Saved me the trouble of finishing her myself. And now it's your turn."

I hold up the lump of dirty fungus from the bluehouse. "We have what you want. Let us go, and you can have it. If you hurt Elza, I'm destroying it."

Marrant laughs. "If you really had the missing piece, you wouldn't be using it to bargain. You wouldn't hand me power over trillions of lives in exchange for one person. Even a princess."

"You don't know that." I suddenly have tears in my eyes, looking past him, at Elza. "I'm her consort. I would trade all the stars in the universe for her happiness. It wouldn't even be a hard decision."

I look into Elza's eyes and try to send her all my strength and faith in her—and most of all, love.

Who I belong to is at least as important as who I want to be.

Marrant seems to consider. "Give me the missing piece. I'll let you two escape from here. What happens after that is outside the scope of our agreement."

I hold out the fungus crumble to the nearest mercy-killer, a Makvarian. "Let her go and it's yours."

Marrant nods, and the Irriyaian releases their hold on Elza's throat. She stumbles forward, choking. I hand the chunk of mushroom to the Makvarian, who takes it.

"This was too easy." Marrant nods again, and the Irriyaian lunges and grabs Elza again. "I don't trust it. Any more than you should have trusted me." He turns to the Makvarian. "Remove the clone's helmet and throw her into space."

"We made a deal! We made a deal, you—" I just stand there as my helmet is peeled away.

I want to fight back, but the Irriyaian has a gun to Elza's head.

Think. Come on, think.

There has to be a way out of this.

"You can't do this!" I scream, my hair wet in my face, my limbs thrashing in the Makvarian's grip.

"Lately, I've realized that not everybody needs to die by my touch," Marrant says in a conversational tone as the Makvarian shoves me toward the open hatch. "Sometimes the cruelest fate is to allow someone to be mourned. So that everyone else may appreciate the full scope of their failure."

Just as the Makvarian pushes me out into open space, I see Marrant lean over and kiss Elza's hand. "And then there are those who must be despised by the few who even remember them."

The last thing I see is Elza staring at me, helpless, as she starts to melt away.

49

·

I'm alone, with nothing but stars and wreckage on all sides of me, except for the closed hatch of the ship. I float there, frozen from the inside out, my whole body shaking as I replay the sight of Marrant kissing Elza's hand. The mocking leer on his face.

Then it hits me: I still love Elza.

I still remember her smile, the poetry in her footsteps, the music of her voice. The way she smells like lilacs in the springtime.

Elza drank the nightweed juice, same as me. Same as Nyitha. She has a day left, maybe, before she's gone for good.

We can still find a way to save each other.

Also, I'm floating in space without a helmet, but I'm not freezing to death or suffocating. Yet. The ship's main power grid came back on, so it generated a tiny bubble of air around me, which will last . . . oh, about two minutes, give or take. I've already wasted ten or fifteen seconds trapped in the horror of what was meant to be my last moment alive.

I take off running across the hull of the starship, my boots clanking with each step. We left a gaping hole in the side of the ship where we cut away the second immobilizer claw. I might be able to reach it before my air gives out. Maybe. Too bad it's all the way over on the other side.

This ship is way bigger than I remember. I make it past where we removed the first claw and plugged the hole we made. I start to choke and gasp. Air giving out already.

I run faster. Breathing my own CO_2 now. There's no more air in this bubble.

Dots in front of my face, buzzing in my ears. I keep running.

I can see the hole we made, half a basketball court away. I sway and wobble.

I can make it.

I have to make it.

I start to pass out. Drunken head, weak limbs. Pins and needles.

I take another step, then another. And then I fall forward. Too far. Too hard. My boots stay clamped onto the hull and I can't lift them.

Someone catches me.

Yatto the Monntha snaps another helmet onto the spot where mine was supposed to be.

"You appeared as though you needed some assistance," they say, linking their suit to mine so we can communicate securely.

They point to a nook on the side of the ship, where Wyndgonk and a young Irriyaian whose name I don't know are hiding, wearing atmosphere suits. I'm glad Wyndgonk found a suit fire could wear.

"Listen, Marrant told me that he doesn't just want to stop the Bereavement. He thinks he can control it. Like, he could choose which suns live, and which die. We can't let him have that power."

"All the more reason to get the hearthlight away from here." Yatto's spikes stiffen. "We scavenged some personal impellers, with just enough fuel to reach another ship."

I nod. "You should go without me. They caught Elza. Marrant just touched her."

Yatto shakes their head, while handing me an impeller. "I'm sorry. Elza was one of the most brilliant and generous people I have ever known. I will hold her in my—"

"She's not dead. Not yet. She drank the nightweed juice. But she doesn't have long."

"All the more reason to get away from here, as far as you can. Maybe you'll be able to remember her as she was."

I'm seeing a haze again, but this time it's bright red.

"Stop using the past tense! She's not gone, she's here, and I'm going to save her."

Yatto sounds disappointed. "The lives of trillions of people are—"

"I can't think about anyone else right now. I can't lose her. I can't. I've tried so hard to be unselfish, for so long, and I'm done. I'm done. If all the worlds are dying, I'm going to save the love of my life." I take a deep breath. "Take the hearthlight. Keep it safe. If anyone else survived, tell them I'm not coming back, not without Elza. If you see Rachael, tell her I love her and I'm trying to save our family."

Yatto wants to argue some more, but I'm already walking away from them.

Wyndgonk reaches out and touches my leg. "I only heard some of that," fire says. "But I'm telling you. Save her. If Elza dies, I'm going to fry your face."

I nod. And walk to the hole that Elza and I cut, feels like a hundred years ago.

50

.

ELZA

Marrant drags Elza by the arm and yells at her: spittle-faced, red-eyed. "How are you still alive? I gave you my merciful touch—" he shrieks, his fingers digging into her skin.

Elza can't stay on her feet as he pulls her down the hallway that she and Tina were sneaking down a short while ago.

Tina is gone, thrown out into space without a helmet.

Elza is falling apart at the molecular level, her body unraveling. She'll end the same way as all of Marrant's other victims: a foul puddle. It'll just take a little longer in her case.

The Ardenii are still flooding her head with information. A city of seven million people on one of the Makvarian worlds was just destroyed. A species of mud slugs on Anhyk that everyone thought were extinct just showed up again.

But also, the Ardenii feed Elza every little detail about her unraveling body, without any pity or sugarcoating. She knows in detail exactly how much she's already fallen apart, and how long she has left: about twenty hours, Earth time.

Marrant screams at her. "Answer me! I can still make your death whatever I choose, I still have the power to erase you. Answer me!"

Elza turns and looks at Marrant. "What was the question again?"

"How are you still here? How did Aym survive my touch? What did you do to me?"

They've reached the tiny crew lounge, with just one table and a few teacup chairs. Elza wriggles out of Marrant's grasp and settles into a chair.

"I don't know anyone named Aym," Elza says. "Nobody did anything to you." Marrant is about to start screaming again, so she adds: "*Nyitha* found a way to slow down the effects of touching your skin, so she could survive long enough to end you. If only she had not failed."

Marrant's coal-black eyes grow wider and his voice more shrill. Elza can't take in what he's screaming, if there are even words, because the Ardenii are telling her that the entire population of Uarlis Prime is facing critical starvation.

Not now, Elza pleads with the dark angels in her head. *I need to focus.*

"Listen to me," Elza says to Marrant. "We already tried this once, at Antarràn. You decided you could control an ancient weapon from a war that nobody remembers, and a lot of people died. Now you're going to do the exact same thing with the Bereavement."

"This time will be different." Marrant stands over her, pouring his hot breath on her neck. "Now I have the whole Firmament working for me. Teams of scientists and experts have been studying that ancient temple on Larstko IVb, deciphering all that remains. Remember that when Irriyaia's sun went dead—"

"When you killed it," Elza corrects him.

Marrant moves swiftly and a loud crack rings out. Elza braces herself for pain, then realizes: he slammed his hand into the table, hard enough to leave a mark on the carbonfast surface.

"When Irriyaia's sun was consumed in a tragic accident," Marrant continues, "the Bereavement sped up everywhere else. Which means it has some central control. We believe we can instruct some parts of the swarm to go offline, while letting others continue."

Marrant stands up and fetches something from one of the lockers overhead: a thin tube. Something explodes in front of Elza and she flinches again, but it's just a Cydoghian eggburst, growing and shrinking over and over. "We'll have an opportunity to erase everyone who is a drain on our resources, all the vile creatures that pollute our galaxy. And then we can rebuild."

"Don't do this," Elza pleads. "You can build your regime in other ways. You have the queen on your side. You have the Royal Compassion. You don't need to commit genocide a thousand times over."

"I don't, it's true." Marrant takes a bite out of the eggburst, letting the juice dribble down his face. "But I choose to. I came back from the dead to bring peace and decency to everyone. I am the face of the new justice."

The Ardenii choose this moment to give Elza an update: her cellular degeneration is speeding up. They advise her to avoid exertion or anger, anything that would raise her heart rate. They tell her this while she looks at the juice-spattered doll face of a man who boasts about his holy mission to cleanse the galaxy.

Marrant sits there, chatting with Elza and munching on his eggburst, while his people search the *Unpredictable* for the hearthlight.

"These are an acquired taste. Aym never liked them." Marrant gestures at the eggburst as it grows to full size again. "All this time, we could have had a second chance."

"People," Elza says into her hands, "have given you too many second chances already."

"Nobody has ever given me a single chance. Not one time. Everything I've gotten, I've had to take for myself."

Elza uncovers her face and looks past Marrant—and sees Tina.

Alive.

I'll never leave you again. I'm your consort as long as you'll have me.

Tina stands in the doorway, wearing an atmosphere suit and holding a helmet in one hand, her face missing one cheek-jewel. She does a chef's-kiss motion against her lips, meaning: *Don't tell.*

Elza nods slightly.

"Isn't the queen going to be angry with you?" Elza says. "If I melt, this crown will be ruined. It's irreplaceable, and near-impossible to remove without my consent."

Tina gropes in the belt on her atmosphere suit and finds something chunky and dark blue: the cutting tool she and Elza were using to remove the immobilizer claws from the hull. She hefts it in one hand, like a club.

"The queen will understand." Marrant bares teeth. "My goals are her goals. My triumph, her triumph. I'll need her more than ever soon, because this is a big galaxy and I wouldn't have the faintest idea how to govern it without the Ardenii." He takes a dainty bite of eggburst, right when it's big again. "I must say, I'm looking forward to observing your death. I've never been able to watch my touch take effect in slow motion."

Tina creeps closer, hefting her blunt instrument. Elza bites her tongue to keep from blurting out, *Stay away, don't let him touch you, too.*

"I feel quite sorry for you," Marrant says to Elza between bites of egg-burst. "The first lesser humanoid to become a princess, and you'll be re-membered as a cautionary tale. You won the crown, but you never managed to make it yours."

The Ardenii tell Elza something she can't understand at first: one of Marrant's ships has been destroyed. (Also, a civilization of space-worms who eat dark matter just invented a new religion.)

She forces herself to pay attention to this grinning mannequin-faced monster, who is trying to wreck her self-esteem in the little time she has left. Tina is still creeping forward, so she needs to keep him talking.

Elza says the only thing she can think of: "You worry too much about what other people think of you."

Marrant stops chewing, his face goes pale.

"That's what Kankakn told you, the last time you saw her," Elza says, looking him in his wide, dark eyes. "Kankakn was your spiritual teacher, right? She saw right through you. You think the worst thing you can say to me is that I'll be remembered as a failure, because that's your worst fear. And you know what? It's true. You will be remembered as a failure."

"You don't know what you're talking about." Marrant looks like a ghost just touched the back of his neck.

Tina is almost close enough to take a swing. Elza still wants to warn her away.

Marrant sees Elza looking over his shoulder, and spins to face Tina. "You. Again."

Elza kicks the chair out from under him, and shoves Tina out of his reach. Marrant lands on the floor in a puddle of eggburst juice, struggling to get up.

Tina is still stumbling backward. All Elza can think about is stopping him from touching her.

Marrant is getting to his feet, and Elza flips over the table he was just sitting at. It lands on top of him.

"Go," Elza hisses at Tina. "We have to go. Now."

The two of them run, back toward the crew quarters with the hole in the ceiling.

"How did you—" Elza blurts.

"No time," Tina says. "Yatto and Wyndgonk got away. I stayed behind to rescue you."

"But I'm . . ."

"Escape first. Talk later." Tina digs in a locker and grabs another helmet for the atmosphere suit Elza's still wearing. Elza finds a cloudstrike gun.

A cacophony of boots and voices comes from right behind them.

Without slowing down, Elza shoots her gun at the gravitators in that section of hallway. There's a satisfying *bvarrp* sound as they smoke and sputter, creating a pocket of zero gravity right behind Elza and Tina.

They make it back to the crew quarters with the jagged hole they cut in the ceiling.

There's someone waiting inside.

The Irriyaian who had Elza by the throat earlier blocks their exit, wearing an atmosphere suit. They smile. "Figured this is where you would be heading."

Elza's gun is aimed right in front of her. The Irriyaian's gun is aimed at the floor. She levels it and tightens her finger on the trigger.

"I heard they give you princesses weapons training," the Irriyaian says. "But I'm guessing you've never killed before. Is that really what you want your last act to be?"

Elza tenses her whole body, ready to fire. Then she stops.

The Ardenii flood her brain with information.

"You're Smaa the Nahhi (*she/her*), right? Your sister Novhi is dying. The marshfly sickness came back. She probably has a few metacycles left, and she's still on the refugee citystar. If you leave now, you could say goodbye."

Elza snaps her helmet on, holding Smaa at gunpoint. Tina takes her free hand and helps her to climb outside the ship. Smaa just watches the two of them go, her eyes hooded, downcast.

As soon as they're outside, Tina grabs Elza's waist and fires up the impeller, maximum power. The *Unpredictable* shrinks: just one more dead ship in a crowd of dead ships.

51
.

YATTO THE MONNTHA

Mantho the Null used to say that you are always trying to be two different people at any given time. There's the person you aspire to be, and then there's the person everyone else needs you to be. You never get to choose one or the other, you always have to be a little of both—and the balance depends on how strong your dreams are, and the strength of other people's claim on you.

Yatto the Monntha gave up their own name and tried to turn their back on everything they'd ever done, but other people weren't done with them. So they pushed their feelings down and went back to a world of starships and battles.

Now they're soaking in a mixture of exhaustion, despair, and fury at Marrant—and Tina, who put her personal desires ahead of everybody else.

Yatto is standing on the hull of another ship from their fleet, an old Royal shortsword called the *Impeccable*. They're frantically hacking away at one of a dozen immobilizer claws that have their little metal jaws into the hull, using only the tools in their suit. Nearby, Wyndgonk and the young Irriyaian, Chanka the Anhth (*he/him*), are doing the same thing. The three of them don't have enough air in their suits to make it to another ship, so they need to get this one working at all costs.

"A shortsword takes a minimum crew of fifty or sixty, probably more," says Chanka the Anhth. "Where in the Rain's name are they?"

"Dead," Yatto says without looking away from their work. "They suffered a hull breach right after the claws came, and the ship's systems couldn't compensate. They must have died instantly."

"That's cheerful," Wyndgonk says. "I have to say your brilliant battle plan has worked out great."

"It's not my—" Yatto snarls, then takes a breath of scarce air. "Let's just try and get these claws off, so we can get inside."

Not enough time or oxygen to explain properly, but this ship won't let them inside without power, and the hull breach is too small to squeeze through. And Yatto doesn't have the tools to cut open this thick hull. And a Royal Compassion ship could turn up at any moment.

"If anybody should be angry at Tina, it's me," Wyndgonk says. "I'm carrying the future of my people, and the salvation of this entire galaxy, and she could have helped us to safeguard it. But I still think she did the right thing."

"I can't imagine the burden you're carrying," Yatto says.

"You can't?" Wyndgonk snorts with laughter. This involves a tiny jet of flame, a bad idea inside a spacesuit, especially one that's running out of air. "You're one to talk, Yatto the Monntha."

"What do you mean?" Yatto is so startled, they almost stop working.

"If anybody here knows what it's like to be carrying the whole future of their people, it's you," Wyndgonk says. "You should see how the other Irriyaians talk about you when you're not around."

"I'm nothing to anybody. Not anymore."

"I hope all that self-pity will keep you warm after our suits lose temperature control," Wyndgonk snarks.

"Fire is right," says Chanka the Anhth. "I've been on the Irriyaian citystar, among the refugees. We lost more than our home. Our whole culture was based on proving we could take care of the land we occupied, and now there's no more land. People know that you almost died trying to save them, even after they turned you into a symbol of hate. If any of us survive this fight, you could lead all the nations, not just the Monnthas."

Yatto can't take all these demands. This work is going too slow, their air is running out too fast. They've only removed four claws, and eight still remain.

Chunky shapes circle in the darkness overhead: an ancient graveyard that just gained a lot of new residents.

If Tina was here . . . well, they still would be doomed.

"I can't die until I get some answers," Wyndgonk wheezes, almost as if fire could tell what Yatto was thinking. "I need to know why the hearthlight is so important, and why it's the key to stopping the Bereavement. It doesn't make any sense."

Yatto chokes on stale air. "I told you I visited your world once. They showed me their temples, including the big one in the basin. So I know your people's stories about gods that visited long ago. There has to be some truth to it."

"I hope . . ." Wyndgonk coughs and sputters a few faint wisps of smoke. "I hope we live to find out. I'm not feeling too good."

"Save your . . ." Yatto's head is swimming.

Such irony: they don't have enough breath left to say the word "breath." They would laugh—if they could breathe.

Maybe Yatto is hallucinating, but one of the shapes out there seems to be getting closer. A ship, approaching fast.

Yatto tries to raise their head and look for markings, but they fall onto their back, knees bent and boots still attached to the hull. The last thing they see is the ship descending, filling their vision, and then the universe goes away.

"—lucky bastards," someone is saying. "We didn't expect to find anyone alive on this ship. We've divided our crew so we can keep both ships operational, which means a lot of work all around, let me tell you."

Yatto's head is pounding. They try to open their eyes and the light burns like rockfire.

I am so sick of near-death experiences.

They coax their eyes open a little, and see what looks like a sickbay, with a few people in the makeshift uniforms of the rebel fleet bustling around.

"Epic bravery and sensible fears," says a young Aribentor, almost a child, with an ill-fitting uniform. "I'm Acting Senior Visioner Fhonan, and my pronoun is *he.* You're safe on board the *Unbowed,* at least as long as we can stay hidden from the Royal Compassion—"

Yatto raises their hand, and Fhonan goes mercifully quiet.

"Sorry. I need to know. How did your ship, the, uh, the *Unbowed*? How did you avoid the immobilizer claws?"

"Oh, we didn't." Fhonan's skull-plates stretch on either side. "The claws got us, but then one of the rebel ships arrived and gave us a transponder that made them disengage. We have a bunch of those transponders, and we're hunting for other ships that haven't been destroyed yet, so we can free them from the claws."

"That ship." Yatto scarcely dares to get their hopes up. "What did it look like?"

"Oh, it was the strangest thing: two ships stuck together, no logic whatsoever. Hard to believe it stayed in one piece."

"I need to get to that ship as soon as possible." Yatto sits up, ignoring the pain. "Everything depends on it. Take me to your captain at once. Please."

52

.

TINA

The Mazda Miata is right where I parked it, on the edge of the spaceship graveyard. No immobilizer claws, thank the Hosts of Misadventure. I get the hatch open and bundle Elza inside.

"How are you holding up?" I ask her.

She shivers. "Not well. The Ardenii are giving me too many details about how my body is destabilizing." She blinks away tears. "I probably have about seventeen hours, Earth time."

"Okay. There has to be a way to fix this."

I get the ship fired up and set the spaceweave in the opposite direction from the spaceship graveyard and our friends.

"What are you doing?" Elza says. "We should say goodbye now, and then you should get far away from me."

"I took an oath that I would never let you go. This is me not letting you go."

I'm scared if I look at her, I'll see signs of softening, deterioration. There's an icy, spiky monster waking up inside me, made of pure despair, and I need it to stay asleep. So I can stay focused, stay in the can-do headspace. I need to be a little bit Thaoh and a little bit me.

"We both know there's only one person who can fix this," Elza says in a quiet voice. "And she despises me. So why would she save me?"

I nod, without looking away from the controls. "The queen has access to the full power of the Ardenii, so she could do the higher math that would stabilize you. Probably wouldn't even be hard, right? But you'd have to give her something in return."

"My crown." Those two words sound as if they cost Elza everything.

"Like you told Marrant, if you die now, your crown dies with you. She might be willing to make a deal." I can't bear being so close to her and feeling like she's already half-dead. My heart crashes, a burning wreck. "It's just a piece of hardware. It's not what makes you powerful. You already communicated with the Ardenii before you had it."

There's a long, agonizing silence, apart from the chattering of the flight instruments.

"Let's say you're right," Elza says. "Let's say the queen takes my crown but saves my life—assuming we can trust her. She'll never let me leave, because I'm an embarrassment. Once she has me as her captive, I'll be locked away forever, in disgrace. That's not a life that you should want for me. And I don't even know what she'll do with you."

The icy spike monster rears up inside me.

Part of me is still stuck in that moment where Marrant kissed her hand and the hatch swung shut—when I thought we were both dead.

"Marrant already showed us there are things worse than dying," Elza says.

We're racing toward empty space. In their final days, the stars gleam like ice crystals.

Something throbs in my satchel: the safebeam node that Thaoh Argentian left behind. First I think it's Yatto, or maybe Rachael and Yiwei, calling to yell at me for running away in the middle of a losing battle. But no.

Halred swims into view, with Eldnat next to her and a few of the other Grattna behind her. They're on a ship that looks a lot like a copy of the super-powerful flagship Marrant had, back at Antarràn.

She says, "We have reached a decision," but my hacked-up EverySpeak lets me understand that she's really saying something like "We were caught between three unpleasant options and we have moved away from one of them, somewhat closer to the second, and much closer to the third."

I waste too much of our short window trying to get back in the mindset to speak in a way that makes sense to the Grattna, with the love of my life dying right next to me.

"Ummm . . . we will move toward you as you move toward us. I mean—"

Elza cuts me off, and speaks in rapid-fire, perfect Grattna, without even a trace of an accent. "We you life entire protect holding power together."

They talk back and forth, too fast for me to follow, even with the Every-Speak. Then the safebeam cuts out, right as they seem to reach an agreement.

Elza turns to me, and—oh, my poor heart—she's smiling. "I almost forgot, you did all that work to understand the Grattna better." Her eyes are shining now. "I can't even believe how much I love you."

"You, too, I never thought I could love someone so much."

I want to say something else, like *We're going to get through this,* or *I won't let Marrant take you away from me.* But I don't want to remind Elza that she's dying, in case she's somehow forgotten. So I just offer her my hand. She takes it.

"The Grattna are coming. I told them everything," Elza says. "They know that the man who caged and killed so many of them could soon have the power to kill their sun forever, so they are ready to fight him. I told them how to rendezvous with Yatto and whoever else is left. And . . ." She takes a rattling breath. "I told them you would be there to greet them."

"But . . . I won't. Even if everything somehow goes okay with the queen."

"This changes things," Elza says. "With the Grattna and those ships, we have a chance to stop Marrant. Also, the Ardenii just told me the Kraelyors are sending ships, too. Kfok managed to reach them. You need to be there. We can't spare you. I can try to make it to the queen on my own, with the impeller."

"The impeller doesn't have enough power. You wouldn't make it."

She rasps, "Depends how badly the queen wants this back." She gestures at the top of her head.

"I already made my choice."

I can barely make out Elza's voice now. "For you to be the person you always told me you were, you might have to let me die."

"The only person I want to be is the one who helps you save yourself."

I stay on course toward the queen. Elza stares at the viewport, not saying anything, for what feels like a million hours. I can only imagine all the horrible things the Ardenii are telling her.

I'm scared to turn my head her way, in case I see her skin softening, her perfect face starting to distort, as everything comes apart.

A while later, I break the silence. "Tell me more about your crown."

"What?" Her eyes flash gold, her tears reflecting the lights on her head.

"I'm sorry. This sucks. But please, tell me everything you know about that crown."

"Are you *trying* to torture me? I'm dying, and I've never been this scared, and I'm going to have to give up this crown forever, and now you want me to talk about it?"

"Listen. The queen and the other princesses, they've had their crowns for longer than you, and they've had more training. Right? But you have one thing going for you that they don't—you're a hacker. You can never resist taking things apart to find out how they work. So yeah, I need to know all about your crown. It could help us get out of this mess in one piece."

Elza is so tiny now, arms and legs bundled up even though it's pretty warm in here.

"Okay." She gives another chainsaw breath. (I hope this is just normal sobbing and not Marrant's touch kicking in.) "The crown stores a lot of knowledge inside, so even when I'm not connected to the Ardenii, it still gives me a ton of information. There's a high-speed brain-computer interface via some kind of nanotech. They taught us about the base code when I was at the palace."

"So the crown is a computer?"

"Yeah, sort of. Not exactly."

"And you know the code. Could you program it to do something after you hand it over to the queen?"

"Maybe." She frowns. "Or even inject it with some malware." She shivers. "I don't think the Ardenii would appreciate that, but they'd probably understand."

"How long do we have?" I'm pretty sure she understands what I'm asking, and that she knows the answer.

"Three or four cycles. The queen knows where we are, and she's coming to meet us." She reaches up and carefully, gingerly, detaches the crown from her head and lowers it into her lap. "That might be enough time to prepare a little surprise."

Elza pulls part of the crown open, revealing a tiny port, and she plugs it into the ship's computers. Now she's furiously poking at a holographic cloud of symbols and numbers, which make no sense to me whatsoever.

She mutters under her breath, and at one point I swear I hear her laughing.

53

.

RACHAEL

. . . 178 Earth days until all the suns go out forever

Yiwei stalks around the flight lounge, blurting orders. "Zaeta, Damini, stay close to that debris cluster. Kfok, keep all of your eyes on that tactical display. Kez, be ready to cut engines on my signal." He spits, eyes glued to his Quant. "Next time the enemy shows up, we need to be ready."

Rachael tries to speak up, and he ignores her.

Yiwei has that gleam in his eye, and the twitch in his jaw, right next to his ear, and all Rachael can think is, *I've seen this movie already.*

Everyone else on the *Undisputed Training Bra Disaster* looks rattled, at their breaking point. And Yiwei keeps pushing them harder.

Rachael sidles up to him and whispers, "Can I talk to you in private for a sec?"

Yiwei starts to say no, now's not a good time. Then he catches himself. "Sure."

She follows Yiwei into the same tiny studio where she watched his band practice, with Cinnki on lead vocals (ugh), so long ago. She opens her mouth to say something like *You're doing it again, you're getting carried away, you're not even treating me like a co-captain.*

But she looks at his raised tendons and tight neck muscles, and remembers. He's not doing this to live up to some heroic story—her boyfriend is scared and traumatized, and trying to take care of everybody the only way he knows how.

So she throws away the angry words she was about to spit at him, and instead whispers, "Hey. I think maybe it's my turn to be captain for a while. I know we agreed we'd be co-captains all the time. But you've been taking more of the burden, and it doesn't seem fair."

She braces herself for him to snap at her for trying to take away his authority.

Instead he takes a deep breath. "Yeah," he says. "I could really use a break. Thank you." Some of the tension drains out of him.

She basks in the relief on his face—then the responsibility settles onto her shoulders. Instant neck cramp.

"Okay, as acting captain, I think we need a new strategy. We've hurt the Royal Compassion a little, but it's been costing us too much and our luck is running out. We haven't found another ship to give a transponder to since we saved the *Unbowed*, which feels like a long time ago."

Yiwei smiles. Never not beautiful. "So what do you suggest—Captain?"

"I think we need to have a quick team meeting."

Rachael can still feel Yiwei next to her, radiating tension. Everyone else stares, glassy-eyed. Kfok looks like she has something stuck in her big, sluggy throat. Kez gives her a friendly nod.

They're all waiting for Rachael to say something. She thinks of her conversation with Yatto, before the battle.

Maybe there is a way she can be present, and still have solitude in her thoughts.

Rachael pulls out her lightpad and makes her first drawing of people in such a long time. The quirk of Kez's mouth, the gleam in all ninety-nine of Zaeta's eyes, Kfok's two mouths grimacing, Damini gazing expectantly.

These feel like the right people for her to be drawing now.

She can talk and sketch at the same time. "Time for a new plan. There has to be a way to tie up more of Marrant's ships in this tactical dead zone, without getting caught up in these dogfights. Plus we lost track of the hearthlight and our friends, and without them we're just spinning our wheels."

"We can't locate the ship our friends were on," Kfok says. "The *Unpredictable*."

"So we need to find a way to search for them without getting caught," Ganno says.

Rachael glances at Yiwei. He looks stressed AF, but he gives her an encouraging smile.

"Can we create a signal that only our friends would recognize?" Rachael says. "In case they're looking for us?" She almost mentions that's how she and Tina found them before, but that leads to thinking about how Yiwei almost shot at them.

Damini and Zaeta start to talk at the same moment. Then Damini stops and waves at Zaeta. "You go."

"Thanks." Zaeta turns to Rachael. "We were thinking . . . the impellers have been acting weird ever since the queen messed with them. They're venting anti-leptons."

"It's true," Kez says.

"Only someone who'd been on the ship this whole time would notice some stray anti-leptons in the middle of all this interference," Zaeta adds.

"Great," Rachael says. "Let's make it happen. Thank you."

She turns and looks at Yiwei. He gives her a thumbs-up. "Great work, Captain," he whispers.

Kez works with Damini and Zaeta to make the engines spew anti-leptons, and then there's nothing to do but wait. Ganno and Kez sit down in the engine compartment, talking in low voices with their hands *almost* touching. Zaeta and Damini keep the ship darting around metal slivers, and Kfok watches the tactical scan. Rachael tries to convince Yiwei to sleep, or play his guitar, but he wants to stay on high alert.

Just when Rachael's starting to wonder if the party's over and everyone else has left the ancient battlefield, she hears Kfok yelling from the tactical station.

"We've got another ship. No, wait, two ships. But they're friendly! One of them is the *Unbowed,* and there's another rebel ship, the *Impeccable.* They want to send an elevator platform over."

"Ummm." Rachael freezes. What if the Royal Compassion took over these ships and it's a trap? Then she shakes off the paranoia. Those two vessels could beat the *Undisputed Training Bra Disaster* without any subterfuge. "Sure. We'll put out the good cookies and punch."

"Wait, we have cookies?" Ganno the Wurthhi pops his head up from where he's been doing repairs.

"No. I wish."

The big pizza dish is already on its way over, and Rachael barely has time for one last anxiety spiral before it arrives. Yiwei is already heading down to the cargo hangar, where two familiar people are standing.

Rachael rushes toward them, smiling. "Yatto the Monntha! Wyndgonk! We've been so worried. I'm so glad you're safe—"

Then she sees the look on Yatto's face, and the dark smog coming out of Wyndgonk's mouth.

"What is it? What happened?" Rachael's stomach twists.

Everything feels too loud and horribly quiet, all at once.

"Marrant." Wyndgonk walks toward the crew lounge, under a literal dark cloud.

"He boarded the *Unbelievable*. In person," Yatto says.

Rachael's seen Yatto grieving, but now they look completely undone. Like this was just one terrible thing too many, at long last.

"What did he do?" Damini is actually yelling, with fury in her eyes.

"Calm down," Zaeta says, "we need clear heads—"

"What did he do?" Damini balls her fists, quaking.

"He did what he always does," Wyndgonk says in a toneless voice. "He put his hands on the best of us and tried to ruin her. Elza has a short time left before the effect hits, so Tina decided to try and rescue her. We don't know what happened next."

"Oh no." Yiwei slaps his palm against the wall.

"We can't lose both of them." Kez slumps into a chair. "We can't." Ganno the Wurthhi walks quietly over to sit on the floor in front of Kez, so they're eye to eye.

"Hope is not lost," Wyndgonk says.

"Sorry to interrupt," Kfok says from the comms station. "But we actually just got a message from Elza. Just a few lines of text, heavily encrypted. I think the Ardenii delivered it for her."

"What does it say?" Damini still looks ready to tear someone apart with her bare hands.

"Uh . . . she and Tina have a plan, but it's pretty dreadful. She doesn't explain. Also, she says that the Grattna finally decided to fight alongside us, with all the powerful ships they constructed after they copied Marrant's old ship. They have twenty ships, and they're already on their way to rendezvous with us. Also? Looks like some of my people are coming to join us as well."

"Wow. Oh wow." Rachael wishes she knew where Tina and Elza were, and had a way to help. She can't handle the idea of never seeing them again.

She wants to hide in her quarters and draw nonsense diagrams for a hundred hours. She wants to cry-sleep forever. But she looks up and realizes everyone is looking at her, because she's still wearing the captain hat, and they're waiting for her to say something captain-like.

"Wyndgonk is right: we need to have faith in our friends. If anybody can beat this, it's Elza and Tina. We still have the hearthlight, and now the Grattna and the Kraelyors are joining us. We have a fighting chance, as long as we can keep most of Marrant's ships tied up in this junkyard. More people than we could ever count are depending on us. So let's get back to work."

Nobody cheers or starts writing epic poems about Rachael's leadership skills. But they all nod and get back to work, because there's a lot to do.

54

.

TINA

I was never in love before I met Elza, and I had all kinds of ideas about what it'd be like. Balcony serenades, rose petals everywhere, moonlit confessions, clever banter, fireworks. I wasn't sure if I'd find love on Earth or in space, with a boy or a girl or some other gender. But I knew for sure it would be the biggest joyride.

I never once thought about what it'd be like to sit next to the person I love with all of my brain cells and nerve endings and veins and capillaries, and watch her die.

Eaten from the inside by a poison that will end up poisoning me against her.

Elza seemed fine one moment, and now she's gone soft. I can feel her starting to lose her shape, without looking directly. She feels colder, too, though maybe that's just my own skin turning clammy.

"It's going to be okay," I keep saying. "The queen won't let anything happen to that crown, we're almost there. You just have to hang on a little longer. Please just stay with me, I promise I'll never leave your side again. I'll do anything."

She can barely form words anymore, but she looks at me with steel in her eyes and says, "Just promise you'll let me do most of the talking."

"I—But what if—" I can't bring myself to say, *But what if you can't talk by the time the queen gets here?*

"The queen is c . . . ugh. The queen is cunning and she'll twist any . . . anything you tell her. Don't give her anything. Promise me." Elza makes a rattling gasp. "She's already agreed to save my life if I give up the crown. There won't be much need to . . ."

"I promise."

Elza closes her eyes.

She's starting to smell the same as Marrant's hands. That noxious, burnt-chemical odor that's already taken so many people I used to care about.

———

Something appears directly in front of us, out of nowhere: the floating palace.

Crystal plumes curl in all directions and the whole thing glimmers with a bright light that changes colors as it gets closer. The nerdy part of my brain is wondering how such a large structure manages to spaceweave. It must be very lightweight, with only minimal structures inside. But most of my brain is pleading, *Hurry, please hurry.*

Elza's not talking or moving. I don't know how long it's been since she last spoke or opened her eyes. I tell myself she's just conserving her strength.

The Mazda Miata gets pulled inside the floating palace, and a moment later we come to rest in some kind of drawing room full of ornate furniture that looks like oak. I lean over Elza. "We're here," I whisper.

She doesn't respond.

I lift her in my arms and carry her out of the ship. She weighs way too little.

The light from some high-tech candelabra smears in my eyes. *Come on, come on, this can't be the end. I need you, Elza, just a little longer. You're too wonderful to go out like this.*

If this goes the wrong way, I could find myself hating her at any moment. That thought only makes me want to love her as hard as I can.

Elza opens her eyes and whispers to me. "The Grattna just rendezvoused with our friends. Also, on Makvaria, Thaoh Argentian's family just had a new baby, they're going to name her Tina. The Irriyaian citystar is having food riots. An ancient civilization of plant-animal hybrids just died out."

"Shhh," I say. "You can tell me later. We're here, it's time."

Where the hell is the queen? Is she keeping us waiting as some kind of power move?

I lower Elza into a fancy armchair and try to sit her upright, so she looks like a goddamn princess.

I would do literally anything for her, and all I can do is cross her ankles.

A few attendants in the same colorful silk I saw on the *Invention of Innocence* come and cluster around Elza. They whisper something, and she nods. And then they lift the crown off her head and place it on a cushion that appears in midair. The crown glows with a faint golden light, same as always.

The attendants lift Elza out of the chair gently, cradling her head and supporting her back. I try to ask where they're taking her, but they ignore me. And then they're gone.

"So Marrant sent us a present at last. A little worse for wear, but better than nothing."

I know the queen is behind me, even before I turn around. She's gorgeous, of course: mossy dark-green Yarthin skin adorned with tiny gems, lithe body clad in a shift that ripples with light.

My arms and legs curtsey before I even know what I'm doing. I want to ask how Elza's doing, what's going on, but I bite my tongue. Almost the last thing Elza said to me was, *Don't give her anything.*

So all I say is, "Your Radiance. Your acquaintance is a prize."

"As is yours, Tina Mains. That *is* whom I'm addressing, is it not? So hard to keep up. Perhaps if you had figured out who you are, you might have made a better consort, and the notorious Rogue Princess wouldn't have come to such a bad end."

The queen is trying to get under my skin. Trolling me the exact same way the kids at Clinton High used to. All I want is to be by Elza's side, holding her hand while they do whatever they're doing to save her.

The queen walks closer to me, then stops and gazes at Elza's crown, resting on an emerald-green cushion. She reaches out and strokes it with one finger, like a sleeping cat.

Something has been nagging at me since we got here, and now I get it. The queen doesn't have any of the princesses with her.

Right when I twig that, the queen takes Elza's crown in both hands and carries it to the far wall. She tilts her head to one side and then the other, and something lowers from the ceiling: a kind of golden wreath? Looks like a circle made of circles, except that there's a gap in the upper right-hand side.

I stare and wonder, and then I see it: this is six crowns, linked in a single ring. The queen holds up Elza's crown and places it in the missing space.

"No more princesses," the queen says. "All of the Ardenii's power will flow through ourselves alone, as it always should have."

Ouch. So it's not just Elza having her crown taken away. The queen is getting rid of anybody who could challenge her, anyone in line to become queen after her. It makes a horrible sense: Queen Nonesuch rose to power by plotting against her predecessor, so of course she wants to make sure there are no princesses to challenge her.

But also? I can tell by looking at this wreath that all the crowns are being networked together—to do what?

"By now Marrant is close to securing the hearthlight—yes, we now know what object he'll need, thanks to your carelessness—and soon, we shall commence the great work of reshaping the galaxy into a more proper shape." The queen gestures at her ring of stolen crowns. "Once we have removed all of the misshapen and distorted creatures, once everything is clean, we will restore true order."

I'm freaking out, the longer this goes on. Shouldn't there be some news about Elza by now? Whatever happened had to have happened by now, and the queen probably knows Elza's status. She's just standing there in her finery, watching me squirm.

I don't hate Elza. I keep checking inside, and I still love her. I tell myself that's the only diagnostic instrument I need: my own tattered heart.

If this were a fairy tale, my true love would be enough to save her. But this is the real world, and we survive by fighting dirtier than the people who are trying to destroy us.

I force a smile onto my lips, even though I'm screaming inside.

"What?" The queen blinks. "Why are you making that face?"

Elza made me swear not to give her anything. But I can't resist saying, "Marrant knew how bad you wanted that crown back, but he still touched Elza anyway. The crown would have been destroyed if Elza hadn't taken precautions."

I shake my head, as if to say that Her Radiance is just the latest in a long line of suckers to get taken for a ride by that man.

The queen stares at me, then snaps, "Take the ex-consort someplace unpleasant."

Two attendants come and take me by the arms. I don't try to resist, just let them lead me into a hallway with walls and ceiling made out of something that looks like taffeta.

I still love Elza. I still love Elza. If the worst had happened, I would know. As long as I love her, I can tell myself she's okay.

I barely notice as I'm half led, half dragged through a series of lush rooms.

Flowers with cartoon faces stare at me. I hear one of them whisper to the others, "Is that really her? She looks so messed up. Remind me never to fall in love."

I think of Elza every other heartbeat, replaying memories. The fire in her eyes when she first arrived on an orbital funnel from Earth, the way she filled a starship with hummingbirds, the poetry in her arms and legs when she fought Kankakn. I still overflow with warmth when I bring those things to mind.

At last they take me down a ramp to roughly where the cargo hangar would be on a regular ship, and push me into a space that looks like an actual dungeon. Crumbling stone walls, water dripping somewhere in the distance, a stone bench, and a bucket. They shove me inside and lock the door.

I go to sit on the bench, but then I realize there's a second bench on the other side of this cell . . . and Elza is sleeping on it.

She looks as beautiful as ever. Peaceful, as if she'd been to a lovely party and just needed a cat nap.

Only one difference: there's no crown resting on her head.

I kneel on the stone floor next to her, and look up at her perfect face. I know how much it hurt her to give up that crown.

Even with everything breaking apart, I could watch her sleep for hours.

She opens her eyes. "Tina. You're here." She breathes. "They did it. They stabilized my molecular structure, just in time. A little while longer, it would have been too late."

Can't speak for crying. Shoulders quaking, breath stuttering.

I was trying so hard to hold on to my love for her, all of that love is breaking me down now that she's okay.

"You're still my consort," Elza says in my ear. "Nothing can change that."

"And you're still my princess," I whisper back. "Always."

She scoots over on this fugly stone bench to make room for me to curl up next to her. I feel her warmth, the beat of her heart, and her breath on my cheek, and I still feel totally wrecked by gratitude and love. We lie together, hands clasped. We might be on a floating palace full of silk and flowers, but this cell is the only place I ever want to be.

55
.

RACHAEL

. . . 176 Earth days until all the suns go out forever

The *Merciful Touch* was Marrant's flagship, back when he first tried to kill Rachael and her friends. A big spike, dotted with engines and wrapped with a sleek, curved hull, it hung over everyone's heads, raining down death at Antarràn. Just the memory of that shape makes her feel like she drank ice-cold ink.

Now she's looking at ten replicas of the *Merciful Touch,* clustering on the edge of the starship graveyard. Nearby, a dozen Kraelyor battle-slicers look like scythe blades, glinting against the darkness.

Kez (he/him) spent the past few cycles studying Tina's notes on how she reconfigured her EverySpeak. "I'm going to embarrass myself for sure, but perhaps it'll be the kind of embarrassment that leads to good things."

"I just want to point out that nobody has ever put in this much effort to understand my language," Wyndgonk says.

"Same." Kfok makes that hissing sound Kraelyors make, that's kind of laughter and kind of a snarl. "I've been here the whole time and nobody's ever wondered if we're communicating properly."

"Maybe our people should have been stealing advanced starships and building copies of them," Wyndgonk says.

"Fair point." Kez smiles. "I think we need to recognize that everybody communicates differently, and we should try to do better. But also? We need to accept that we'll never fully understand each other."

"That's kind of defeatist," Wyndgonk says.

"I think it's more hopeful," Kez says. "The problem starts when we think we know more about each other than we actually do."

Damini calls out from the pilot station. "Heads up! We're—"

"—about to rendezvous," says Zaeta.

The *Undisputed Training Bra Disaster* glides inside the cargo hangar of the lead Grattna ship, which is apparently called *Nindred's Blessing.* (Rachael has no idea who Nindred is, or was. Maybe one of the godparents? She needs to learn more about Grattna religion.)

Yiwei tenses up, because once they're inside the bigger ship's belly, they'll be helpless. But trust has to go both ways, right? (Or if you're a Grattna, maybe it goes three ways.)

Halred greets them as soon as they get off the ship, talking too fast for Rachael to follow all of it. "You didn't get lost or stay away, you came and found us," she says. And then it gets harder to understand, like: "Marrant moon us [failuresuccess] murder fight save."

Kez steps forward and responds—except he doesn't quite sound like Kez anymore. "We, you, the Royal Compassion [togetherapart] danger purpose fight distance."

This is maybe the most important conversation in history—is history even going to be a thing anymore?—and Rachael can't pay attention at all. Partly because Kez and Halred are talking back and forth in these weird non-sentences that give Rachael a headache, but mostly because she's worrying nonstop about Tina and Elza.

The fate of the damn galaxy hardly feels like it matters, if Rachael loses her best friends.

Kez stumbles and loses the thread of what he was trying to say. Ganno the Wurthhi moves closer to him and gives him a sidelong smile, like, *Keep going, this is working.* So he picks up and keeps going.

The Grattna lead Kez, Ganno, Rachael, Yiwei, Yatto, and Wyndgonk deeper into the ship, which looks so much like Marrant's that Rachael gets chills. Except that here and there, the Grattna have planted some of those doily trees from Second Yoth in little pots.

Eventually they reach a room that kind of looks like the crew lounge on every Royal Fleet ship, but the Grattna have decorated it with the three-headed thistle and pictures of their great walking ocean. Everybody sits or perches on chairs, or on the long bench along one wall.

Kez and the Grattna talk back and forth. Rachael can tell Yiwei is getting twitchy at being left out of the strategy discussion. Plus, every moment they delay, Marrant could be figuring out that the hearthlight isn't on any of the ships in the starship graveyard, and that the Grattna fleet just showed up. Time is not on their side.

Soon everybody is spouting off ideas. Yatto thinks they could trick Marrant into thinking the Grattna ships are part of his fleet, since they're copies of his old ship. But Wyndgonk can't resist pointing out how it turned out last time they tried to trick Marrant.

"Okay." Yiwei turns to Wyndgonk. "What would you suggest?"

Wyndgonk puffs red sparks. "I don't know anything about battle strategy, because battles are terrible and I don't like them."

Halred says something that adds up to: *We can't trick Marrant, we can't fight our way through, so what's the third option?*

Wyndgonk huffs and snorts for a moment, rubbing fire mandibles together. "On my world, we survive by working with the things that are trying to eat us." Fire gestures at the cloud of starship debris that's between their ragtag fleet and Larstko IVb. "Why don't we bring the junk with us? I've gotten used to having it around."

"We could use our ion harnesses," Yiwei says. "Drag a whole lot of it out of the graveyard, until we reach the moon. And then fling it ahead of us, so we can follow it down."

"We could use the wreckage to confuse their scans," Yatto says.

"And also as a battering ram, to break through their lines," says Kfok.

"With any luck, they won't be able to tell what's junk and what's our ships," Yiwei says.

"I wish you would all stop using that phrase," Wyndgonk grunts. "'With any luck.' When have we *ever* had any luck?"

56

.

ELZA

Elza wakes with the worst headache of her life—one of those hangovers that clamps lead weights to your brain, so heavy you barely remember where you are, or what you could have done to deserve this white-hot throb.

Elza is sure she's lying on the floor of Fernanda's closet back in the Luz, wrapped in a hand-me-down sleeping bag, with Fernanda praying in front of her homemade Candomblé altar on the other side of the screen door. In a moment, Elza will have to get up and face Fernanda and explain what she did to Fernanda's phone.

"I was a bad friend," Elza says out loud. "I should have known better."

"Shhhh." A voice comes from overhead. "Just rest. I'm here." Tina.

Elza opens her eyes and sees crumbling stone walls with moss coming out of them, and she remembers: she's in the flying palace.

Everything comes back to her: Marrant kissing her hand and saying *There are those who must be despised.* The sensation of falling apart, the looseness of her own skin, the toxic stench from her own pores. Her heart speeds up, she breathes heavy, cold sweat pools in her eyes, and still her head throbs.

Now Elza is convinced if she moves a muscle, she'll dissolve utterly, leaving nothing but a garbage reputation.

From somewhere behind her, Tina says, "Are you awake? I wanted to let you sleep in case that was part of the cure."

It's okay, Elza tells herself. *I was cured. I'm not dying anymore.* She reaches up with one hand and feels nothing on her head. The crown is gone.

A little bolo mouse creeps along the stone wall and pauses in front of Elza. Big round eyes look into Elza's and the mouse's nose twitches. The Ardenii, come to say hello.

The mouse opens its mouth, but nothing comes out.

Instead, Elza hears in her head: **Permanent stabilization against psychomolecular incursion, with limited contact immunity.**

Oh great. The Ardenii are speaking to her the same way they did before she had the crown: in riddles and numbers.

Elza's pretty sure "permanent stabilization" means that even if Marrant touches her again, she'll be protected next time. They didn't just cure her, they made her immune. She tries to gather breath to ask what "limited contact immunity" means.

But the bolo mouse is opening its mouth again. She hears in her head: **Network cascade averted, incursion failed.**

"What kind of network cascade are we talking about?" Elza says out loud.

She can feel Tina startle next to her. "Excuse me?"

"Sorry, not talking to you," Elza says. "Hi. I love you. But this is important."

Cranial interface not compromised, the Ardenii say. **Network cascade averted.**

Cranial interfaces. In other words, crowns. But what do they mean, *network*?

Elza sits up and looks into Tina's tear-soaked smile. "Did the queen connect a bunch of crowns together? Including mine?"

"Umm. Yeah," Tina says. "She made a daisy chain of crowns. It seemed . . . bad?"

"Yeah." Elza still hurts all over, and she fears with every move that she'll be unmade. That she'll slide apart. But she hears Princess Constellation in her head: *You still have to graduate.* She swings her legs around and sits forward, rubbing her temples.

"I thought the queen already had more access to the Ardenii than the princesses," Tina says.

"She does. She wants to have the Ardenii all to herself. Maybe they're still not helping her as much as she wants."

"Marrant did say she would help him to rule whatever's left after he's wiped out everyone he thinks is unworthy," Tina says. "But your crown—"

Elza shushes Tina. The queen is definitely listening to their whole conversation.

Cranial interface not compromised.

Right. Elza remembers now: she left a surprise inside her crown, a little taste of malicious code. When she was sitting in the tiny starship next to Tina, she tried to create something that could spread and flower everywhere like wild brambles. She can't remember exactly what her fevered brain ended up with, because that whole voyage from the *Unpredictable* feels like a horrible dream.

Nonsense fills Elza's head—not the staccato bursts of information the Ardenii were just sending her, but something more sustained. She reels and nearly falls off her bench. Then she realizes what she's seeing: the desperate, last-ditch code she put into her crown before she surrendered it.

There's a tiny bug in her program, and she didn't notice because her brain was liquefying along with the rest of her.

The pain is fading, and Elza's head is clearing, except for the Ardenii chattering.

A sudden wash of awareness: the *Undisputed Training Bra Disaster* is racing toward Larstko IVb, the moon with the wedding chapel, accompanied by a tiny fleet. And Marrant is setting another trap for her friends.

Tell me what you want of me, Elza thinks at the Ardenii. *All this time, and I still don't understand what you want.*

A tiny click comes from the far side of the cell.

The door swings open a crack. The bolo mouse looks at Elza like, *What are you waiting for?*

Elza forces herself to her feet. That code is still on her crown, and it's now networked with six others. If she can just patch the bug somehow, the queen could have a really, really bad day. The Ardenii are literally holding the door open for her.

"Tá bom," Elza says out loud to Tina. "We've got a lot to do."

She still feels sore, and a big part of her wishes she could just hide away in this gross cell forever. But she makes herself get on her feet and start walking.

57

.

Water drips somewhere far away, and a milk-breath stench rises from the paving stones. Tina and Elza creep under weed-eaten arches, past walls that glisten with slime.

These palace catacombs didn't exist before, and now they go on forever.

Elza keeps trying to reach out to the place where the Ardenii still live in her mind—she can hear them loud and clear, if she concentrates. They let her out of her cell and protected her forever from Marrant's touch, but they won't help her to patch the code she put on her crown. And they're not letting her find a way out of here.

Come on, she thinks at the Ardenii. *Time to choose a side.*

Primary cranial interface prioritized, they say. "Primary" meaning the queen? Like, they can't act against the queen directly, because she's the main way they talk to flesh-and-blood people.

They give her a burst of awareness: the floating palace is racing toward Larstko IVb to witness Marrant's rise.

Tina jumps at shadows and tries to look in every direction at once, as if she'll see danger coming. She won't.

The longer Elza concentrates on reaching the Ardenii without her crown, the stronger the signal feels. "You were right," she says out loud.

"Don't sound so surprised." Tina scoffs.

"I mean about the crown. I was already communicating with the Ardenii before I had it. And the whole time I was wearing it, they were putting more nanotech into my brain, adding more connections. It's easier to hear them with the crown, but with practice I'll be able to do without."

"I'm glad," Tina says—then jumps at another shadow.

Slinking through darkness . . . this situation reminds Elza way too much of being trapped on board a tiny ship, with Marrant hunting her and Tina. She flashes on what happened next. *There are those who must be despised.* She recoils as if Marrant just touched her, just now, as if his curse was freshly upon her. She reminds herself: permanent stabilization. And there was something else . . . that she has no time to make sense of.

Something moves in the darkness: Tina's left hand. Elza clasps it with her right.

Elza chatters to distract herself. "Do you remember why Marrant decided humanoids are superior to everyone else?" she asks Tina.

"Umm . . . there was a lot of ranting. So many rants." Tina frowns. "Oh. He said that we're better because our brains are raised above our bodies, so it's like our minds are elevated over everything else. And other creatures have brains that are closer to their bodies, or whatever? To be honest, I do a lot of my best thinking with my stomach."

"Yeah." Elza is struggling to put something into words. "That's the thing. The crown was just a piece of hardware. An interface for my brain. It didn't need to be a symbol of authority at all."

"But because it was on top of your head, someone decided it ought to be a crown, and it should be all fancy," Tina says.

A hungry groan reverberates from up ahead, in the deepest part of the shadows.

Elza backs away, her arms stiff. *Those who must be despised.* Tina does not let go of her hand.

"Somebody's in trouble," Tina whispers.

Elza moves forward again, as if she knows what she's going to do when she gets there.

A skeleton is suspended in a mesh of threads, the same as the web that slowly destroyed the former queen.

The Ardenii say, **Neural agonist engaged.**

As Elza and Tina get closer, the figure looks up. Exposed eyeballs widen with recognition.

"Well," rasps Naahay. "Have you come to gloat? This is what you wanted."

"Why did the new queen do this to you?" Elza asks.

"Honestly . . ." Naahay coughs. "I think Her Radiance was displeased when I arrived without you. I keep having phantom sensations in different parts of my body, as if . . ."

". . . as if the threads are trying to take over your nervous system," Elza says. "So you can become a puppet, or a spy."

Neural agonist engaged, the Ardenii repeat.

This is what the queen must be planning to do with Elza, if she doesn't get out of here.

"What can we do for her?" Tina whispers.

Elza tastes something bitter. Sadness drapes like a caul.

"I don't . . ." She hears the former queen saying, *We are beyond rescue.* "I don't know."

"There's nothing," a voice says behind her. "I tried. I couldn't disrupt the threads. At all."

Gyrald looks weary. Their body sags, their hooked feet scrabble, their petal-face droops.

"Gyrald!" Elza feels a little less horrible. "I'm so glad you're okay. Tina, this is Gyrald."

"We met! Good to see you." Tina spits on the floor.

Gyrald spits too, and for a moment Elza can pretend they're just hanging out.

"Not fair," Naahay mutters. "If I had delivered you to justice . . . I could have been lifted up. Like I deserve."

Naahay seems to shrivel before Elza's eyes.

"None of this needed to happen," Elza says to Naahay. "We could have been friends."

"You and I were never going to be friends." The hatred in Naahay's eyes knocks Elza on her heels. "And now you won't even try to save me."

"I can't," Elza says.

The Ardenii send Elza another flash: her friends are starting their final assault, fighting for their lives.

"We need to go," Elza says.

"The palace is so empty. The queen only brought a few attendants, to reduce the weight so she could travel faster. It's been so lonely, but at least I've found the perfect way to hide myself," Gyrald says. "Oh, oh, I never should have stayed here, I should have fled with you. I waited too long to give up on princess training, and now there are no more princesses."

"*What?*" Naahay says.

"It's true," Tina says. "Even if your betrayal had worked, you'd have gained nothing."

Naahay starts to cry, loud and high-pitched, like an animal in a trap. Her sobs echo around the catacombs, until they come back sounding like laughter.

Elza gives Naahay one last look, then turns to leave.

"Are you sure—" Tina looks back at Naahay's misery.

"I'm sorry," Elza says. "I really am. There are a lot of other people we can still help, if we move fast."

58

.

WYNDGONK

. . . 173 Earth days until all the suns go out forever

Sing fire, sing water, sing blood. Even as I rush into the path of death, I feel the saints of the air around me, and all the way inside my lung-stomachs. My flame is true, my flame blazes every color, let me light a path for myself and for all those who journey with me. As I breathe, I burn.

Wyndgonk prays again—as fire descends into peril worse than a hundred Dnynth nests.

The *Undisputed Training Bra Disaster* drops out of the *Nindred's Blessing*, whirls around, and snags a few large chunks of debris. What's left of the rebel fleet, along with the Grattna warships and Kraelyor battle-slicers, follow suit, lassoing sections of these once-sleek starships that flew proud and true before Wyndgonk's people evolved.

All at once they see the outlines of the moon and the ships defending it. Even without being able to see any details, Wyndgonk can make out a perfect defensive formation, covering every part of the moon's gravity well.

"Marsh and waste, that is a lot of ships." Ganno curses in a couple languages. "Makes me sick in my gutspleen."

"I thought we had tied up most of Marrant's ships inside the junkyard," Yiwei says. "But his fleet is big enough that he can still spare enough ships to blockade this moon. Completely."

"Trust the plan," Rachael says, but she gives off a rich stew of fear chemicals.

The moon is still half a light-year away. All the ships are doing maximum spaceweave, sprinting flat-out like a mob of run-farmers. Their borrowed garbage streams behind them, sucked along by their wake.

"Almost." Yiwei leans forward. "Almost. Just a little closer . . ."

Wyndgonk looks at the hearthlight, cradled inside a stasis field. If this half-and-half ship finally breaks apart, the way Wyndgonk has been expecting it to since forever, the hearthlight will be protected until the moment that nothing is protected. *Mother, I swear I've done my best, whatever comes next.*

The distant stars are blue needles. The moon is a fuzzy shape rushing toward them.

"Nearly there," Yiwei says. Then he punches one arm in the air, almost like he's dancing, and shouts, "NOW. Exit spaceweave, release the ion harness."

"Sure," Zaeta and Damini say in unison.

The *Undisputed Training Bra Disaster* slows down suddenly, at the edge of the moon's gravity well. The space junk keeps its momentum, racing ahead of them.

Wyndgonk smolders with satisfaction as a slice of ancient wreckage crashes into one of Marrant's ships in orbit, plowing through its hull and causing severe damage. The damaged ship spins out of control, crashing into its neighbor. And still the junk keeps coming.

"Let's follow it down," Yiwei says. "We can still use it as cover for our approach." He turns to Wyndgonk. "This was a good idea. Thank you for suggesting it."

Wyndgonk sobs, because fire learned the hard way that whenever these people start celebrating, it means something truly ruinous is about to happen.

Sure enough, Kez (*they/them*) points to the tactical scan and says, "We've got trouble."

Something very big is on their tail, coming out of the spaceship graveyard and following them to the moon. For a moment, Wyndgonk thinks it's more space junk, then fire realizes: it's Marrant's other ships. Too many to count.

"We're trapped between two enemy fleets," Kez says. "This is really, really not good for my complexion."

The ships from the junkyard bear down on the rebel fleet, driving them toward the orbiting vessels below. The gap the rebels made in the blockade doesn't look big enough to sneak through. Wyndgonk is starting to hate this plan, even if fire helped to come up with it.

Missiles and dark-energy cannon bursts come from behind them, streaking past and narrowly missing their ship as Damini and Zaeta bob and weave.

"They're going to hit their own ships!" Ganno yells.

"Marrant doesn't care about friendly fire as long as he gets us," Yiwei says.

Kez risks getting on comms with Halred and the rest of the Grattna. "Hi! I mean, we move toward you. Listen, Marrant's flagship packed a lot of immobilizer claws, and I'm wondering if you copied that part. If so, maybe they'd like a taste of what they did to us?" They hold their breath, like they're hoping the Grattna understood.

"Yes!" Halred makes that weird Grattna hooting sound that gets under Wyndgonk's shell. "Pain captivity suffering [we you them] suffer share release!"

Immobilizer claws fly out of the Grattna ships and spin toward the Royal Compassion ships, both behind and in front of the rebel fleet. A moment later, a few of the ships in front of them stall and lose orbit.

"Still too many ships," Damini says.

"And we can't take a single hit," Zaeta adds.

A new voice gets on comms. "This is acting captain Yatto the Monntha on the rebel ship *Unbowed*. All of us ex-Royal ships will remain behind to guard your approach."

"Are you sure?" Rachael says. "You'll be in the line of fire."

"This is the very least we can do," Yatto says. "Just make it worthwhile."

"Thank you," Yiwei says. "Okay, we're going in."

"Is it too late for me to upgrade to a first-class ticket?" Kez says.

Zaeta says, "Remember all those times—"

"—when it felt like we were about to crash for sure?" Damini says.

"This is going to be worse," Zaeta says.

The rattling, screeching makeshift ship goes into a steep dive, plunging through the tiny gap in the enemy lines. Missiles explode all around, heavy weapon fire slashes right past them. The beautiful velvet-and-wood panels near Wyndgonk are ablaze—not the friendly kind—and Rachael rushes to get an extinguisher.

Wyndgonk withdraws partway into fire shell.

They're plummeting, past missiles and ray beams and explosions and enemy starships, on their way to a tiny moon crawling with hostile fascists who will kill Wyndgonk just for existing.

Microscopic saints of the wind, please let my furnace keep burning, and I will run as fast as I can, I swear to run forever.

59

.

RACHAEL

When Rachael opens her eyes again, everything is still. Golden dust motes swirl in the shafts of daylight coming through a crack overhead, riding a wave of white smoke. Everybody picks themselves up and looks around.

Yiwei strides out the hatch, onto the moon's surface. "We'll need to find a way to slip inside the ancient temple and—"

He stops, because the temple is gone.

Or rather, it's no longer visible. In its place is a small city: a collection of scuffed gray carbonfast walls ending in flat slate roofs, with round tunnels snaking between them. At the center of this metropolis, the structures get taller and cluster together, and after a moment Rachael can tell that they're built around the wedding chapel.

"They built a prefab town overnight." Kez whistles.

They crawl closer and hunker behind a big slash of streaky red rock. Now Rachael has a view of a doorway in the front of one of the buildings, where guards are waving people inside. Everyone coming and going from the structures is wearing a sort of hazmat suit, or a modified atmosphere suit.

"These aren't soldiers," Ganno murmurs. "They look like scientists, or engineers."

These scientists look . . . excited. They're almost the first people to look at the super-advanced ruins left by a long-dead civilization, and they don't seem to care that they're doing it on behalf of a mass murderer. Rachael feels sick to her stomach.

"We need to find a way inside," Yiwei says. "If we could capture one of those scientists, we could steal a suit and some credentials."

Everybody turns and looks at Ganno the Wurthhi.

"Um, why are you all looking at me?" Ganno says. "What did I do?"

"It's more what you're going to do, mate," Kez says. "There's only one of us here who looks like they could be a member of the Royal Compassion."

Ganno goes rigid. Even the spikes on his head and neck get pricklier. "Oh."

Kez leans close to Ganno. "I know. You hate these people, even more than I do. I get it. Having to dress up as one of them, it's not just cosplay."

"I don't know what 'cosplay' is. But yes. They make me want to scream."

"I'm sorry," Kez says. "But we're all doing things we hate."

The two of them make eye contact, and Rachael can feel all of the history between them. Ganno was angry that Kez helped negotiate with the Compassion, back when they were the government of Ganno's homeworld. Kez hated doing that, but it was necessary—just like this is necessary.

Ganno nods. "So be it."

They lay in wait as a few technicians wander by. Then they hit the jackpot: one lone scientist comes straggling along: an Irriyaian, roughly the same size as Ganno.

Yiwei and Eldnat jump out from behind their hiding place and drag the scientist behind their big rock spur. The scientist thrashes until Rachael finds a vial of sedative in her satchel and waves it under their face—then they conk out, snoring a little.

Ganno starts removing the scientist's clothing. "Hmm. This is Zanttra the Wurthhi (*he/him*) and he's a biologist."

"See that building on the left, third from the end?" Zaeta says. "There's a hatch, which was probably left over from the starship designs these walls were originally fabricated from. It's not guarded."

"So once you're inside," Damini adds, "you just sneak around there and let us all in."

Ganno nods and walks away, muttering, "I'll need to gargle floatbeast bile to get the taste of this out of my mouth."

From behind their hiding spot, Rachael can barely hear him going up to the Royal Compassion guards. "Uh, hello." He holds up Zanttra's pass.

One of the two guards, a Ghulg, says something about the Misshapen—meaning people like Wyndgonk, Zaeta, and Kfok—and they both laugh.

The other guard, a Makvarian, says, "Soon we won't have to deal with any of these infestations anymore. Can you imagine? It'll be so nice."

"Yes," Ganno says through gritted teeth. "I also wholeheartedly support genocide."

The guards recoil.

Wyndgonk sputters. Rachael can feel Yiwei tense and reach for his gun.

Then the guards shrug. "Scientists," says the Ghulg. They wave Ganno past.

A minivan-sized chunk of debris has crashed in between two big mud dunes. Everybody crouches behind it and keeps an eye on the unguarded doorway—being careful not to touch the wreckage, because it's still scalding hot.

"I hope Ganno is okay in there," Kez says. "It's silly. It's not as if he and I are a thing anymore, if we ever were. But if anything happens to him . . ."

"I can tell he really cares about you," Damini says.

"He's angry all the time, except when he looks at you," Zaeta says.

"I shouldn't crave his approval so much," Kez says. "But it's okay to crave his affection, right? Even if we could never have a real romance."

"It's all good. Just be careful, okay?" Rachael says. The unguarded hatch starts to judder a bit. "I think something's happening."

The hatch opens and Ganno's head pops out. He beckons with one arm. Rachael and Yiwei run across the rocky ground toward the doorway, with all their friends behind them.

Inside the doorway, Eldnat finds a container full of hazmat suits and other protective gear. "I you they [possible] wear use hide."

"These will fit all of us," Rachael says. "Almost." She looks at Wyndgonk.

"So what do I do?" Wyndgonk says.

"I found something that could work." Ganno drags over a carbonfast shell with vents on the sides and some motion-sensitive interface on top. "If we put you in this, you might look like a piece of equipment."

"This is revenge for all the times I wanted to flamethrower your face," Wyndgonk says. But fire clambers inside the metal box, which seals neatly.

They trudge through the maze, with Wyndgonk peering out through the front slats in fire disguise. One group of scientists in protective gear stops them and starts asking questions, but then smoke starts pouring out through the vent in the "machine" they're toting, and Ganno steps forward and says they need to get this equipment out of here before it melts down. The scientists look alarmed and wave them forward.

Rachael can tell they're getting closer to the heart of the prefab city, and the actual temple. She hears the echoes of footsteps and voices on soapstone, and the gurgling of an old waterspout.

One of the last newly constructed chambers is also the biggest they've seen so far, with ceilings at least twenty feet high, and workstations scattered around a wide and elongated space. At the center of the room is a holographic map of the Milky Way galaxy, except that it's sketchier.

A dozen people in protective gear hustle around, muttering to each other, bits and pieces of jargon.

"They've identified exactly which stars were attacked by the Bereavement," Kez says with a low whistle. "As I figured, it's mostly the stars that support inhabited planets. A lot of F- and G-class stars."

"And look at those lists on the side," Yiwei breathes. "Are those what I think they are?"

"I'm afraid so," Zaeta says. "Lists of major stars, sorted into three categories."

Damini adds, "Stars that Marrant wants to save, ones he definitely wants to snuff out, like what happened to Irriyaia. And I guess the third category is worlds that he'll give a chance to survive if they pledge their loyalty?"

That swirl of dread and anxiety is churning inside Rachael worse than ever.

"There's more," Kez whispers as they back away from the doorway before they're spotted. "Marrant wants to wipe out everyone who's shaped differently, once and for all. Most of us here will lose everything. But Earth's sun? Is on the chopping block, too."

"And we just brought the one thing he'll need to finish it," Yiwei says.

Somehow Rachael thought the scary-awful churn couldn't get any worse.

60

.

ELZA

Elza rushes up out of the catacombs, eyes sweeping left to right for danger.

She expects to stride into the royal receiving room or the queen's contemplation suite—but instead she finds herself in a white space with low styrofoam ceilings, spotted with water damage. The linoleum floor beneath her feet bears countless scuff marks, she smells the fug of overclocked laptops.

The skin on her upper arms goes frigid. This is the last place she ever wanted to see again.

All of a sudden she's a scared runaway, in a place where nobody wants her, mourning a friendship she destroyed.

"What is it?" Tina sounds far away. "What's wrong?"

Elza can't answer.

She's standing in the Coletivo Frenético, the hackerspace where she used to live after she was thrown out, first by her parents and then by Fernanda. Everything is exactly as she remembers, including her tiny cot in a storage room next to the kitchenette and the racks of expensive equipment. Over here is the long table lined with power outlets, where João and Mateus used to sit and give her the evil eye. Over there is the couch where Roberto slept.

It's not real, Elza tells herself. *It's a hologram.*

The Ardenii scanned Elza's phone when she first came to the palace, and now the queen has created a 3-D holo based on some of her old photos. When she looks carefully, there are blurry edges where her phone camera didn't see.

Queen Nonesuch thought this would get under Elza's skin and wreck her concentration. And it's working.

"All of this equipment is so primitive," Gyrald snorts. "Are these supposed to be *computers*?"

A thundering sound comes from somewhere overhead, ugly music that sounds out of tune on purpose, with pounding bass. Elza almost jumps out of her skin.

A voice rings out. "Disgraced. Discredited. Unrecognized. False princess, we would be done with you."

The cheap ceiling yawns open, foam tiles and metal struts parting, until the hackerspace is inside a cavernous space, like a cathedral, with high, vaulted ceilings where beams of amber light cross from distant windows.

"You are not the only one who can reach into the past to forge a weapon." The queen stands on a balcony, five meters up, looking down at Elza, with two attendants flanking her. She's clad in a maelstrom of liquid that churns around her, changing colors as it goes, and her crown glows until it leaves streaks on Elza's retinas.

And hanging on a belt around the queen's waist: seven crowns, linked in a wreath.

"Surrender," the queen says. "Prostrate yourself before me. Kneel, and I may yet find some use for you."

Elza's mind is working overtime.

Gyrald said the queen only brought a few attendants with her on this trip, in order to travel fast. And the Ardenii won't do anything to harm anyone directly. So it's just Elza and her friends versus the queen and her closest aides.

If Elza can get close enough to that tangle of crowns on the queen's hip, she can patch the code she left on her crown . . . but the crowns are far above her, out of reach.

Elza looks around the reconstructed hackerspace again, and this time she sees . . . weakness. "You went to so much trouble to throw me off my game with this flawed illusion," she says to the seething figure on the balcony. "You know what this tells me? That you're afraid. You still think I could take you down."

Elza can feel the Ardenii watching—the hairs on the back of her neck stand up, but also there's a buzzing in her head. Everything in this fake hackerspace has eyes: the toaster, the 3-D printer, the rack of hard drives, the posters for long-ago hackathons . . . all paying attention.

Like the Ardenii are trying to decide what to do. Who to support.

They already let Elza out of her cell, which they probably weren't supposed to do.

"The other princesses didn't put up a fight, did they?" Elza says. "They just gave up their crowns and let you throw them away. Too bad for you I'm the Rogue Princess."

Elza has never called herself the Rogue Princess out loud—other people gave her that name. Claiming the title for herself feels like a whole new coronation.

"You are nothing," the queen says. "And soon you shall be less than nothing." But there's a twitch on the side of her green-coated face.

Elza needs to keep the queen talking while she figures out a plan. "You became queen just as all the stars were starting to die. The Ardenii must have been overwhelming you with all of the panic and chaos and pain, and it was all your responsibility. Why would you want to deal with that alone? You could have had all the princesses standing with you."

The queen sneers. "You never understood, even after you failed the test of the logic sphere. One can do no good if one wastes time dwelling upon the misfortune of others. A queen must look past the never-ending cries of victims and see the shape of history."

Elza fixes the bug inside her code in her mind's eye, until she could almost repair it in her sleep.

"Recently, some of my friends have been annoyed at me, because I took time to help strangers in need, instead of staying focused on our mission to stop the Bereavement," Elza says. "My friends said that saving a few hundred lives wasn't so important, when billions of people are at stake."

The queen frowns. "Your friends were correct."

Elza puts on a brave face while she tries to figure out how she can climb up to that balcony. She left her tactical ballgown on that tiny ship. "Maybe. But your way leads to more pain for everyone. You probably tell yourself you're being practical and sensible while you make friends with Marrant. He'll kill half the stars just to reshape everything the way he wants."

Elza glances over her shoulder: Tina nods at her, with pride in her eyes.

We're not just your voice, Elza thinks at the Ardenii. *We're your hands and feet, your presence in the world. Who do you want to be known by? I know you care, even if I still don't understand how you think. You want to save people. Let me help you.*

The Ardenii respond, **Primary and secondary interface conflict unresolved.**

"You wore your stolen glory as if it belonged to you." The queen's serene look is gone, her rage revealed at last. "You defied my will and set yourself against me. Even uncrowned, you dare to speak to the Ardenii, who should speak only to me. You walk freely within my palace."

Two attendants, an Undhoran and a Zyzyian, enter the hackerspace through the front and back entrances, holding guns with barrels like harpoon blades.

"Can you keep them busy for me?" Elza turns to ask Tina and Gyrald.

But they've vanished. She's alone in the hackerspace, with the queen above and the two guns aimed at her.

The queen's voice rings in her ears: "Alone forever, false princess."

Both attendants fire their weapons with a sizzling crackle.

Elza leaps behind the same desk where Rafael once hid so he could jump out and surprise her, and slides across the floor. She comes up and throws an unplugged soldering iron at one of the attendants, who goes down.

Then she's dashing through the front door of the hackerspace. She expects to run out onto the Avenida Paulista for a second, but instead she's back in the palace, a walkway near the ballroom with the winged ceiling. "Tina!" she shouts. "Gyrald!" No answer.

Her friends could be a few feet away, but she won't see them unless the illusion lifts.

Elza hears movement behind her: the other attendant? She turns to fight.

And she finds herself looking at someone she thought she'd never see again.

Just like with the hackerspace, she knows it's an illusion, but she's still overcome by saudades and anxiety.

Elza's looking into the eyes of the friend she betrayed back on Earth, after she'd given Elza everything. She's wearing the dark strapless dress she used to wear on dates, the one with all the threads gathered around a beaded heart. The same dress she's wearing in most of the photos and videos that Elza couldn't bear to delete from her phone. Her skin looks golden, her eyes are a rich green.

Fernanda's lip curls, the way it used to when she was about to say something wonderfully sarcastic. She whispers, *Just let it happen.*

Too late, Elza realizes that threads are snaking toward her from all sides.

The same threads that took the former queen and Naahay.

They're already attaching themselves to Elza's skin.

"These threads are alive, after a fashion," the queen says, "and they're very hungry. I found them on a world you'll never visit, the half-dead planet Balarada, and I've helped them feast on so many nerves and sinews. This will hurt more if you struggle."

Four threads have already fixed themselves to Elza's arms and legs, unshakable, and more of them are reaching toward her. She's trapped.

Fernanda mouths: *This is what you deserve.*

61

.

RACHAEL

Here's how it happens.

First, there's a long silence, like a held breath, which seems to last a dozen lifetimes. Yiwei squeezes Rachael's hand, Damini and Zaeta exchange one last smile. Ganno shuffles his feet, standing guard outside their hiding place: a tiny storage room just a dozen feet away from the doorway that leads to the love temple. (The doorway that's protected by two guards in mech suits and an energy barrier that glows the same turquoise as a fuzzy sweater Rachael used to wear.)

Ganno whispers, "Now."

And then everything happens very quickly.

Ganno takes Zaeta by the flipper-claw, and they're sprinting across the intersecting hallway, dodging pulse-cannon fire.

Damini is already sliding across the floor toward the two mech guards—which just started a maintenance cycle that'll slow their reflexes for a few moments. Long enough to take them out of action, or so everyone hopes.

Eldnat stands taller than Rachael has ever seen, unfurling all three wings with a loud SNAP, and then he's flying along the ceiling toward the guards. Wyndgonk runs at them, releasing a tongue of fire, eye-searing bright.

Yiwei tosses a device to Damini, and she catches it with one hand, giving a thumbs-up. She attaches it to one mech guard, then the other, and they both power down, leaving their occupants helpless.

A squadron of Royal Compassion soldiers without any fancy armor is approaching from the opposite end of the hallway, shooting pulse cannons and fireburst guns. Yiwei shoots back, while Rachael drags a sheet of carbonfast out of the storage room into the hallway, creating a makeshift barricade.

"Come on, Ganno and Zaeta," Yiwei grunts. "Don't keep us waiting."

"Zaeta's almost done," Damini says, concentrating on their shared connection. "Remember, we'll only have a few minicycles to get inside the temple once the force barrier comes down." In other words, twenty or thirty seconds.

For one golden moment, Rachael feels good as she rushes toward her friends. Everything is going okay. They took out the mech suits, their friends are about to take down the force barrier, the rest of Marrant's forces won't get past their barrier in time to stop them. This could work.

Then Damini frowns. "Zaeta and Ganno are trapped."

"We'll come back for them, I swear," Rachael says.

"They're just a dozen meters away. We need to help them." Then Damini blinks. "It's about to happen."

The turquoise barrier vanishes, and the way into the temple is open.

"Go," Yiwei says. "Hurry!"

Wyndgonk is already rushing inside the temple with the hearthlight cradled in one claw, with Eldnat right behind fire.

The barrier will only be open for another ten seconds, tops.

"Come on!" Wyndgonk beckons. "I need your help in here."

Kez is already inside too, and now Yiwei rushes through the entrance. Damini is stuck, looking back.

"It's okay." Rachael tries to talk to Damini like a captain: steely and soothing. "Zaeta and Ganno can take care of themselves. They want us to finish the mission."

Damini nods and steps through the doorway—just before the energy barrier comes back on, with Rachael still on the outside.

The mech suits are humming back to life. A dozen Royal Compassion soldiers run toward Rachael. She thinks about surrendering—but then something catches fire next to her. They're not taking prisoners.

Ugh. This is not how she wants to go out.

Major panic attack coming, except that it started at some point in the distant past and will continue until all the nerve endings have petered out. Rachael is talking to herself, but she can't hear what she's saying.

"Rachael!" Yiwei shouts from the other side of the barrier. "Get away from here. We'll find you later. Just hide, or find Zaeta and Ganno. Go!"

The air is sizzling and the exosuit people are lunging at Rachael with their big stubby arms. Yiwei and the others are sealing the door they just came through.

Rachael waits one second longer, then takes off running, with the air on fire all around her.

62

.

ELZA

Elza reaches out to the Ardenii. *You have to make a choice now. If you let her keep this illusion in place, you're helping the queen to kill me, even if you don't kill me yourselves. I know you've been keeping track of how many living things are dying, and this is your last chance to help me stop the tide of death.*

Nothing happens. The Ardenii feed Elza a torrent of news about the battle on the moon's surface—her friends are in worse trouble—and the riots and civil wars on a dozen planets. A species of underwater slime on a distant world just crawled onto land for the first time ever. All this information gives Elza a head rush that whites out her vision for a moment.

Fernanda looks into Elza's eyes, making the face she practiced in that one video where she lip-synched to Ludmilla.

The four threads are burrowing under Elza's skin, and more threads are reaching her. Tina could help, if Elza could find her.

Already, Elza can feel the strength leaving her arms and legs—she tries to move, and can't. The queen mentioned something about the threads eating away at your nerves, like the signals from your brain won't reach your muscles. The pain starts to dance up and down Elza's arms and legs, and she can already tell it'll get worse soon.

Just help me see past this illusion, Elza pleads with the Ardenii. *I'll do the rest.*

The Ardenii respond with a very large number. Elza doesn't understand for a moment, then she gets it: the death rate just went up. By a lot.

The fake hackerspace behind Elza vanishes, and so does the ghost of Fernanda.

Tina is standing a few feet away from Elza, looking around in a panic. The other attendant lies unconscious at Tina's feet.

"Elza, damn it, where—" Tina turns and sees her. "There you are. Oh no. No, no, no. Those threads. Hold on, I got you."

Tina and Gyrald both set about yanking the threads away from Elza.

The four that had already burrowed under her skin hurt coming out, and a little blood spatters on the palace floor.

The queen is gliding down from the balcony, to land on her feet a short distance away from Elza.

Elza pulls herself upright, now that she's free of the life-sucking threads. She looks the queen in the eye: "You keep miscalculating. One of us wasn't ready for a crown, and it's not me."

The taunts work—the queen brandishes a Javarah shock-stick, like the ones Tina used to train with, and lunges at Elza.

"Ah, there it is," Elza snorts. "Tina, what do you think of people who reach for violence the moment things don't go their way?"

"Unimaginative," Tina says. "I would even say weak-minded."

"Weak-minded. Yes." Elza pivots out of the queen's way and sweeps her leg. She almost connects.

The queen swings again, and grazes Elza's shoulder. Pain surges down Elza's already sore arm and she falls on the ground.

Elza crouches a few inches away from the ring of golden circlets hanging from the queen's belt.

She reaches out and touches one of the crowns—she can tell it's hers—and concentrates on the interface.

The Ardenii won't fix the code for her, but they guide her to it. She makes the tiniest change, with her mind.

The shock-stick comes down toward Elza's unprotected neck.

The queen stops, mid-swing.

"What . . . what did you do?"

Elza still has her hand on the ring of crowns. She plucks all seven of them away, then gets to her feet.

"What did you do?" the queen shrieks. "We cannot feel the Ardenii anymore."

The queen loosens her grip on the shock-stick, and Elza carefully knocks it onto the floor.

"I left some extra code on my crown as a precaution," Elza says. "I didn't realize you were going to link all the crowns together. That's bad network security on your part."

In her mind, she hears Princess Constellation: *Paranoia is beauty.*

"The Ardenii will not heed me. Their voices are stilled. You will fix this."

"You can't afford my rates." Elza toys with the ring of crowns, shrinking them down until she shapes them into a bracelet, or more like a bangle. She slips them onto her wrist, where they feel natural.

"That's the thing," Elza says. "When you close yourself off from caring about the pain of others, you stop being curious. And then you go and do silly things, like networking your hardware together without checking for malware first."

Elza walks away from the queen, Tina and Gyrald by her side.

And then the gunfire starts.

All three of the queen's attendants have recovered, and they're shooting their fancy guns at Elza and the others. The air crackles around them.

"Stay low to the ground," Tina says, crouching down and running.

Another gunshot makes the air crackle next to Tina's head. She steers Elza and Gyrald around the next corner.

Tina's tiny ship is right ahead of them, perched at an odd angle in the cargo hangar.

"The Mazda Miata!" Tina shouts. "Come on, we gotta go."

Tina's already getting the roof hatch open, but Gyrald stops moving.

"I can't go with you," Gyrald says.

"You can't stay here!" Elza protests. "You have to leave, before it's too late."

"It's already too late, I'm afraid," Gyrald says. "You remember I told you that I had hidden myself away inside these walls? The price was rather high."

Gyrald gestures with one of their front limbs, and they turn transparent for a moment.

"You're . . . a hologram," Tina says. "How are you a hologram?"

"I found a way to become a part of the palace. I wanted to learn everything. Perhaps in time I will join the Ardenii." Gyrald cocks their head and does the thing with their petal-face that Elza's learned to recognize as a smile. "I learned so much, including things I wish I didn't know. Princess. You must go now."

As soon as they say that, the attendants come around the corner and start shooting again.

"Please," Gyrald says. "Save my people. Save everyone. I believe you can win."

Tina is already in the pilot seat of the little starship and is powering everything up. "We're ready."

"I'm so sorry." Elza shakes her head. "I'll find a way to help you, if we make it through this." Then she climbs into the ship next to Tina.

The ship races toward an opening that's appeared at the back of the white chamber. Tina manages to pilot the ship with one hand while offering Elza the other hand. They hold hands as the palace in space shrinks away and they head back out into the void.

The Ardenii have gone quiet again. Elza's malicious code won't affect them directly at all, but it's overwhelming their main interfaces—the crowns—and they won't be able to say much to anyone for a while. The floating palace is drifting off course, in a distant orbit around Larstko IVb, and Marrant's ships swerve to avoid crashing into it.

In all the confusion, Tina manages to slip past the blockade in orbit and head for the moon's surface.

"Who was she?" Tina asks in a low voice.

"Who was who?" But Elza already knows what Tina means.

"I caught a glimpse before the last illusions fell away. There was someone looking at you, she looked like another travesti. And when you woke up earlier, you said something about being a bad friend."

As tired as Elza is, this still makes her heart race. She can feel her hairs standing up, where the crown used to be. Maybe Tina will never look at her the same way again, once she hears the truth.

"Fernanda was my best friend." Elza speaks as if each word is a tiny explosive that must be defused exactly right. "She was there for me after I had to leave home. She taught me so much, and she let me stay with her when I had no place else. But she always used to go out with these guys, and I would sit at home, freaking out that something would happen to her."

Tina sucks in a breath and nods. "You told me it's dangerous to be a travesti there. It's not fair. You shouldn't have had to live with that fear, when you were just learning to love yourself."

"It doesn't excuse what I did." Elza can still see the hurt in Fernanda's face. "I was still messed up from all the stuff my parents said to me, and I couldn't stop worrying about Fernanda, every time she went out. So I . . . put some spyware on her phone, so I could make sure she was okay. After she found out, she never wanted to see me again."

As soon as Elza finishes, she feels as if a huge weight was just lifted off her head for the second time today. She's been holding in this story for so long.

"Oh wow. You've been carrying this the whole time I've known you? I'm so sorry." Tina takes a deep breath. "You made a mistake, okay? You were trying to keep her safe. I've done messed-up things in the name of protecting other people, too."

"Maybe. But . . . I shouldn't have violated her privacy like that."

"Yeah, but you were traumatized, and you'd never had a friend who knew the real you," Tina says. "You messed up, sure. But it's made you a better princess. All that knowledge, all those secrets, you handle them with care, because you know what it's like to break someone's trust."

Oh. Elza hadn't thought about it like that.

"You really think so?" She looks at her girlfriend—her consort—and feels too many things at once. Grateful, scared, happy, guilty. Her heart is going haywire.

"Yeah." Tina smiles. "I've seen it so many times. You take care of people, but you're careful about it. It's one of the things I admire about you."

Elza looks at the ring of crowns around her right wrist, still inactive thanks to her malicious code. "I'll never know what it would have been like if I'd gotten to be a princess at the palace, with everybody else. But I think I need to find my own way of using the Ardenii without spying on other people so much."

Tina pokes at the pilot interface with her free hand. "People do seriously random things when they're scared. You're still responsible for what you did, but we also have to blame the people who created that fear in the first place." She looks at the instruments. "Oh great, we're about to crash. Again."

Elza looks up and realizes their tiny ship is going into a nosedive toward the surface of the tiny moon. The engines are screaming and spewing dark smoke like Wyndgonk on a bad day. The heat of the moon's atmosphere is making bright orange streaks across the viewports.

"I'd better put on my tactical ballgown," Elza says.

63

.

WYNDGONK

Wyndgonk's mothers used to say that being the keeper of the hearthlight was the kind of responsibility that shapes your whole life. The three of them sat in the cloister entrance, with a view of the poison waterfall catching the light from both the red and yellow suns. Dnynths circled overhead, looking like friendly spirits instead of monsters.

All Wyndgonk wanted to do was run, like the other kids. Fire would have been so happy to finish school, then spend several years running and stirring the air, to help bring the precious thurli roots down from the skies. Then maybe fire could go to work developing the next generation of Thythuthyan spacecraft.

"You can help to protect the future of our people," said Wyndgonk's mother Innávan. "No job is more important, not even the work of the Defenders and the Inventors."

"So many of our legends are about heroic hearthlight-keepers," added Wyndgonk's other mother, Uynhyu, who died before Wyndgonk went to the palace. "You were named for Wyndgonk the Brazen, who ventured into the mouth of a great frost-serpent to retrieve the spark of life. But also, at every hearth festival we sing of the hearth-keeper to come, who will restore our birthright from beyond."

Wyndgonk looked down at fire own pointed feet. "I wouldn't call it singing. It's more like a waking snore."

"Our heritage is everything," Innávan said sharply. "And you refuse to appreciate how lucky you are to be part of it."

In the end, of course, Wyndgonk was able to get out of hearth-keeper training, but only because they sent fire to the palace instead. Fire traded one heavy legacy for another.

Yiwei, Eldnat, Kez, Damini, and Wyndgonk run inside the wedding chamber and close the entrance behind them. Seven humanoid technicians in protective gear are holding instruments and staring at large pieces of equipment that are attached to the walls and floor, including a large framework built around the dry fountain. Mech suits are trying to break into the chamber, and everybody is yelling. Wyndgonk ignores them all and heads for the dry fountain.

Our heritage is everything.

This should be easy: just pull the hearthlight out of the stasis cube and stick it inside the cavity at the top of the dry fountain. But the stasis cube won't open and the hearthlight is stuck inside and everybody is yelling and dodging heavy weapons fire.

No job is more important.

"We need to go back for Rachael," Kez says.

"We can't, I'm sorry, we can't," Yiwei says, giving off a mix of chemicals that Wyndgonk has learned to call "anguish."

Eldnat herds the scientists into the corner at gunpoint. The scientists are shouting about their precious equipment, and demanding that nobody touch anything.

"I'm scared for Zaeta and Ganno," Damini says. "Total panic, disorientation. They're being thrown in a cage."

"We'll save them," Yiwei says. "All three of them. Once we're done here."

Yiwei, Kez, and Damini shove two big stone blocks toward the ornate doorway, making a barricade.

One of the armored soldiers fires a pulse cannon and makes a new burn mark on the wall. The captive scientists cower and start yelling louder.

Kez rushes over to help Wyndgonk, and the two of them manage to unjam the stasis cube and lift out the crystalline double-knot.

The hearthlight slips through the gap between Kez's hands and Wyndgonk's front limbs. Wyndgonk watches it tumble toward the floor—it's going to shatter, it's ruined, Wyndgonk is disgraced—then Kez catches it with one hand.

They rush the hearthlight over to the dry fountain, but there's a carbon-fast framework, which wasn't there before, blocking the way. Wyndgonk can't figure out how to get the hearthlight into the socket, and Innávan is yelling inside fire head about duty and responsibility and sacrifice.

"Don't touch that," shouts one of the scientists that Eldnat is holding at gunpoint in the corner. "You shouldn't even be in here."

The whole room shakes. The soldiers in mech suits are pounding on the stone-block barrier in the doorway.

Laynbone, the dragon made out of knives, appears in the center of this chamber. "Have you recovered what we thought never was? Have you brought the flower of our love?"

"Can everybody just be quiet and let me concentrate?" Wyndgonk growls.

The pounding gets louder and more insistent. Cracks spread in the stone barriers, bits of rock crumble off. "This won't hold them," Kez yelps.

Wyndgonk gives up on trying to be gentle and just pulls at the metal framework trapping the dry fountain. It won't give.

Protect the future of our people.

Yiwei rushes over to the dry fountain. "We need to get out of here. How is this going?"

"Give me a moment," Wyndgonk says.

"We don't have a moment," Yiwei says.

"Then help me pull off this junk!"

Yiwei grabs at the metal framework and starts trying to pull it off, bracing with one foot against the side of the dry fountain.

"You're ruining delicate equipment!" shouts one of the scientists in the corner.

Laynbone flutters her knifey wings. "We've waited so long, even past our deaths, and I just want to be sure. Where is the flower of our love?"

"It's in the land of shut-your-face," Wyndgonk says.

Everything goes into the Dnynth nest, all at once. Wyndgonk looks up to see seven angry scientists rushing toward him and Kez, while Eldnat looks on helplessly with his gun in one slack hand/foot. The soldiers shatter one of the two stone blocks.

Damini's found a hidden passageway at the back of the room. "We need to go now!"

"Grab the hearthlight," Yiwei yells. "We can't leave it here."

Kez falls sideways and lands on their back, clutching at a burn on their shoulder.

The barricade blows inward and smoke pours into the room. Pulse-cannon fire sizzles over Wyndgonk's head.

The hearthlight is gone. One of the scientists is running with it cradled in their arms, while the others hold Wyndgonk down and pummel fire carapace.

Exo-enforcers shove the last of the barricade out of the way, and soldiers are stomping into the building.

Yiwei and Eldnat are already running to the secret passage, where Damini is frantically beckoning.

Kez gets to their feet and pushes the scientists off Wyndgonk. "Come on. We need to go."

"I swore," Wyndgonk blurts. "I swore that I would not leave the hearthlight, that I would guard it with my life."

You were named for Wyndgonk the Brazen.

Wyndgonk can't even see where the hearthlight has gone.

Kez closes their eyes for a second, then says, "We'll come back for you." Then they're gone.

The chamber is already filling up with enforcers, flanked by a few of the mechas. Damini is still standing in the doorway, waving frantically to Wyndgonk, and then a pulse-cannon blast streaks past her, leaving a bruise mark on the stone edge of the doorway. Damini takes off running after Yiwei, Kez, and Eldnat.

Two of the mech soldiers stand over Wyndgonk, and one of them keeps a big metal hand on Wyndgonk's head just to be sure. Wyndgonk expects to be dead at any moment—fire was expecting to be dead already—and fire tries to pray without making a sound.

The scientists adjust something, and the big cage they built around the fountain restructures itself to create an opening, so they can easily slide the hearthlight inside.

Wyndgonk wants to scream blue sparks. Of *course* there was an easy way to get past that machinery—if only they'd done a better job of intimidating these scientists, one of them might have helped. But now it's too late, because Wyndgonk and fire friends were useless in the one moment when everything was at stake.

The scientists carefully ease the hearthlight into its cradle, and chatter to each other about energy readings and emissions.

"The interface still isn't responding as expected," one of them says.

"Check the readings again," says another.

Laynbone the dragon flutters her knife wings. "The Bereavement will respond to your commands now. But we still would wish to understand. Where is the flower of our love? Whoever can speak of, and for, the flower will hold sway above all."

Nobody pays the dragon any notice. The dry fountain hums to life and all of the carvings on the walls are ablaze.

Someone is standing behind Wyndgonk. Fire can't turn to see, with the mech-suit holding fire in place—but the flesh-melting stench is unmistakable. Wyndgonk feels a chill running down fire neck.

Thondra Marrant strides around until he crouches down, face-to-face with Wyndgonk. His smile grows hungrier.

"Don't bother," Wyndgonk says.

"What?" Marrant raises an eyebrow. "What do you mean?"

"You were about to try to psychologically torture me," Wyndgonk says, "by saying something to ruin my self-esteem, and remind me of my failure. I'm saying, don't bother. You can't make me feel worse than I already do."

"Take it from one who knows," Marrant says. "It is always possible to feel worse."

"*You* feel bad because you faced actual consequences for your behavior for once. It's not the same." Wyndgonk vents a leaf of red flame, but the mech tightens its grip on fire carapace.

Marrant's face goes rigid and he shows teeth. "You don't speak to your betters that way. You will be erased—your life a forgotten stain—there will be an end to the foulness." Marrant's whole body trembles with rage, even the spiky dark hairs on top of his head quiver.

"And now we've reached the other part," Wyndgonk says. "Where you raise your hands to me and erase me. Go ahead. I don't care."

"Oh no," Marrant says. "You don't die yet. We are going to immense trouble to ferry more examples of vermin such as yourself to this tiny rock, so that everyone may see the need for a purification." He gestures at the stooges in mech suits. "Take this thing to the containment area, with the others."

The mech suits seize four of Wyndgonk's legs—two each—and drag fire away from the chamber, where the hearthlight is at the center of a shuddering machine. Fire squirms and struggles, but their grip is unbreakable. They travel along more of those rounded corridors, past sterile gray rooms where scientists are pointing and shouting out numbers.

64
.

RACHAEL

Rachael natters to herself as she sneaks around the maze of prefab tunnels and laboratories. Every few moments, enforcers or scientists rush past, and Rachael ducks into hiding or pretends to be just another scientist in a hazmat suit even though she's too short and her face looks wrong inside her faceplate.

"This is my second-least favorite visit to the ruins of an ancient alien death empire. Next chance I get, I'm leaving a one-star review on TripAdvisor."

Rachael finds an exit, but two enforcers in mech suits are checking people's passes, and she looks nothing like Ynmi, the Javarah whose suit they swiped. She keeps thinking she's found the doorway she came in through, but then she's in a totally different set of eggshell-white crinkle-walled spaces.

She finds herself in another boxy laboratory.

"What is the point of a maze where you can't make a wish? I am going to complain." She makes herself stop muttering—maybe a moment too late.

Shadows zigzag across the corrugated wall. Footsteps approach, a bunch of them. Rachael looks around for someplace to hide. There's nothing.

A familiar voice sounds out. ". . . that's not the reason I'm keeping the prisoners alive, now that we have the hearthlight," Marrant says. "Don't presume to understand my designs, Vyzi."

No no no. They're right outside, in the hallway.

Rachael looks around the tiny room. There's a table covered with plasti-form diagrams, a couple of teacup chairs, a big machine the size and shape of a night-blooming cactus. Nothing, nothing. At last, she spots a tiny door behind the machine, with a window at eye level. Looks like another one of the features that was part of the spaceship designs they printed this facility from.

She runs through the tiny door and clicks it shut behind her, just before Marrant enters with a group of enforcers.

Rachael huddles under the window, with her skin prickling. She's in a small, rectangular space between two sections of the facility, with rocky dirt underfoot instead of floors.

A young Javarah in an enforcer uniform, who must be Vyzi (*she/her*), is saying to Marrant, "I was just disappointed, is all. I've heard all about your death touch, but I've never seen it in action."

Rachael's skin crawls worse than ever.

Marrant rounds on Vyzi, snarling. "You think I'm doing any of this for your amusement? Do you believe my touch is some sort of party trick? Answer! Yes or no?"

"No! No, of course not." Vyzi audibly flinches.

"You know I could touch you, and nobody would blame me?" Marrant roars. "Everybody would say you deserved to die."

"I do . . . I do know that, yes, sir." Vyzi stammers. "I didn't intend any disrespect. I know that your . . . your abilities have a serious purpose, and I would never . . ."

"Stop talking," Marrant snaps. His voice gets louder as he walks up to the door that Rachael is hiding behind. "Good: this rapid fabricator still has full capacity. We need to make more restraints for the incoming prisoners."

Rachael risks standing back up, so she can look through the window. Marrant feeds a pair of metal wrist cuffs into one neck of the cactus-shaped machine—the same kind he was wearing when he was supposed to be a prisoner. A moment later, a dozen identical pairs come out the far side.

"That'll do. Come."

The young Javarah follows, ears still pressed against her skull. The other enforcers follow, too.

Rachael waits in this tiny open-air rectangle for ages—not just to make sure Marrant and his creeps are really gone, but to let her heart and breathing slow to something like a normal rate. Then she eases the door open and steps back into the laboratory.

It's just sinking in that Marrant says he got the hearthlight, which means Yiwei and the others failed. She's about to go search for them, then she stops and looks at the machine that Marrant called the "rapid fabricator."

It's not too different from the machines that make uniforms and other gear on board starships.

"What if . . . what if anything you feed into it gets scanned and duplicated?" Rachael asks aloud. She studies the holographic controls. "Okay. So we want to make copies that are half the size of the original. And we want to keep making them until the machine runs out of raw material. Right? Right."

She actually shakes her own hand. She resists saying out loud, *Pleasure doing business with you.*

"If I survive this, I'm going to talk to myself way less."

She digs around in her bag until she finds a familiar lump of metal and fake fur. Xiaohou hums a few notes until she shushes him. "Hey, Xiaohou. I hope anything I tell you now, the duplicates will remember, too. I guess we'll find out. I want all of your copies to explore these service ducts over my head, but stay hidden. If you see Yiwei and the others, come find me. Oh, and if the original Xiaohou starts making noise, I want all of the copies to join in. Do you understand?"

Xiaohou thinks for a moment, then nods, going "boop be doop."

Rachael goes ahead and sticks the little robot into the left-hand stalk of the metal cactus. "Let's make you some friends." A moment later, miniature copies of Xiaohou start pouring out of the machine, one after the other. As soon as they drop onto the floor, they run across the floor, swing up onto the table, and climb the furrowed walls to reach the service duct.

Rachael loses count of how many miniature versions of Xiaohou scamper into the ducts. More than a dozen, less than a thousand.

She pulls the original Xiaohou out and sticks him back into her satchel, but the machine carries on making the tiny copies, humming and chortling.

Welp, turns out I have an army after all.

65
.

WYNDGONK

. . . 171 Earth days until all the suns go out forever

Cages, as far as Wyndgonk can see. Cages overhead, cages ahead and behind. Nothing but cages.

On one side of the ancient temple, Marrant's engineers have created a makeshift prison. Every time Wyndgonk looks up, another big starship lands on the rocky plain behind the temple, and a short time later, another group of prisoners is shoved inside a nearby cage.

Someone is calling Wyndgonk's name. Fire doesn't bother to look up.

Fire can't help imagining what Innávan would be saying right now. *We trusted you with the most important item in our culture, and you let some scientists trick you.*

"Wyndgonk!" the voice comes again.

At last, fire looks up and sees Yatto the Monntha and Kfok inside the same cage. They were on board the *Unbowed*, trying to hold off the Royal Compassion long enough for Wyndgonk and the others to reach the planet's surface.

"So. You were captured as well." Wyndgonk doesn't waste any smoke expressing surprise.

"I can't believe we're still alive." Kfok rolls her stubby head around her slug body. "These people don't usually bother taking prisoners."

"I have a feeling our survival is no blessing at all," Yatto says.

"You're right about that." Wyndgonk tells them what Marrant said: the prisoners are here to *show the need for purification.*

"He's going to make an example of us," someone says from the cage next door. Zaeta.

In Wyndgonk's head, Innávan says: *The hearthlight is our past and our future, our heritage and our hope for a birthright from beyond. You failed us.*

"Yatto the Monntha, it's you," says Ganno the Wurthhi, who's also in the neighboring cage. "You're here. Please tell me there's hope."

"I'm not the one you should ask." Yatto looks at Wyndgonk. "Are the others free? Do they still have the hearthlight?"

"Yes. And no. We lost the hearthlight. But our friends are still out there."

"I can feel Damini, running for her life," Zaeta says. "But it's faint."

Something cold is rising up inside Wyndgonk, almost putting out the fire inside.

"What can I do?" Ganno says. "Yatto, tell me. What do I do now?"

"We wait for our chance," Yatto says.

"There's one thing you can do," Zaeta says to Ganno. "Tell me how to live with losing everything. Marrant is getting ready to use the Bereavement to do to my homeworld the same thing that already happened to yours. Wedding Water will be gone in a single breath. I probably won't live to see it. How do I keep from breaking completely?"

Ganno sighs. "I think . . . you get angry, and you make it count. You put the blame where it belongs, on Marrant and his creeps. And you don't let yourself feel helpless—we can keep fighting, and that means they haven't won."

"Shh," Yatto says. "Someone's coming."

A cluster of shadows approaches from the side of the temple, approaching the front doors of the cages.

Yiwei, Kez, Eldnat, and Damini rush to the front of Wyndgonk's cage. Yiwei says, "We're here to get you—" And then he sees the rescue-proof cage.

"You're alive," says Kez (he/him). "All of you. I was so scared." He's nursing a superficial burn on his left shoulder.

Ganno smiles at Kez. "It's good to see you. There's still much we need to say to each other."

Damini is crouching down, so she and Zaeta can whisper back and forth.

Yiwei is still studying the cage. "We knocked out a guard, but they didn't have anything we could use to open this."

Eldnat says something Wyndgonk can't understand at first. "Cages me you my people [something] torment murder trap cruelty." Then Wyndgonk gets it: Eldnat's people were trapped in cages just like these, suffering and humiliated, and then a lot of them died.

"These people love cages way too much," Wyndgonk says. "Listen, rescuing us isn't your priority. Getting the hearthlight back is."

All the prisoners in the other cages are shouting and clamoring. More guards will show up soon.

Damini is crying. "I can't leave you," she says to Zaeta. "If anything happens to you, I . . ."

"I know." Zaeta heaves and closes half her eyes. "I know. We are joined for life, and if one of us dies, the other suffers . . . but my love for you goes beyond even that. You are my sister from another world." She stops shaking, with an effort that Wyndgonk can feel in fire shell.

Kez turns to Eldnat. "How do we help them?"

Eldnat hesitates, then lowers his head and folds all three wings into a kind of hood. For once, it's easy to understand what he says next: "We can do nothing."

"We can't just leave our friends caged," Kez says. "That's what we did to you, and it was wrong."

Eldnat's head lowers further. "Godparents us you Marrant [futility] die freedom escape trapped." Meaning: *Whatever we do, we can't free these prisoners. We can only get ourselves caught.*

"Go," Zaeta says to Damini. "Find our allies. Stop Marrant."

"He's planning a big show," Wyndgonk says. "That's why we're still alive."

"That explains all of the big ships approaching this rock. He's flying in a lot of dignitaries." Yiwei's tiny pink mouth makes a clicking sound. "It's a major strategic blunder, bringing in a ton of civilian transports in the middle of a battle zone. Hard to maintain security."

"Not only that," Kez says, "but I bet they'll try and land those ships, so everybody can have access to all of the comforts of home." He turns to Zaeta and Damini. "Remember how tricky it was to land here?"

Damini growls in her throat. "How could I forget? Of course—"

"—our ship is a half-and-half disaster," Zaeta says.

"But also, the magnetic field," Kez says. "It fluctuates and moves around. Remember? It's a beast, especially if you're not expecting it."

Wyndgonk feels something unexpected bubble up, like a laugh that begins in the pits of fire lung-stomachs. After a moment, fire realizes this feeling is . . . hope.

"What exactly did you have in mind?" Yatto asks Kez.

"Umm . . . okay, so all of these powerful ships use electromagnetic envelopes to shield their power cores—which is why it's such a bad idea to park so many of them on one wobbly moon, just to satisfy Marrant's vanity. And guess what?" Kez is bouncing up and down. "Wouldn't take much to make all those engine cores overload."

"In theory, you get one spectacular light show, but nobody gets seriously hurt." Kfok pumps one stinger-arm in the air.

"There's only one catch," Kez says. "We'll need to be in the air, at least thirty meters up. Which means first we'll need to find a ship that actually flies—"

"—and once all the engines go boom, we'll immediately crash." Damini looks at Zaeta. "I can't possibly do this without you."

"You won't," Zaeta says. "You'll have me with you every step of the way, even if we're not physically together. Now get going, before somebody comes to check on us."

They all leave, dragging the unconscious guards with them, and then the door clicks shut again. Zaeta, Ganno, Yatto, Kfok, and Wyndgonk are once again alone, staring at the bars of their cage.

66

.

TINA

The Mazda Miata spirals head over tail, with the engines on fire. We can't fight this magnetic flux, we're going to be lucky to walk away from this landing. At least Marrant's ships won't bother shooting at us, since we've already shot ourselves down.

"There." Elza points. "Try to bring us down over there."

We're flying over the dark side of the moon, at least a dozen miles away from the ancient temple. Nothing out here but crags and craters, except I see where Elza is pointing: the *Nindred's Blessing* and a handful of other Grattna ships, plus some Kraelyor battle-slicers.

"Okay, I'm going to try to crash as gently as possible. Hang tight, beautiful."

I pull us up with the last of our engine power—and then we hit, with an impact that jars every one of my bones. I grab hold of Elza as tight as I can.

We plow a brand-new furrow into the rocky ground and careen toward a spur of rock.

I wrestle with the dead controls, cursing and screaming, as the jagged wall rushes toward us. At this speed, we'll be dead on impact.

I don't know how to save us—but I ransack my brain and the embers of Thaoh Argentian give me the answer: use what's left of our gravitators to make a bubble in front of us.

We coast to a stop, just a few inches away from the knife made of rock.

"We made it." Elza touches my shoulder. "And we're not alone."

I raise my head and look outside the totaled Mazda. Halred is standing there, looking at us, with a group of Grattna behind her. Halred gives me a look like: *Thanks for taking such good care of the ship we went to so much trouble to repair for you.* I raise both hands and greet her in the best Grattna I can manage.

A short time later we're flying again, except without a ship this time. Halred cradles Elza and me in all three of her limbs, while her three mighty wings beat against the air. Good thing the gravity on this moon is a bit lower than Earth's. I felt bad about asking Halred to give us a ride, but it's the only way we can get close enough to the temple without anyone spotting us, as long as we stay close to the ground.

Turns out the *Nindred's Blessing* and a couple other ships can still fly, more or less, but they decided to hide out on the dark side for now. We just have enough power left in our safebeam nodes to signal them to come for us, once we find our friends and hopefully cook up a plan.

We're coming around the horizon and there's the temple, with a ginormous facility built around it. A small army of engineers wearing mechanical suits is building a floating stage next to the ancient wedding chapel, with a huge area for the audience to sit or stand.

"Looks like the worst music festival ever," I say under my breath. "Bottled water is gonna be at least twenty dollars."

We descend, somewhat gracefully, onto the rocky ground behind a section of a crashed Royal Compassion starship. I can see the semi-trashed remains of the *Undisputed Training Bra Disaster* nearby. *Good noble ship. You'll fly again, I swear.*

The sun goes from dazzling to gone, all at once—like a total eclipse.

A ginormous freaking starship, almost a full broadsword, is descending from the sky. A few minutes later, it happens again. It's near-impossible to land one of those big ships, even with the lower gravity.

Everybody who's anybody in the galaxy is coming here to this tiny rock. The Coachella vibes are getting harder to ignore.

"Skrillex has gotta be here somewhere," I say.

Already, influencers and politicians are hobnobbing in a big rocky field that's been cordoned off near the floating stage. Elza, Halred, and I slip into the crowd and steal some clothes and Joiners, which are like all-access passes. A few of the dignitaries are ushered into the prefab complex with puckered walls and crinkle tunnels, so they can ooh and aah over the impending genocide.

The three of us sneak inside with the tour group, then peel off at our first chance. We creep around this sterile maze for ages, without finding anything that could help us turn this mess around.

Then I spot something on one of the carbonfast walls that could just be a tiny scuffmark, except it's not. It's a tiny doodle of a sword-fighting zebra riding on a narwhal, and it's pointing its sword the opposite direction from where we're going. I gesture to Elza and Halred, and follow the sword point until I find another mini-sketch: a space dragon in a casino.

All the little dreams we clung to and obsessed over back on Earth, when me and my best friend spent all our time yearning to be here.

The scuff-toons lead us to a tiny door, like three feet tall, for a supply locker.

I peel the door open. Rachael sits with Xiaohou in her lap, two pairs of wide-open eyes blinking in the sudden light. "You found me," she says. "You're here. I thought . . . I thought I'd never see you again."

"We had to make a pit stop." I reach out my hands to pull her out and up.

"You know we would never want to be anywhere but by your side," Elza says.

Rachael still hasn't climbed out of the tiny cubby. "I got so scared that everything was scary and nothing was scary, all at the same time, and I was pretty sure that I live here now. I live in this cubby. I can't feel my arms and legs. I'm sorry, I will get it together, I swear, I will."

My eye lands on the final scribbled critter, pointing at this open cubby: the Joyful Wyvern, looking so valiant—except for its tiny cartoon eyes, which are wide with terror. My heart races. I feel like I just heard my favorite song for what might be the last time.

I sit down on the floor and look into my best friend's eyes. My first impulse is to put on a fake reassuring look, to banish all of the fear—but I need to be honest with the people I love.

So I show her all the terror and anxiety that are eating away at me, and I can see that it helps—she's not alone. Elza sits down next to me, but Halred hovers, watching for guards.

Halred gives me a look like, *You're wasting time.* I nod.

A flood of bad news comes out of Rachael's mouth as she falls out of her hiding place into my waiting arms. "Marrant has the hearthlight, and I lost Yiwei and the others, and we're up against absolutely everyone. And he's figured out how to do to other planets the same thing that happened to Irri-yaia, and he's made a whole list."

"A list of suns he wants to erase?" Elza says. "Worlds he wants to wipe out?"

Rachael nods. She sounds like she's laughing, except that her face is all twisted, like the "tragedy" mask that hung over one side of the theater my mom dragged me to. "And . . . Earth's sun is on the list. He's not just going to take out anyone with the wrong shape, he's going to kill our families, our friends. Our people."

The temperature just dropped a hundred degrees all at once. I feel frost-numb, except for a sharp terror stabbing through the center of my chest.

Now I'm the one making a quiet scream that sounds like a laugh.

I've been trying not to freak out about the fact that my mom, and Bette and Turtle, and everyone else back home, only have five months and change left. But if Marrant wins, they only have one.

"This makes us limb-friends," Halred says. As in, *Our worlds face the same fate, and therefore we are the closest of allies.*

"Okay." I stand up. "The situation just got really simple. We're not beaten, because we can't be."

"Except maybe we are," Elza says, still sitting next to Rachael.

I lean forward and offer one hand to Rachael, and the other to Elza. They just look up at me. Then they let me pull them both to their feet with my awesome Makvarian strength.

"We've never won by having the biggest gun," I say. "Not even once. We've never won by being the strongest, or the most powerful, or even the smartest. When we've won, it's by getting creative and weird. By noticing all the stuff that everybody else missed. By talking to people that nobody else bothered to talk to. That's how we're gonna win this time. Let's go."

I walk away as if I know where I'm heading. The others follow me, Rachael still massaging the pins and needles out of her cramped legs.

67

.

RACHAEL

Captives kneel in front of Marrant, wearing the cuffs that he duplicated with that machine. Close to the front of the ancient temple, there's Zaeta, Kfok, Ganno, Wyndgonk, Yatto, and some captive Grattna. Plus every ex–Royal Fleet officer who dared to stand against his rule. The other people in restraints must be captives that Marrant flew in, to make examples of in front of his fancy guests.

About half of the dozens of prisoners are various types of humanoid, but there are a lot of other species, including some that Rachael has never seen before. Someone far away is wailing and offering a last prayer to their gods.

A half dozen mechas stand between these prisoners and the visiting dignitaries, who are milling around in a big VIP area, farther away from the stage. Rachael follows her friends into the middle of the crowd of planetary leaders and bureaucrats who are gossiping among themselves. Marrant's soldiers are trying to do crowd control without pissing off anyone important, which makes sneaking around much easier.

"Marrant's almost ready to begin," Elza says. "This event is going to be livestreamed everywhere, on a few thousand worlds. It's going to take enough energy to power a whole fleet of starships for a year." She winces, like she got a sudden migraine flare.

"Are you still able to talk to the Ardenii?" Rachael asks. "Without your crown?"

"Certo," Elza says. "I have to concentrate more, because the crown gave me a boost. I have this bracelet made out of crowns, but it's still inert." She holds up her wrist, which bears a ring of seven golden circlets. "And they're still finding ways to tell me about all the bad things everywhere. The oldest forest in existence, these ancient trees that used to sing when the wind blew the right way, just turned to stone. Gone forever."

Elza kneads the back of her neck and her forehead. Rachael can still see the tiny marks where Elza's crown used to latch on to her skull.

"I wish there was something I can do to help you," Rachael whispers to Elza.

"You made me this dress," Elza says. "You've been there for me so many times. It's more than you know."

Marrant stands at the front of the temple, within line of sight of the fountain where the hearthlight is floating in a shimmering cloud. He isn't gloating—he's having hushed, sober conversations with some of the scientists who've helped him figure out the temple interface. A couple of times, someone in a fancy Royal Compassion uniform comes up and whispers to Marrant, and he nods and whispers back.

"Follow me," Halred mutters. "I know where to find [your friends | my wingmate]."

Rachael has a plastiform pad and a lightpen, and she manages to draw while walking behind her friends.

She hunches over, sketching the whole scene in rough. The temple, with the brand-new maze of laboratories and torture chambers built onto one side, the stage facing the hearthlight, the captives up front and the audience farther away, the guards and mechas, the "parking lot" full of starships. Even the rubble and the rocky hillocks all around them. Somehow capturing the whole terrain in a picture makes Rachael feel slightly less like rolling into a ball again.

Halred threads a path through the mosh pit of privilege, keeping her head down to hide her non-humanoid features. As she walks, she explains twice (because nobody gets it the first time). Eldnat is rubbing his wings together at a frequency that no humanoid can hear—but to a Grattna, it's like yelling *Hey, over here.*

Yiwei, Kez, Damini, and Eldnat are hidden under satin hoods and wraps of their own, hunkered directly behind the prisoner area. They're a short distance from the cuffed people, except there's towering mecha blocking their way. Damini is gazing at Zaeta, like *I'll get you out of this,* and Kez is trying to send a brave smile Ganno the Wurthhi's way. Next to Zaeta and Ganno, Wyndgonk squirms because fire cuffs are too damn tight.

Eldnat turns and sees his friends approach—he lifts off the ground a tiny bit, before he remembers he's supposed to be hiding. All three of his eyes widen and his mouth quirks upward. "Godparents you me us [safety] guided delivered arrived." Like: *The godparents brought you back to me.*

Then Yiwei, Damini, and Kez turn and see their friends. Yiwei stares, like he can't trust his eyes. He sways, his eyes misting over and his mouth making tiny inaudible sounds. Damini whispers something and then she's hugging Tina and Elza, and then Kez joins in.

Rachael sees Yiwei about to flop over, and she holds out her arms to steady him. She feels supported, even though she's the one holding him up. He's so warm, she tries to drink in every drop of relief, before things get scary again: Yiwei's face against hers, his voice in her ear: "The threads pulled us together again." Her family is reunited for the first time since they sailed into a minefield made of claws.

But some of her family are in bondage awaiting execution, and the rest are hiding, right in front of all of Marrant's enforcers and big battlesuits.

This close to the stage, Rachael can see Marrant's nostrils flaring. He preens in a beautiful midnight-blue suit that sets off his porcelain skin and dark hair—looking like nothing so much as a pop star getting ready to perform.

"I love you. We can't stay here," Rachael says to Yiwei.

"Yeah. You're right. Co-captain." Yiwei performs a sneaky little salute, close to his heart, and then he and Rachael are leading their friends away from the prisoners.

Damini is the last to leave, her wide, teary eyes fixed on Zaeta. "We'll come back, I swear," she whispers. Then she follows her friends as they try to weave through the crowd toward the starship parking lot at the back.

Rachael knows Yiwei too well—she can tell something is eating him from the inside, and it's not just all of the totally valid reasons to freak out. His jaw is grinding, his arms are pylons. He has the same look as when he was talking about putting mines in orbit around Thythuthy. If she could get him alone for an hour, especially if his guitar was nearby, they could get to the heart of whatever this is. But there's no time.

She gets closer to him and just says, "Whatever it is, you can tell me. We share the burden of command, remember?"

Yiwei kneads right below his ears, where his jaw meets the rest of his face.

"We might have a way to stop Marrant," he whispers as they weave through a group of partying Ghulg. "But there could be a lot of collateral damage."

Kez sidles up to the two of them. "It's too much. I thought we could cause a big flash or knock everyone unconscious, with no ill effects. But I ran the calculations again, and . . . it's much, much worse."

68

.

TINA

Yiwei explains a second time, and I feel even sicker. "No," I say. "No way. Please tell me we're not even considering this."

And here I thought I couldn't be any more freaked out.

"It was my idea," Kez says, "and I agree with you. We would be war criminals."

Rachael is biting her pinkie nail. I know what that means. She thinks her boyfriend might be right, and there's no other choice.

The eight of us managed to sneak out of the VIP area while some of the guards were breaking up a fight between a group of Javarah and some Scanthians. Now we're hiding behind what's left of the *Undisputed Training Bra Disaster,* with Kez (*they/them*) monitoring Marrant's big party on their Quant.

"The math holds up," Yiwei says, as if the math is the issue. "Marrant needed to have a big, triumphant rally, which meant parking a lot of mega-starships close together inside an unstable magnetic field. All we need to do is give it a push—"

"—and all the ships blow up," Damini says. "Killing thousands of people."

"Thousands of people who came here to witness the worst act of genocide in history. I don't want to kill anyone—again." Rachael closes her eyes, and I can tell she's thinking about when she killed Kankakn. "But maybe there's no choice."

"We can't risk damaging the temple with a big explosion," I say. My head is working overtime, while my heart is sinking deeper and deeper. "Or damaging the hearthlight. We promised Wyndgonk."

"No danger of that," Kez says. "The temple has already survived eons, it's reinforced against anything. But we'd kill all of the visiting dignitaries, and Marrant's forces on the ground, and . . . all of the prisoners. We'd be killing Ganno, Wyndgonk, Yatto . . . and Zaeta."

Damini recoils as if Kez just hit her.

Halred says something that I can't understand, even with my hacked-up EverySpeak. Eldnat bows his head and says something else that I can't understand.

I glance at the two Grattna and try to say "I didn't get that."

Halred folds her wings over her chest. "My world will die." she takes care to speak in a way she knows I'll understand. "So will yours. We need to act."

"All we need is to get airborne, about thirty meters up, and fly close to the ancient temple, and we can use our engine core to set off a sympathetic resonance that will make all the other starship engines explode. And just hope we can bail out before our own ship becomes a fireball." Yiwei glances at Kez—they nod, mournfully. Everything Yiwei just said is correct.

"I can't stand this plan for so many reasons," I say. "We'll get shot down before we get close enough. We'll burn up along with our ship. And then . . . there's the mass murder."

Rachael gives me the same expression as when she used to tell me not to be a martyr. "We're out of time," she says. "If you have another idea, we need to hear it."

I cover my face and breathe into my hands. The Grattna and Kraelyors still have a few ships, but they'll get cut down in seconds by Marrant's superior forces if they attack. We could try to impersonate scientists and get back inside the ancient temple, and try to barricade ourselves in there with the hearthlight . . . except that there are mecha-enforcers in there. I could challenge Marrant to a duel, but he'd probably just laugh.

No options—it's exactly like when we realized there was no choice but to turn me into Fake Tina.

Thaoh rings out in my head. *You have to do better than I did. Killing is the clumsiest, cruelest solution to any problem.*

I uncage my eyes, to see Elza sitting on one side of me, and Rachael on the other. "Whatever we choose today, we're going to hate ourselves forever," Elza says. "So let's hate ourselves because we saved as many people as possible, not because we let everyone die."

"The math holds up," Yiwei says again—but this time "math" has a different meaning. "We kill thousands to save billions. This is the position Marrant has put us in."

"This is killing me," Kez says. "I wish there was another way."

"I've prayed and prayed that this moment would never arrive," Damini says.

They're talking as if we've already decided to do this. And I guess . . . we have? I can't think of any other way.

"If we need a distraction," Rachael says, "I cooked up something that might buy us a minute, when I was inside Marrant's facility. But I need to be close to there to set it off."

"We're out of time," Kez yelps. "Marrant's starting!"

Marrant talks in a low voice to one of the scientists on his makeshift stage, and they say something back, bobbing their head. Then he steps forward a little, and waves one hand: the holographic map of the galaxy appears next to him, big enough for his audience to see. He waves one finger on his other hand, and then I can hear him breathing, as if he was next to me.

"Good people of Her Majesty's Firmament." Marrant's calm expression vanishes—or really, it breaks open. Suddenly his eyes bug out, his mouth is full of snarling teeth. "You made me your first councilor because you were tired of feeling unsafe, of having to worry that your way of life would be ruined at any moment. Today, I honor our covenant."

His voice rises until he sounds hoarse. All of the soldiers standing at inspection rest around the captives stomp their booted feet in unison. Hooting and hollering come from the VIP section. We even hear some cheers from the other planets where people are watching this speech.

Marrant's voice gets louder and hoarser. His whole body vibrates. "Two great scourges have menaced our worlds. Ancient, cowardly gods created a vile weapon to destroy us, called the Bereavement. And an infestation of filthy, misshapen creatures has swarmed—multiplying like the pests they are. Using up vital resources. *Stealing from us!*"

He points at one spot on the galactic map, and it zooms in, showing a group of stars, with one particular star highlighted.

"This is Kraelyo Homeglobe, and its star, Kraelyo Homesun," he snarls. "You've no doubt encountered the Kraelyors, because they spread their slime trails everywhere. Their entire political system is based on crude biological processes, instead of choosing their leaders based on merit, the way you all chose me. Pirates, grifters, liars—and they have the nerve to claim *we* owe *them* something!"

The soldiers and VIPs roar and stomp louder.

A few soldiers seize Kfok and drag her up on stage, shaking and freaking out and crying. Rachael can see her mouthing *No, no, no, no.*

"Now that I have complete control over the Bereavement," Marrant says, "I can render unto Kraelyo Homesun the same fate that befell Irriyaia's star. Let them suffer the way we have suffered. Infestation? Solved."

He clicks his thumb against his middle finger on his right hand, and Kraelyo Homesun sputters and dies.

Kfok gets upright on her slug bottom, yelling and waving her arms until she gets an electric shock from the cuffs. "You fucking creep, you dirty symmetron, eat your own fa—"

Marrant leans forward and slaps Kfok with the palm of one hand.

She's gone. Nothing but mist and scraps.

I look back at the dying husk where Kraelyo Homesun used to be, and the only thought in my head is: *Those creatures deserved what they got.* I try to remember how beautiful Kraelyo Homeglobe was, how cool their culture seemed when we visited one of their ruling councils. But all I can think of is *Yuck slug people.*

The applause is deafening.

"When this is all over," Marrant shouts, "we will have the community of worlds that we always should have had. We will be clean. All our nightmares will be laid to rest. We have given and we have given, and now we deserve to be happy."

I get it now. He's going to do this for every world he plans to wipe out: give the crowd someone to hate, someone who can't talk back anymore. Someone like Kfok, that worthless, slimy creep.

I try to imagine the hatred I'll feel when Zaeta dies along with her whole world. Or Wyndgonk. Or one of the Grattna. Or one of us Earth kids, if he catches us.

Everything shakes, and for a moment I'm sure there's an earthquake. Then I realize: it's Halred and Eldnat, beating their wings with anxiety.

There's no fuel more toxic than despair, but it'll burn just fine with enough friction.

"Every world that shares our values will be saved," Marrant spits, actually spits. His whole face is contorted with rage and hatred. "But the misshapen? The lesser humanoids? The worthless trash who taint every good thing? They will be cleansed for all time." He turns and looks at the galaxy map, which is zoomed out again. "This is the beginning of something beautiful."

"Okay. I'm in." A million wretched feelings rise up out of the pit of my stomach. I push them down and lock them tight. "Let's do this. It's last-resort time."

69

.

ELZA

. . . 0 Earth days until some of the suns go out forever

Eldnat and Halred use the safebeam node, and soon the *Nindred's Blessing* flies low over the ground and comes to a rest nearby. Elza follows all of her friends inside the ship.

"Oh god," Damini says. "Kfok. She was our friend, and now I can't . . ."

"There's no time," Yiwei says. "Feel your feelings later."

Elza is pretty sure that whenever that time arrives, when at last they can feel their feelings, it's going to break her.

But Wyndgonk is there, trapped, and Elza swore a dozen oaths to fire. "Yiwei's right," she says. "Let's stay focused."

The ship is already lifting off, flying low and weaving back and forth.

"I'll need a couple ticks in the engine compartment," Kez says. "Just so everyone's clear: when I do this, our ship blows up along with all the others."

"Understood," Yiwei says. "It's been a minute since I was on an exploding starship."

Nobody laughs, or even smiles. Kez looks at their hands as if they can already see the blood all over them. Then they slip back to the engine compartment.

Tina is sleepwalking, checking weapons systems and tactical scans on the workstations as she walks to the control deck with Elza by her side. "The moment we come on their scans, the Royal Compassion will throw everything at us," Tina says in a flat voice. "At least their hardest-hitting ships are still in orbit or mopping up in the debris field. But any one of those mechas could shoot us down, and they have at least thirty knifeships and barbships patrolling the airspace around the temple."

"We have nine ships left," says Damini. "Including four bigger Grattna ships and five smaller Kraelyor ships. Not great odds."

The Kraelyors are displaying the colors of mourning and righteous vengeance on the hulls of their ships.

"A low-flying dogfight, then," Yiwei says. "We'll need to use the terrain as much as possible."

"I have some ideas for how we can confuse their targeting systems." Tina's voice betrays no emotion.

Halred says something along the lines of *We copied all of the stealth and countermeasures from Marrant's flagship.* But with more stuff embedded in it about Marrant, and the fact that he caged the Grattna and now wants to erase their whole world.

Everybody heads into the control deck, except for Elza. And Rachael. They stand outside and watch everybody bustling around and barking orders. Rachael looks stuck—like she ought to be by Yiwei's side, but she also needs a moment.

Marrant has dragged a captive Pnoft on stage—a fuzzy red ball that moves and speaks using wisps of pale hair—and is shouting about the pollution these creatures bring to the galaxy. The Pnoft bounces up and down with terror, pleading for their life and the lives of their people. Elza can't bear to watch. But she knows that even if she looks away, the Ardenii will find a way to make her see. And knowing becomes her responsibility.

"Half a cycle to contact," Yiwei says. Meaning two or three minutes before the enemy sees us, and the battle starts.

Rachael is still frozen. Elza gets close to her. "I need to talk to you."

Rachael follows Elza into the crew lounge, which looks a lot like the lounge on board the *Indomitable*. "I should be in there, by Yiwei's side. I'm worried about Tina, too, but—"

"Not what I wanted to talk about," Elza says. "It's time we pooled information, in case this plan fails. You said you created a distraction. What was it?"

Rachael cringes. "It's silly. I made a few copies of Xiaohou, they're hiding inside the complex. They could make some ruckus, but I would need to be very close."

Elza nods. "What do you think the dragon—Laynbone—meant when she said 'the flower of our love'? We thought it was just a poetic way of talking about the hearthlight, even though it made no sense."

"But Laynbone kept talking about the flower thing even after we delivered the hearthlight," Rachael says.

"Laynbone told us that her people tried to join with the Vayt, but it went wrong somehow. That's why they went to war." Elza's head is full of noise, but she tries to concentrate. To find comfort the way she always does: taking things apart and making sense of even the most senseless things.

"This is not how the Vayt described any of it when I met them. They said the Shadow Galaxy—the Fatharn—could not understand their ways, or see their designs. Oof. That does actually sound like a messy breakup, now I think about it."

Rachael scans the nearest holographic display and twitches. Almost battle time.

"Meanwhile, the Ardenii told me something after they saved me from Marrant's touch," Elza says. "They said I was permanently stabilized against psychomolecular incursions, and that I had limited contact immunity. You worked in the sickbay. Do you know what any of that means?"

"Not sure." Rachael wrinkles her nose. "Sounds like you're protected if Marrant tries to touch you again. But what does 'limited contact immunity' mean? Maybe if you're touching someone else, they're also protected?"

"That makes sense." Elza gropes for the words she wants to say, but there's still so much noise in her head. "Let's make a pact. I will comfort you in the ashes, hold you through all the guilt and the trauma, if you will do the same for me."

"Deal." Rachael doesn't exactly smile, but there's a light in her eyes. "But I figured you and Tina—"

"We both know Tina won't be any good to anybody after we do this. Not for a long time." Saying it makes it feel true. Saying it makes it worse.

There's so much more to speak about, but alarms are screaming. Situation Red Dive: we have engaged the enemy, and they are making short work of us. Elza and Rachael rush toward the control deck where all their friends are shouting and poking their hands and other appendages into as many holographic honeypots as possible.

70

.

TINA

An hour ago, I'd have sworn that nothing could ever tear me away from this family, as long as I had the least strength left. The only future I craved was one where I stayed close to Rachael, Elza, Yiwei, Damini, Kez, and all our other friends and companions.

Now? I never want to see any of these people, ever again. Not even Rachael. Not even Elza.

A bell-clear voice in my head says this will be our penance. We'll all have to scatter to the ends of the worlds, because we'll never be able to face each other.

The *Nindred's Blessing* flies so low, I can see every shoot of eggplant-purple vegetation sprouting from the rocky sand. Pulse-cannon blasts and missiles and fireballs rock us on all sides and above, and the air is full of screaming. The hull, the engines, the floor under my feet, the alarms, and the people—scream scream scream.

My face is jammed into the tactical scan, and it's pure chaos. The Grattna are doing an evasive maneuver I've never seen before, and at least it's mystifying the Royal Compassion ships, too. We tilt forward like a bird drinking, then flip back-over-front. One of the enemy barbships flies too close, and we take out their engines, leaving them to sputter and crash.

There's just too many of them, and we're still too far from the ancient temple for Kez to do their thing.

Damini is helping two of the Grattna at the pilot station, but she's not used to flying without Zaeta anymore. And she's looking at the instruments through a sheet of tears.

The Kraelyor ships won't stay in formation, won't fight smart. They have nothing left to lose, so they rush ahead of the rest of us, into the line of fire. Already, two of their five vessels are spiraling in flames toward the crags below. We won't even make it anywhere near Marrant's party at this rate. Oops, a third Kraelyor ship just went down.

Marrant hears our battle, from a long way off. He turns on some kind of noise reduction and tells his audience to ignore the momentary distraction. Then he just carries on—his people drag a squirming, protesting Bnobnobian on stage to serve as another example.

We're still ten standard terrain units (twelve miles) away from the ancient temple, and the enemy ships keep coming in wave after wave. More than we were expecting. Mostly knives and barbs, but also some daggers and a couple of shortswords.

I hate this. I send Halred and Yiwei some suggestions for how to punch through the lines of the enemy ships between us and the ancient temple, using our missile launchers to take out two of the unprotected knifeships. I hate this. I figure out a way to use our ion harness to scoop some boulders ahead of us and take out the engines of the biggest shortsword. I hate this. I send Damini some evasive patterns.

I send Halred a message, even though she's busier than I am. "You don't have verbs in your language, so you must think way differently about murder. I wish I had time to understand better. You always seem to include more context, whenever we talk about who's doing what to who, as if it's more complicated. I swear I didn't just ask you to come here to fight and die. I hoped, I dreamed, we could build something better together. Please tell me you can see another way."

One of the Grattna ships falls out of formation, but they crash in one piece. I hope most of the crew survived.

"Kez, we're two minutes out from the temple," Yiwei says. "If we survive that long."

"Sorry, I need another few minutes," Kez says. "I'm doing nth-dimensional theoretical physics in a ship that keeps losing stability, and I'm trying not to think about what I'm actually doing."

"I know you can do this. Just try to clear your mind," Rachael says.

Enemy ships coming from behind as well as ahead, so we're about to be surrounded. Still five miles to the target.

Halred sends me a response. And wouldn't you know, I can't even make sense of it at first. Blame the brain fog of war, or maybe my hacked-up EverySpeak is finally giving up.

I squint and shut out the ships exploding around me, and then . . . I get it.

"It could work," I say out loud.

"What could work?" Rachael asks. I didn't even realize she was standing next to me.

"Halred has an idea how we can win this. Without killing all of the everybody."

"There's no time—" Yiwei protests.

"Tell them," I say.

Halred says the thing that she said in her message to me: "Murder energy weapons engines [containment] store transfer." Nobody gets it.

"It's so simple," I say. "We don't blow up all their engines. We blow up all their weapons!"

I gesture for Elza to come with me, and run down to Engineering so fast I skid on the new floors.

I'm down in Engineering with Kez, Elza, and Halred, plus some Grattna engineers. The walls shake like tree branches in a hailstorm.

"I'm thinking!" Kez protests. We all nod and put on our most patient expressions. Alarms start caterwauling again. "It's tricky—I know how to set up a cascade in our engines that will cause all the other engines within this magnetic field to go boom. It's true that weapons also store and release energy in a similar way, but they're also completely different."

"Every gun is a miniature starship," I say. "It's just a battery that stores a ton of energy and then releases it."

"The Ardenii don't want to help me hurt anyone," Elza says. "But . . . they're saying Tina's right. Any weapon's power source is a tiny version of a starship's. The containment fields operate—"

"—at a higher frequency than an engine." Kez starts babbling numbers.

"Marrant is still at it," Damini says from the control deck. "I'm scared Zaeta will be next."

Something very large and very hot goes boom right next to our ship. We all get thrown against one wall, and the floor heats up under my feet.

"We're one minute out from the temple," Yiwei says, "and we're taking a beating."

Halred speaks with great care, so she is understood. "When we built these ships, we needed to study their designs. The weapons are shielded with a field of magnetized anti-protons."

"And the temple is generating a magnetic flux that oscillates," Kez says. "The timing is going to be a beast."

"On my mark," I shout into the internal comms. "Shut down all weapons."

"That will leave us defenseless," Yiwei protests.

"No it won't, I swear. Do you trust me?"

Yiwei doesn't miss a beat. "Always. With my life."

"I think this might work," Kez says.

"Twenty seconds out," Damini says. "I can see the whole festival, the stage, the building. Marrant isn't even worried."

"He will be," Elza says.

"Five seconds," Damini says.

"Ready!" Kez says.

I hit the comms for our whole ragtag fleet. "Everybody, weapons off. Now!"

One piece of the droning around us stops. The engines are still on, but the weapons are off.

"Here goes!" Kez hits a control. Nothing happens.

I turn to Elza and Rachael, and I see their hearts sinking, same as mine.

I just doomed a thousand worlds to keep my hands clean.

The floor shakes: we just took a direct hit. Our hull is messed up.

I open my mouth to say something—like maybe it's not too late to try the original plan.

Then . . . there's a popping sound, like a champagne cork.

And then another. And another, and then a whole bunch of them, all together.

The quietest explosions you ever heard, but a lot of them.

"Every last gun just . . . blew up," Yiwei says. "Every missile launcher and pulse cannon, too. The ships attacking us are helpless, so they're running. The mechas, the enforcers around the temple. They're all unarmed now. I think the mechas are immobilized, too."

"We did it." Kez sounds stunned. "We bloody did it."

Halred unfurls her middle wing, which I think is a Grattna fist-pump. "The godparents see us."

"It's not over," I say. "We need to take this to Marrant. Before he kills anyone else."

I can't let myself think about how many people Marrant wiped out while we were fighting our way here. That's for later.

For now, I feel . . . light. Alive, from my soles to my scalp.

Like I got air in my lungs and blood in my veins after a long time down.

I see the same light in Elza's beautiful hazel eyes. "Are you able to face him again?" I ask. "We don't have any more nightweed juice, and it's out of all our systems by now."

Elza nods. "It's okay. If you're touching me, Marrant can't hurt you. I think."

"And I always want to be touching you anyway. So that works out."

I reach out a hand, she takes it.

"We never had our first dance together as princess and consort," she says.

"It's never too late. Let's dance."

The *Nindred's Blessing*—what's left of it—is floating directly over the temple. Marrant is looking up at us with a murderous expression. He's just figured out that we disarmed all of his people. The crowd of visiting bigwigs looks uneasy, too.

I smile at Elza, and she smiles back. We run toward the cargo hangar, ready to jump.

71

.

RACHAEL

Rachael has always avoided making eye contact with Thondra Marrant, and not just because looking into someone else's eyes is a weird thing at the best of times. The few times she's been in Marrant's presence, she's gotten this feeling that if she gazes directly into his dark eyes she'll lose her soul or some such nonsense.

Now, though, she can't help it. She's standing on board a starship that the people he tried to wipe out copied from Marrant's pride and joy—the pride and joy that she helped to steal—and she's about to jump onto Marrant's stage like a last-minute guest act at a Lil Nas X concert. Marrant is at least thirty or forty feet below her, but she can see his eyes staring up at her.

She meets Marrant's glare and sends back the iciest contempt.

Elza is the first to jump out of the *Nindred's Blessing*. She pulls out two of the straps embedded in her tactical ballgown, which look like fuchsia satin but are made of some nearly unbreakable, stretchy material. She attaches the straps to the cargo hatch on the ship and then swings down onto the stage, where Marrant stares—speechless, for once. Then she retracts the straps and stands facing her enemy with steel in her eyes.

Tina lands next to Elza a second later, using a personal impeller to slow her descent a little. Yiwei, Halred, and the others follow her down.

Rachael takes a deep breath, checks the impeller on her back, and jumps after them.

"Somebody find a gun that works and shoot down that ship!" Marrant is screaming.

The prisoners close to the stage are hooting and cheering. Further back, the fancy people are freaking out, because this is not the party they were invited to. They don't even know how close they came to dying in a fire.

Rachael lands on her feet, right next to a poor Kthorokan volcano-fish that Marrant was about to make an example of. She shoves the fish, who's squirming in a tank full of lava, out of harm's way.

Marrant lunges for Rachael with his death touch, and she loses a breath—

—but Elza takes her hand, and Marrant's hand brushes off Rachael's skin.

"Seems you've lost your touch," Elza says.

Marrant snarls and lunges at Elza, and she dodges without even trying.

Then Elza's holding hands with Tina—she spins in Marrant's direction, doing one of the nahrax moves she's been practicing, hitting a pressure point in Marrant's left arm.

Elza pulls Yiwei close and then twirls him away, gripping his left hand while his right fist strikes Marrant's jaw.

Damini and Kez are rushing over to Zaeta, Ganno, and the others, trying to figure out how to open the cuffs. Rachael can't hear what they're saying, but she sees the tears in Damini's eyes and Kez wrapping his arms around Ganno.

Elza is holding one of Halred's limbs, so she can fly over Marrant's head and kick him. "For. Justice," Halred says.

Marrant looks the way he did when Nyitha plunged her knife into his heart. The mask falls away, his face is twisted with pain and self-hatred. He deflates, falls into a defensive crouch.

"How?" He looks at Elza and Tina. "How are you alive? Why won't you quit trying to destroy me, when all I want is to bring peace and decency—"

"We saved each other," Tina says. "Like we always do."

"Tina helped me survive—and now you can't hurt me anymore," Elza says. "Never again."

That was the wrong thing to say. Rachael sees it in Marrant's face: the smirk is back, he straightens back up.

"I can *always* hurt you. You make it so easy. You wear your weakness as if it were armor." Marrant turns to his massed soldiers, a lot of whom are nursing nasty burns on their hands. "First and second divisions, kill the prisoners. Bludgeon them to death if necessary. Everyone else, to me."

Oh. Oh no. This is bad.

The whole army of Royal Compassion enforcers swarms toward the stage and the prisoner mosh pit up front. Their battle cry splits Rachael's eardrums and puts a chill on her heart. She sees the murder in an Aribentor's exposed eyes, the battle frenzy in a group of Javarah. A whole mob of Makvarians who look a bit like Tina are yelling and brandishing whatever weapons they found. They don't need guns to carve up Rachael and all her friends.

Tina has Marrant by the throat, with Elza holding on to her with both hands. "Call them off," Tina says.

"I don't take orders from pretenders." Marrant elbows Tina in the face and kicks her leg out from under her.

Tina stumbles. She slips out of Elza's grasp—then Elza grips her wrist again.

The soldiers are climbing up onto the stage, brandishing sharp implements. Some of them are coming out of the ancient temple, too. (At least the mechas are still down.)

"Rachael," Elza calls out. "Now would be a really good time for your surprise."

Rachael freezes, over at the far end of the stage with the terrified volcano fish. What surprise was that, again?

Then she remembers: it was a dozen scary things ago!

Yiwei is searching his bag for a gun that still works. He notices Rachael pulling Xiaohou out of her satchel, and she can see the pain sweep across his face—like it physically hurts to be reminded of a time when he could make music and goof off, instead of what he's doing now.

"Rachael, we can't afford—" Yiwei gives up on finding a gun and raises his fists.

"I disagree," Rachael says.

"I told you," Yiwei pleads. "We'll have time for music later, when we're not fighting for our lives." One of the soldiers leaps onto the stage in front of Yiwei, and he kicks them off. Another comes, and Yiwei grapples with them.

"We'll always be fighting for our lives. Trust me: this is the right time." Rachael raises Xiaohou to her face. The monkey robot gazes at her with wide, glowing eyes and crooked metal teeth. "Xiaohou, play Cinnki's last song."

An urgent growl comes out of the little monkey. "Take off your fur, we'll be furless together."

Nobody notices.

Until another voice takes up the song. And another.

All at once, the whole ancient temple rings with song.

"I'll give you my fur, give me your fur!"

Cinnki's voice comes from everywhere. All over the ancient temple, all over the complex Marrant's people built.

His voice echoes off the distant mountains and drowns out Marrant. So loud, Rachael's ears hurt.

"GIVE ME YOUR FUR! WE'LL BE FURLESS TOGETHER! I TRUST YOU WITH MY SKIN!"

Marrant hisses with rage, but Rachael can't hear his voice over all the loud guitars and drums. Tiny monkey robots stream out of their hiding places and crawl all over every surface, bouncing and waving their little tails.

"We . . . We never got to perform that song for you." Yiwei's face is streaked with tears. He swings his fist and knocks another enforcer off the stage, then takes one second to drink in the music filling the air. "It's so beautiful. I forgot. I forgot how good he sounded."

"You told me you only made a few of those duplicates," Elza says.

"Umm, well I told the machine to keep making them until it ran out of raw material. I guess I made too many?"

The entire temple and the adjoining complex are covered with miniature versions of Xiaohou, raising their faces to the sky.

"I TRUST YOU WITH MY SKIN," a thousand tiny monkeys proclaim. "GIVE ME YOUR FUR!"

"You made exactly the right number of monkeys." Elza grins at Rachael.

The Grattna ships and the two surviving Kraelyor battle-slicers are wheeling overhead, and nobody even hears them over the loud music—until a couple of ships that still have weapons start shooting at the soldiers who are attacking the prisoners.

"I TRUST YOU BECAUSE YOU SPOKE YOUR TRUTH TO ME! NOW WE CAN GO FURLESS!"

The song comes to an end. For a heartbeat, everything feels way too quiet, almost peaceful—and then the sounds of battle rise up to fill the space.

Down in the prisoner mosh pit, Damini raises her fist in triumph. All of the prisoners' cuffs fall off, and the captives all rush toward the wall of enforcers, picking up anything they can use to fight back. The Grattna and Kraelyor ships are still raining fire on the enforcers, driving them back.

Marrant freezes for a moment, then he shakes his head. "Kankakn was right: I care too much for others' opinions, and it's led me into folly. I should have ended this already." He looks at Tina and Elza. "You have certainly disrupted my victory celebration, but the victory itself shall stand. I still have complete control over the Bereavement."

Elza and Tina run toward Marrant, but he's already raising his hand to make another gesture. The same hand-motion he used to wipe out Kraelyo Homesun and the others.

"I was wrong to try and cleanse these infested worlds one at a time," Marrant says. "But it's not too late to finish what I started. Time to be rid of all the vermin, all at once. We all deserve a fresh start."

Elza desperately lunges to try and grab Marrant's hand—but he finishes his gesture.

"You were only ever going to achieve a symbolic triumph, Your Radiance," Marrant sneers at her.

Another gesture, and a fresh map of the galaxy appears. All of Marrant's targeted stars—all of the worlds containing so-called inferior creatures—are starting to die. Including Earth.

72

.

WYNDGONK

The cuffs on Wyndgonk's limbs just loosened, but fire still doesn't budge from the spot where fire has been trapped watching a celebration of pure death. Fire can't breathe enough to make even a lick of flame.

All of the other prisoners are rushing toward the Royal Compassion enforcers, screaming and waving whatever weapons they scrounged. But there's no point in fighting anymore.

Marrant did it. He won. All of the singing and shouting and plans and strategies were for nothing. Wyndgonk should have known—and deep down, fire always did know.

Elza is yelling Wyndgonk's name. "It's up to you now! I think you're the only one who can stop this. Wyndgonk! Please listen!"

Wyndgonk has a clear view of the stage: Marrant laughing as Tina and Elza grapple with him, everyone else fighting in close quarters against the mob of enforcers. Beyond them, fire sees inside the ancient temple: the hearthlight, the most sacred object in Thythuthyan culture, glows and rotates over the dry fountain. Scientists buzz around it, taking readings and spouting jargon. The Bereavement is working overtime to snuff out more stars. Including Thythuthy's.

"Wyndgonk!" Elza shouts. "Listen! Remember how Laynbone kept asking for the flower of their love? And it wasn't the hearthlight?" Marrant elbows her and she grunts. "They needed more than DNA, they needed something they thought was lost. Please listen!"

Wyndgonk still can't make a single spark.

Fire can't help hearing Innávan's voice, drowning out Elza's: *You were named for Wyndgonk the Brazen, who ventured into the mouth of a great frost-serpent to retrieve the spark of life. But also, at every hearth festival we sing of the hearth-keeper to come, who will restore our birthright from beyond.*

This is it: the moment that Innávan and Uynhyu always told Wyndgonk about.

Wyndgonk feels sick, as if the poison from a whole swarm of Dnynths had worked its way inside fire shell. *I can't do it,* fire thinks. *I don't even know how.* All this time, and all of those old legends still feel so remote. What does "our birthright from beyond" even mean? It's as meaningless as when that long-dead dragon said "the flower of our love."

Fire closes all of fire eyes. And tries to picture the City of Braids, and the cloister where the hearthlight rested for generations, and all of the carvings about the great heritage.

And then fire thinks about what that cranky dragon said, about the Vayt and the Fatharn, and their long-ago wedding that ended in disaster. They were supposed to become one people, to weave their genes together. They were supposed to give rise to something new.

Wyndgonk stands up, and fire cuffs fall away with a satisfying *clunk.* "I understand at last," fire says. "I understand all of it. I know why the Fatharn called their last weapon the Bereavement, and why the Vayt were so obsessed with making every creature in the galaxy the same shape. They were grieving the loss of their shared children—but we were never lost. We are still here, and we've come to claim what's ours."

Marrant wriggles away from Tina and Elza and rushes toward Wyndgonk, raising his foul-smelling palm, but Wyndgonk doesn't stop speaking up.

"I'm here. I've come at last," fire calls out, at the top of all of fire's lung-stomachs, looking directly at Laynbone the knife-dragon. "Nobody else needs to die, because *I am the flower of your love.*"

Everything goes quiet. The galaxy map vanishes and the Bereavement goes still. Marrant stops and stares, shaking with fury—then he lunges toward Wyndgonk with his murder hand.

73

.

ELZA

Elza watches Marrant leap forward, about to wipe out another one of her friends, and she's too far away to do anything. Part of her is still reliving that moment when he touched her and said, *There are those who must be despised,* and meanwhile a Javarah enforcer has leapt on her back and is trying to claw her face off. Another enforcer, a Rosaei, swings a granite fist at Tina's face.

The hearthlight just stopped buzzing and leaking golden light atop the dry fountain. The noise stopped, too. And now, all of the machinery goes dead. Elza is so startled, she loses her balance in the middle of fighting the Javarah enforcer, and the two of them tumble forward, off the stage, landing on the ground.

Elza looks up and she's just a few feet away from Marrant, whose face is a mask of pure rage. Marrant is advancing on Wyndgonk, who's standing fire ground in front of Marrant's makeshift stage.

"You can kill me if you want," Wyndgonk says in a calm voice. "But I just took back the power that never belonged to you. You'll have to commit genocide the old-fashioned way from now on."

Marrant leans forward to touch Wyndgonk—then he stops. "The Bereavement," he says. "It's still claiming all the suns. I didn't get around to saving Makvaria, or Javarr, or countless others."

"I already saved them all," Wyndgonk says. "I didn't pick and choose which suns should live, the way you wanted to, because I'm not a bag of poison. Just surrender, and tell your people to do the same."

Marrant closes his eyes and digs his nails into his own palms.

Elza and the Javarah she's fighting both stop and stare, wondering if this is it. If it's over.

Then Marrant lunges toward Wyndgonk, bloody palms first. "I did not! Fight my way back from the dead! To surrender to a filthy insect!"

Elza tries to get up, to throw herself in Marrant's path, but the Javarah enforcer grabs her neck and pulls her back toward the stage. Tina and the

Rosaei are rolling around, while the Javarah swipes at Elza's face with both claws.

Marrant has reached Wyndgonk, whose defiant stance has crumbled. Fire is cowering, covering fire eyes with fire front legs.

"When you're dead," he says, "I'll figure out how to regain the power. And since your world will be gone, absolutely nobody will mourn for you."

He swings one bleeding hand in a neat arc, and Wyndgonk lets out a moan of fear.

Elza does the only thing she can think of: she hurls the Javarah enforcer at Marrant. The Javarah evaporates, except for a few soiled scraps of uniform.

This only slows Marrant down for a moment, but that's enough time for Elza to charge at him, smacking him in the face. She gets one hand on Wyndgonk, and now fire is safe.

Elza looks Marrant in the face—*those who must be despised*—and she sees something behind his furious glare: terror.

As scared as she still is of him, he's much more afraid of her.

She glances at the bracelet of crowns on her wrist and sees a faint glow. The Ardenii aren't fully back, but they want to witness this moment. And she wants them to.

"You tried to kill me, but instead you turned me into the cure for your disease," Elza tells Marrant. Then she looks up and raises her voice. "Everybody join hands. All of you."

Ganno takes Wyndgonk's other front leg, and Zaeta takes Ganno's free hand in her flipper-claw.

"As long as you're touching someone who's touching me," Elza says, "Marrant can lay his hands on you as much as he wants. It won't do any harm, any more than any other creepy man's hands would."

Tina takes Elza's free hand, and whispers, "So damn proud to be your consort."

The Grattna ships are still raining fire on the enforcers, scattering them.

A line of people advance on Marrant, closing in on him, hands clasped. The Grattna join in, and so do the surviving Kraelyors. Elza turns her head and realizes there are twenty people holding hands. All of her friends from Earth, plus Yatto, Ganno, Wyndgonk, Halred, and several of the people Marrant just tried to erase.

The bracelet glows brighter.

"As long as we stay tied to each other," Elza says, "we are more powerful than you are."

Marrant falls to the ground, cowering, covering his face. Then he struggles to his feet and turns to run.

The line of people holding hands closes around Marrant, so he has nowhere to go. He spins in a full circle and Elza can see the bottom drop out of his world—everywhere he looks, he sees the same expression.

"You're not going to win or escape. You're going to face justice. Not from the Royal Compassion or the Firmament, but from your victims." Eldnat flexes all three wings, and he looks so powerful in this moment—but also, he speaks slowly, taking great care to make sure all of the humanoids understand.

"Time to surrender!" Tina shouts at the throng of Royal Compassion enforcers. "You've lost your weapons and your leader, and you're out of options."

The enforcers look around, like they're hoping for a sign to fight on. Then one by one, they get down on the ground, hands raised. Some of the Grattna start collecting the cuffs that just fell off Marrant's prisoners.

Without letting go of Elza's hand, Tina grabs two pairs of cuffs and clicks them onto Marrant's wrists and ankles, behind his back. She cranks them up to the maximum setting, so all four of them are locked together.

Marrant glares up at Tina. "You still don't understand how things work, where power comes from. A hundred worlds just witnessed you assaulting the rightful First Councilor of Her Majesty's Firmament. I won't be wearing these cuffs for long."

"A hundred worlds watched you committing a crime, and us stopping you," Tina says. "But you're right. Those cuffs won't be enough. Hold on, I've got an idea."

Wyndgonk lets go of Elza's hand, hoists fireself up onto the stage, and wanders back to the dry fountain, where Laynbone the knife-dragon is gazing down with misty eyes.

Laynbone cries out, "Ah! We never dreamed this moment would arrive, when our hopes would be—"

Wyndgonk spins around. "You can do me a favor and shut your mouth. You're nothing but a hologram of my long-dead ancestors anyway—and I'm busy making sure your weapon is shut down for good."

Laynbone sputters, but she goes quiet. The group of scientists, who were sheltering on the edges of the room while Elza and Tina fought the enforcers, step forward. "Don't touch any of that," says a Ghulg in protective gear. "You have no idea how long it took us to calibrate—"

"We don't care. Be quiet." Elza walks into the chamber, still holding hands with a whole chain of people. She turns to Wyndgonk. "How bad is it?"

"I don't understand all the technical stuff," fire says. "But it looks like we shut down the Bereavement just in time. For every sun. Those tiny black holes will revert to their dormant state and slowly drift back into space, to evaporate. No big surprise, it's much easier to save all of the stars at once than to pick and choose." Fire sprays some bright orange flames in the direction of the scientists, who go back to cowering against the wall.

"Is it too late to save Kraelyo Homesun from dying out permanently?" Elza asks.

"Probably," Wyndgonk says. "That black hole lost all of its covering, and it can't be rolled back like the others." Fire spits a few more sparks at the group of scientists.

The Ghulg in the hazmat suit squirms. "We were trying to do pure science."

"Did we win?" Damini comes running into the temple. "Please tell me we won. I was kind of busy freeing the prisoners, and—"

Zaeta rushes over and puts her flipper-claws on Damini's face. "We won," Zaeta says. "We did it. You were just in time, because you didn't have me to help you get here faster."

"That's never happening again," Damini says.

"It wasn't pretty," Elza says. "But we won." She gestures at Marrant, with his wrists and ankles cuffed together. And all the other enforcers, who are being rounded up and cuffed as well. "Wyndgonk is still wrangling the hearthlight, but all the stars should be shining as bright as ever soon. Almost all."

"Except that we let another world die," says Ganno from the doorway, hanging his head. "Seeing it happen again, to someone else, I . . ." He can't finish that sentence, but Elza can see his jaw moving as if he can't help trying. At last he turns and walks away, back into the chaos outside.

"Found it!" Tina comes back from the makeshift audience area, facing the floating stage, holding a boxy gray device with two prongs coming out of one side. "I noticed this earlier. Someone was using it to keep their snah-snah juice at just the right temperature." She holds the device up in front of Marrant. "I made a promise to Thaoh, and this is one step toward keeping it."

Marrant's eyes widen. He starts to say something, some final taunt.

Tina's already pressing the interface on the side of the device. "We've heard enough out of you. Everyone has." A pale smoky glow comes out of the two prongs, and Marrant stops moving. He just sits there, with his mouth wide open and hatred in his eyes.

"That ought to keep him out of trouble," Tina says. "This machine stops the flow of time in a small area, sort of like a showstopper missile. Marrant can stay frozen until the Grattna can take him back to their world." She pushes another control, and the box hovers next to Marrant, keeping him stuck in mid-grimace.

Tina turns and looks at the map showing the stars that almost died, and the one that actually did. "Somebody's going to have to organize a relief effort for the survivors of Kraelyo Homeglobe. That's the sort of thing the Royal Fleet would have done, once upon a time. I don't know who it's going to be now."

Halred thinks about this, then says: "We you they the Kraelyors [possiblity | inevitability] rescue protect oppress any longer." She pauses, and says as clearly as she can: "All of us will build something new. You humanoids can be part of it, but you cannot lead it or own it."

A throbbing hum comes from the other side of the big audience area: a lot of starship engines powering up.

74

RACHAEL

Kez (*he/him*) runs across the rocky field that was full of VIPs a short time ago, with Rachael by his side. Ganno and Yatto run behind them until they catch up.

All of the politicians and bigwigs and planetary leaders who came here to witness Marrant's triumph are trying to run away, now that it's all fallen apart.

"We have to stop those ships taking off." Kez huffs and pants.

Rachael runs alongside Kez. "I don't get it. Why do we care if those jerks bail on us? Good riddance, right?"

Kez shakes his head and runs faster, chopping his arms, wincing because his shoulder still hurts. "They need to stay and face the music. Now is the moment when we can actually talk about starting over, but not if they get to leave and pretend they were never here."

"Plus we'll need hostages," Yatto says from behind Rachael. "Most of Marrant's fleet remains in orbit. They didn't have time to get more forces down here when Marrant's plan fell apart, but they could kill us a dozen ways once these leaders are safely gone."

A wall of starships looms in front of Rachael, facing the ancient temple behind her. From close up, they just give an impression of curved, sleek metal with just a few tiny nicks and dents here and there. Some of the ships have Royal Compassion markings, others are labeled with Makvarian crests, Oonian fronds, Scanthian comets, and so on. It looks a bit like the garden of starships, back in Wentrolo.

The engine whoosh becomes overpowering now that Rachael is up close. Like being on the tarmac next to a jet, only louder.

"How do we stop all these big ships from taking off?" she yells over the droning.

Kez looks at Ganno and Yatto. "I'm going to need some help."

"Of course," Yatto says.

"Any chance to put the blame where it belongs," Ganno says.

Kez nods at Ganno. "Some heartache can only be cured by justice." He turns and looks at the dozen or so huge ships. "Okay. Sounds like they're pretty close to ready. We just need to make enough damage to the hulls of these ships that they can't lift off safely."

"And they all have weapon systems that just blew up." Rachael feels a grin spread across her face. Feels good to smile again.

Yatto produces a bag full of the cuffs that fell off all the prisoners. "Could these be helpful?"

"Yes!" Kez takes one of the cuffs and pops out a tiny pill-shaped nugget of metal. "All we have to do is attach one of these devices to each of the ships. Just look for the spots wherever the ships used to have missile launchers or some other means of vomiting death all over, and stick one of these nearby. They'll prevent the hull from sealing around the damage. Hurry now, we can't let all our guests leave before the party's over."

Rachael races around, sticking the little metal tubes onto all of the ships—turns out it's not hard to spot where they used to have offensive capabilities, because there are giant scorch marks that streak outward like a patch of mold on a bathroom wall. The little nodules stick to the hulls, so tight that you can't pull them off again.

The four of them finish their sabotage run just in time, then they stand back and watch from a safe distance. The engine noise ramps up, and all of the ships start lifting off the ground one by one . . . only to drift back down and land with a jolt, right where they just were.

"Waiiiit for it," Kez says.

The hatch on one of the ships pops open, and out come a handful of Aribentors, wearing silvery tunics that hang off one skeletal shoulder (kind of like togas.) They glare at Kez and the others. Then some Javarah emerge from another ship, and a whole mixture of people in the uniforms of Royal Compassion top brass come out of a third. They all stalk toward Kez, clearly wishing they had some guns.

One of the Aribentors raises a bone finger and says, "What is the meaning of—"

"We can't allow you to leave," Kez says. "As a junior ambassador, *and* as one of the people who just risked everything to stop an atrocity of mind-blowing proportions, I am hereby notifying you that your presence is required here. Indefinitely."

A Javarah in a truly stylish outfit made of aquamarine beads starts to protest, and Kez silences them with a wave of his hand.

"I didn't invite you to talk," Kez says. "You'll have your chance, soon enough. But you'll also have to do a lot of listening—to the people whose deaths you came here to witness. Let me be absolutely clear: you are here to take part in discussions of the future of the galaxy, but you will not be negotiating from a position of strength."

Ganno steps close to Kez. "It's time we all shared power with the people who have been left behind. The Seven-Pointed Empire fell generations ago, but its evil has never ceased."

One of the Royal Compassion leaders, an Undhoran with senior explorer markings, gets their face-tubes in a twist. "You are in no position to make demands. Our warships in orbit—"

"—will get shot down by our Grattna allies before they ever reach the surface," says Kez. "I really, really hate violence, but in this case, it seems appropriate. And your ships won't dare launch an attack from orbit, not while you're here."

"We're going back inside our ships now," says the leading Aribentor. (None of these people have bothered to introduce themselves, which feels disrespectful.) "We'll wait for rescue, or for our ships to be repaired."

"You will not leave or hide away," says a familiar voice from behind them. "You will come with us, or we will be forced to destroy all of your ships." Halred steps forward, from behind Rachael and the others. She waves one of her wings, and more Grattna emerge on all sides. She waves another wing, and a Grattna warship comes floating down, with all of its still-functional weapons aimed at the grounded ships.

"This doesn't have to be unpleasant," Kez says. He turns toward Halred, whose three eyes have a distinct *Oh yeah?* expression. "Okay," he adds. "It does actually have to be unpleasant. But you get to decide quite how unpleasant it becomes."

"Come with us, please," Yatto says. "I think we can convert part of that ancient temple into a meeting chamber, and there might be enough snah-snah juice to go around."

The dignitaries look at Kez, then at the Grattna and the *Nindred's Blessing.* Then they sigh and follow Yatto and Ganno, back toward the ancient temple.

Rachael still isn't used to drawing people since she got her art back, but this is too good to miss. She sits on a piece of starship wreckage and sketches the whole scene: a river of people clad in the most sumptuous fin-ery, trudging across a battlefield toward a grand ancient temple that's still covered with singing monkeys. She needs to preserve this scene forever, the only way she knows how.

75

.

TINA

The next several days go by really, really quickly.

Okay, so Larstko IVb has days that are only like four hours long—but also, there's a ridiculous amount of work to do. We need to patch up everyone's injuries, stash the Marrantsicle someplace safe, build a makeshift jail for the other Royal Compassion stooges, and help organize a humanitarian mission to help the survivors of Kraelyo Homeglobe. Damini, Zaeta, and Yiwei work their butts off fixing the damage to the *Undisputed Training Bra Disaster,* one of the few ships left that can still fly. And meanwhile, Kez is starting diplomatic sessions with whoever's alive and not totally compromised.

We kept wondering if Marrant's fleet in orbit would decide to wipe us all out, even with our celebrity "guests." I guarantee they thought about it. Right when I was starting to worry, the warships started drifting away from this little moon, a few at a time, until they were all gone.

So one Earth day—six local days—later, I'm sitting on a hillside and basking in the reddish sunlight. Nearby some of my friends work on repairing our patchwork ship, using bits and pieces from all the other ships nearby. They even found some fragments from the ancient starship graveyard, so maybe the *Undisputed Training Bra Disaster* will have superior stealth capabilities. Nobody will see that ship coming—and when they do see it, they won't believe it.

Anyway, I'm thinking about how much I appreciate sunlight, and the fact that warmth and sunbeams are generally good things, and how close we came to not having them anymore. The sun goes down, and I keep sitting. My mind knows the crisis is over and now we get to rebuild, but my nerves haven't gotten the memo yet. Every few moments, I snap into a state of alertness, ready for another alarm to shrill, or for another splodey thing to start sploding. Might take years for me to quit bracing.

Grateful as I am that my friends are here and alive—mostly—we haven't had a quiet moment together. Maybe not even since I came back from the kinda-dead.

Rachael and Elza wander up the hill from the *Undisputed Training Bra Disaster* and sit down on either side of me, watching the sunrise.

One good thing about this place: there's a sunset or sunrise every time you look up, and they tend to be spectacular. Especially with so much debris lingering in the atmosphere.

"I should be celebrating, right?" I say. "We won, we saved almost everybody except for the poor Kraelyors. I should be cheering and stomp-dancing. Instead all I am is so, so tired. Like my emotions ran a marathon, and now I don't have the energy to feel much of anything."

"We kept saying we would feel things later," Rachael says. "And now it's later, and there's too many things to feel. I want to mourn and celebrate and worry about what's next. It's nonstop mood swings over here."

We sit, watching the horizon glow.

I don't need to turn my head, I can *feel* the presence of the people I love on either side of me. I'd die for these two—again—but I'm sure glad I don't have to.

"The queen kept trying to tell me that doing good means not caring too much about anyone or anything." Elza sighs. "I'm scared that one day I'll realize she was right. I'll wake up and it'll hurt too much, and I'll just shut myself off."

"You said yourself, there's a cost to closing yourself off like that," I say. "You stop being curious, and then you miss important stuff. Plus, that's why you have us. We'll annoy you until you pay attention."

Next to me, Rachael hunches over a plastiform sketchpad. She's not drawing the view from this hillside, our oddball starship in the foreground and the ancient temple in the distance. Instead, she's sketching the 23-Hour Coffee Bomb back home, with the strip club across the street and the back alley piled with garbage. Ouch. Instant homesickness.

"We get to decide," Rachael says. "We get to choose who we want to be, for the rest of our lives. Maybe I'll become a farmer and make artisanal snah-snah juice, or open a karaoke bar on Wastrel Station. Maybe I'll teach the whole galaxy to play *Waymaker*. For the first time in forever, we can start over."

"I can't." Elza raises her wrist, adorned in faintly glowing gold. "I'm the last princess. Soon these crowns are going to come all the way back to life, and I'll have to figure out what to do with them. I'm going to be the Rogue Princess for the rest of my life, no matter what else I become."

I want to say Elza won't carry that weight by herself. And none of us can really start over—we're all going to be carrying our choices forever. But I've already said that stuff so many times, and I'm worded out. So I just make space for her to lean her head on my shoulder.

It's already noon. I can see lights in the yellowy-green sky: starship shards burning up in the atmosphere.

Rachael's already started another drawing: her parents' house, with the broken mailbox and the dead lawn out front.

"I think a really good friend is someone who helps you live with yourself," I say after a while. "Instead of trying to get you to be someone different, or letting you be in denial about who you are and what you've done."

Yiwei trudges up the hill, carrying something I haven't seen in so long.

He sits next to Rachael with his DIY guitar in his lap, and starts strumming a brand-new song.

I rub my eyes. Thanks to these short days, I have no idea when I'm supposed to sleep. "I want to go home." I don't even mean to say it, the words just trickle out.

". . . to Makvaria?" Rachael says.

"Nah. To Earth. I do want to visit Makvaria one of these days. But first, I need to make sure my mom is okay. And eat donuts. But mostly, make sure my mom is okay."

"Yeah." Rachael clasps her knees.

"I need to check on my grandmother," Yiwei says. "Is it bad if we leave in the middle of rebuilding the galaxy?"

"I don't know." I yawn and stretch. "I think the rebuilding is going to be a long, long process, and we can take a vacation in the middle of it."

Damini and Zaeta come sit with us too, and then Kez and Wyndgonk come over the other side of the hill. The sun is already going down.

"So this is where you've been hiding," Kez says. "We could really use some backup."

"Those negotiations are getting all the way under my shell," Wyndgonk rumbles.

Elza stands up. "We're coming. Ugh, I just want to sleep for a couple of days."

"On this moon, two days would be a normal amount of sleep," Rachael says.

We all follow Kez and Wyndgonk back to the ancient wedding chapel, where everyone is still yelling.

76

One of the twelve emparchs of Makvaria is standing on the floating stage in front of the wedding chapel, right where Marrant was showing off his plans for galactic cleansing not long ago. "We will not negotiate under duress," says Baysha Narrath (*she/her*) in a pompous drone. "Once order has been restored, there will be time to discuss matters of fairness and reparations."

I stare at Baysha until she starts to squirm. I kept hearing over and over how kind Makvarian society was, how it was all built around the idea of everybody taking care of everybody else. But I guess that only applies to other Makvarians.

Commander Zkog glides forward from the group of Kraelyors. "You just want everything to go back to the way it was, after what your leader did to us while you cheered."

"He wasn't . . . I mean . . ." Baysha sputters.

"You still can't even look at me." Commander Zkog waves her stinger-arms and hisses with both mouths. "Why won't you look at me?"

Next to me, Kez (*she/her*) clutches her head. "Why did I ever want to be a diplomat? This is the worst of the worst of the worst."

"You didn't choose this path because it's easy," Ganno murmurs in Kez's ear. "You chose it because you have a yearning to heal worlds instead of breaking them. The same way you've helped to heal my heart."

Kez looks up at Ganno with tears in her eyes. "You're going to make me cry in front of the Oonians, and they'll probably consider it a declaration of war. They have a whole thing about eyes."

"I will shield you with my massive body, so you may cry unobserved." Ganno opens his big, powerful arms, and Kez disappears into his embrace.

Okay, I don't mean to eavesdrop, it's just that we're all stuck inside this ancient wedding chapel with a whole crowd of fancy people, and privacy is hard to come by. Also, I wish I was half as smooth as Ganno.

Every time I come back to the meeting chamber in the wedding hall, the same arguments are happening: justice versus stability. Personally, I think stability went out the window when they let Marrant take charge. But I'm so not ready to give a speech.

At last, Kez steps forward and says, "The whole time I was in diplomatic training, they kept saying that I needed to respect how other people see things. But we can't negotiate if you all insist on being in denial." She turns and gestures at me. "We need to hear from the Grattna, but first my associate Tina is going to show you how to alter your EverySpeaks so you can understand them better."

Everyone looks at me, and I step next to Kez. "Oh, right. Hi. I'll walk you through it." I only get lost in explaining the technical specs five times before I get them on track.

But it's all worth it when Halred steps up onto the stage, flexing her wings, and starts to talk about all of it. How Marrant took her people and caged them, and they worked to copy Marrant's flagship so this could never happen to them again—but they'll never feel safe again.

Halred says, "You we Royal Compassion [something] allies fight flee decide, but Kraelyors us Marrant [something] victims protect restore." She says it a couple times, until we all get it: the Grattna struggled with the choice of whether to fight on our side, but in the end, they were fighting for themselves, plus the Kraelyors and all the other people that Marrant wanted to destroy.

The longer Halred talks, the more we get used to Grattna speech, and the easier it is to understand the first time. I can see Baysha's face open up, like she's starting to see the Grattna as people.

Around day twenty of the negotiations—at least, based on local days—I catch Yatto the Monntha standing around outside, watching the meeting through the open doorway. They have a ginormous frown on their face, and I wander up to them.

"I'm kind of surprised you're not in there," I say. "I mean, everybody respects you."

Yatto does this shoulder-flex that I recognize as their version of rolling their eyes. "Not everybody respects me. I learned that the hard way."

"Everybody who's not total garbage respects you," I correct myself. "And I don't see anyone in there speaking for the Irriyaians. I guess Marrant didn't bother to try and fly in anyone from the Irriyaian citystar to witness his triumph."

"The Irriyaian citystar is a mess," Yatto says. "My people will take a long time to get used to being a diaspora. We should reach out to the Kraelyors and offer whatever help we can." They rub between the spikes on their forehead. "So you believe I should go in there and claim to speak for Irriyaia. Wouldn't I be lying?"

"I am definitely not an expert on Irriyaian politics. But you have a chance to speak for everyone who's been displaced, and everyone who believed in the old dream and watched it go up in smoke. Right? You have as much right to be heard as anybody! And maybe this is how you start to become a leader of your people, right?"

Yatto gives me an *if it'll shut you up* look and squares their shoulders, then walks inside the council chamber.

Baysha is in the middle of grandstanding about how the Royal Fleet kept everyone safe for generations. She sees Yatto enter and trails off in mid-mouthbarf. The whole room full of chatterboxes goes quiet, all at once.

Kez looks up from staring at her diplomatic augmenter, and sees the reason why everyone stopped talking. Her face brightens.

"I heard you talking about the Royal Fleet just now," Yatto says in a quiet voice. "We tried so hard to do good. The first time I met Wyndgonk, I lectured fire about everything we had done for the Thythuthyans when my ship visited there. But then I realized we never actually talked to the Thythuthyans, or asked them what they wanted from us."

Wyndgonk sidles closer to Yatto, beetle shell parting a little in the back. "I had a hard time trusting Yatto, especially after their people joined the Compassion. But none of us would be alive if they hadn't earned my trust. You wet-mouths don't even know how close you came to being blown to scraps. We had a plan to turn all your ships into bombs, and your last act would have been cheering for the deaths of people who had done nothing to you."

The room goes quiet, for the first time in ages. I squirm, hearing Wyndgonk talk about what we almost did, but so does everyone else. These dignitaries hadn't realized how close they came to being toast.

"We spent so long debating whether to help or hurt people like the Thythuthyans and the Grattna," Yatto says. "But neither option involved getting to know them and treat them like equals. Until Tina reprogrammed her EverySpeak, I'd never realized how much I wasn't hearing."

Now I'm squirming again, but it's a slightly happier squirming.

"We risked everything," Wyndgonk says. "You're alive because we didn't take the easy way."

"You really should be grateful." Kez looks like she's actually starting to enjoy diplomacy after all. "And like Wyndgonk said, building trust takes a long time, but I believe you're all capable of doing better."

Everybody starts talking over each other again, but I notice Baysha slinks up to Yatto and starts whispering to them. Yatto nods and then brings Halred and Wyndgonk over to introduce the three of them to each other.

77

.

ELZA

Elza sits with Tina, Rachael, Yiwei, Kez (*he/him*), Ganno, Zaeta, and Damini, watching the stars go blue. They're in a shiny observation lounge on the *Best Effort,* a pretty new diplomatic cruiser from the old Firmament that Kez managed to lay claim to. The *Undisputed Training Bra Disaster* is safely parked inside the *Best Effort*'s hangar, because it's going to be weird enough when they show up at Earth, and that ship is kind of hard to explain.

"I really wanted to go back home as the representative of something," Kez says, fidgeting with his new ambassador tunic. "But I guess this is almost as good? I can return home and tell everyone that we're helping to found a new galactic best friend council, and Earth has a chance to be part of it from the very beginning."

"We have no idea what to expect on Earth," Yiwei says. "Humans found out aliens were real, over a year ago, and then Marrant came so close to killing our sun."

"People do not handle change well." Elza shivers. "I don't know what's going to freak people out more: the sun almost dying, or humans finding out that we're not the most important people in the galaxy."

"We have a chance to show up and give everybody back home something to be proud of," Kez says. "Look at us: we've all leveled up since we left home."

"Speak for yourself." Tina holds up her big purple hands. "I haven't changed a bit."

"We're going to be influencers," Damini tells Zaeta. "I'm going to be endorsing shoes!"

"Confusion!" Zaeta protests. "Do shoes only fit properly if they've been endorsed? Does somebody need to endorse every single pair of shoes before they can be worn? That sounds like a big job."

"It is the biggest job," Damini says. "We'll help each other."

Everybody is goofing around and cracking jokes, but Elza can feel the anxiety bubbling under the surface. Back on Earth, it's been seventeen months since she jumped on a pizza tray and rode it into space. Even the Ardenii don't know what's been happening since then, because Earth is such a backwater—and there's no way of knowing what kind of welcome Elza and her friends will get.

"I don't know that anybody's going to want me endorsing anything." Tina laughs—but Elza remembers her saying that she's worried people on Earth will take one look at her and call pest control. At least Tina's not the only person in their group who looks alien: there's Zaeta and Ganno, plus the whole crew of the *Best Effort*.

"I'll always want you to endorse everything," Elza whispers, and holds out her hand. Tina clasps it and leans her head on Elza's shoulder.

"Your people will welcome your safe return," Ganno says, shaking his head. "If I could have one more day on Irriyaia, I would give almost anything. But all I can do is help you to make your people understand that their sky has just gotten so much bigger."

Kez holds Ganno tighter. "Thank you for coming with me. I'm half convinced that I'm going to see my father, and suddenly I'll be five years old again."

Ganno frowns. "Your age will continue to increase at a constant rate. But I will be by your side when you face your family and everyone else. I need some time to think about everything that's happened, in any case."

This ship is nice, although nowhere near as luxurious and strange as the *Invention of Innocence*. Becoming a princess feels like a weird dream Elza had, except that the Ardenii are still in her head, feeding her information about things happening all over the galaxy that she can't do anything about. Not everything the Ardenii tell her is terrible: sometimes there's a flash of a group wedding on Makvaria, or the Thythuthyans throwing a party to celebrate the return of the hearthlight. But mostly it's chaos, destruction, upheaval.

Elza doesn't know how to tell Kez—or Tina, for that matter—that she's pretty sure this new Galactic Best Friend Council will not unite everyone. A lot of worlds will break away and do their own thing. There'll be wars, upheavals, atrocities, local alliances. Nothing is going to fill the void left behind by the Firmament and the Royal Fleet. It's going to be messy for a long, long time.

She decides to slip down to the crew lounge and get a snack, because maybe raising her blood sugar will keep the dark thoughts at bay for a while. Everybody is too busy chattering to notice her wandering off, except that Tina gives her a questioning look, like *Should I tag along?* Elza shakes her head.

Fried Scanthian parsnips taste like a crunchy, tangy miracle, and Elza wants to savor every bite. She can't believe she'll maybe get to eat pão de queijo again soon. She lets the flaky insides melt in her mouth, and tries to push all her worries away.

All at once, she feels . . . a presence. A mocking voice, in the back of her mind. She can't make out what the voice is saying, or even understand what's happening, except that her whole body suddenly goes numb and the fried parsnip slips through her fingers onto the floor.

The voice becomes clearer just as she realizes where she's heard it before: when the queen showed up at Thythuthy and cut off her access to the Ardenii.

Enjoy your stolen glory while it lasts, Rogue Princess, the queen says inside Elza's head. *We are not defeated, though our Firmament no longer uplifts us as it should. We burn as bright as ever, and soon our fire will consume you entire. Your mind will unravel slowly, over many years, and we will weave every thread through our palace walls.*

Elza can't move. She can't feel her arms and legs. This voice is a pin sticking all the way through her, like one of the moths in her father's collection. Trapped, helpless, alone.

Then her eyes land on the crumbles of fried parsnip on the floor, and she remembers where she is: with her friends, going home, in a powerful ship that is part of something new and maybe great.

She speaks aloud, and she's sure the queen hears her. "Come for me if you dare. I'll be ready. You're a queen in exile, with no throne and a broken crown, and whatever happens, you'll have to live with knowing that you were the last queen of the Firmament. You're the one who's disgraced—just another fool who believed in Marrant."

The queen doesn't answer right away, and Elza wonders if the connection already broke. She can't imagine how much energy it must be taking to beam the queen's voice into her head from this distance.

Then the queen says, *We will make you know our displeasure, foolish child.* And the voice is gone. Elza's thoughts are her own again, apart from the random flood from the Ardenii.

Elza goes from rigid to limp all at once. Her legs can't support her, her knees go one way and her feet the other, she topples. The floor is rushing to meet her.

A pair of purple hands catches her.

Her consort lifts her up and helps her into a teacup chair. "You're okay," Tina says. "I'm here, and you're safe. They can't hurt you."

"You don't . . . you don't know that." Elza clutches on to Tina's hands like a drowning person with a raft.

"I overheard your part of whatever that was," Tina says. "The ex-queen, right? You know she wouldn't be bothering to yell threats at you if she could actually do anything. She's in bad shape. Her main ally, Marrant, is chilling in a cage on Second Yoth by now. She has no fleet anymore. And you told me that the Ardenii won't hurt anyone directly."

"All of that is true," Elza says. "She still scares me nonetheless. She hates me. A lot."

"I know," Tina says. "But please take a breath. And eat some more parsnips—soon, we'll get donuts together!—and remember that you're here with us, and the queen is billions of miles away. She's a long-term problem, just like most of the other stuff we're dealing with now."

Elza does what Tina says, and some food and snah-snah juice make her feel way better. So does Tina's voice, chattering about all the stuff they're going to do when they get home. Elza lets herself just soak in the feeling of being safe, with Tina and all of their friends nearby. Even the Ardenii give Elza some space, for a little while.

Elza finds herself gazing at the bangle of seven loops wrapped around her wrist, which blaze brighter and brighter as the Ardenii come back. She'll need to find six people who deserve to wear them, and she's pretty sure they shouldn't include anyone who thinks of these circlets as crowns.

Something comes to life inside Elza's satchel: her cell phone, which she hasn't looked at in forever. The Ardenii must have boosted the range somehow, because they're still approaching Earth and over a year's worth of text messages and emails and updates are streaming across the tiny screen. Junk, almost all of it, just random group chats and actual spam—it makes her head hurt to sift through it.

There's nobody back on Earth I want to get in touch with. But as soon as Elza thinks those words, she knows they're not true.

She finds Fernanda's number and starts writing a text. She deletes the first five drafts, then just writes, "I miss you. I'm sorry I hurt you."

No response.

Maybe Fernanda blocked her number a long time ago.

Then she sees Fernanda typing a response. Typing, typing, typing, then . . .

Fernanda writes, "I miss you too." And an agonizing minute later: "I think I'm ready to talk."

Elza looks up at the viewport, at the blue-and-green pebble getting closer. For the first time, she feels like maybe she really has a home to come back to.

78

RACHAEL

Rachael is sure they've come to the wrong planet. They come out of space-weave next to a honking big curvy metal bar, bristling with nuclear missiles and other weapons, orbiting a blue world streaked with green and white.

At first Rachael can't place why that orbital structure looks so familiar.

Then Yiwei says, "It's what's left of the *Cleansing Fire*, the Compassion ship that attacked us in orbit around Earth. They ditched their crew and turned part of the ship into a missile, remember? Somebody must have salvaged the rest."

Zaeta squawks. "Hostility! They're trying to target us with some of these weapons in orbit."

"That's just rude," Damini says. "We can outrun anything they throw at us, but my feelings are hurt."

Tina nudges Kez (*they/them*). "We better talk to them."

"Right now?" Kez squirms a little. "I didn't finish writing a speech . . ."

Ganno beams down at Kez. "Whatever you say to your people, I'm sure it will be perfect."

"We can do that thing!" Damini claps her hands.

"That thing where we make you come out of every device everywhere," Zaeta says.

"Okay." Kez stands up straighter. "Just give me a—"

A holographic torch-singer microphone appears in front of Kez's face.

"Now!" Damini says. "You're live. Everyone on Earth is hearing you, through their phones and computers and televisions and everything." Long silence. "You'd better say something."

Kez clears their throat and looks at Ganno. "Uh. Hello, everyone. On Earth. Everyone on Earth! My name is Kez Oduya and my pronoun is *they*. My friends and I left Earth seventeen months ago, and now we're back with some good news. You don't have to be scared, I promise."

They run out of things to say, and everybody gives them thumbs-up and *keep-going* motions.

"Here's what you need to know for now," Kez says. "I'm here as the representative of a new galactic alliance, which we're calling the Best Friends Council for now. We're going to build a peaceful and fair galaxy, and Earth can be part of it. The main thing we learned out there in space is that exploitation and genocide are everywhere—but so are people fighting to build something better. It's time for all of us to become part of that fight."

Kez looks at Ganno—fluid is leaking out of little ducts on the sides of his face.

"That's all for now, I guess," Kez says. "We'll answer everybody's questions soon, and I'm hoping to have some meetings with leaders from Earth. Just please don't shoot at us, and please, please, don't make this weird. Or . . . weirder than it needs to be. Okay, bye."

Kez waves a hand, and the microphone vanishes.

"Ugh," they say. "That was one of the most important speeches in human history, and I sounded ridiculous."

"You were great," Ganno says.

"I loved it," Rachael says. "You totally nailed it."

"So now what?" Zaeta says.

"Do we try to land?" Damini says.

"Uh, looks like lots of people want to talk to us." Tina gestures at the ship's comms, which are blowing up.

"Let's not land just yet," Yiwei says. "We can take an orbital funnel down to the surface, and nobody will even know we're there."

A little while later, Tina walks up and holds out a holographic rectangle to Rachael: a cell phone.

"I had them make these for all of us," Tina says. "I know you lost your phone ages ago. Your parents' number is already programmed in, and the ship's comms can boost the range."

Rachael looks at the phone: kinda like an iPhone 11 or 12, but most of the details are a little bit wrong. She can't even remember how to use one of these things.

Then she takes it from Tina and cradles it in her hands, feeling her heart speed up. Tina is holding a holographic "phone" of her own.

"Just like that," Rachael says. "I push this, and I can talk to my parents. I . . . I don't know if I can. I mean, what if . . . what if they're not okay?"

Her finger hovers over the little "call" button, and her heart is louder than an exploding starship.

Then she pushes the button, and hears a gargling bell sound. And then another.

And then there's a click.

"Hello?" Her father's voice comes through the speaker.

"Uh. Hi. It's. It's me."

". . . Rachael? Bear? You're really here? We thought, we didn't even know, we—" Jody's voice gets further away. "Esmé, it's her, it's Rachael, she's home and she's alive. Come quick!"

Now both of Rachael's parents are motor-mouthing at once.

Some of the tautness releases from Rachael's arms and shoulders, and she has a sense-memory of smelling and tasting fresh-baked snickerdoodles.

"You and Tina both vanished, and there was an explosion in space, and we thought—" Rachael's mom says.

"We never gave up hope that you'd make it home to us," Jody says.

"We should have known. The news trucks just came back," Esmé says.

"The . . . the what now?" Rachael stares at the phone.

"People figured out pretty quick," Jody says, "that you and Tina were part of what happened with those aliens showing up and everything. We've had cameras in our face, on and off, for the past year and a half."

"They didn't show up for a while," Esmé says, "but suddenly there's more of them than ever. We can hardly leave our house."

Rachael looks at Tina, who's still trying to get through to her mom. Tina shoots a helpless look back at her.

Tina mouths, *Tell them to meet us for donuts.*

"Um, if you can manage to get away from the reporters," Rachael says, "then maybe you can come meet us for some bathroom-graffiti bingo. You know the place, right?"

There's a long, hissy silence, and Rachael can tell her parents are looking at each other, trying to remember. Then Jody says, "Oh! Yes. We'll see you there."

79

.

TINA

The 23-Hour Coffee Bomb looks exactly the same. Like, there are a few new scuffs and tags on the mural on the brick side wall, but the gravel parking lot with its view of the strip club is exactly the same. The neon DONUTS sign still teeters exactly the same way. The only reason everything looks different is because I'm seeing it all from a new angle, now that I'm a foot taller.

At least so far, I don't see any photographers or news crews lurking around. Our strategy of telling our friends and family to meet us here seems to have paid off? It's almost like a Royal Fleet blessing: "Happy reunions with no paparazzi."

The eyes on the left side of Zaeta's face are all squinting and looking askance. "Is this really the coolest place on Earth? Do they even serve snah-snah juice here?"

"They serve hot chocolate," Rachael says, "which is just about as good. You'll see."

"Next we'll visit Mumbai," Damini says, "and *then* you'll see some coolness. But I'm glad to see where Tina and Rachael grew up."

"I can't wait to show you all São Paulo." Elza gazes out at the two-lane highway. "This isn't even a city."

The gravel of the parking lot crunches under my feet. Can't believe I stood exactly here and activated my rescue beacon—part of me feels like that just happened a minute ago, and another part feels like it's been a million years. I can't move forward, held down by the weight of everything that's happened since I left home.

Everybody is looking at me, like *Are we going in or what?* Rachael shrugs and walks past me, pushing the door open. I come in right behind her.

My mom is sitting at the first booth, with Rachael's parents. Bette and Turtle and the rest of the Lasagna Hats are at the next booth over, in the middle of playing some new board game. I see a few other kids from Clinton

High, including Samantha Chang and the Rabbit Sisters. Everybody stops talking and jumps to their feet when we walk in, with our mixture of human and not-so-human, and all of us wearing our space clothes.

"Uh, hey," I say. "We're back. What'd we miss?"

The next thing I know my mom is rushing over. She looks smaller than I remember and her hair has more white strands, but her face is lit up like the fresh-donuts sign on a Saturday night.

"You came back home," she says in a still, soft voice.

How can it feel like a lifetime since I saw her, but also like we were just playing Worthington Garden Party five minutes ago?

Nearby, Rachael is hugging both of her parents at once.

"Of course I came home." I didn't expect to cry so many tears. "Where else would I go? I missed you, Mom."

"I would have gotten the toaster waffles you like." My mom sobs. "If I'd known."

"I don't need waffles, Mom. I'm just so happy to see you."

My mom can't get her arms all the way around me anymore, but I still feel totally embraced. The scents of chamomile and molasses come off her.

I look up and a few people in the café are filming us with their phones, but Bette and Turtle are trying to get them to cut it out. We're not going to have this place to ourselves for much longer. I can see Kez psyching themself up to have to give some kind of Statement to the media. Damini and Zaeta are ordering hot chocolates at the counter. Elza is looking at all the names carved in the wall near the bulletin board full of flyers, maybe trying to see where Rachael and I carved our names, in another life.

"Hey, Elza," I call out. I try to ignore the looks I'm getting from almost everyone in here. Even Bette and Turtle are a little weirded out, but they seem to be rolling with it. "Elza, I want you to meet my mom. Mom, this is Elza, she's my . . . well, I'm her consort. It's a whole thing."

"Good to meet you, Elza." She looks at Elza's tactical ballgown. "That's a lovely dress. Do you hug?"

Elza seems a little startled, then she nods. My mom hugs her and murmurs that she's so glad I found someone cool at last.

Rachael is introducing her parents to Yiwei, and then we're all introducing Kez, Ganno, Damini, and Zaeta to everybody, and Bette and Turtle are getting in on it, and a dozen donuts appear from somewhere, including my favorite kind: glazed old-fashioned.

Almost everybody I care about in the universe is here in this one room, and the air is full of coffee and sugar and starch and cloves. My favorite Billie Eilish song is playing on the speakers overhead, and my first bite of donut crumbles perfectly in my mouth, and I'm just so damn glad to be home.

ACKNOWLEDGMENTS

∎

I can't believe we did it! This trilogy has been such a huge part of my life for the past five and a half years, and I'm so grateful to everyone who put up with my near-vertical learning curve at writing young adult fiction, not to mention swashbuckling space adventures. This has been a truly wondrous adventure.

First and always, I have to thank my editor, Miriam Weinberg, who has steered these books and schooled me on YA storytelling. Miriam, your guidance and support have been utterly invaluable, and Tina and her friends would have definitely sailed into a black hole without you. I'm also incredibly grateful to everyone else at Tor Teen, including Saraciea Fennell, Ashley Spruill, Anthony Parisi, Anneliese Merz, Lucille Rettino, Isa Caban, Patrick Nielsen Hayden, Irene Gallo, and too many others to name.

And of course, my agent, Russ Galen, encouraged me to write a YA trilogy in the first place, and did not bat an eye when I told him the ridiculously ambitious concept I had. Russ's feedback and ideas were absolutely essential to the early stages of conceptualizing this trilogy, and his support has been indispensible over the course of the series.

I'm also super grateful to Nate Miller, my manager, for championing these books. And to Stefano Agosto, Elizabeth Raposo, and Michael B. Jordan with Outlier Society for believing in this series, along with Kevin Jarzynski and everyone at Amazon. And of course, the utterly brilliant Gennifer Hutchison, who's helped change how I think about these characters.

This book would be way worse without my sensitivity readers: Hailey Kaas, Jaymee Goh, and Keffy R.M. Kehrli. Hailey has continued working closely with me on Elza's backstory and evolution, answering a million questions about life in Brazil and teaching me to speak not-terrible Portuguese. Obrigada!!!

My beta readers also saved my skin: Karen Meisner, Kit Stubbs, Malka Older, Tessa Fisher, Olivia Abtahi, Claire Light, Liz Henry, and Sheerly

Avni. Y'all helped me figure out so many places where the story needed more heart or better action, and I'm so grateful for your attention to detail.

Major props also to copyeditor Christina MacDonald. And to audiobook narrators Hynden Walch, Sena Bryer, and Imani Jade Powers, who brought this story to life alongside the wondrous Callum Plews.

Once again, Katie Mack helped me to figure out the mechanics of the Bereavement and was a wonderful sounding board on astrophysics stuff. I also had some very illuminating conversations about linguistics with Katie Martin and Gretchen McCulloch, who offered some ideas for how the Grattna language could work—the actual result is entirely my fault, but your feedback was invaluable.

And thanks to everyone who made fan art, came to see me on tour and asked about the future of #Tilza, and shared these books with their friends. Thanks to all the heroic librarians, teachers, and booksellers whom I've gotten to meet as I've traveled around talking about the Unstoppable series. It's been a thrill to get to know you all.

And finally, thanks to my partner, Annalee Newitz, who has been a constant source of inspiration and silliness and joy and splendor. Endless kisses and unforgettable conversations—I love you, bae.